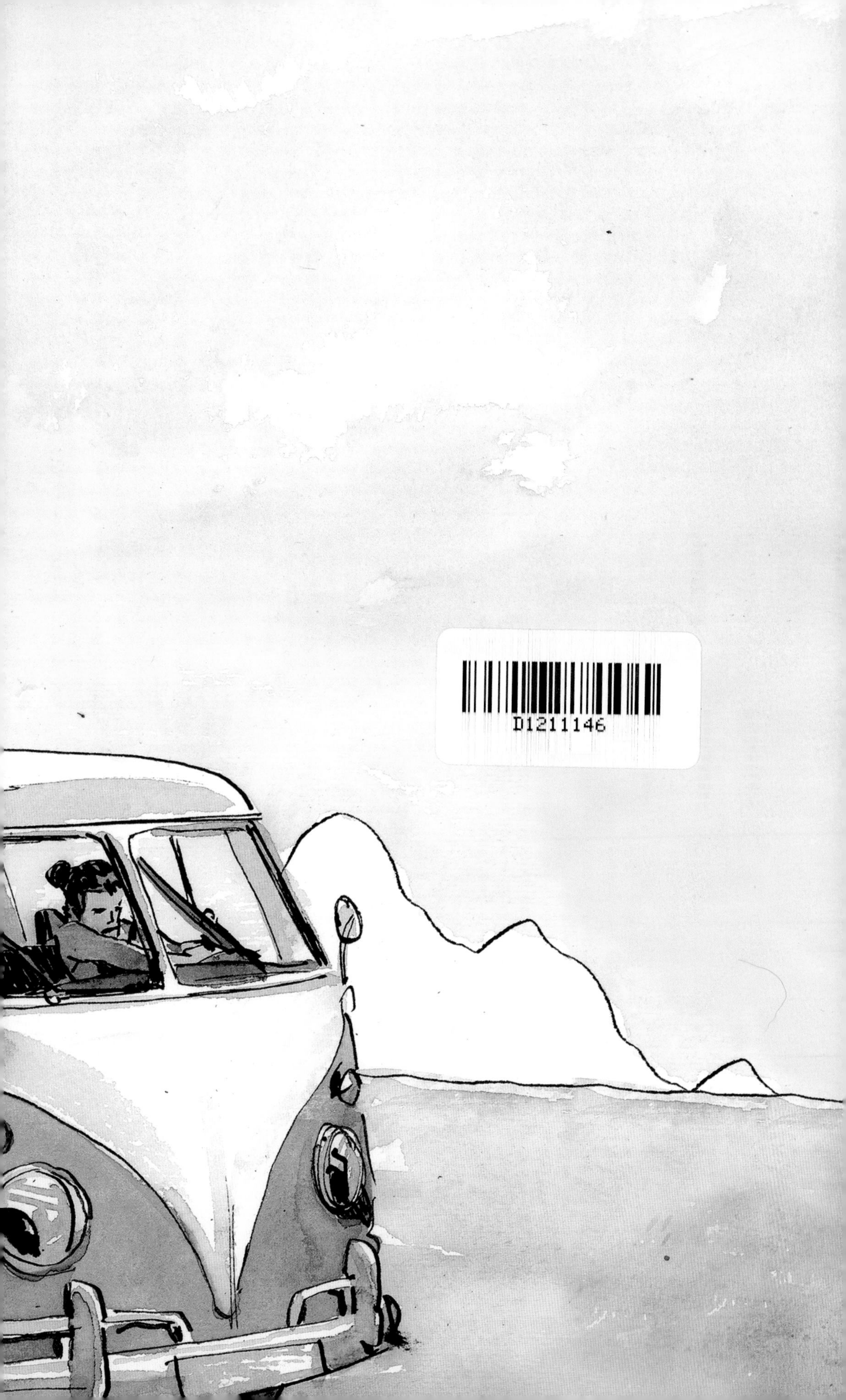

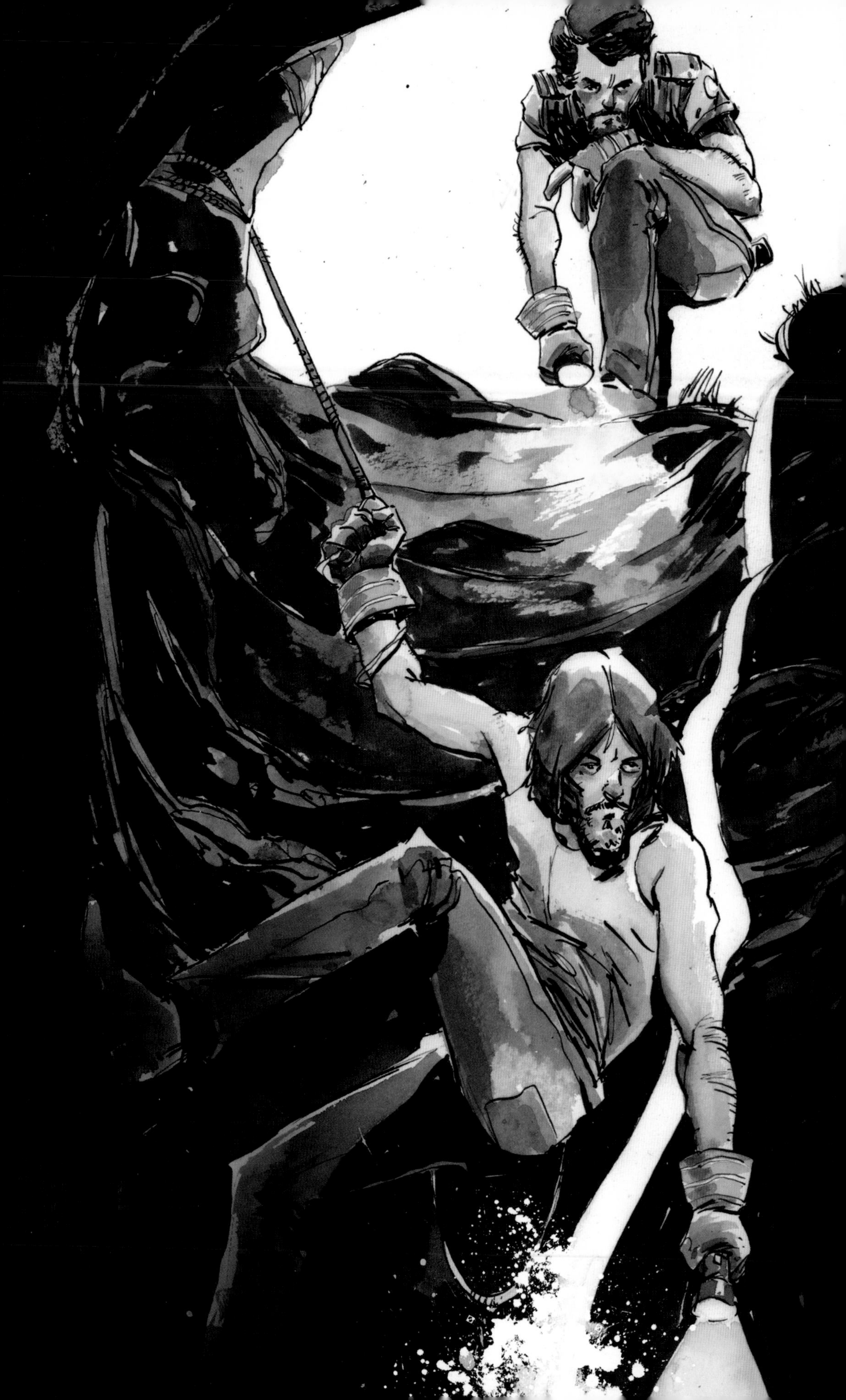

matt kindt   tyler jenkins   hilary jenkins

G R A S S ⚊ K I N G S™

volume three

BOOM! STUDIOS

GRASS KINGS Volume Three, March 2020.
Published by BOOM! Studios, a division of
Boom Entertainment, Inc. Grass Kings is ™ &
© 2020 Matt Kindt & Tyler Jenkins. Originally
published in single magazine form as GRASS
KINGS No. 12-15. ™ & © 2018 Matt Kindt & Tyler Jenkins. All rights reserved.
BOOM! Studios™ and the BOOM! Studios logo are trademarks of Boom
Entertainment, Inc, registered in various countries and categories. All characters,
events, and institutions depicted herein are fictional. Any similarity between any
of the names, characters, persons, events, and/or institutions in this publication
to actual names, characters, and persons, whether living or dead, events, and/or
institutions is unintended and purely coincidental. BOOM! Studios does not read
or accept unsolicited submissions of ideas, stories, or artwork.

BOOM! Studios, 5670 Wilshire Boulevard, Suite 400, Los Angeles, CA,
90036-5679. Printed in China. First Printing.

ISBN: 978-1-68415-492-0, eISBN: 978-1-64144-650-1

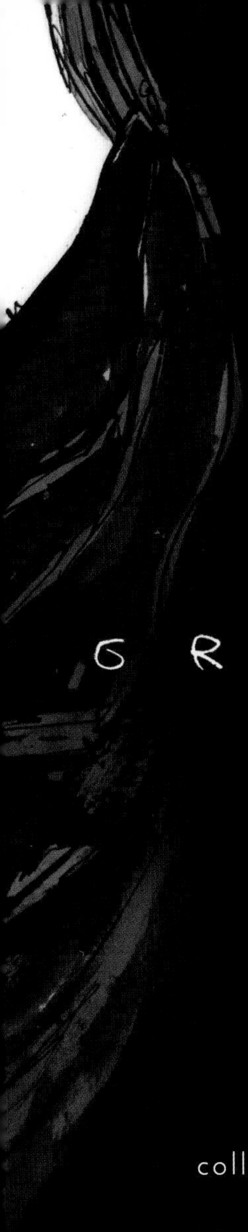

GRASS KINGS™

created by **matt kindt + tyler jenkins**

written by **matt kindt**
illustrated by **tyler jenkins**
with colors by **hilary jenkins**
lettered by **jim campbell**
cover by **tyler jenkins**

series designer **grace park**
collection designers **scott newman + chelsea roberts**
editor **eric harburn**
special thanks **jasmine amiri**

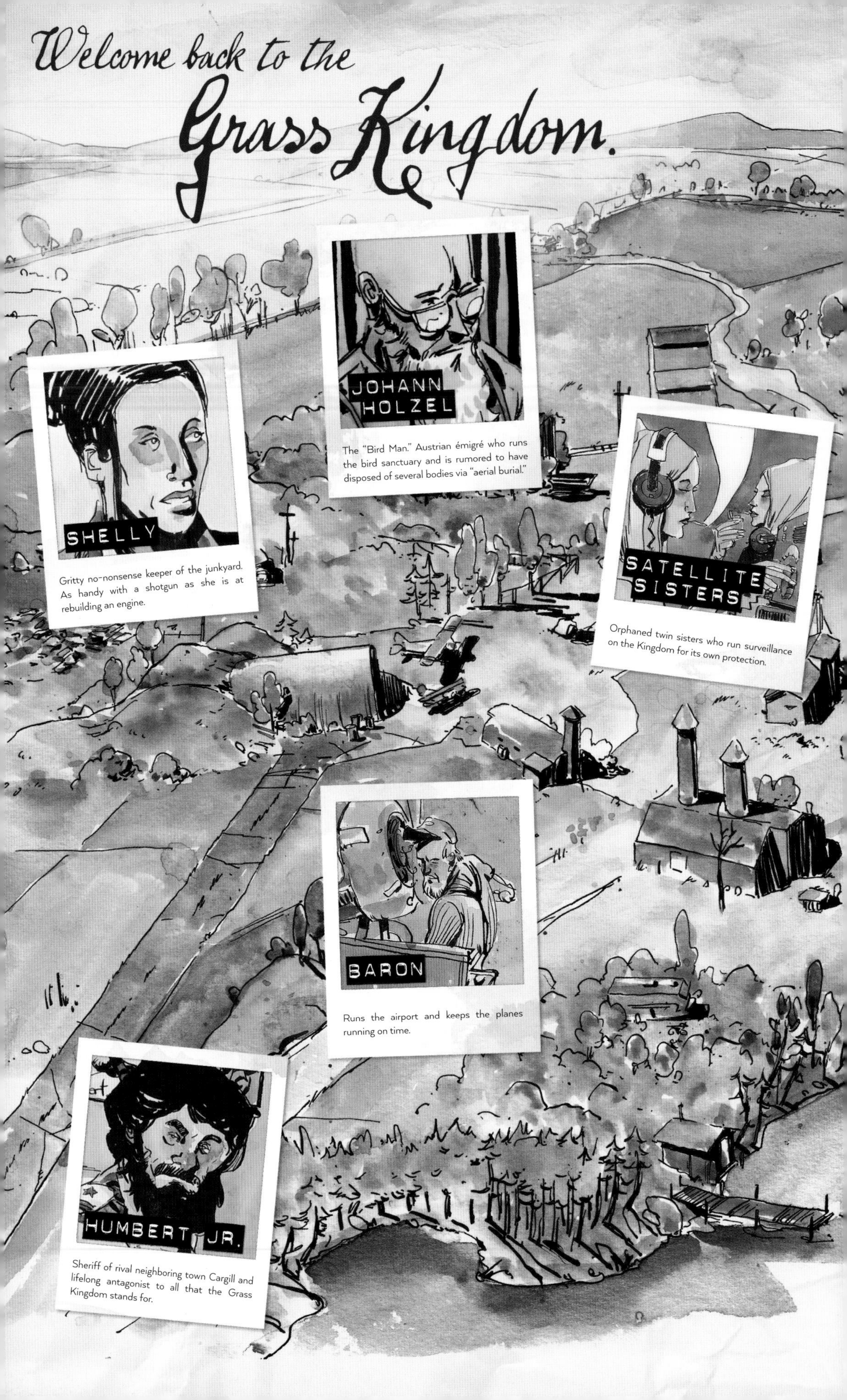
Welcome back to the Grass Kingdom.
JOHANN HOLZEL
The "Bird Man." Austrian émigré who runs the bird sanctuary and is rumored to have disposed of several bodies via "aerial burial."
SHELLY
Gritty no-nonsense keeper of the junkyard. As handy with a shotgun as she is at rebuilding an engine.
SATELLITE SISTERS
Orphaned twin sisters who run surveillance on the Kingdom for its own protection.
BARON
Runs the airport and keeps the planes running on time.
HUMBERT JR.
Sheriff of rival neighboring town Cargill and lifelong antagonist to all that the Grass Kingdom stands for.

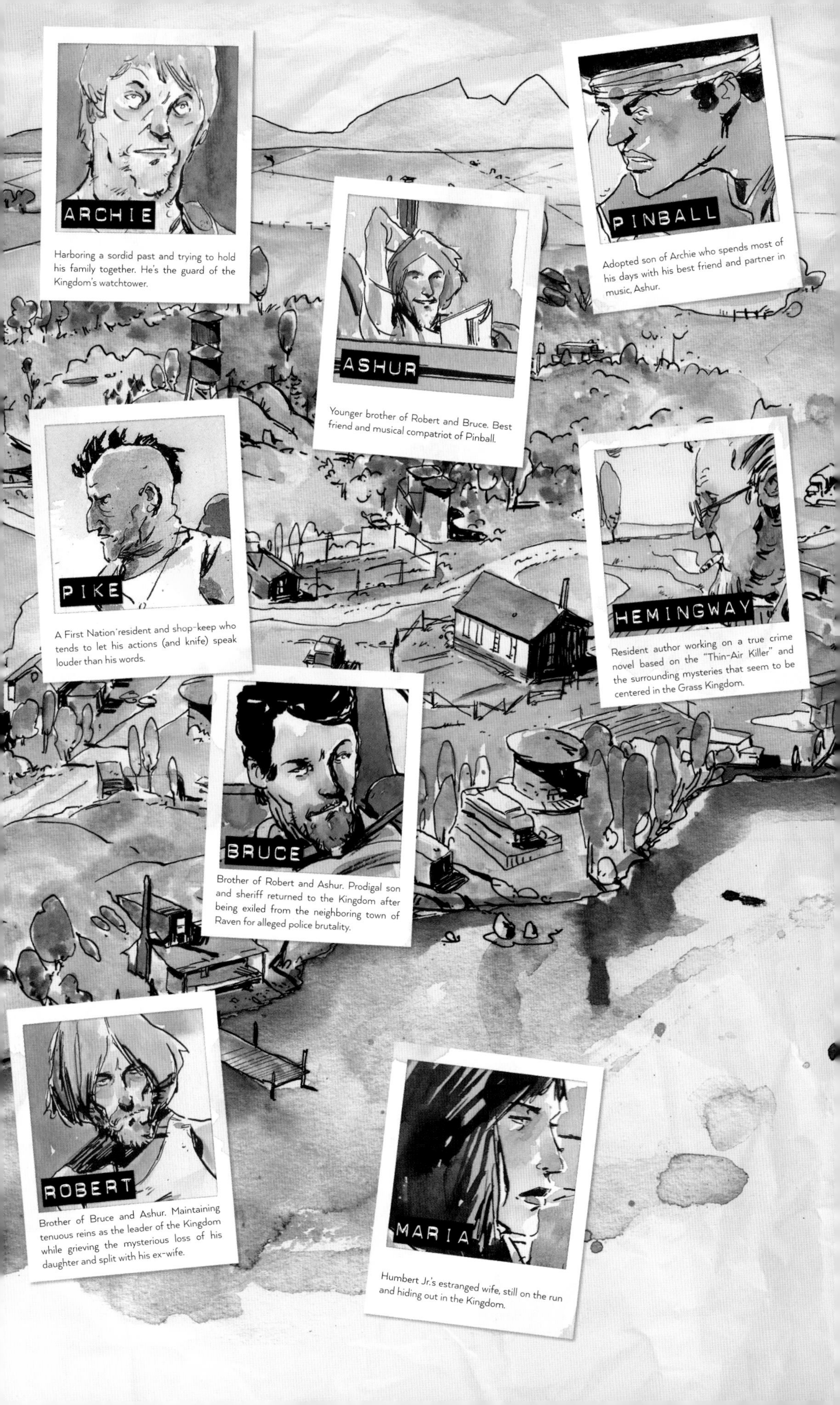

ARCHIE
Harboring a sordid past and trying to hold his family together. He's the guard of the Kingdom's watchtower.
ASHUR
Younger brother of Robert and Bruce. Best friend and musical compatriot of Pinball.
PINBALL
Adopted son of Archie who spends most of his days with his best friend and partner in music, Ashur.
PIKE
A First Nation resident and shop-keep who tends to let his actions (and knife) speak louder than his words.
HEMINGWAY
Resident author working on a true crime novel based on the "Thin-Air Killer" and the surrounding mysteries that seem to be centered in the Grass Kingdom.
BRUCE
Brother of Robert and Ashur. Prodigal son and sheriff returned to the Kingdom after being exiled from the neighboring town of Raven for alleged police brutality.
ROBERT
Brother of Bruce and Ashur. Maintaining tenuous reins as the leader of the Kingdom while grieving the mysterious loss of his daughter and split with his ex-wife.
MARIA
Humbert Jr.'s estranged wife, still on the run and hiding out in the Kingdom.

chapter twelve

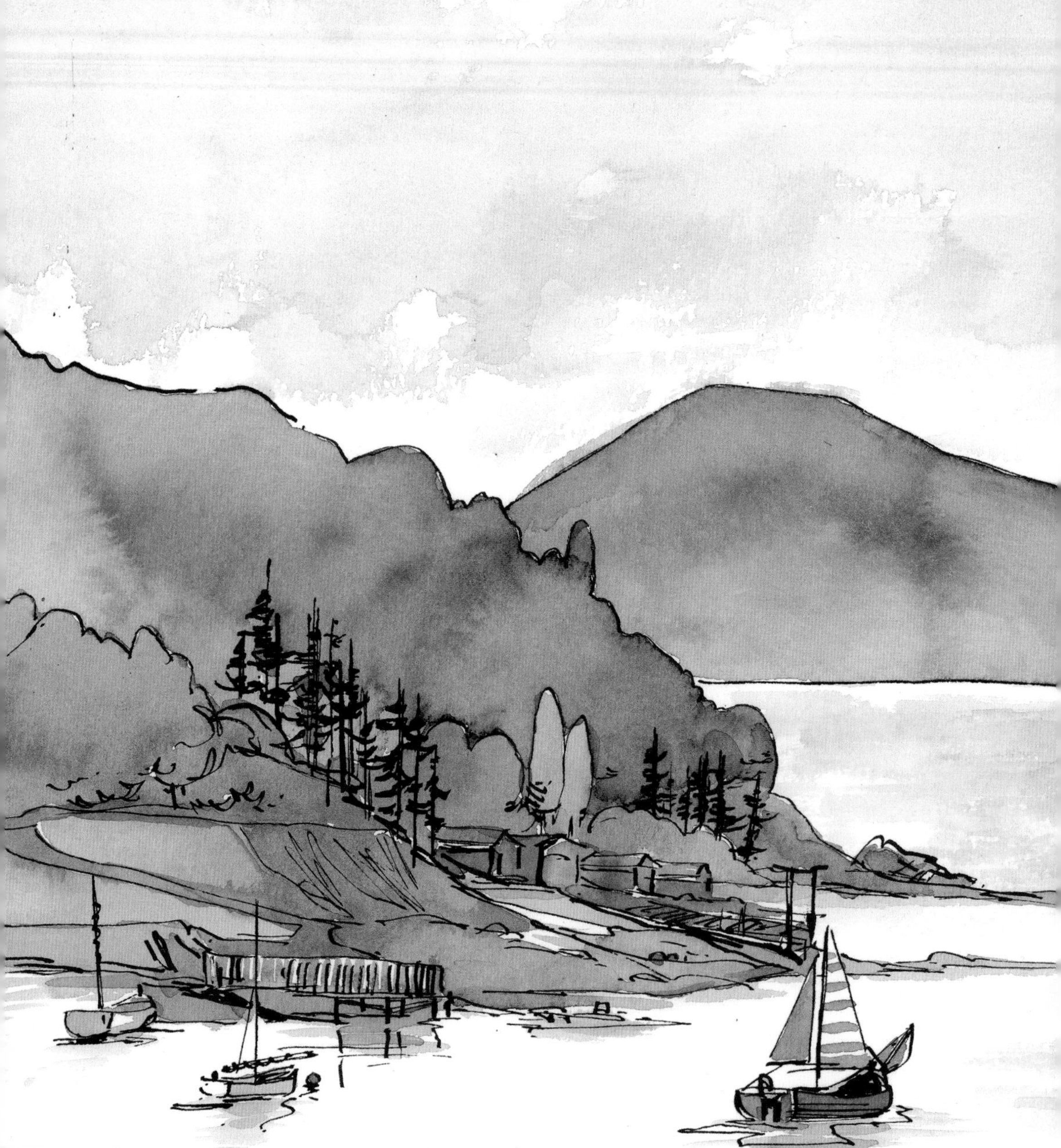

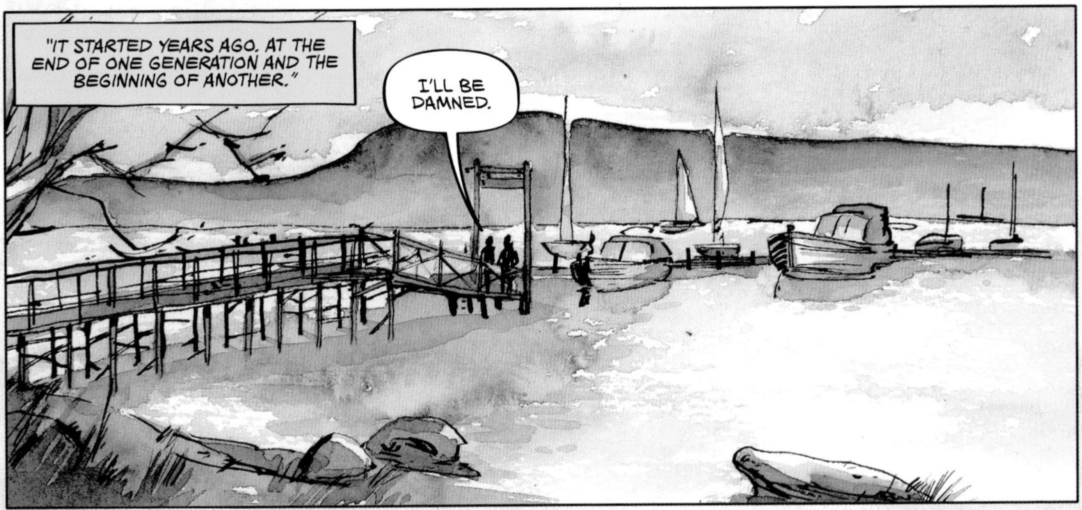
"IT STARTED YEARS AGO. AT THE END OF ONE GENERATION AND THE BEGINNING OF ANOTHER."
I'LL BE DAMNED.
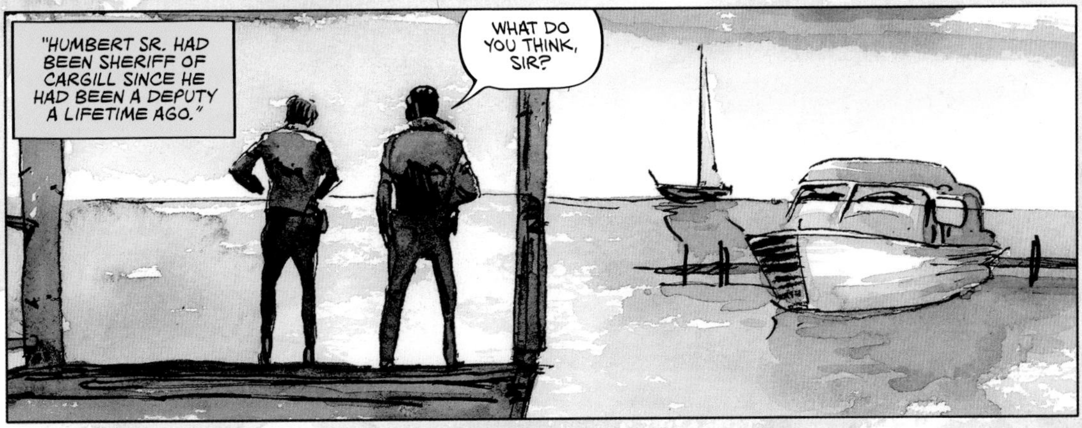
"HUMBERT SR. HAD BEEN SHERIFF OF CARGILL SINCE HE HAD BEEN A DEPUTY A LIFETIME AGO."
WHAT DO YOU THINK, SIR?
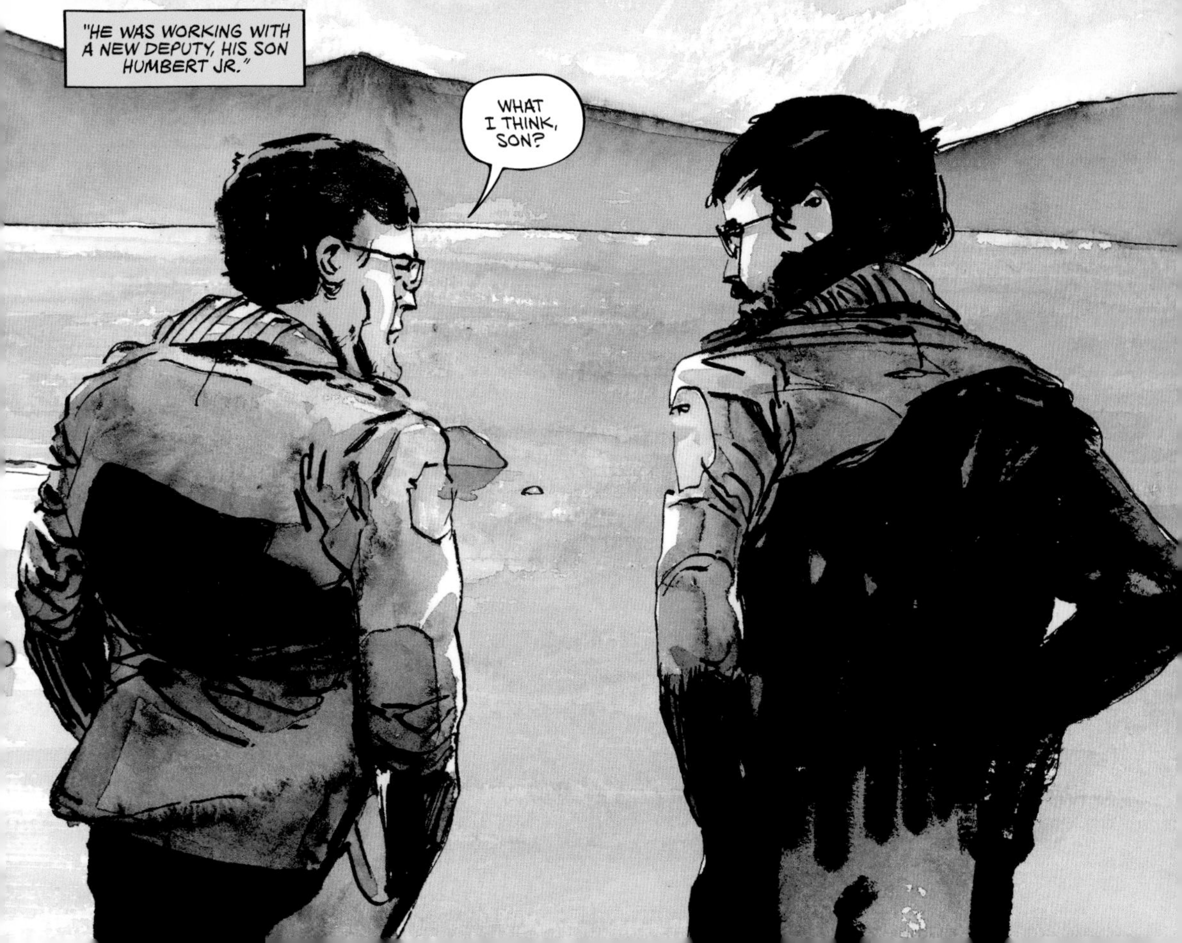
"HE WAS WORKING WITH A NEW DEPUTY, HIS SON HUMBERT JR."
WHAT I THINK, SON?

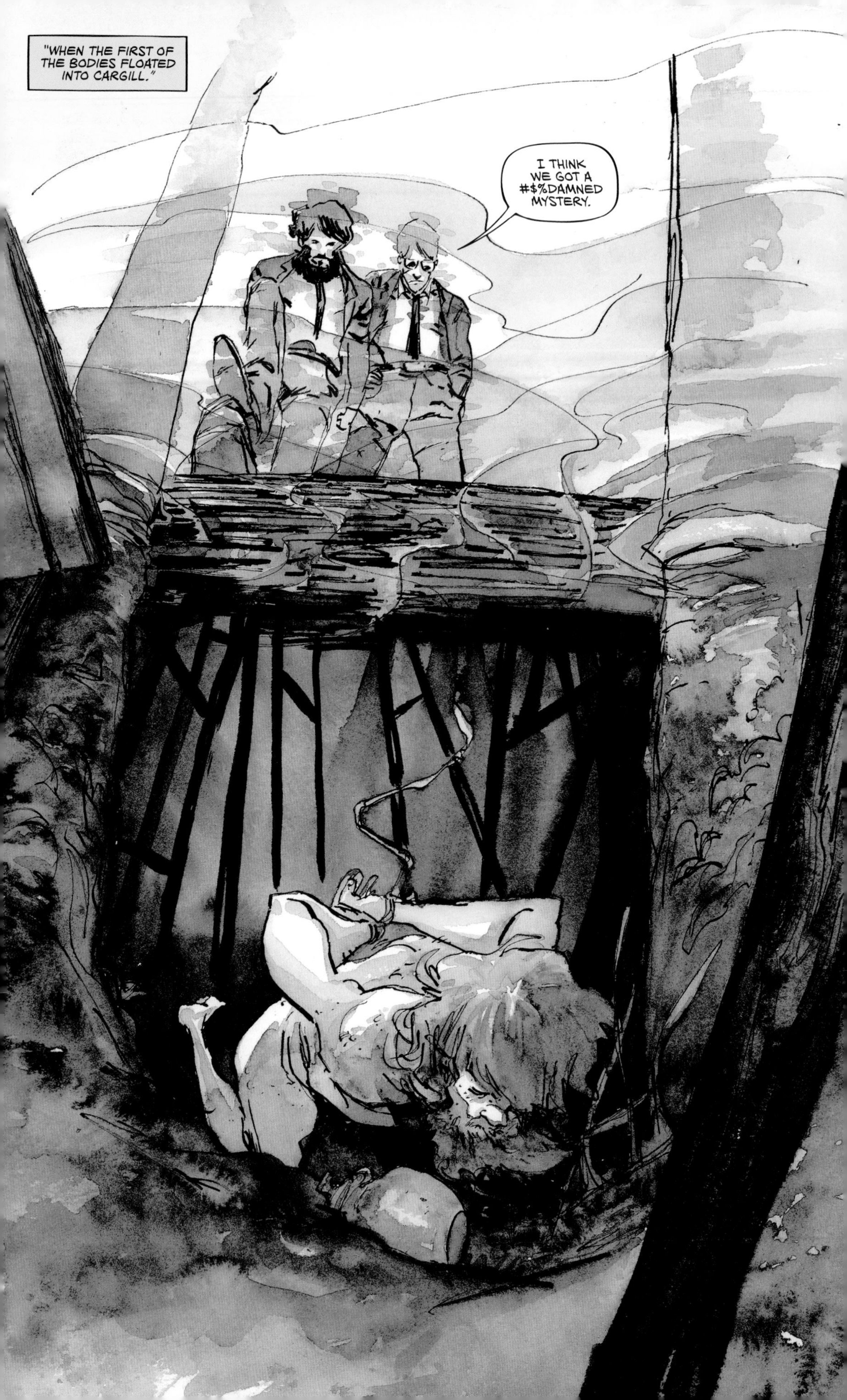
"WHEN THE FIRST OF THE BODIES FLOATED INTO CARGILL."
I THINK WE GOT A #$%DAMNED MYSTERY.

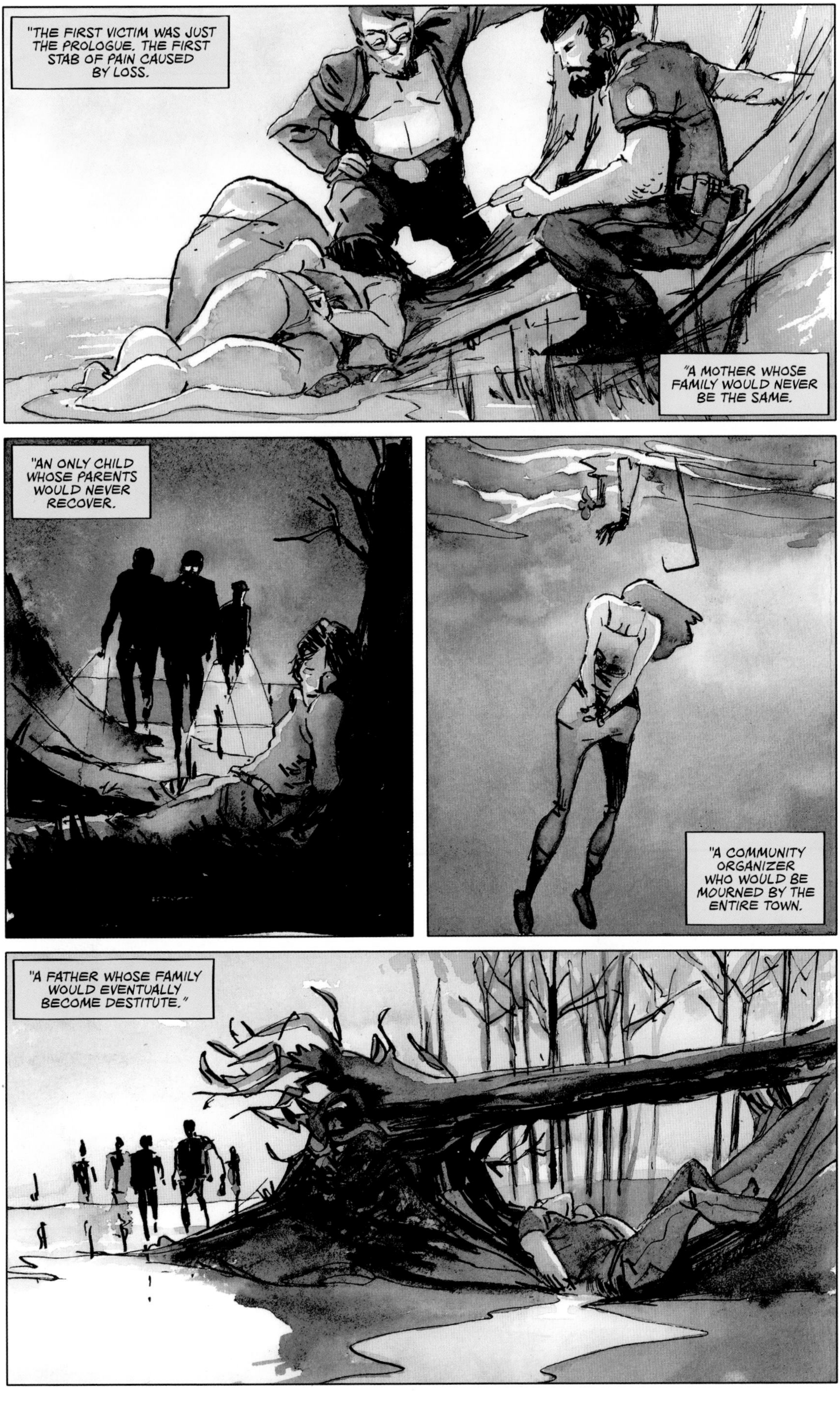
"THE FIRST VICTIM WAS JUST THE PROLOGUE. THE FIRST STAB OF PAIN CAUSED BY LOSS.
"A MOTHER WHOSE FAMILY WOULD NEVER BE THE SAME.
"AN ONLY CHILD WHOSE PARENTS WOULD NEVER RECOVER.
"A COMMUNITY ORGANIZER WHO WOULD BE MOURNED BY THE ENTIRE TOWN.
"A FATHER WHOSE FAMILY WOULD EVENTUALLY BECOME DESTITUTE."

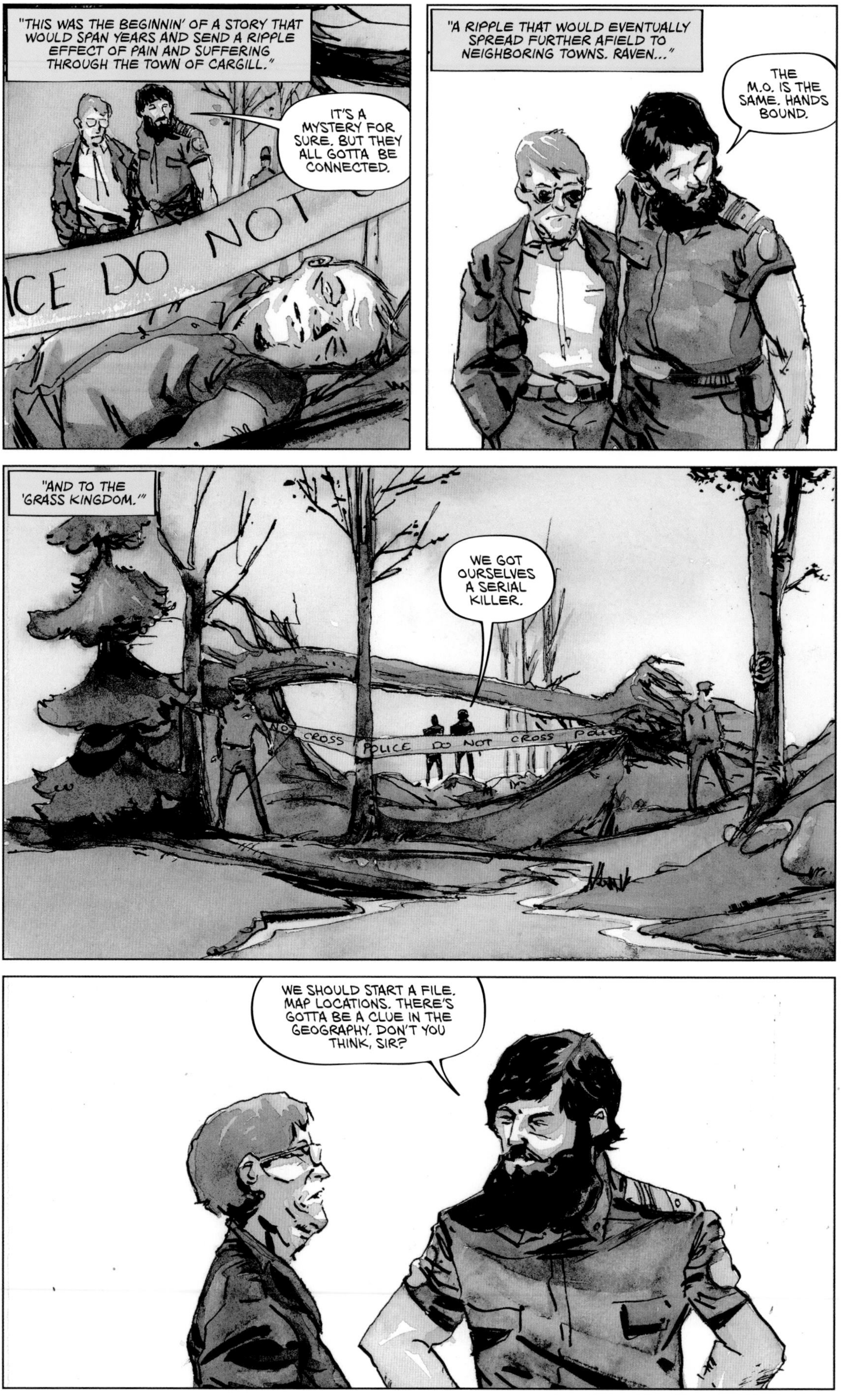
"THIS WAS THE BEGINNIN' OF A STORY THAT WOULD SPAN YEARS AND SEND A RIPPLE EFFECT OF PAIN AND SUFFERING THROUGH THE TOWN OF CARGILL."
IT'S A MYSTERY FOR SURE. BUT THEY ALL GOTTA BE CONNECTED.
ICE DO NOT
"A RIPPLE THAT WOULD EVENTUALLY SPREAD FURTHER AFIELD TO NEIGHBORING TOWNS. RAVEN..."
THE M.O. IS THE SAME. HANDS BOUND.
"AND TO THE 'GRASS KINGDOM.'"
WE GOT OURSELVES A SERIAL KILLER.
WE SHOULD START A FILE. MAP LOCATIONS. THERE'S GOTTA BE A CLUE IN THE GEOGRAPHY. DON'T YOU THINK, SIR?

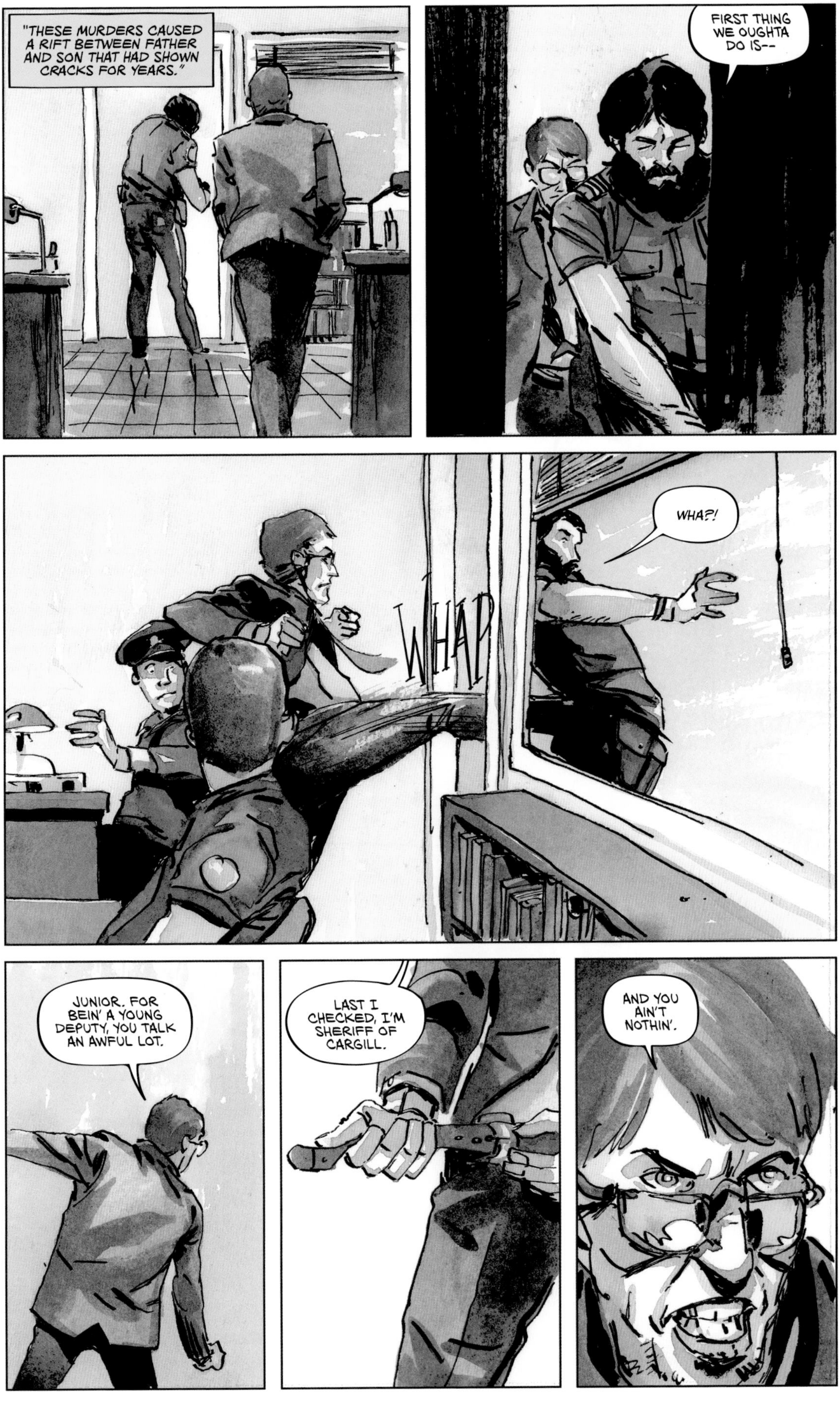
"THESE MURDERS CAUSED A RIFT BETWEEN FATHER AND SON THAT HAD SHOWN CRACKS FOR YEARS."
FIRST THING WE OUGHTA DO IS--
WHAP
WHA?!
JUNIOR. FOR BEIN' A YOUNG DEPUTY, YOU TALK AN AWFUL LOT.
LAST I CHECKED, I'M SHERIFF OF CARGILL.
AND YOU AIN'T NOTHIN'.

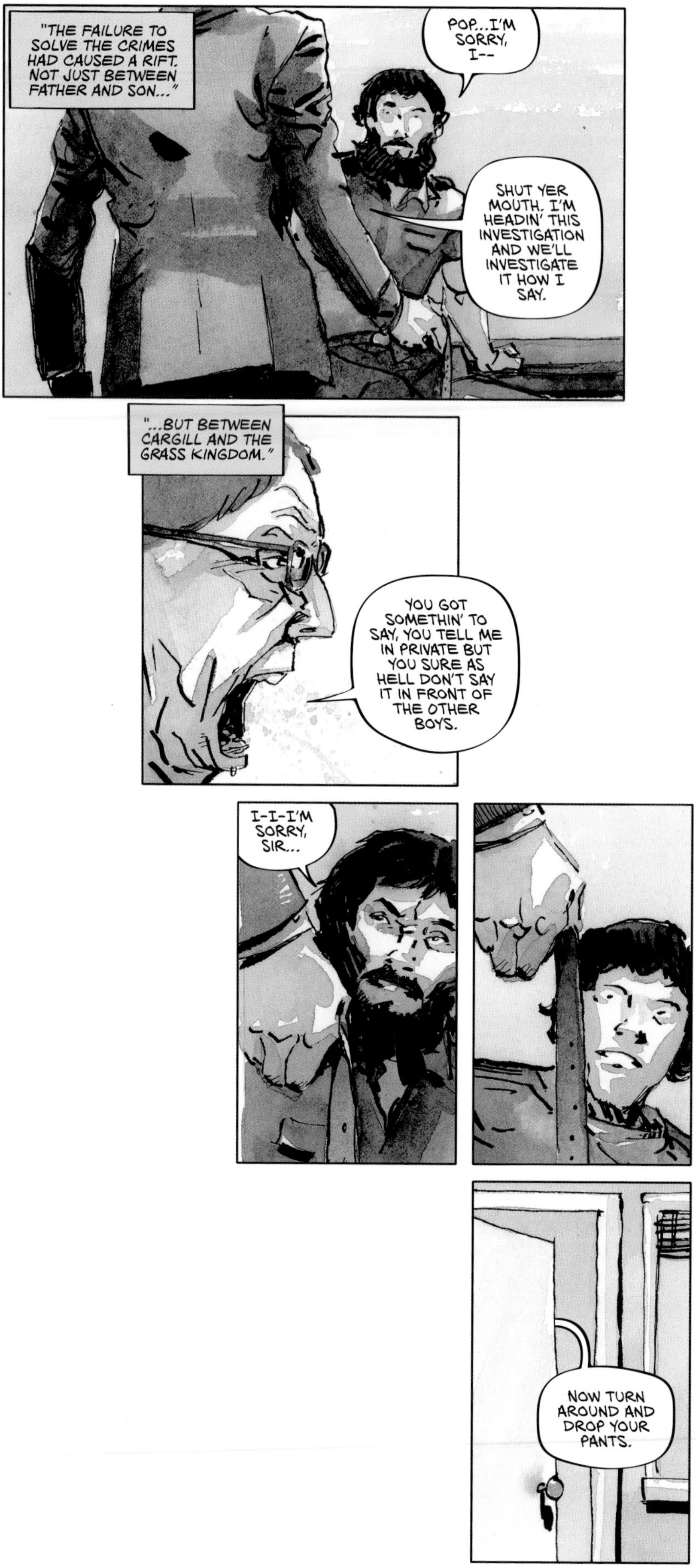
"THE FAILURE TO SOLVE THE CRIMES HAD CAUSED A RIFT. NOT JUST BETWEEN FATHER AND SON..."
POP...I'M SORRY, I--
SHUT YER MOUTH. I'M HEADIN' THIS INVESTIGATION AND WE'LL INVESTIGATE IT HOW I SAY.
"...BUT BETWEEN CARGILL AND THE GRASS KINGDOM."
YOU GOT SOMETHIN' TO SAY, YOU TELL ME IN PRIVATE BUT YOU SURE AS HELL DON'T SAY IT IN FRONT OF THE OTHER BOYS.
I-I-I'M SORRY, SIR...
NOW TURN AROUND AND DROP YOUR PANTS.

YOU WANT A BEER, DAD?
DAD?
YOU SLEEPIN? WE AIN'T HALFWAY THROUGH THE BEERS YET.
I'LL BE DAMNED.
HEART FINALLY GAVE OUT ON YA.

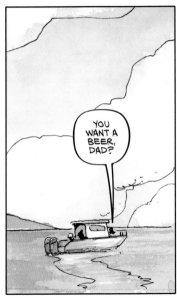

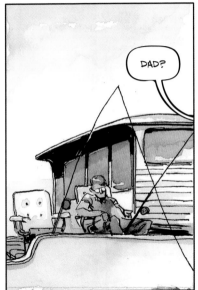

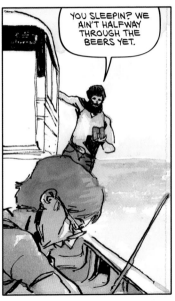

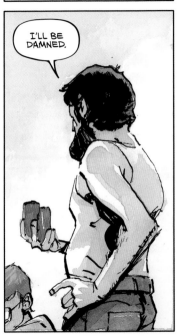

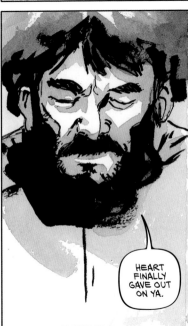

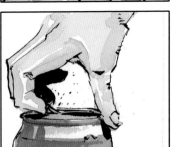

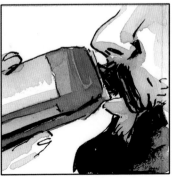

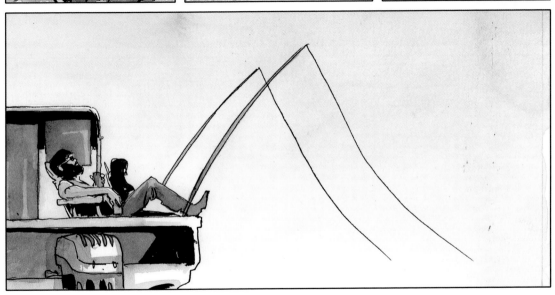

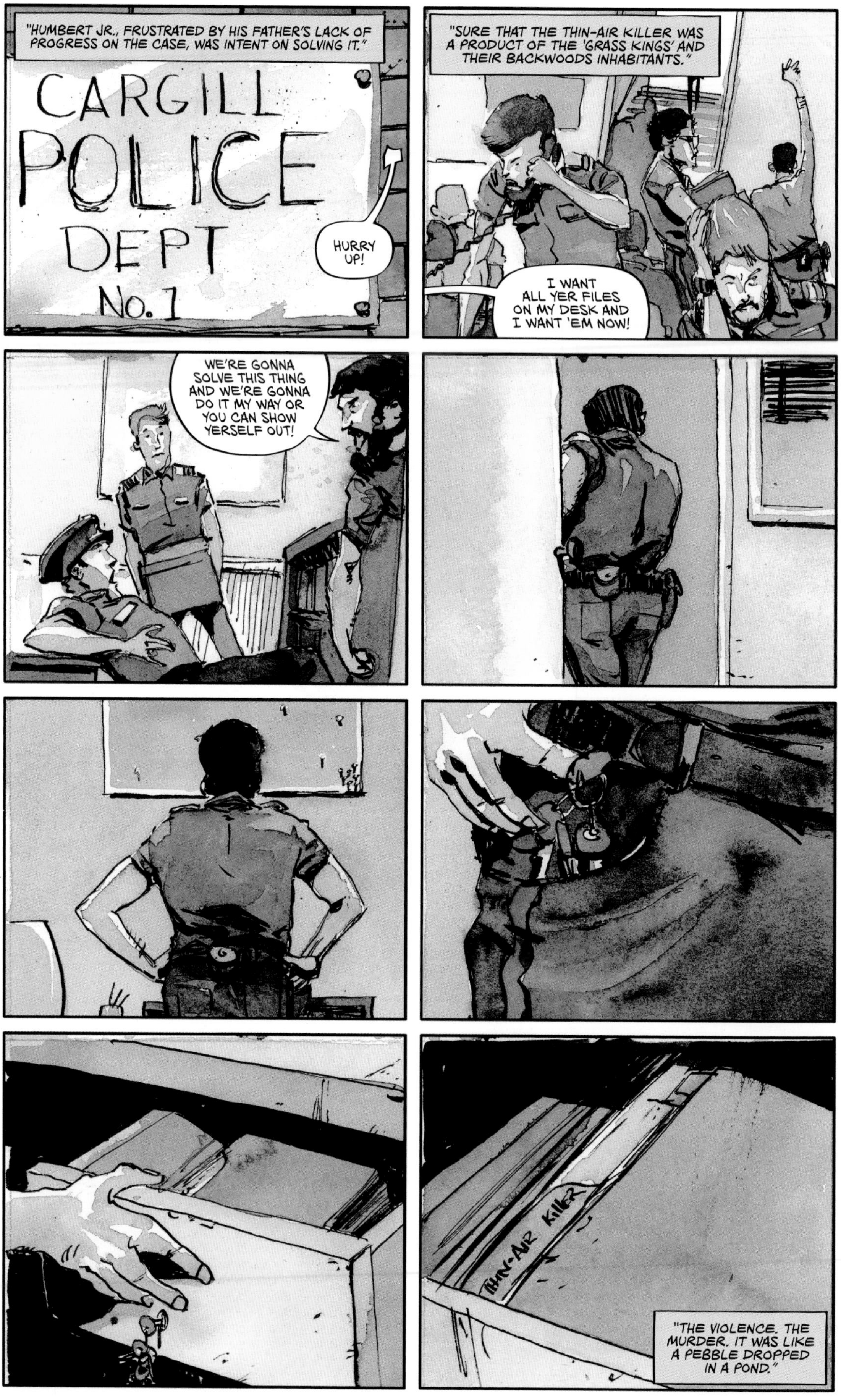
"HUMBERT JR., FRUSTRATED BY HIS FATHER'S LACK OF PROGRESS ON THE CASE, WAS INTENT ON SOLVING IT."
CARGILL POLICE DEPT No. 1
HURRY UP!
"SURE THAT THE THIN-AIR KILLER WAS A PRODUCT OF THE 'GRASS KINGS' AND THEIR BACKWOODS INHABITANTS."
I WANT ALL YER FILES ON MY DESK AND I WANT 'EM NOW!
WE'RE GONNA SOLVE THIS THING AND WE'RE GONNA DO IT MY WAY OR YOU CAN SHOW YERSELF OUT!
THIN-AIR KILLER
"THE VIOLENCE. THE MURDER. IT WAS LIKE A PEBBLE DROPPED IN A POND."

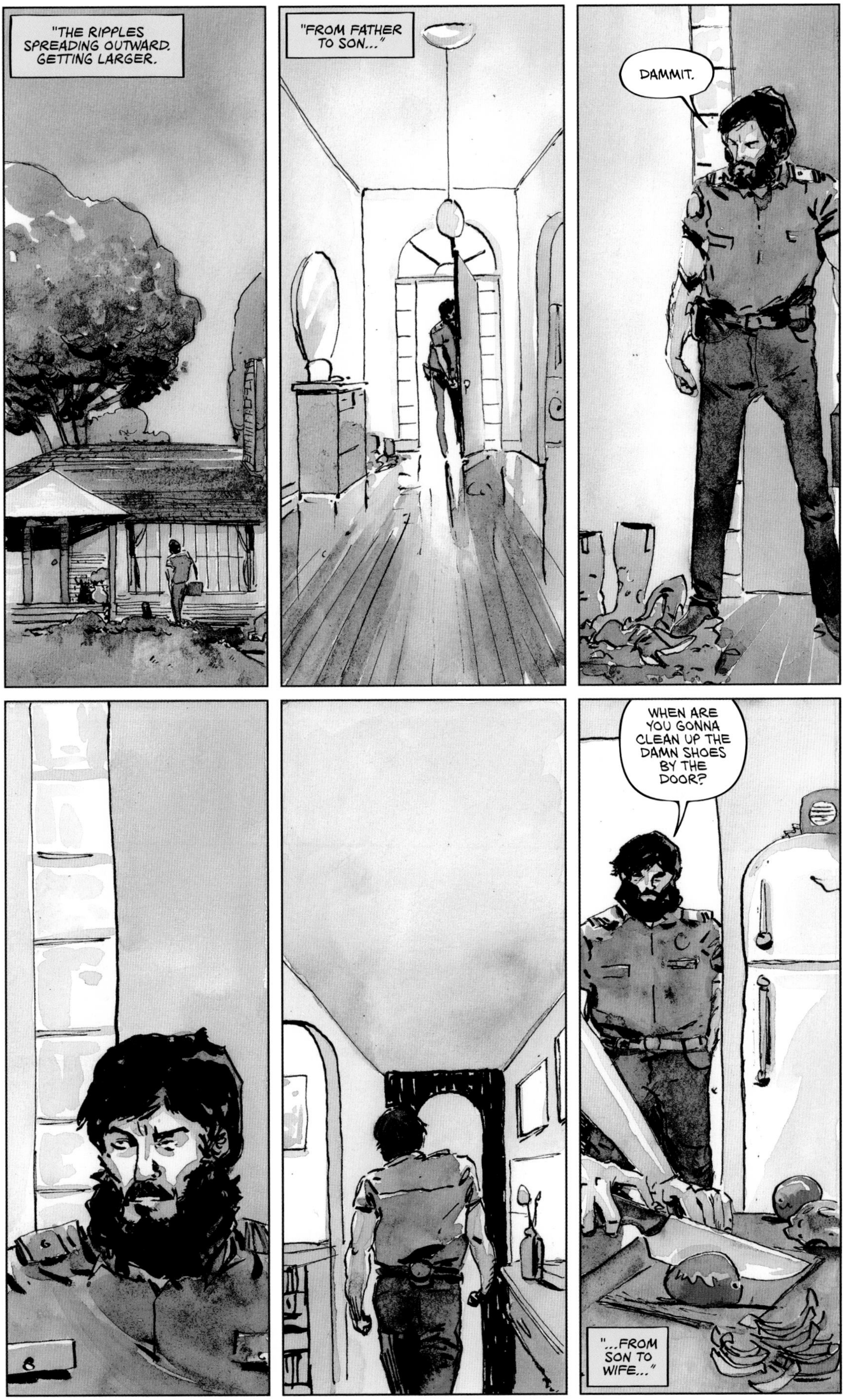
"THE RIPPLES SPREADING OUTWARD. GETTING LARGER.
"FROM FATHER TO SON..."
DAMMIT.
WHEN ARE YOU GONNA CLEAN UP THE DAMN SHOES BY THE DOOR?
"...FROM SON TO WIFE..."

SORRY--
I LOST TRACK OF
TIME. I'LL GET
THEM RIGHT
AFTER--

@#$%. BETWEEN
THE KNUCKLEHEADS
AT WORK AND
YOU HERE AT
HOME...

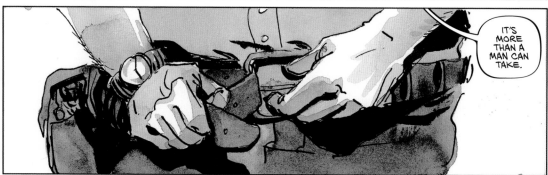

IT'S
MORE
THAN A
MAN CAN
TAKE.

BUT THINGS
ARE GONNA BE
DIFFERENT
NOW.

THAT
I CAN
PROMISE
YOU.

WELCOME TO
CARGILL

"...AND FROM
TOWN TO TOWN."

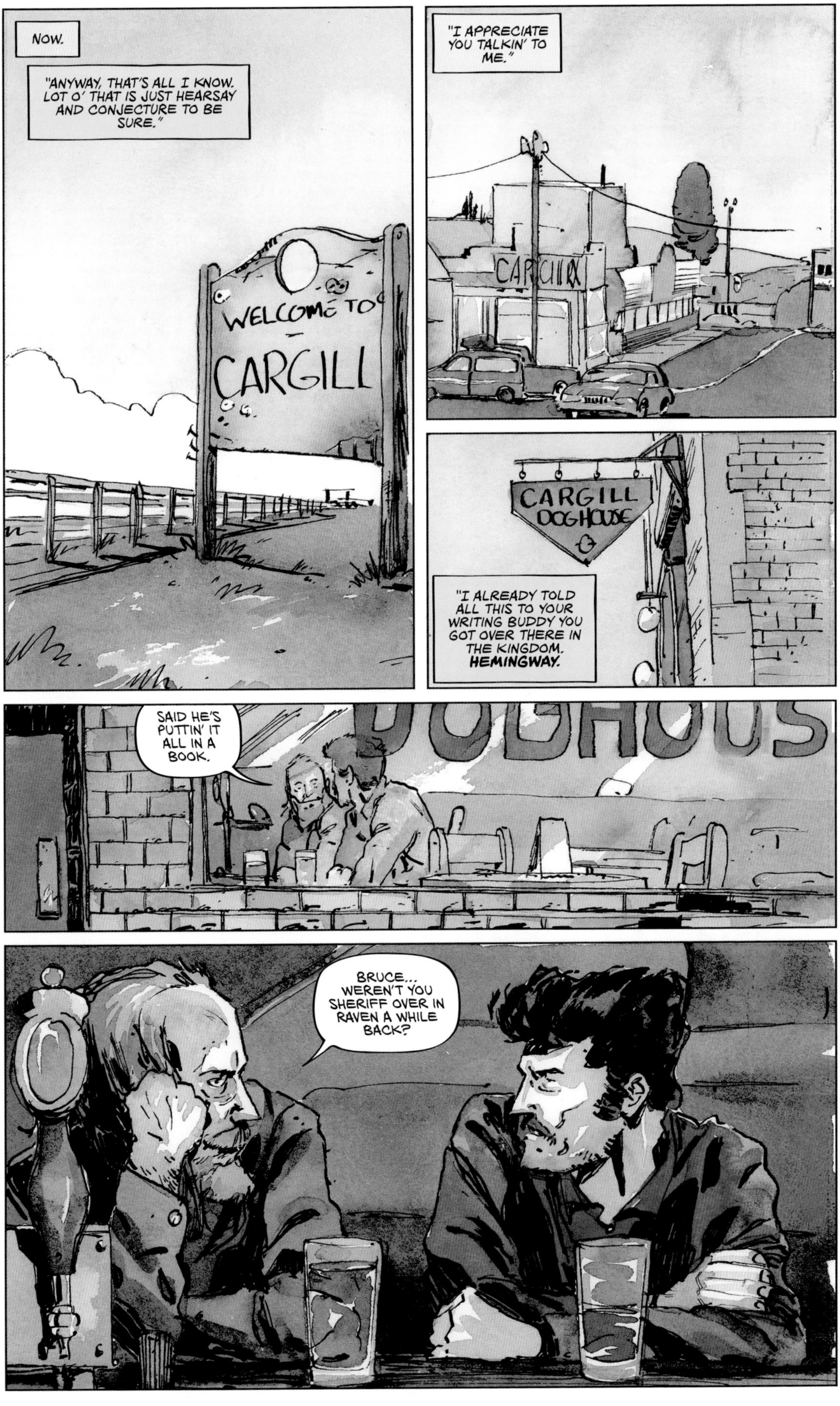
NOW.
"ANYWAY, THAT'S ALL I KNOW. LOT O' THAT IS JUST HEARSAY AND CONJECTURE TO BE SURE."
WELCOME TO
CARGILL
"I APPRECIATE YOU TALKIN' TO ME."
CARGILL DOGHOUSE
"I ALREADY TOLD ALL THIS TO YOUR WRITING BUDDY YOU GOT OVER THERE IN THE KINGDOM. **HEMINGWAY.**
SAID HE'S PUTTIN' IT ALL IN A BOOK.
BRUCE... WEREN'T YOU SHERIFF OVER IN RAVEN A WHILE BACK?

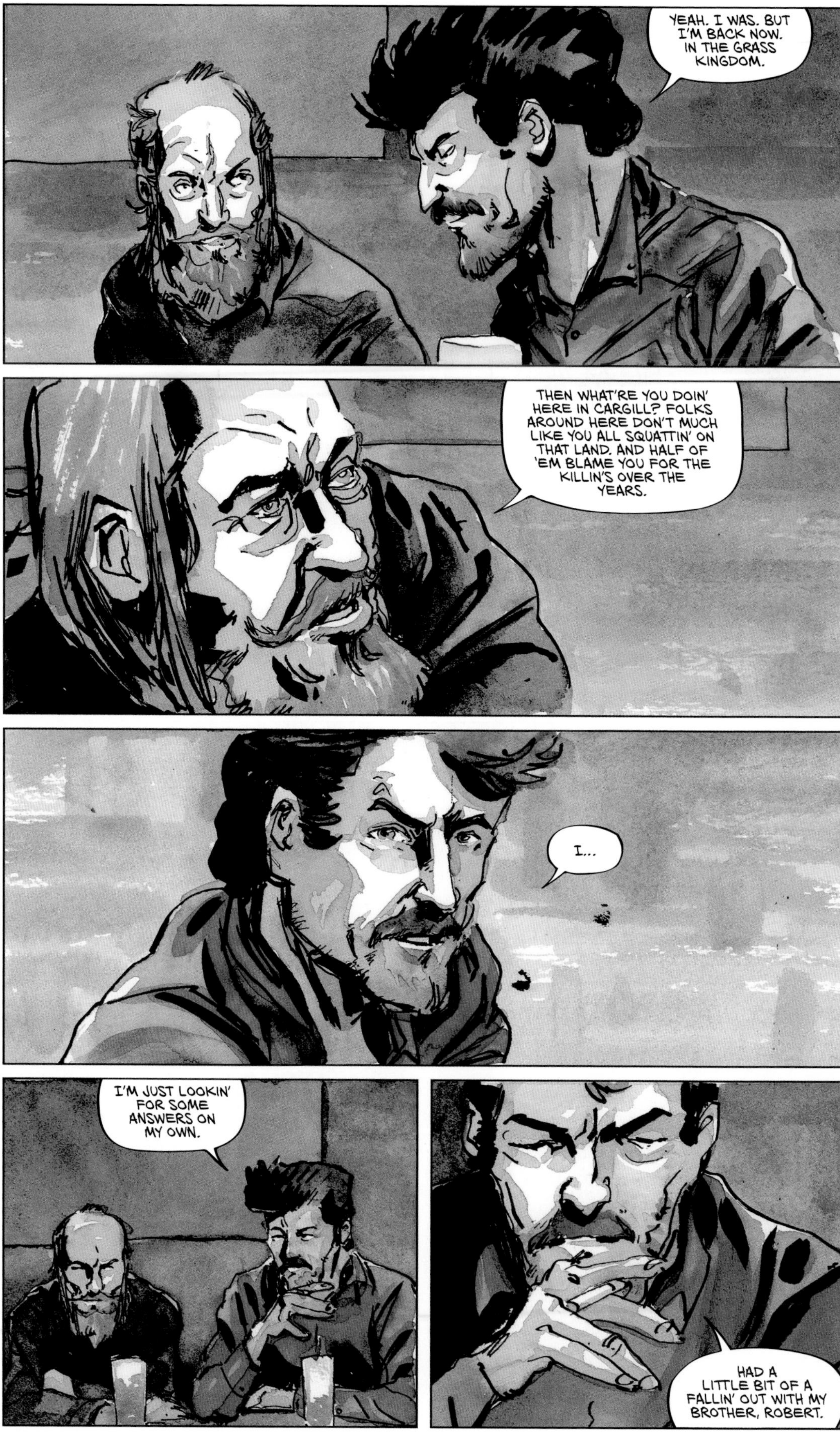

YEAH. I WAS. BUT I'M BACK NOW. IN THE GRASS KINGDOM.
THEN WHAT'RE YOU DOIN' HERE IN CARGILL? FOLKS AROUND HERE DON'T MUCH LIKE YOU ALL SQUATTIN' ON THAT LAND. AND HALF OF 'EM BLAME YOU FOR THE KILLIN'S OVER THE YEARS.
I...
I'M JUST LOOKIN' FOR SOME ANSWERS ON MY OWN.
HAD A LITTLE BIT OF A FALLIN' OUT WITH MY BROTHER, ROBERT.

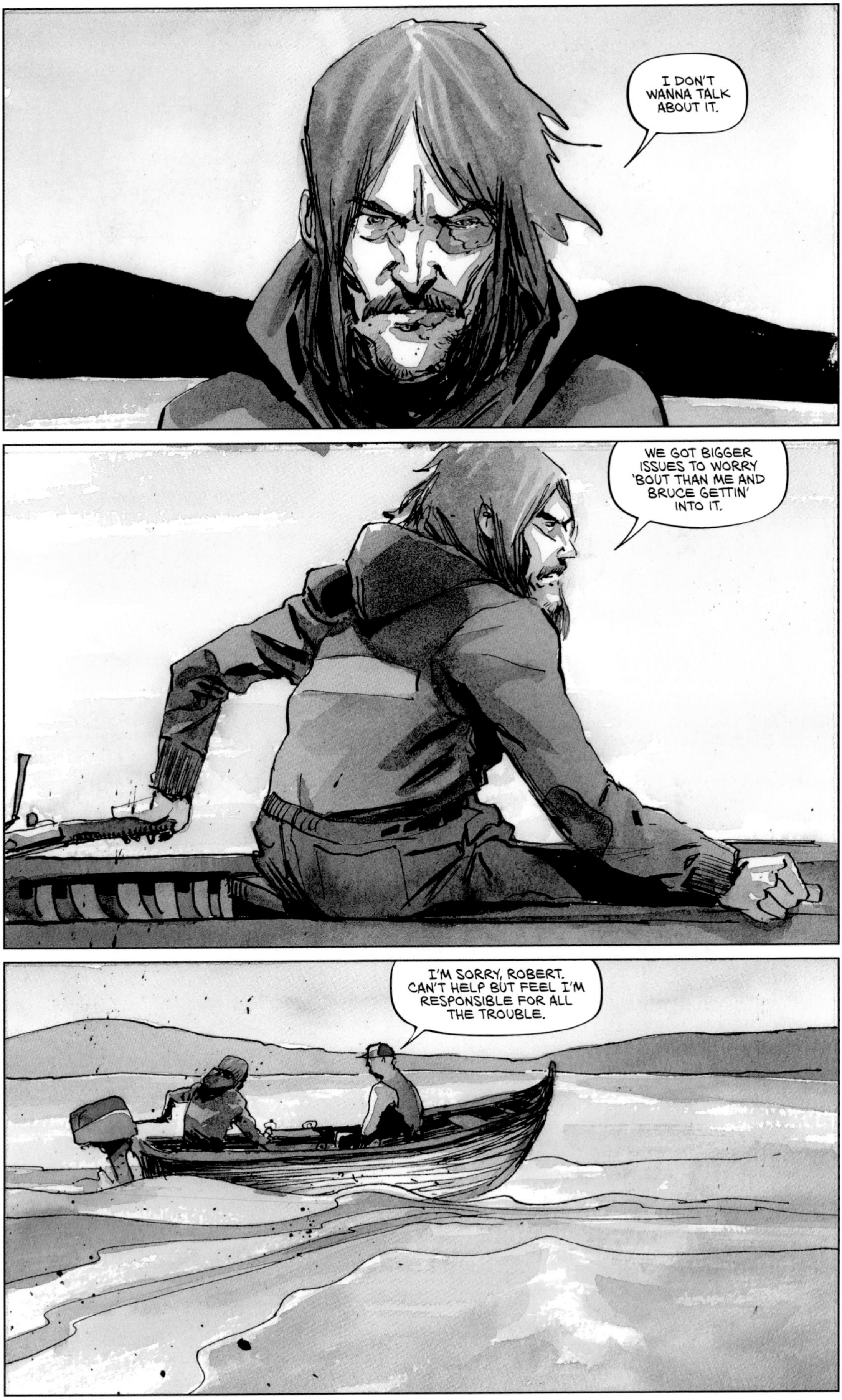
I DON'T WANNA TALK ABOUT IT.
WE GOT BIGGER ISSUES TO WORRY 'BOUT THAN ME AND BRUCE GETTIN' INTO IT.
I'M SORRY, ROBERT. CAN'T HELP BUT FEEL I'M RESPONSIBLE FOR ALL THE TROUBLE.

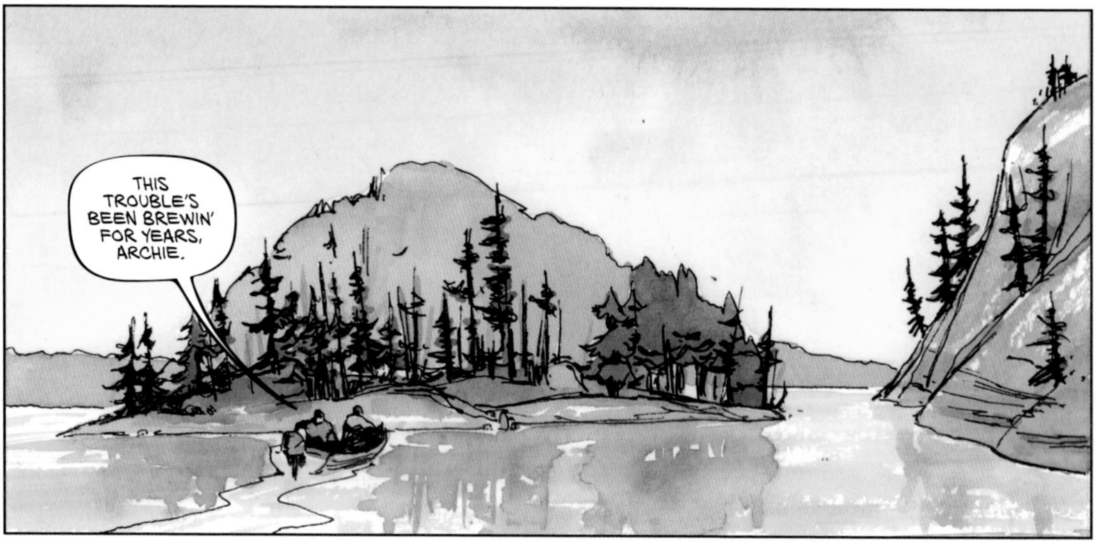
THIS TROUBLE'S BEEN BREWIN' FOR YEARS, ARCHIE.

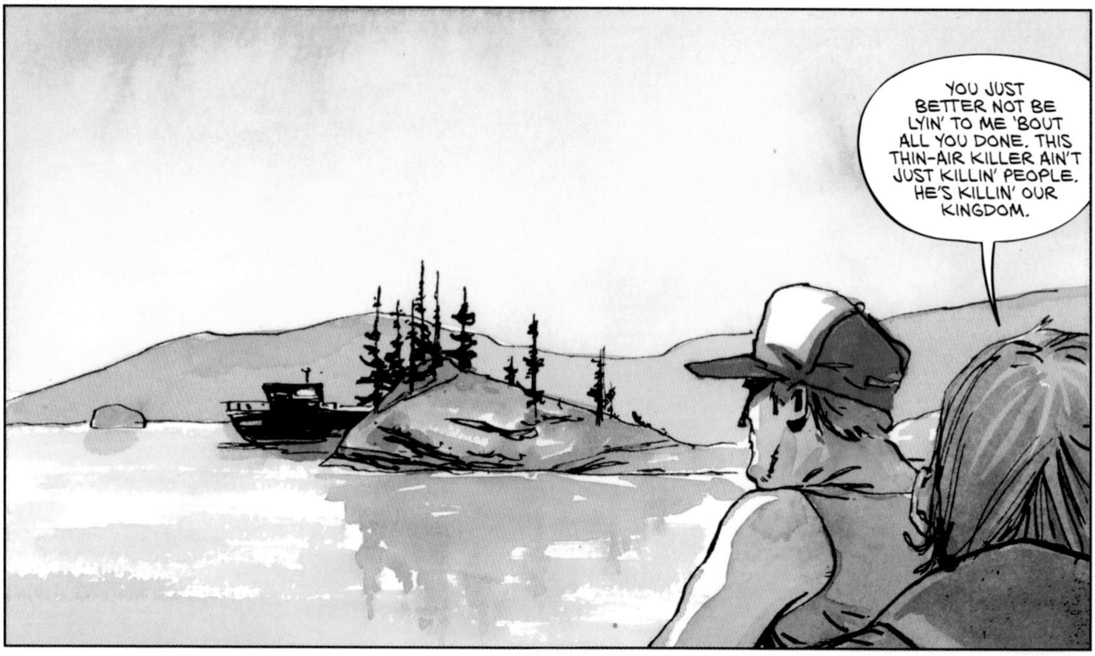
YOU JUST BETTER NOT BE LYIN' TO ME 'BOUT ALL YOU DONE. THIS THIN-AIR KILLER AIN'T JUST KILLIN' PEOPLE. HE'S KILLIN' OUR KINGDOM.

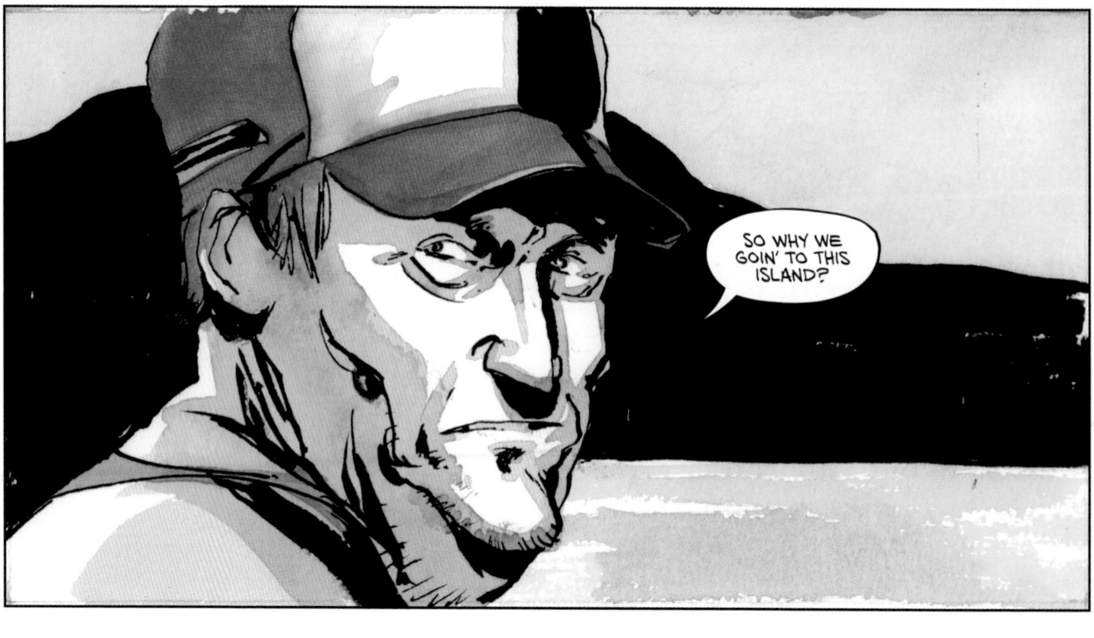
SO WHY WE GOIN' TO THIS ISLAND?

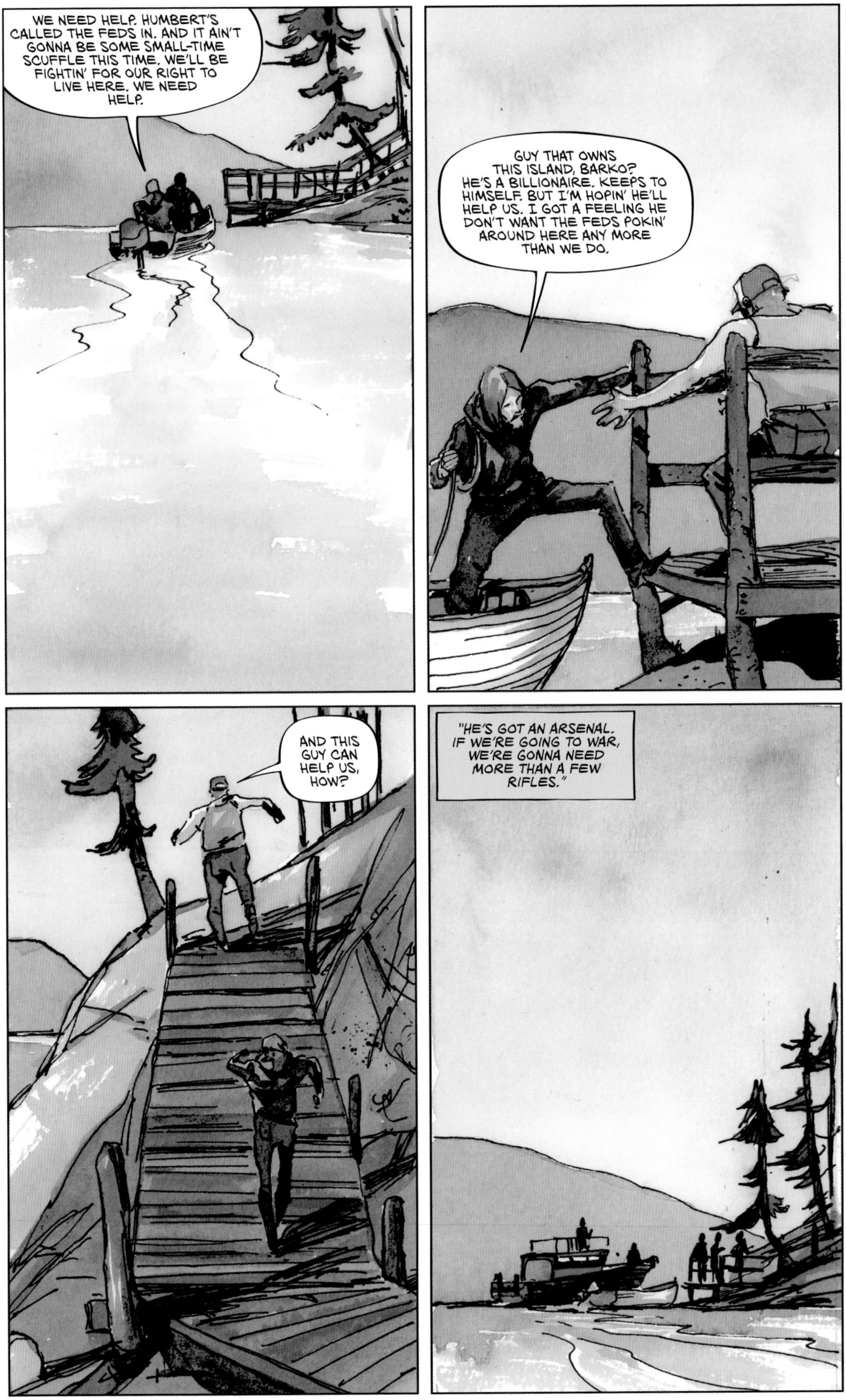
WE NEED HELP. HUMBERT'S CALLED THE FEDS IN. AND IT AIN'T GONNA BE SOME SMALL-TIME SCUFFLE THIS TIME. WE'LL BE FIGHTIN' FOR OUR RIGHT TO LIVE HERE. WE NEED HELP.
GUY THAT OWNS THIS ISLAND, BARKO? HE'S A BILLIONAIRE. KEEPS TO HIMSELF. BUT I'M HOPIN' HE'LL HELP US. I GOT A FEELING HE DON'T WANT THE FEDS POKIN' AROUND HERE ANY MORE THAN WE DO.
AND THIS GUY CAN HELP US, HOW?
"HE'S GOT AN ARSENAL. IF WE'RE GOING TO WAR, WE'RE GONNA NEED MORE THAN A FEW RIFLES."

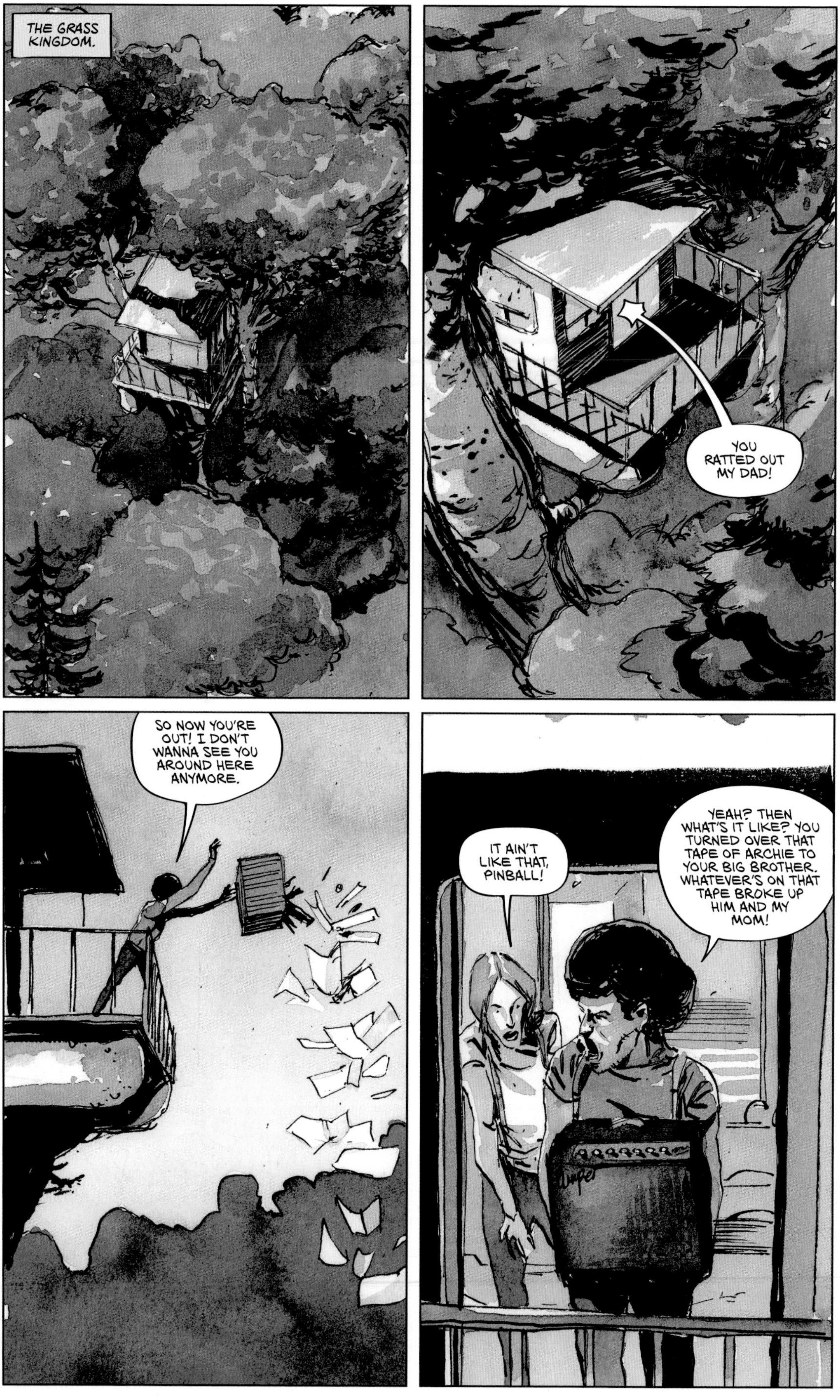
THE GRASS KINGDOM.
YOU RATTED OUT MY DAD!
SO NOW YOU'RE OUT! I DON'T WANNA SEE YOU AROUND HERE ANYMORE.
IT AIN'T LIKE THAT, PINBALL!
YEAH? THEN WHAT'S IT LIKE? YOU TURNED OVER THAT TAPE OF ARCHIE TO YOUR BIG BROTHER. WHATEVER'S ON THAT TAPE BROKE UP HIM AND MY MOM!

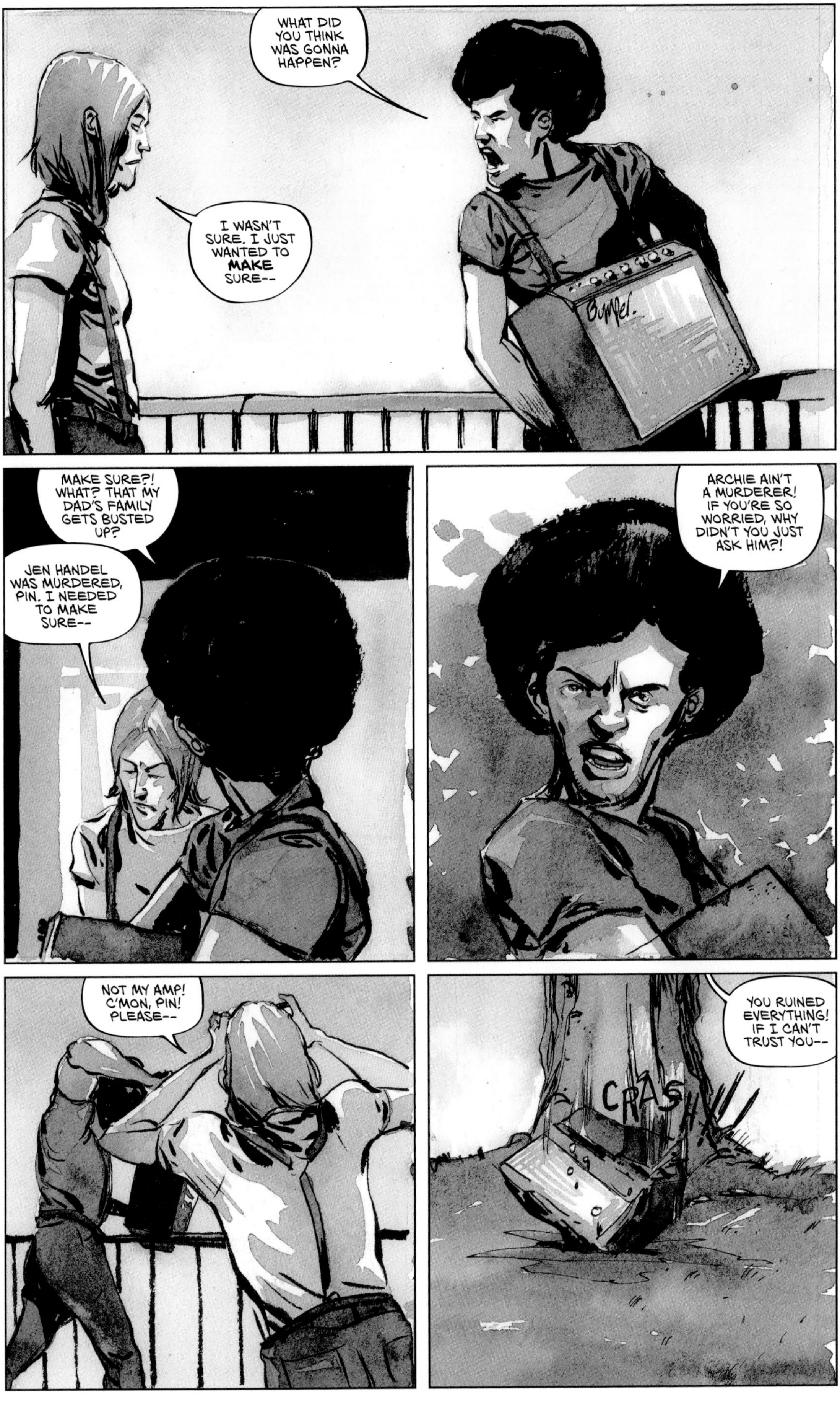
WHAT DID YOU THINK WAS GONNA HAPPEN?
I WASN'T SURE. I JUST WANTED TO **MAKE** SURE--
Bummer.
MAKE SURE?! WHAT? THAT MY DAD'S FAMILY GETS BUSTED UP?
JEN HANDEL WAS MURDERED, PIN. I NEEDED TO MAKE SURE--
ARCHIE AIN'T A MURDERER! IF YOU'RE SO WORRIED, WHY DIDN'T YOU JUST ASK HIM?!
NOT MY AMP! C'MON, PIN! PLEASE--
YOU RUINED EVERYTHING! IF I CAN'T TRUST YOU--
CRASH!!

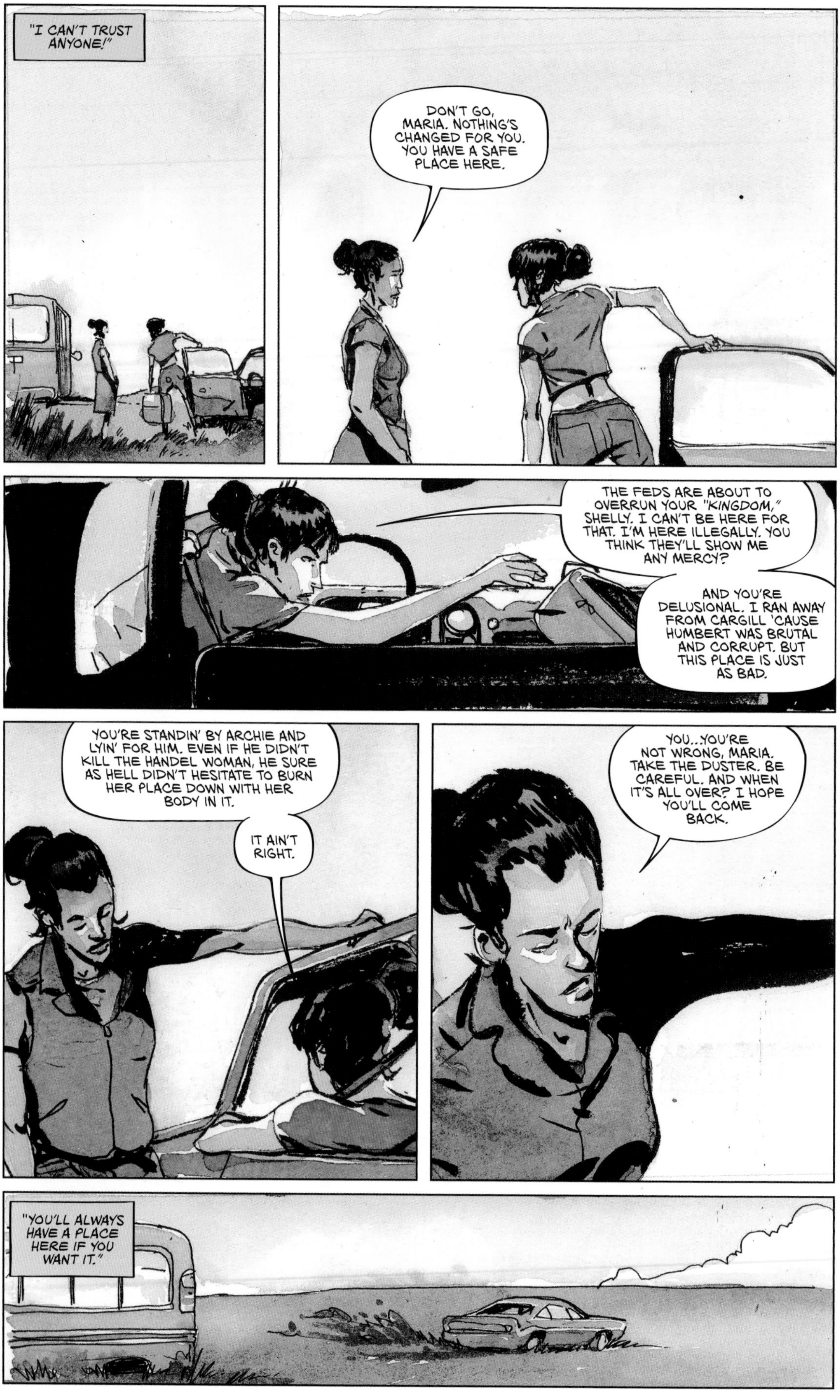

"I CAN'T TRUST ANYONE!"
DON'T GO, MARIA. NOTHING'S CHANGED FOR YOU. YOU HAVE A SAFE PLACE HERE.
THE FEDS ARE ABOUT TO OVERRUN YOUR "KINGDOM," SHELLY. I CAN'T BE HERE FOR THAT. I'M HERE ILLEGALLY. YOU THINK THEY'LL SHOW ME ANY MERCY?
AND YOU'RE DELUSIONAL. I RAN AWAY FROM CARGILL 'CAUSE HUMBERT WAS BRUTAL AND CORRUPT. BUT THIS PLACE IS JUST AS BAD.
YOU'RE STANDIN' BY ARCHIE AND LYIN' FOR HIM. EVEN IF HE DIDN'T KILL THE HANDEL WOMAN, HE SURE AS HELL DIDN'T HESITATE TO BURN HER PLACE DOWN WITH HER BODY IN IT.
IT AIN'T RIGHT.
YOU...YOU'RE NOT WRONG, MARIA. TAKE THE DUSTER. BE CAREFUL. AND WHEN IT'S ALL OVER? I HOPE YOU'LL COME BACK.
"YOU'LL ALWAYS HAVE A PLACE HERE IF YOU WANT IT."

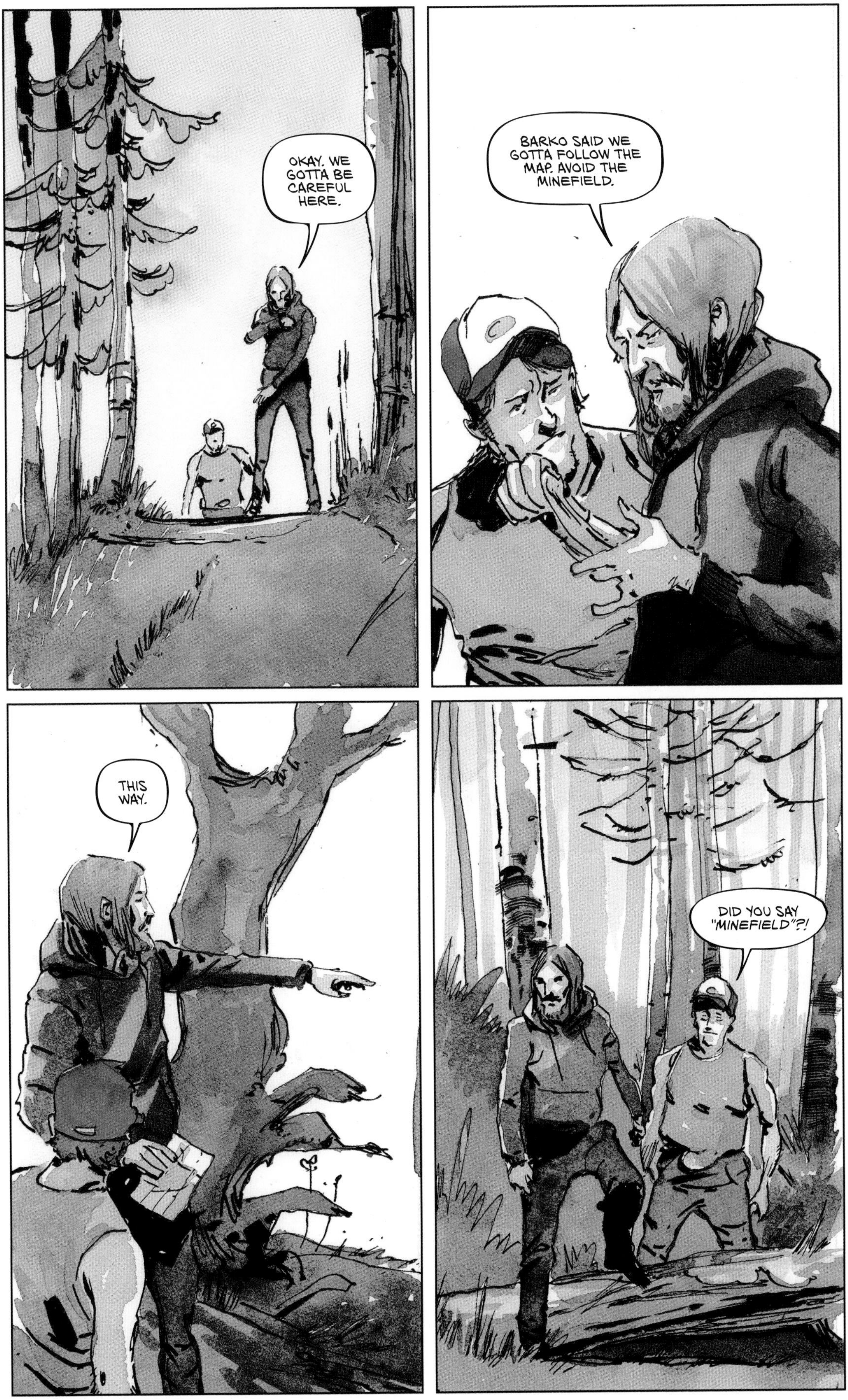
OKAY. WE GOTTA BE CAREFUL HERE.
BARKO SAID WE GOTTA FOLLOW THE MAP. AVOID THE MINEFIELD.
THIS WAY.
DID YOU SAY "MINEFIELD"?!

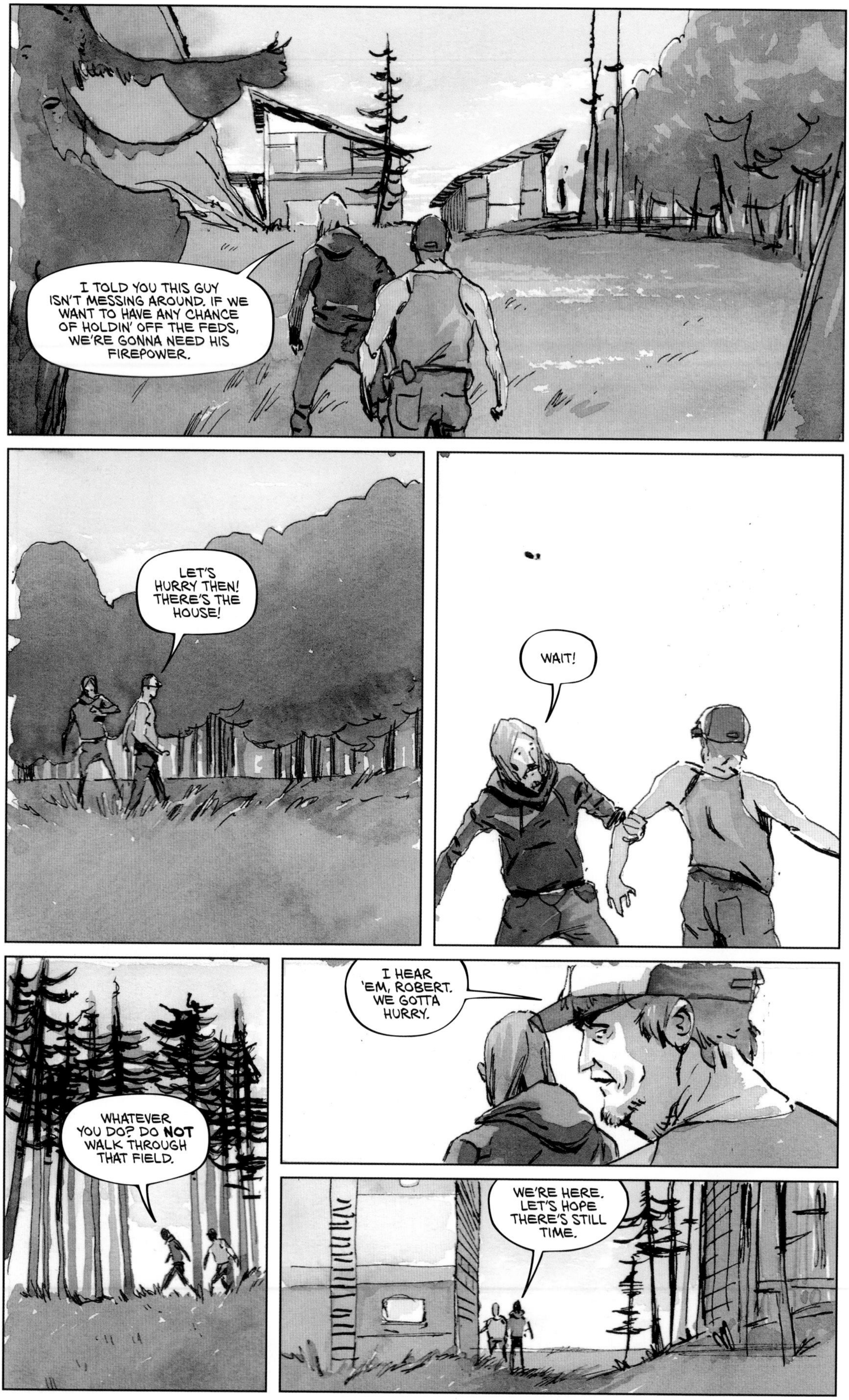
I TOLD YOU THIS GUY ISN'T MESSING AROUND. IF WE WANT TO HAVE ANY CHANCE OF HOLDIN' OFF THE FEDS, WE'RE GONNA NEED HIS FIREPOWER.
LET'S HURRY THEN! THERE'S THE HOUSE!
WAIT!
WHATEVER YOU DO? DO **NOT** WALK THROUGH THAT FIELD.
I HEAR 'EM, ROBERT. WE GOTTA HURRY.
WE'RE HERE. LET'S HOPE THERE'S STILL TIME.

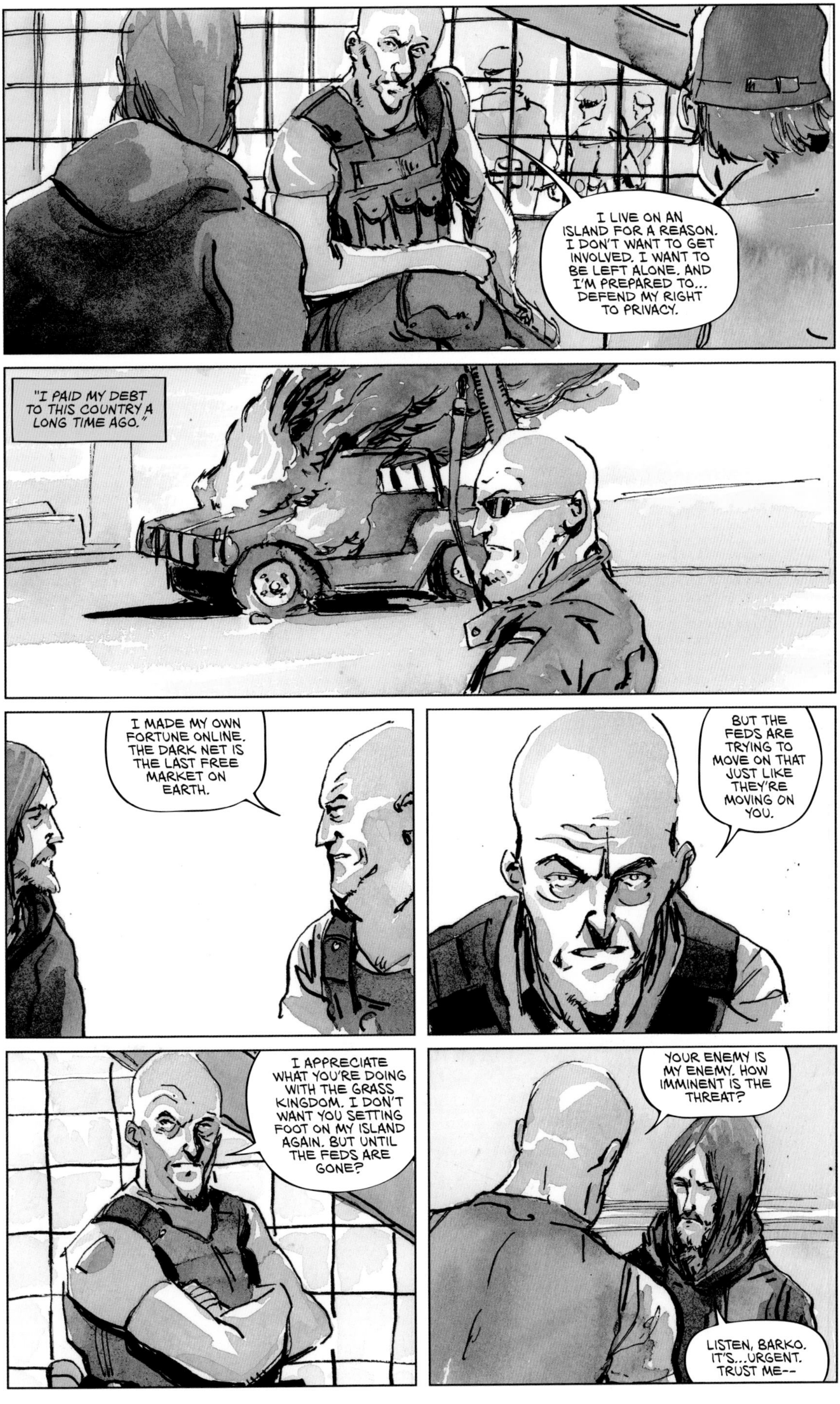
I LIVE ON AN ISLAND FOR A REASON. I DON'T WANT TO GET INVOLVED. I WANT TO BE LEFT ALONE. AND I'M PREPARED TO... DEFEND MY RIGHT TO PRIVACY.
"I PAID MY DEBT TO THIS COUNTRY A LONG TIME AGO."
I MADE MY OWN FORTUNE ONLINE. THE DARK NET IS THE LAST FREE MARKET ON EARTH.
BUT THE FEDS ARE TRYING TO MOVE ON THAT JUST LIKE THEY'RE MOVING ON YOU.
I APPRECIATE WHAT YOU'RE DOING WITH THE GRASS KINGDOM. I DON'T WANT YOU SETTING FOOT ON MY ISLAND AGAIN. BUT UNTIL THE FEDS ARE GONE?
YOUR ENEMY IS MY ENEMY. HOW IMMINENT IS THE THREAT?
LISTEN, BARKO. IT'S...URGENT. TRUST ME--

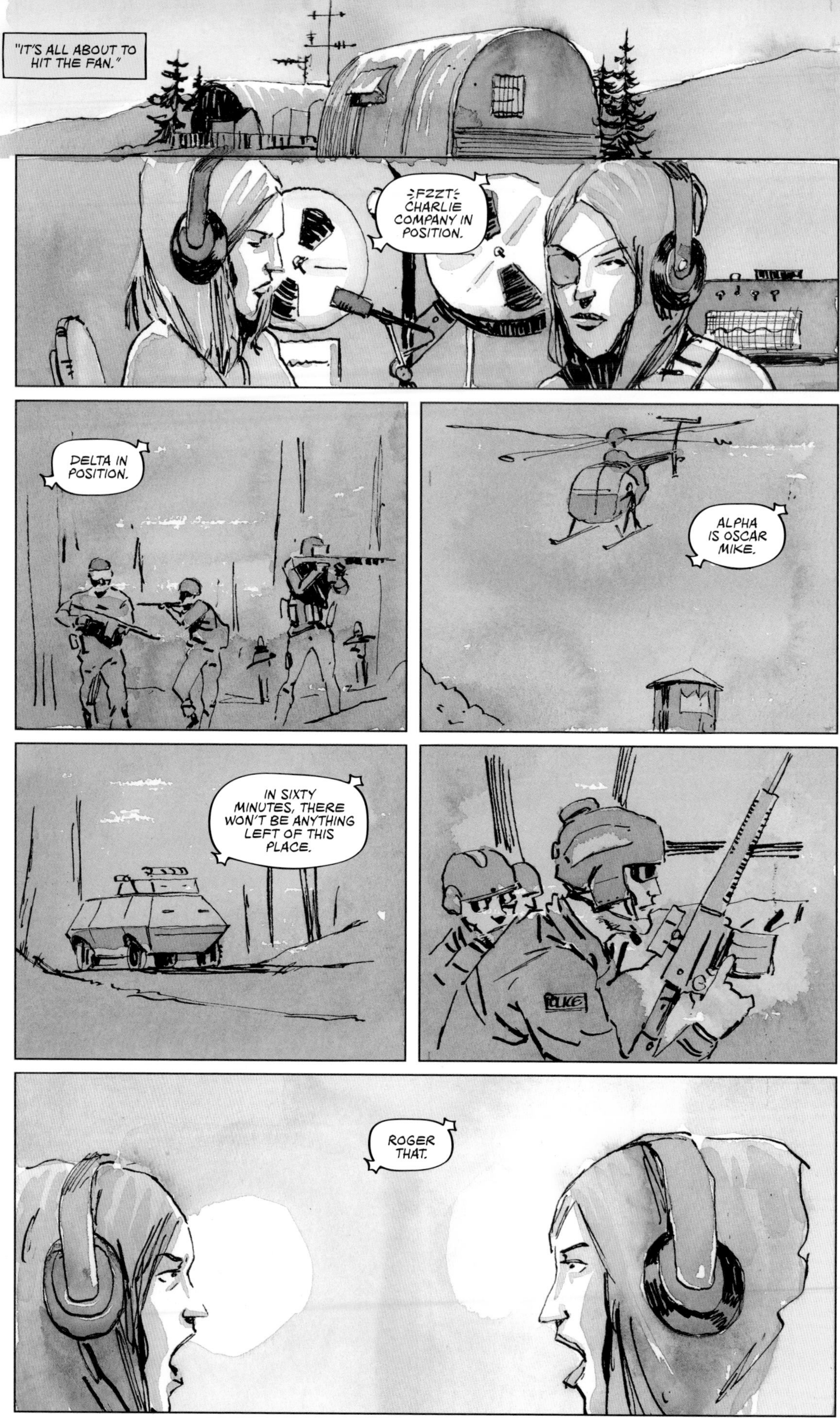
"IT'S ALL ABOUT TO HIT THE FAN."
⚡FZZT⚡ CHARLIE COMPANY IN POSITION.
DELTA IN POSITION.
ALPHA IS OSCAR MIKE.
IN SIXTY MINUTES, THERE WON'T BE ANYTHING LEFT OF THIS PLACE.
POLICE
ROGER THAT.

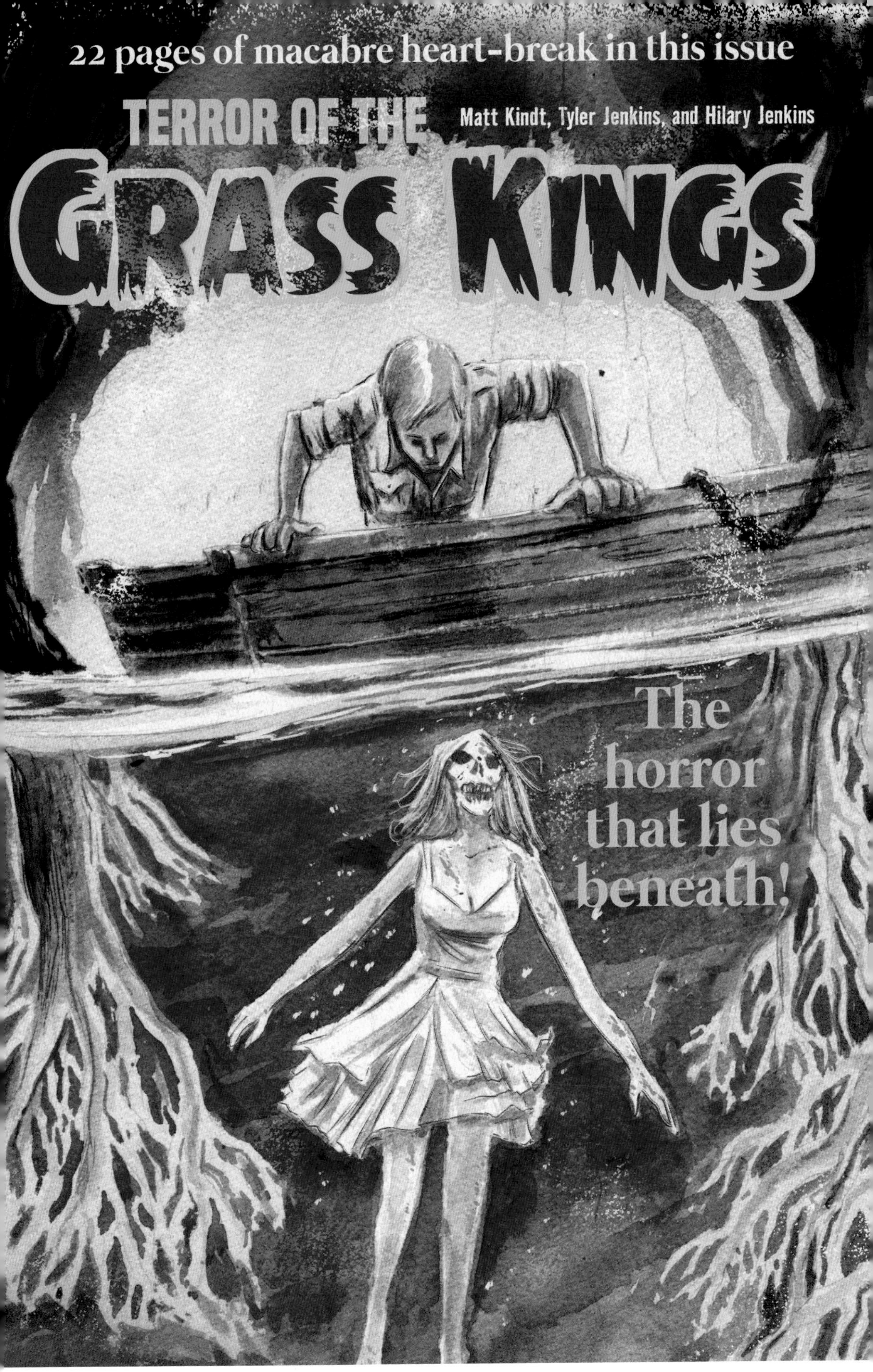
22 pages of macabre heart-break in this issue
TERROR OF THE
Matt Kindt, Tyler Jenkins, and Hilary Jenkins
GRASS KINGS
The horror that lies beneath!

issue #12 cover by matt kindt

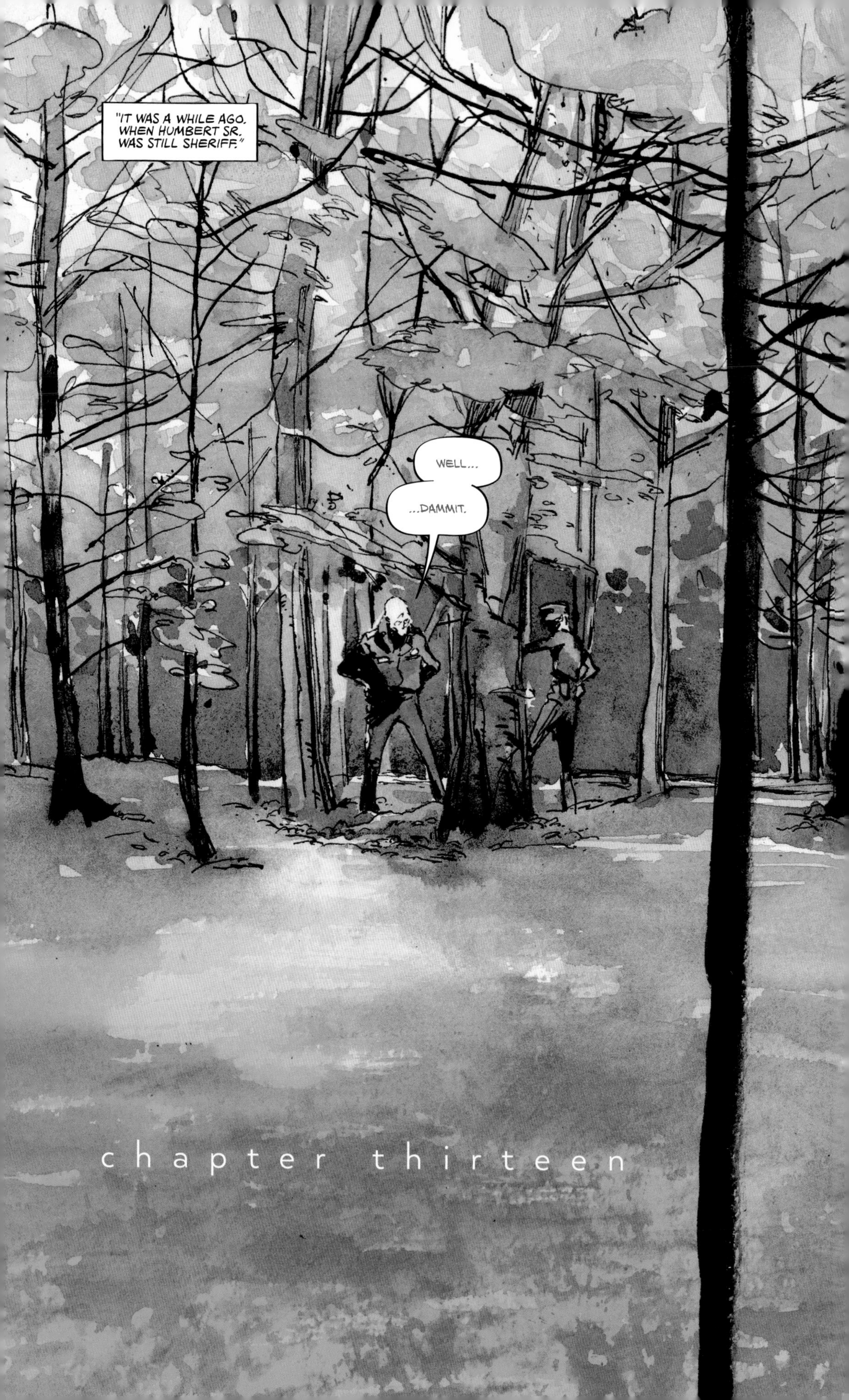
"IT WAS A WHILE AGO, WHEN HUMBERT SR. WAS STILL SHERIFF."
WELL...
...DAMMIT.
chapter thirteen

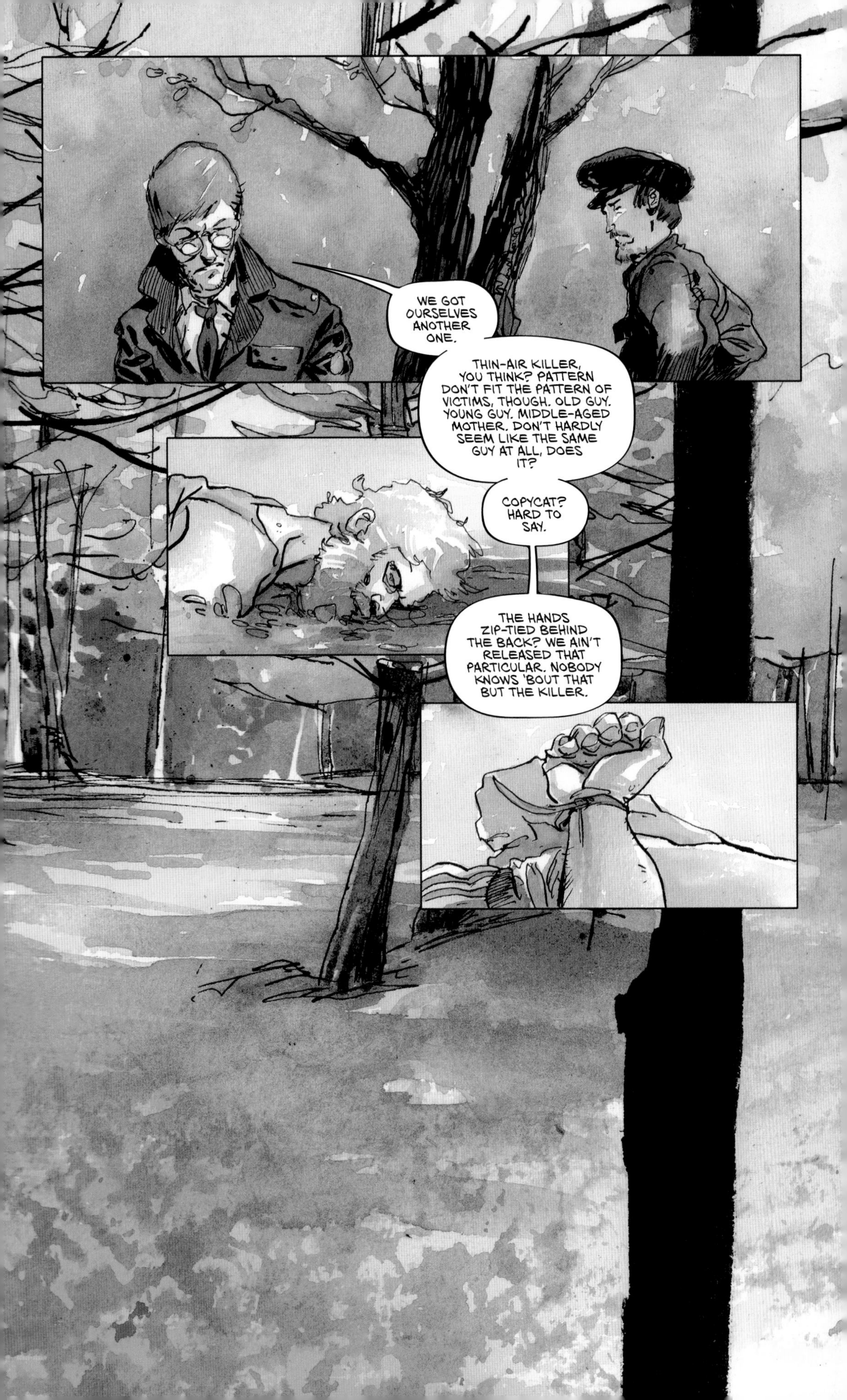
WE GOT OURSELVES ANOTHER ONE.
THIN-AIR KILLER, YOU THINK? PATTERN DON'T FIT THE PATTERN OF VICTIMS, THOUGH. OLD GUY. YOUNG GUY. MIDDLE-AGED MOTHER. DON'T HARDLY SEEM LIKE THE SAME GUY AT ALL, DOES IT?
COPYCAT? HARD TO SAY.
THE HANDS ZIP-TIED BEHIND THE BACK? WE AIN'T RELEASED THAT PARTICULAR. NOBODY KNOWS 'BOUT THAT BUT THE KILLER.

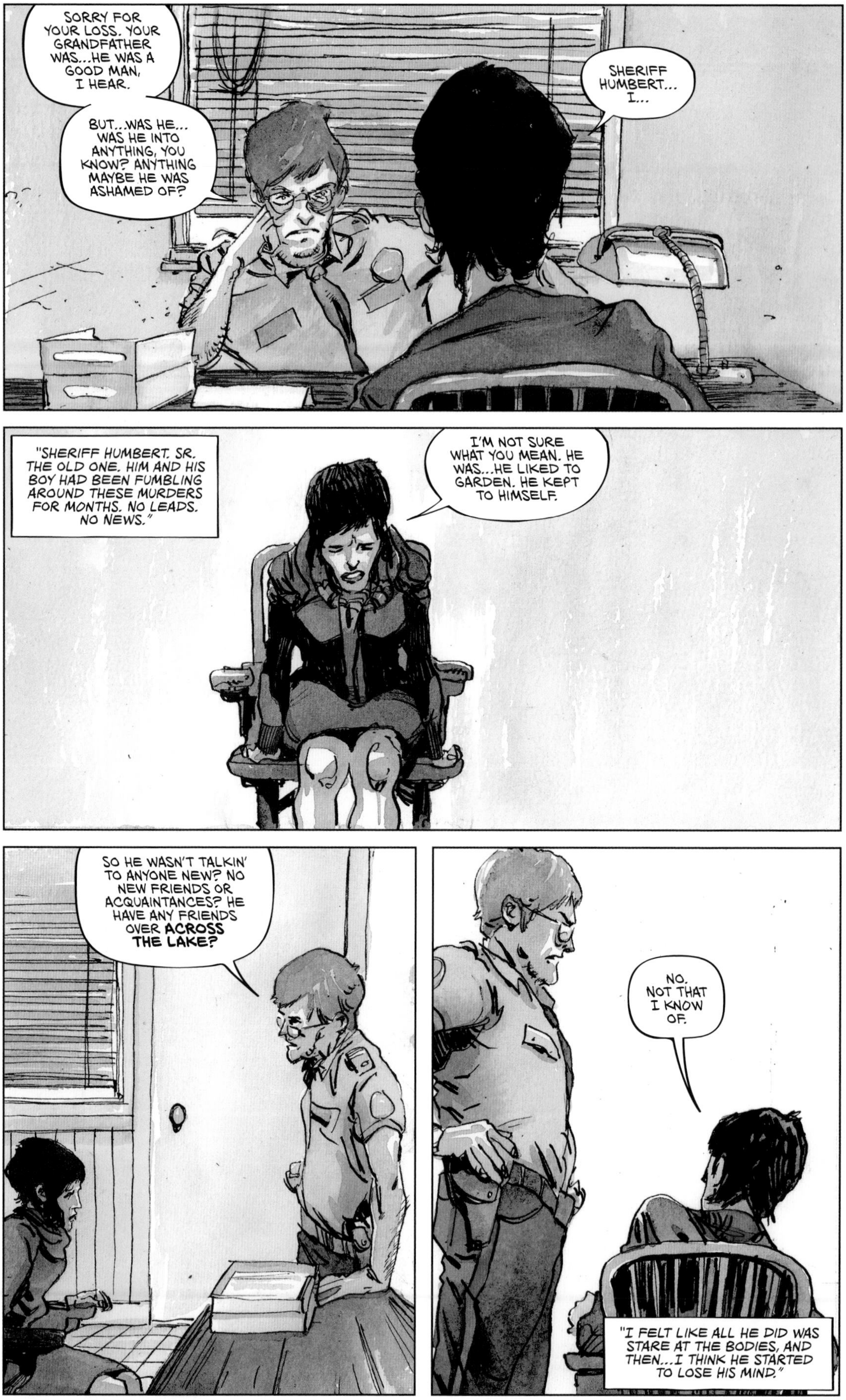
SORRY FOR YOUR LOSS. YOUR GRANDFATHER WAS...HE WAS A GOOD MAN, I HEAR.
BUT...WAS HE... WAS HE INTO ANYTHING, YOU KNOW? ANYTHING MAYBE HE WAS ASHAMED OF?
SHERIFF HUMBERT... I...
"SHERIFF HUMBERT. SR. THE OLD ONE. HIM AND HIS BOY HAD BEEN FUMBLING AROUND THESE MURDERS FOR MONTHS. NO LEADS. NO NEWS."
I'M NOT SURE WHAT YOU MEAN. HE WAS...HE LIKED TO GARDEN. HE KEPT TO HIMSELF.
SO HE WASN'T TALKIN' TO ANYONE NEW? NO NEW FRIENDS OR ACQUAINTANCES? HE HAVE ANY FRIENDS OVER **ACROSS THE LAKE?**
NO. NOT THAT I KNOW OF.
"I FELT LIKE ALL HE DID WAS STARE AT THE BODIES, AND THEN...I THINK HE STARTED TO LOSE HIS MIND."

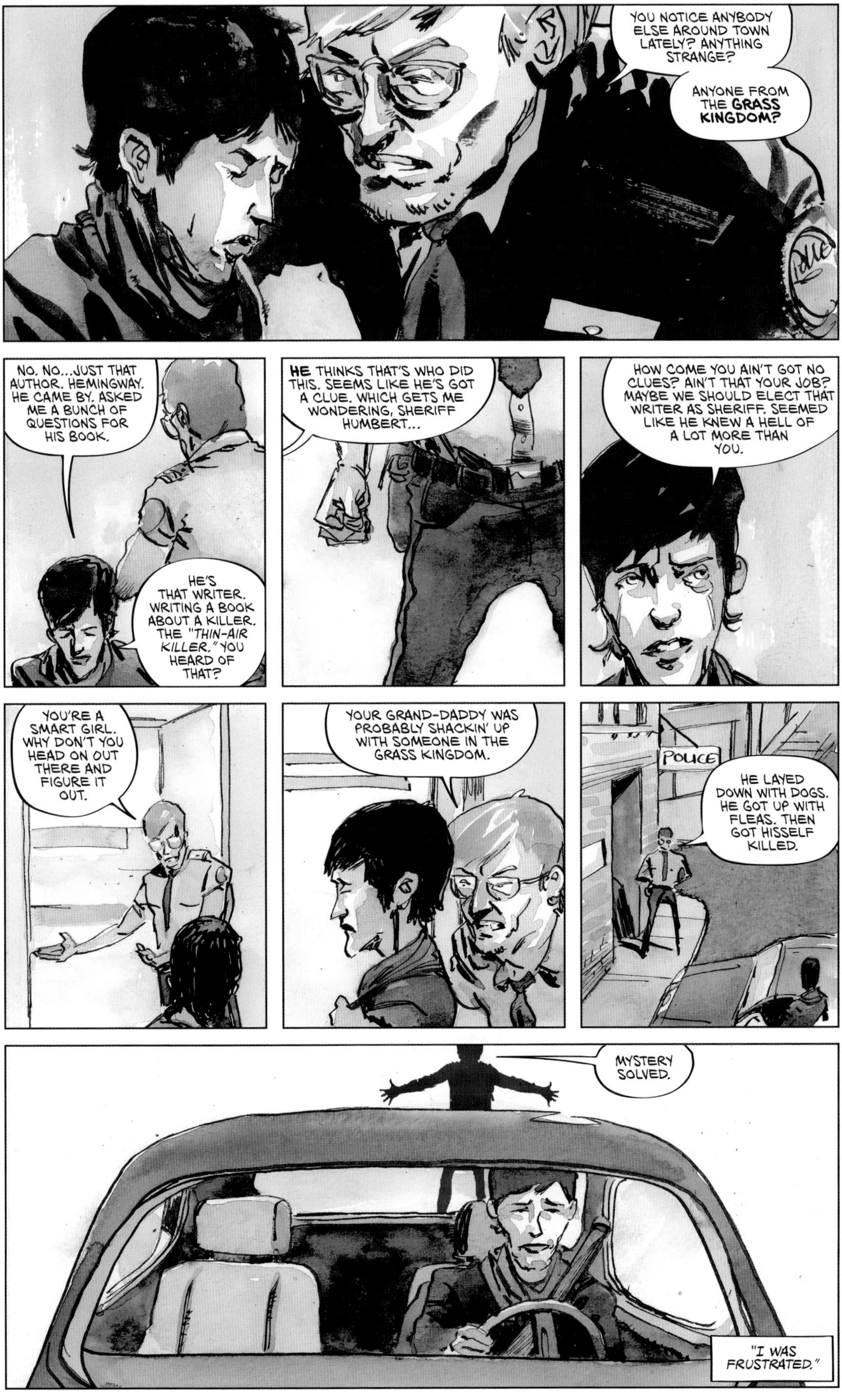
YOU NOTICE ANYBODY ELSE AROUND TOWN LATELY? ANYTHING STRANGE?
ANYONE FROM THE **GRASS KINGDOM?**
NO. NO...JUST THAT AUTHOR. HEMINGWAY. HE CAME BY. ASKED ME A BUNCH OF QUESTIONS FOR HIS BOOK.
HE'S THAT WRITER. WRITING A BOOK ABOUT A KILLER. THE "*THIN-AIR KILLER.*" YOU HEARD OF THAT?
HE THINKS THAT'S WHO DID THIS. SEEMS LIKE HE'S GOT A CLUE. WHICH GETS ME WONDERING, SHERIFF HUMBERT...
HOW COME YOU AIN'T GOT NO CLUES? AIN'T THAT YOUR JOB? MAYBE WE SHOULD ELECT THAT WRITER AS SHERIFF. SEEMED LIKE HE KNEW A HELL OF A LOT MORE THAN YOU.
YOU'RE A SMART GIRL. WHY DON'T YOU HEAD ON OUT THERE AND FIGURE IT OUT.
YOUR GRAND-DADDY WAS PROBABLY SHACKIN' UP WITH SOMEONE IN THE GRASS KINGDOM.
POLICE
HE LAYED DOWN WITH DOGS. HE GOT UP WITH FLEAS. THEN GOT HISSELF KILLED.
MYSTERY SOLVED.
"I WAS FRUSTRATED."

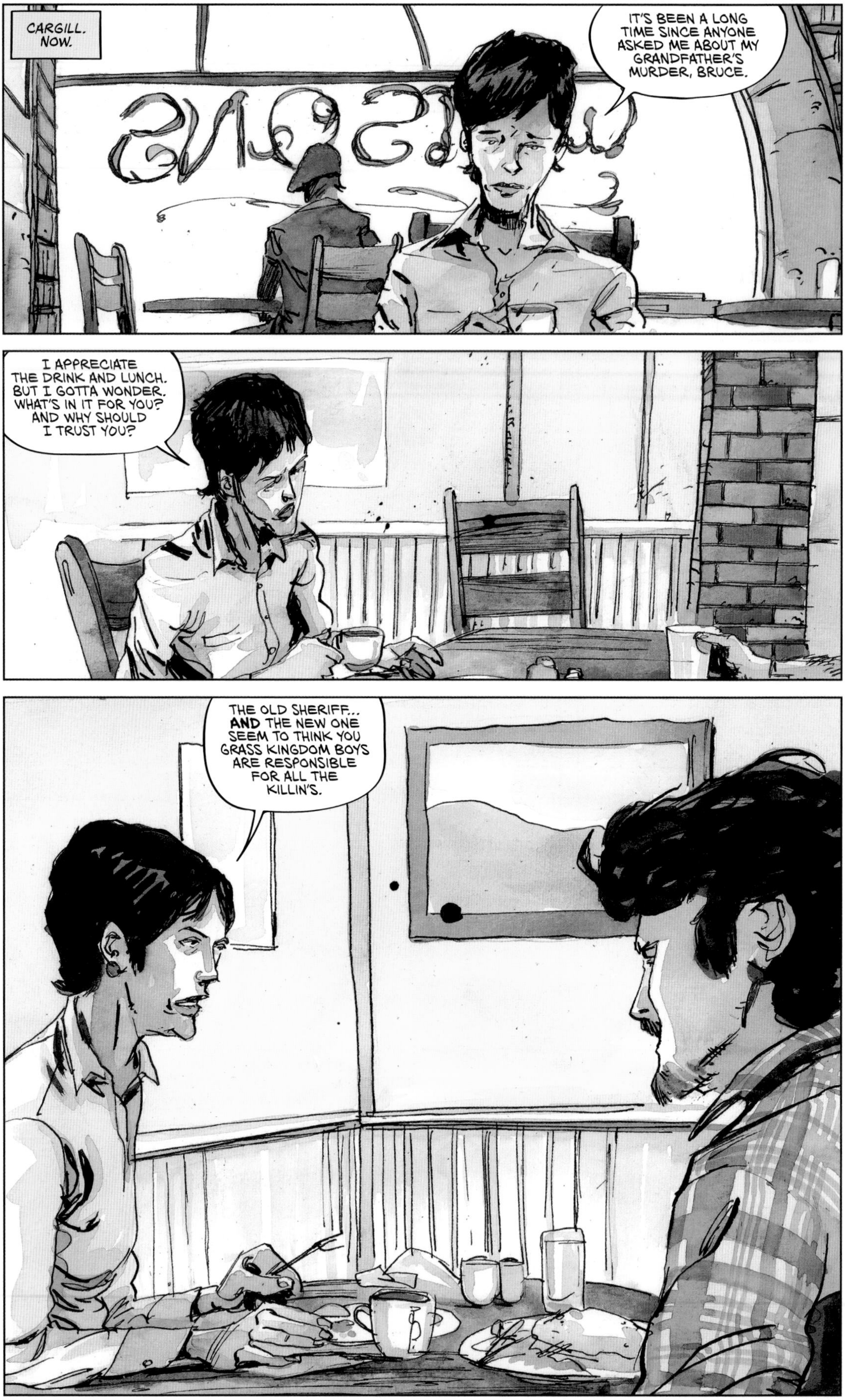
CARGILL. NOW.
IT'S BEEN A LONG TIME SINCE ANYONE ASKED ME ABOUT MY GRANDFATHER'S MURDER, BRUCE.
I APPRECIATE THE DRINK AND LUNCH. BUT I GOTTA WONDER. WHAT'S IN IT FOR YOU? AND WHY SHOULD I TRUST YOU?
THE OLD SHERIFF... **AND** THE NEW ONE SEEM TO THINK YOU GRASS KINGDOM BOYS ARE RESPONSIBLE FOR ALL THE KILLIN'S.

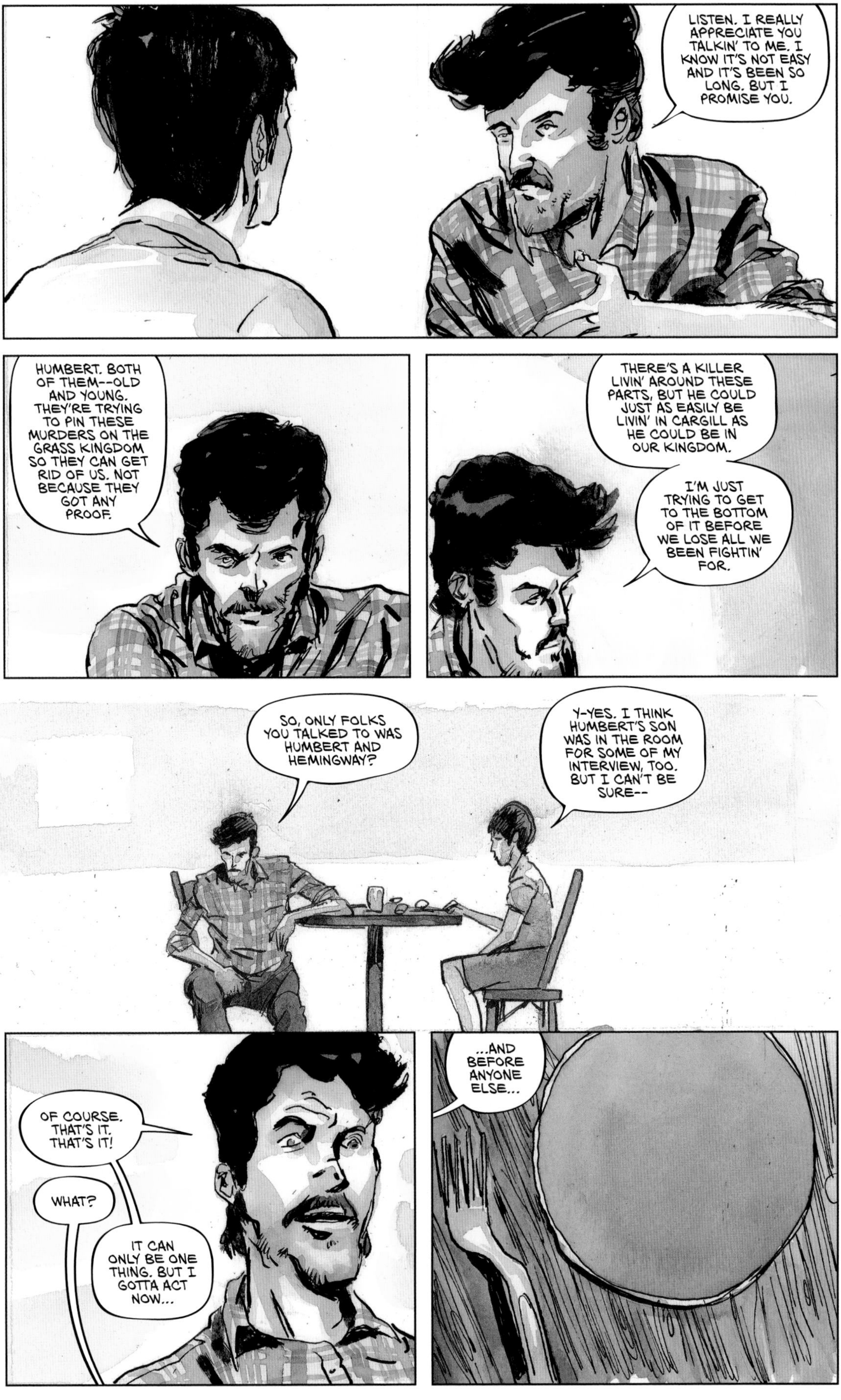
LISTEN. I REALLY APPRECIATE YOU TALKIN' TO ME. I KNOW IT'S NOT EASY AND IT'S BEEN SO LONG. BUT I PROMISE YOU.
HUMBERT. BOTH OF THEM--OLD AND YOUNG. THEY'RE TRYING TO PIN THESE MURDERS ON THE GRASS KINGDOM SO THEY CAN GET RID OF US. NOT BECAUSE THEY GOT ANY PROOF.
THERE'S A KILLER LIVIN' AROUND THESE PARTS, BUT HE COULD JUST AS EASILY BE LIVIN' IN CARGILL AS HE COULD BE IN OUR KINGDOM.
I'M JUST TRYING TO GET TO THE BOTTOM OF IT BEFORE WE LOSE ALL WE BEEN FIGHTIN' FOR.
SO, ONLY FOLKS YOU TALKED TO WAS HUMBERT AND HEMINGWAY?
Y-YES. I THINK HUMBERT'S SON WAS IN THE ROOM FOR SOME OF MY INTERVIEW, TOO. BUT I CAN'T BE SURE--
OF COURSE. THAT'S IT. THAT'S IT!
WHAT?
IT CAN ONLY BE ONE THING. BUT I GOTTA ACT NOW...
...AND BEFORE ANYONE ELSE...

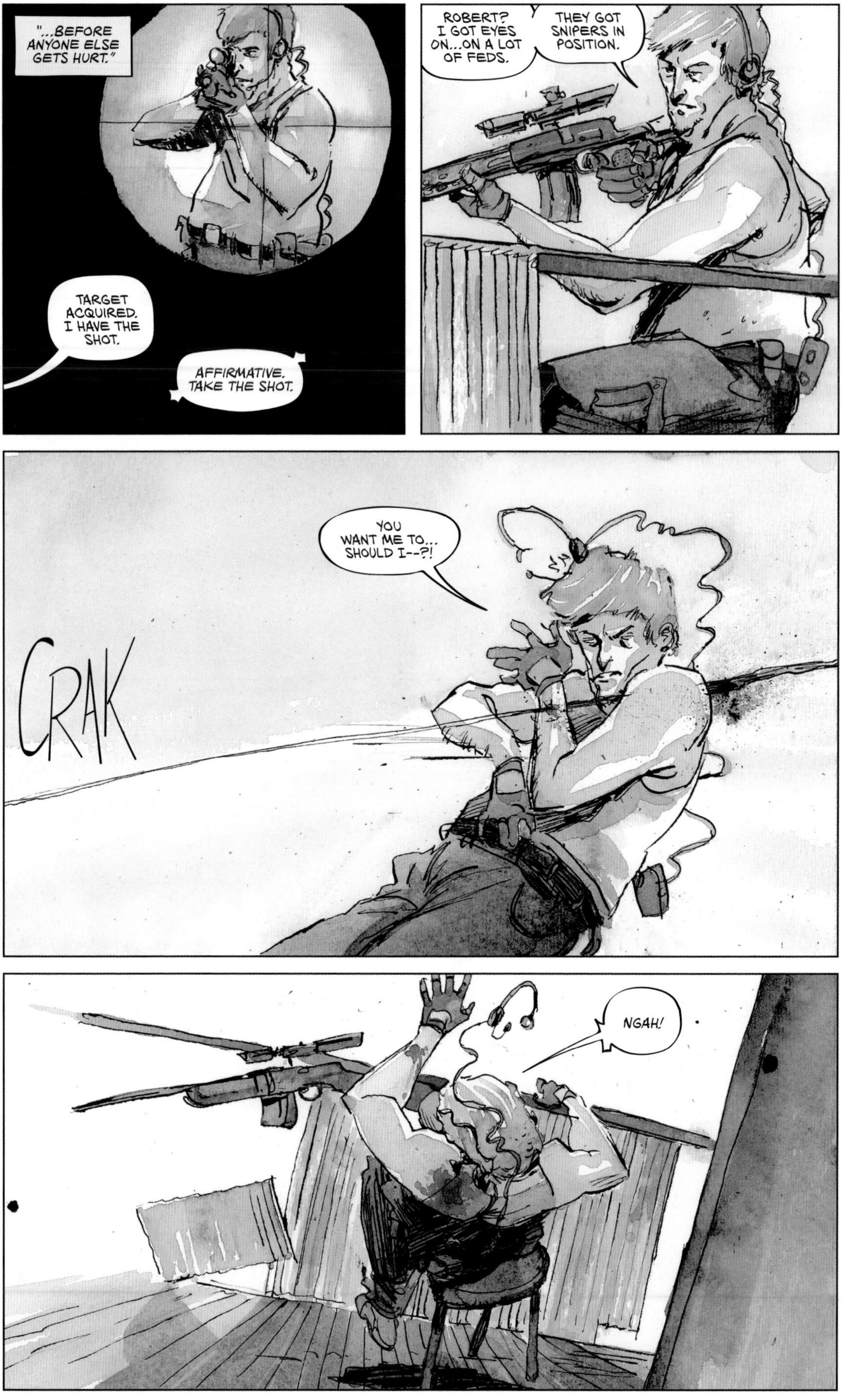
"...BEFORE ANYONE ELSE GETS HURT."
TARGET ACQUIRED. I HAVE THE SHOT.
AFFIRMATIVE. TAKE THE SHOT.
ROBERT? I GOT EYES ON...ON A LOT OF FEDS.
THEY GOT SNIPERS IN POSITION.
YOU WANT ME TO... SHOULD I--?!
CRAK
NGAH!

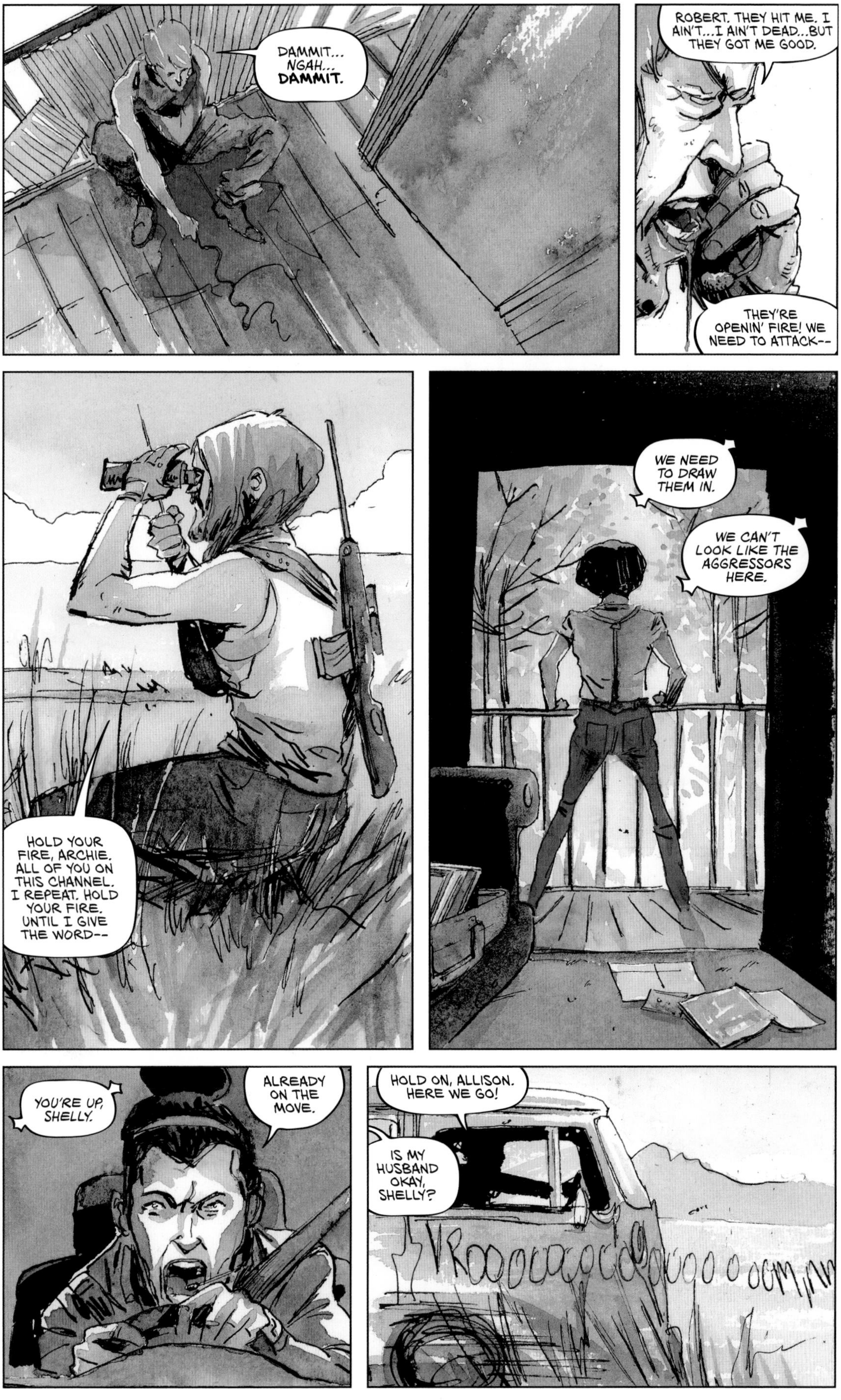
DAMMIT... NGAH... DAMMIT.
ROBERT. THEY HIT ME. I AIN'T...I AIN'T DEAD...BUT THEY GOT ME GOOD.
THEY'RE OPENIN' FIRE! WE NEED TO ATTACK--
HOLD YOUR FIRE, ARCHIE. ALL OF YOU ON THIS CHANNEL. I REPEAT. HOLD YOUR FIRE. UNTIL I GIVE THE WORD--
WE NEED TO DRAW THEM IN.
WE CAN'T LOOK LIKE THE AGGRESSORS HERE.
YOU'RE UP, SHELLY.
ALREADY ON THE MOVE.
HOLD ON, ALLISON. HERE WE GO!
IS MY HUSBAND OKAY, SHELLY?
VROOOOOOOOOOOOOOOOOM

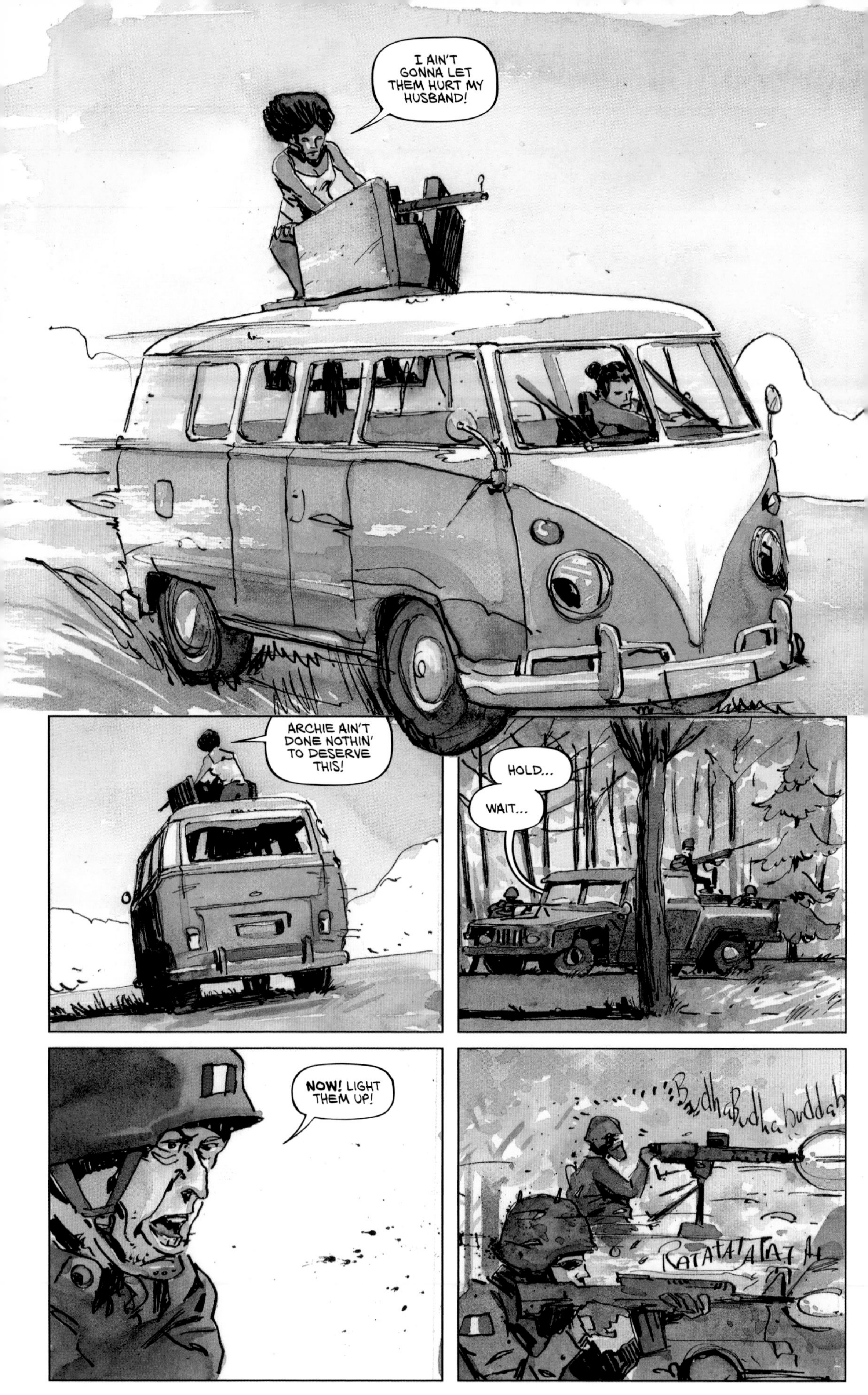
I AIN'T GONNA LET THEM HURT MY HUSBAND!
ARCHIE AIN'T DONE NOTHIN' TO DESERVE THIS!
HOLD...
WAIT...
NOW! LIGHT THEM UP!
BudhaBudhabuddah
RATATATATAT

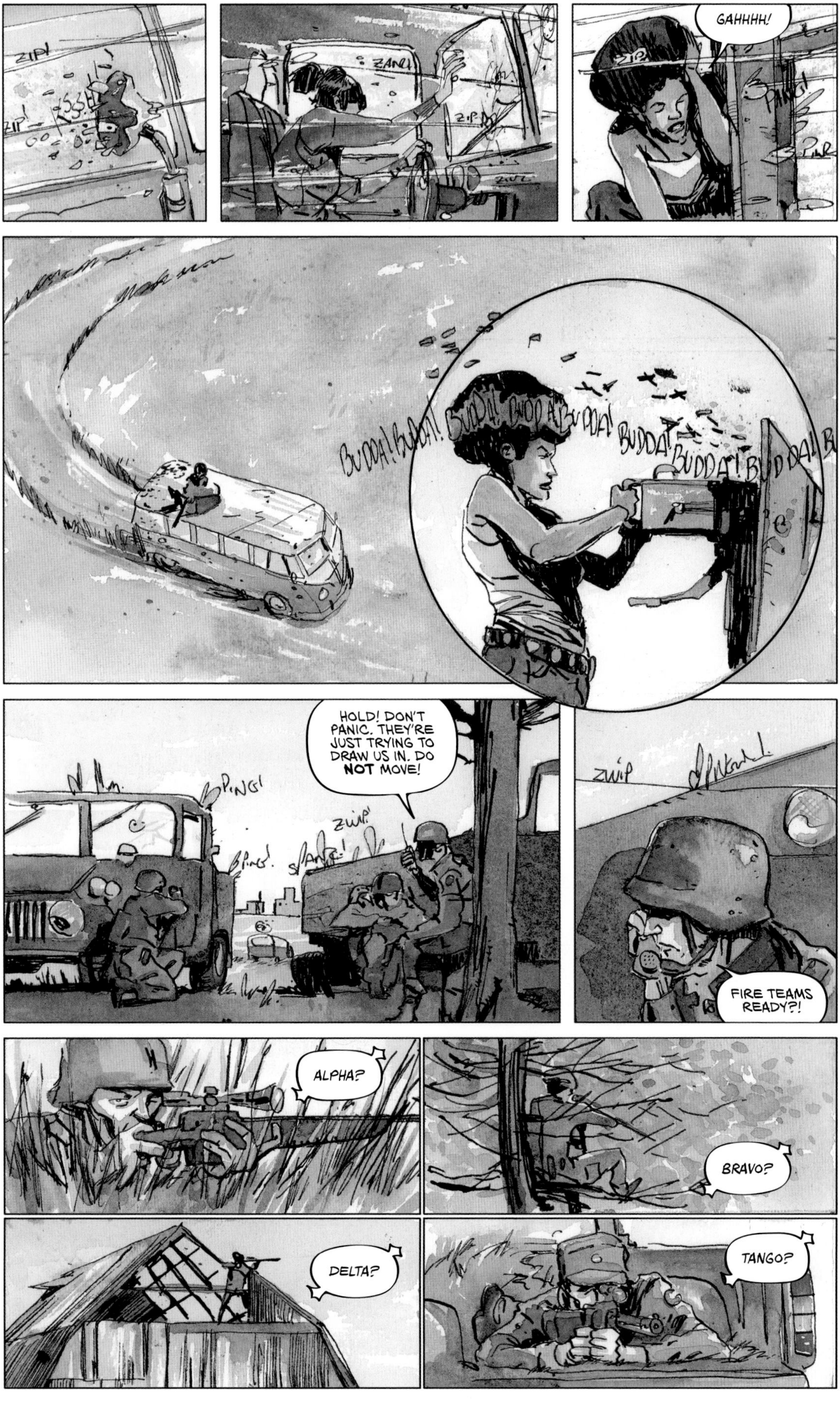
ZIP!
ZANG!
GAHHHH!
PANG!
BUDDA! BUDDA! BUDDA!
PING!
ZWIP!
SPANG!
HOLD! DON'T PANIC. THEY'RE JUST TRYING TO DRAW US IN. DO **NOT** MOVE!
ZWIP
FIRE TEAMS READY?!
ALPHA?
BRAVO?
DELTA?
TANGO?

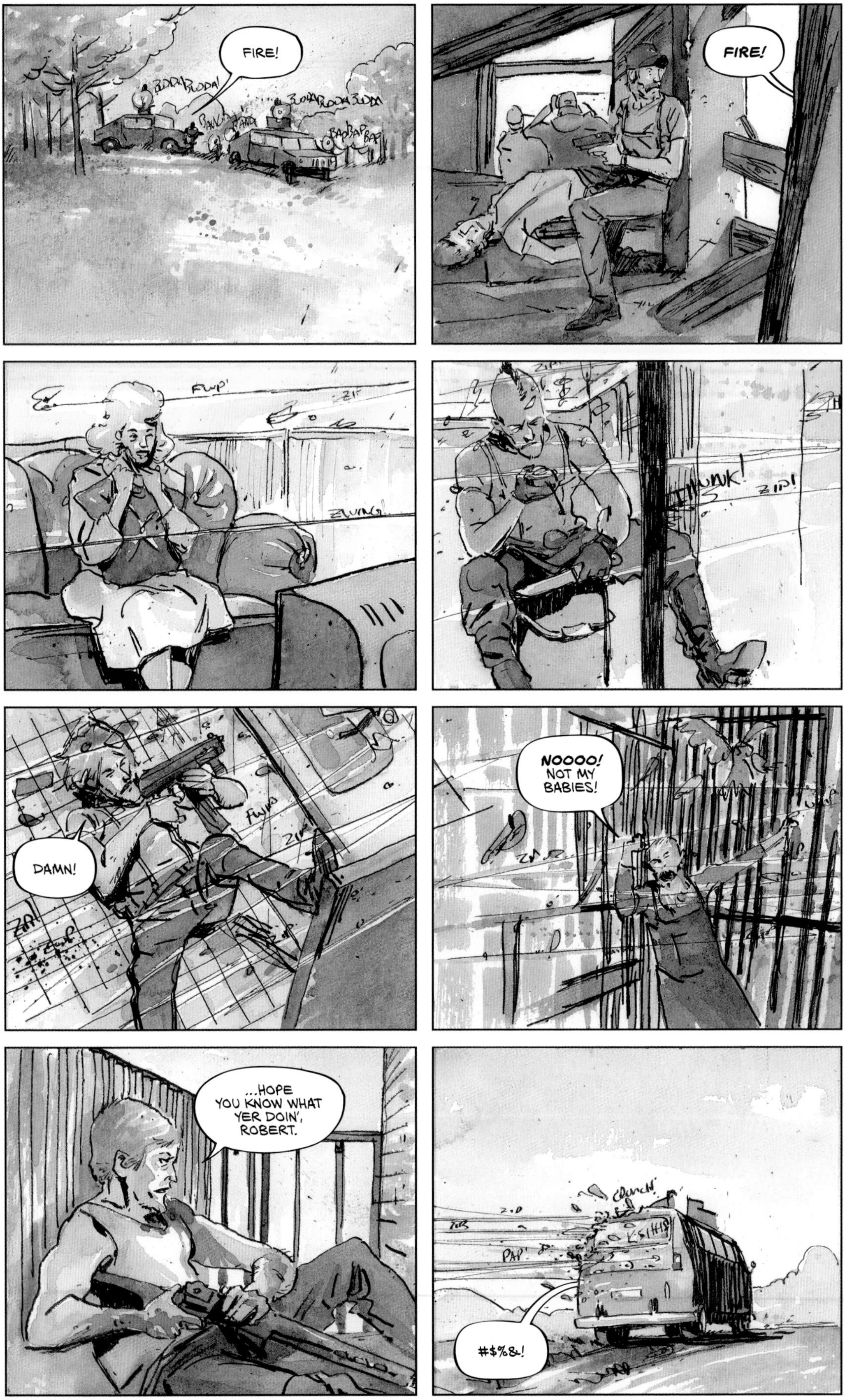
FIRE!
FIRE!
DAMN!
NOOOO! NOT MY BABIES!
...HOPE YOU KNOW WHAT YER DOIN', ROBERT.
#$%&!

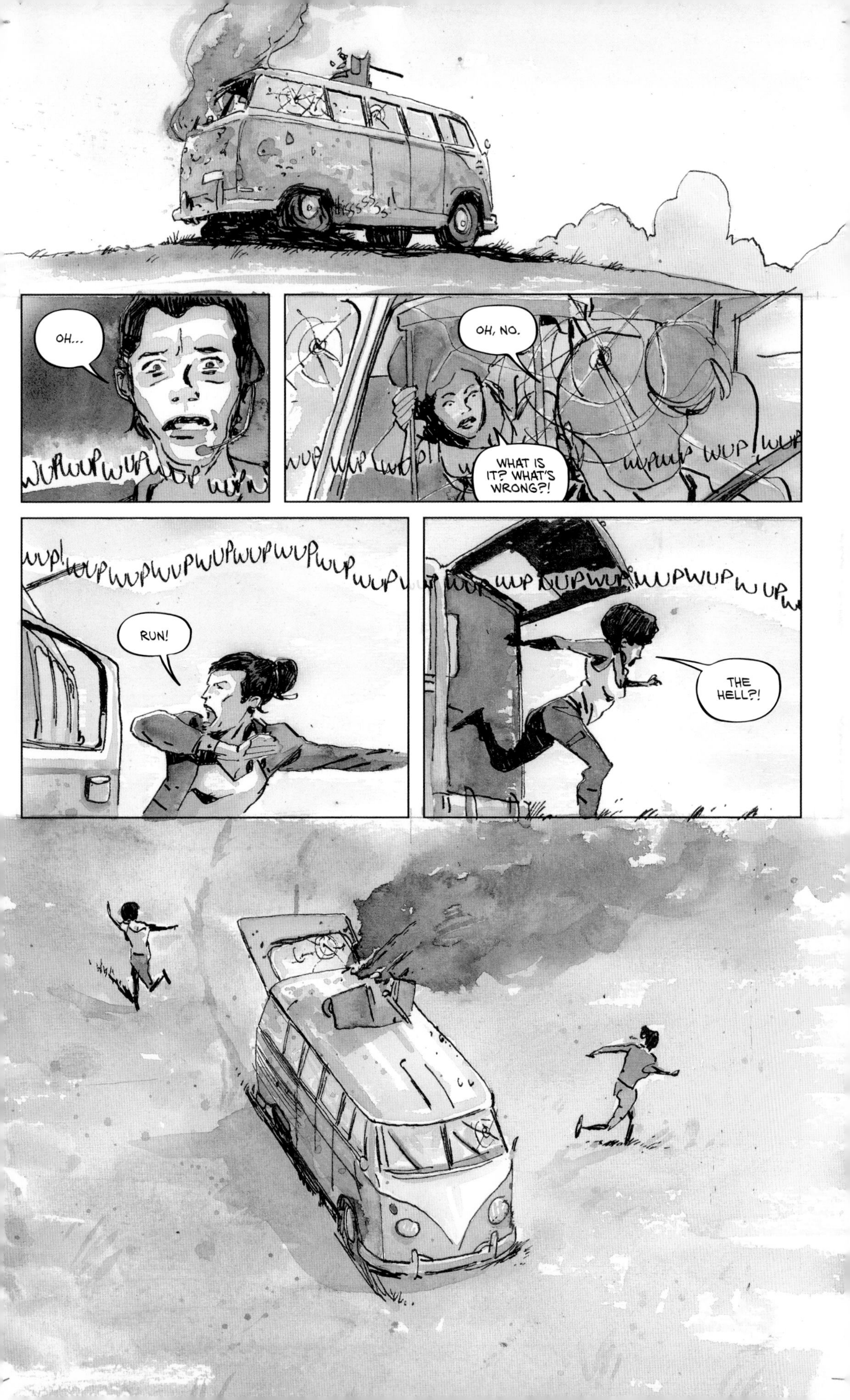
HISSSSSS!
OH...
WUPWUPWUPWUP WUPW
OH, NO.
WUP WUP WUP
WHAT IS IT? WHAT'S WRONG?!
WUPWUP WUP WUP
WUP! WUPWUPWUPWUPWUPWUP WUP
RUN!
WUP WUP WUPWUP WUPWUP WUP WUP
THE HELL?!

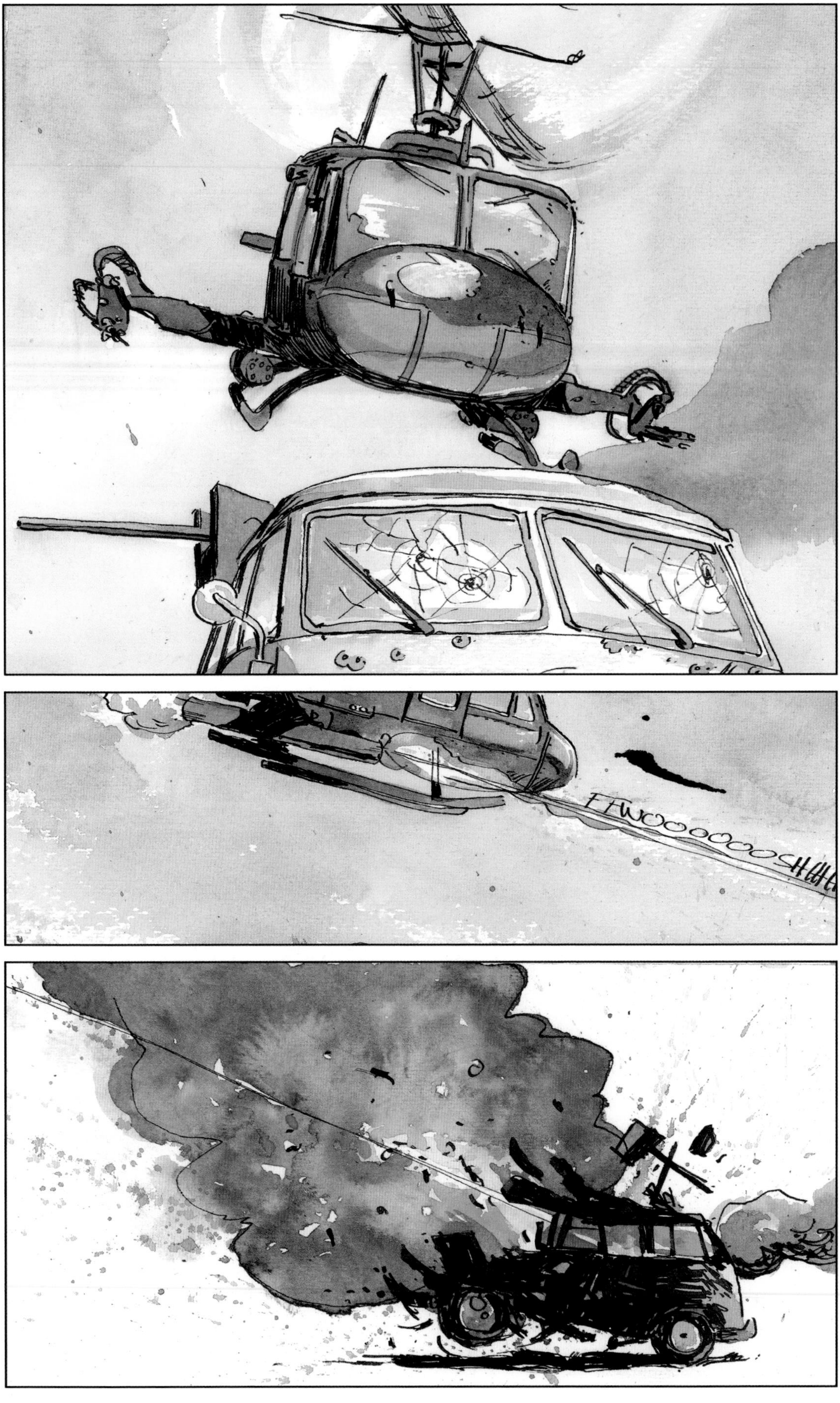
FFWOOOOOOOSHHH

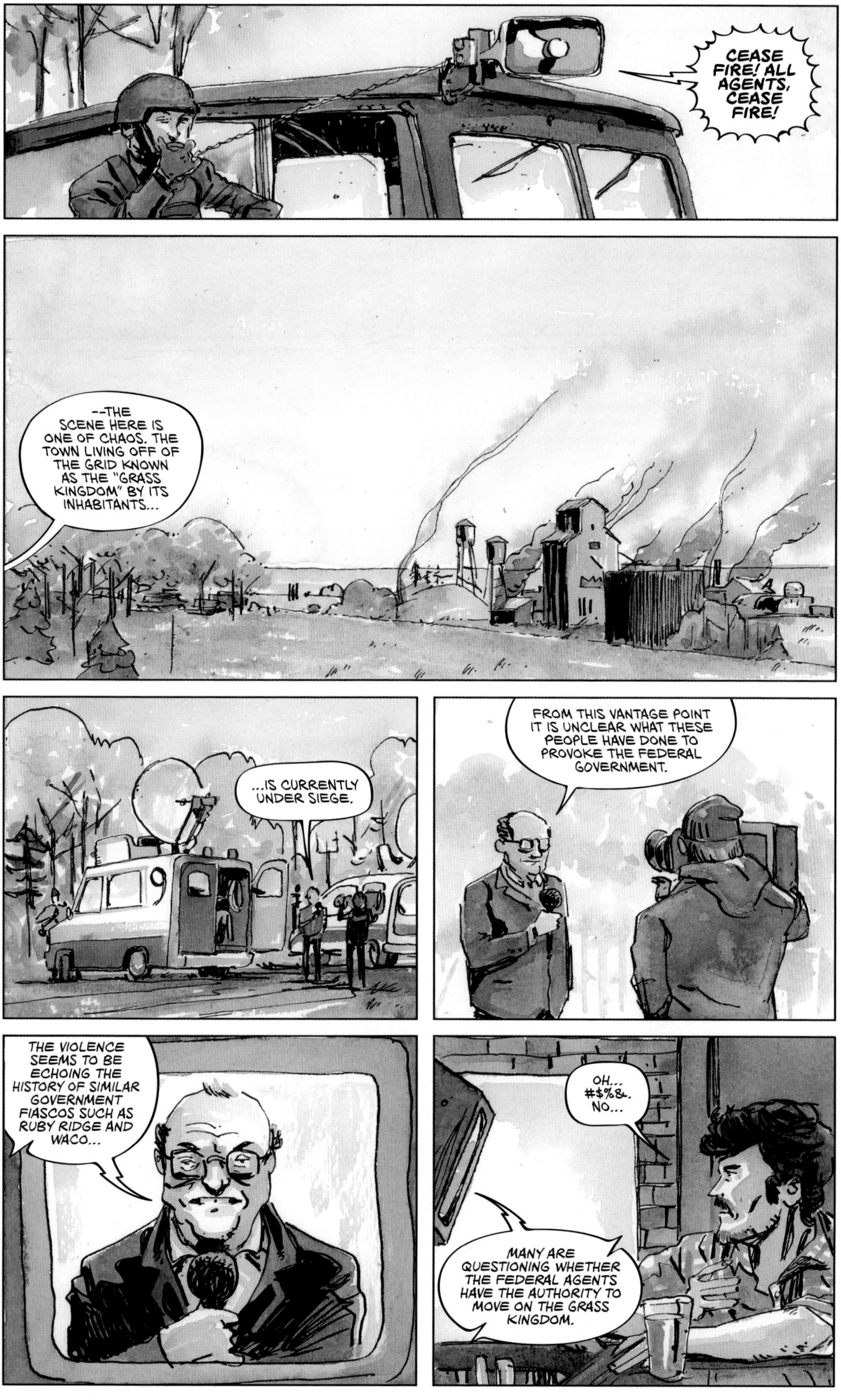
CEASE FIRE! ALL AGENTS, CEASE FIRE!
--THE SCENE HERE IS ONE OF CHAOS. THE TOWN LIVING OFF OF THE GRID KNOWN AS THE "GRASS KINGDOM" BY ITS INHABITANTS...
...IS CURRENTLY UNDER SIEGE.
FROM THIS VANTAGE POINT IT IS UNCLEAR WHAT THESE PEOPLE HAVE DONE TO PROVOKE THE FEDERAL GOVERNMENT.
THE VIOLENCE SEEMS TO BE ECHOING THE HISTORY OF SIMILAR GOVERNMENT FIASCOS SUCH AS RUBY RIDGE AND WACO...
OH... #$%&. NO...
MANY ARE QUESTIONING WHETHER THE FEDERAL AGENTS HAVE THE AUTHORITY TO MOVE ON THE GRASS KINGDOM.

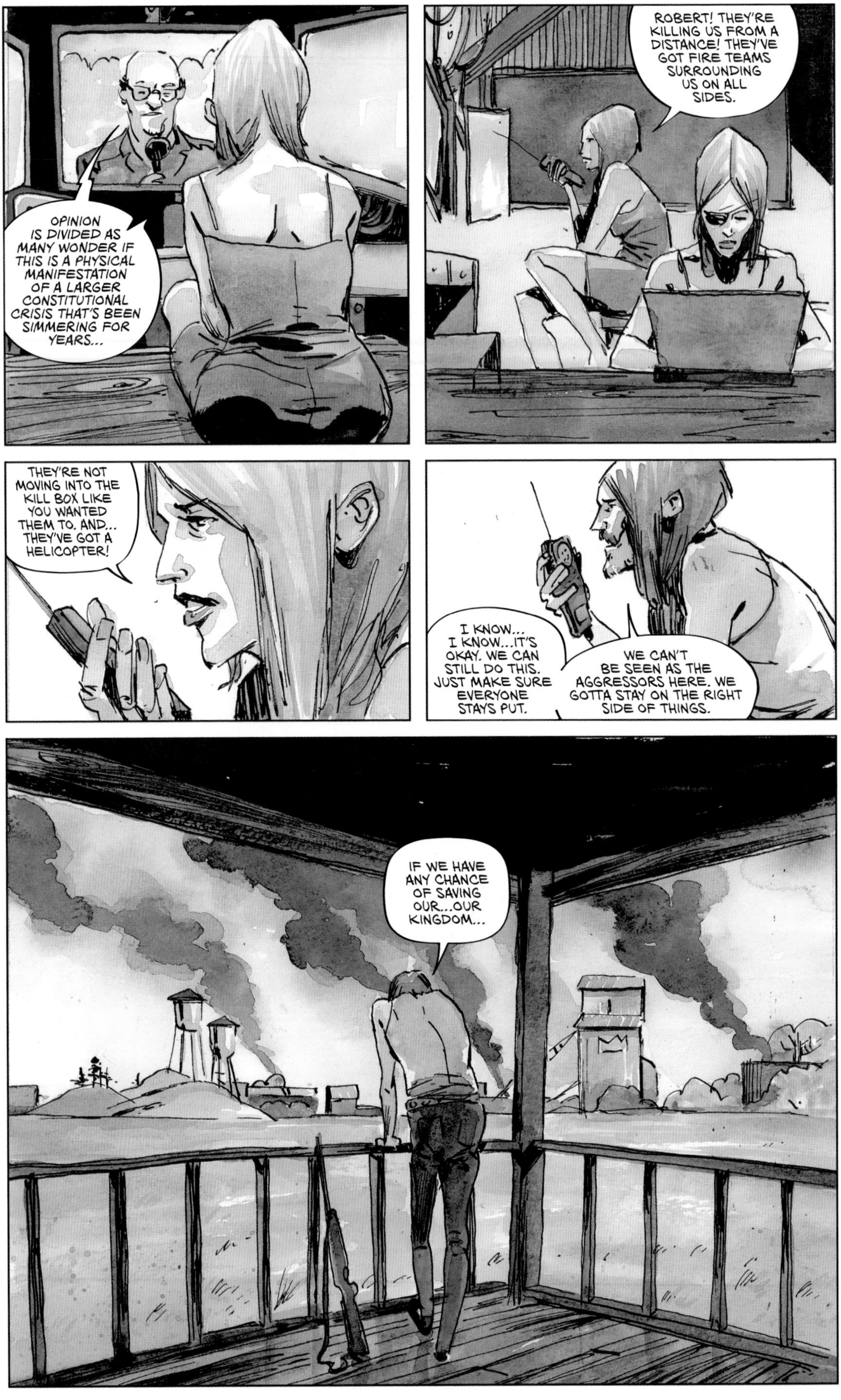
OPINION IS DIVIDED AS MANY WONDER IF THIS IS A PHYSICAL MANIFESTATION OF A LARGER CONSTITUTIONAL CRISIS THAT'S BEEN SIMMERING FOR YEARS...
ROBERT! THEY'RE KILLING US FROM A DISTANCE! THEY'VE GOT FIRE TEAMS SURROUNDING US ON ALL SIDES.
THEY'RE NOT MOVING INTO THE KILL BOX LIKE YOU WANTED THEM TO. AND... THEY'VE GOT A HELICOPTER!
I KNOW... I KNOW...IT'S OKAY. WE CAN STILL DO THIS. JUST MAKE SURE EVERYONE STAYS PUT.
WE CAN'T BE SEEN AS THE AGGRESSORS HERE. WE GOTTA STAY ON THE RIGHT SIDE OF THINGS.
IF WE HAVE ANY CHANCE OF SAVING OUR...OUR KINGDOM...

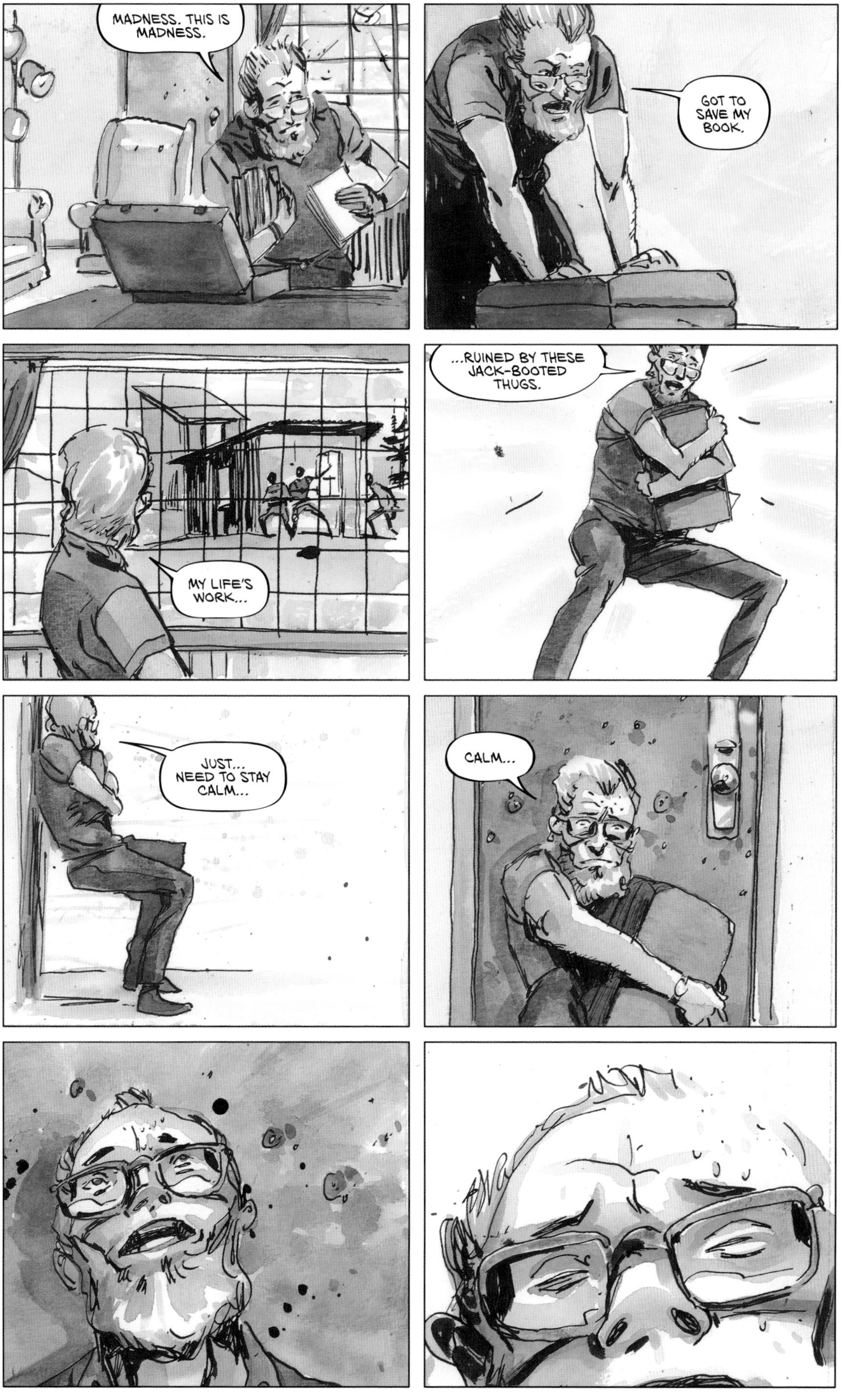
MADNESS. THIS IS MADNESS.
GOT TO SAVE MY BOOK.
MY LIFE'S WORK...
...RUINED BY THESE JACK-BOOTED THUGS.
JUST... NEED TO STAY CALM...
CALM...

"IT SEEMS AGES AGO.

"WE WERE JUST LOOKING FOR A LITTLE CALM. PEACE.

"MY HUSBAND AND I... WERE YOUNGER THEN. WE HAD ENERGY. WE BELIEVED IN THINGS.

KLIK! KLIK! KLIK! KLIK. KLIK. KRKHK! r-KLIK.

"LITTLE ROBERT AND BRUCE DIDN'T KNOW ANYTHING BUT THE KINGDOM.

"WHERE OTHERS SAW FLY-OVER COUNTRY AND FIELDS OF NOTHING? WE SAW FREEDOM. WE SAW A KINGDOM.

"THE ISOLATION WOULD BE OUR WALLS AND MOAT.

"AND THE BONES OF THE OLD HOUSE WOULD BE OUR CASTLE."

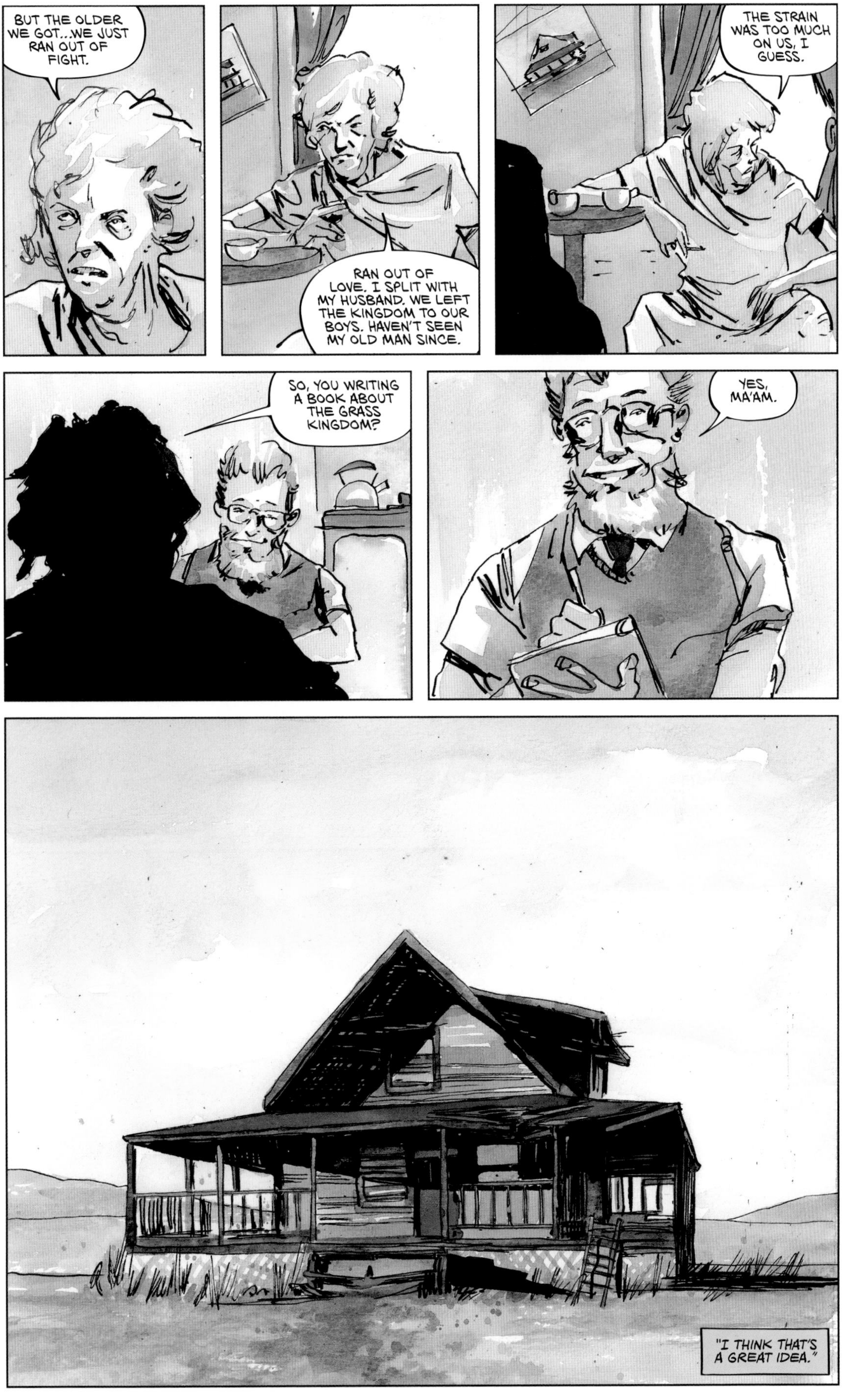
BUT THE OLDER WE GOT...WE JUST RAN OUT OF FIGHT.
RAN OUT OF LOVE. I SPLIT WITH MY HUSBAND. WE LEFT THE KINGDOM TO OUR BOYS. HAVEN'T SEEN MY OLD MAN SINCE.
THE STRAIN WAS TOO MUCH ON US, I GUESS.
SO, YOU WRITING A BOOK ABOUT THE GRASS KINGDOM?
YES, MA'AM.
"I THINK THAT'S A GREAT IDEA."

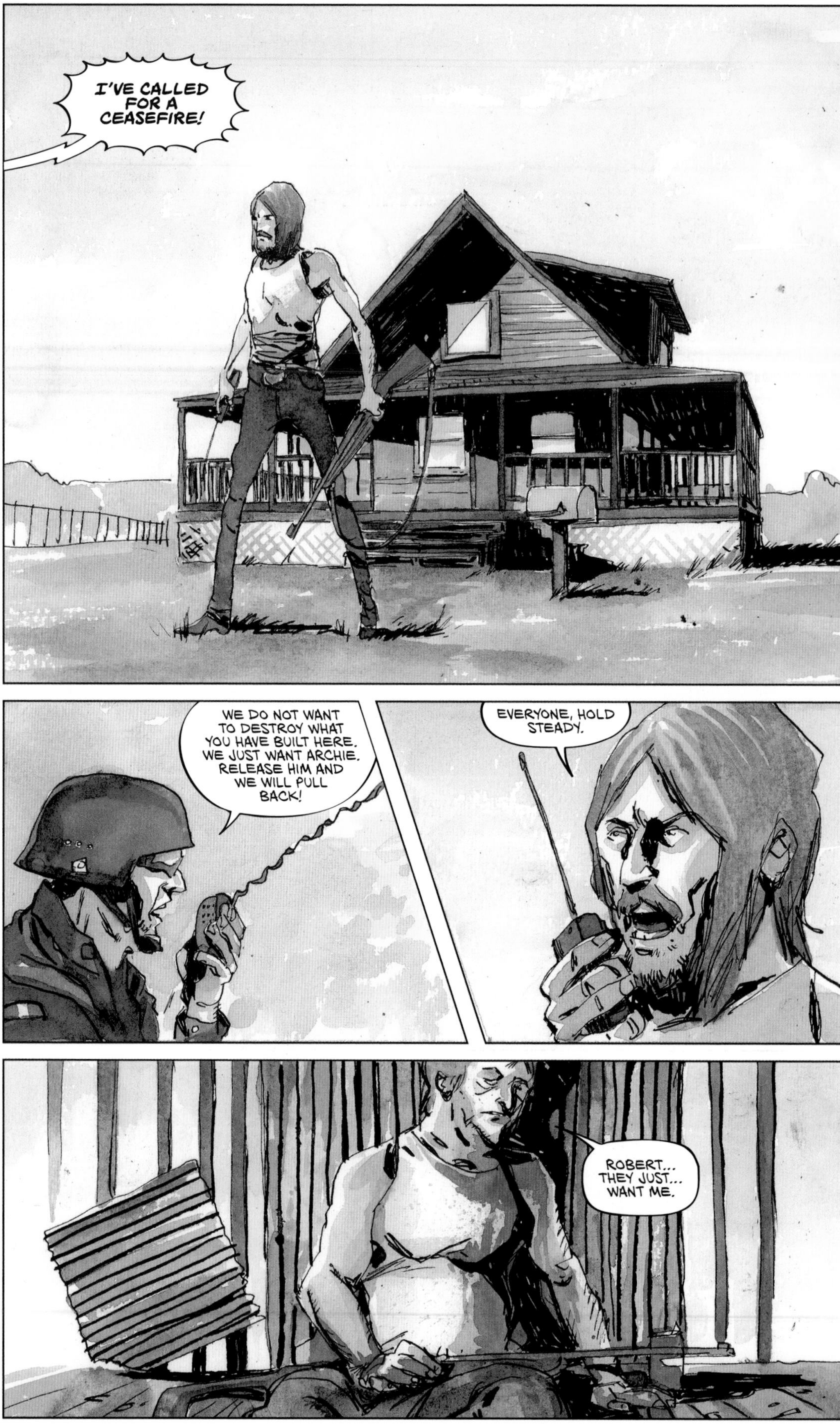
I'VE CALLED FOR A CEASEFIRE!
WE DO NOT WANT TO DESTROY WHAT YOU HAVE BUILT HERE. WE JUST WANT ARCHIE. RELEASE HIM AND WE WILL PULL BACK!
EVERYONE, HOLD STEADY.
ROBERT... THEY JUST... WANT ME.

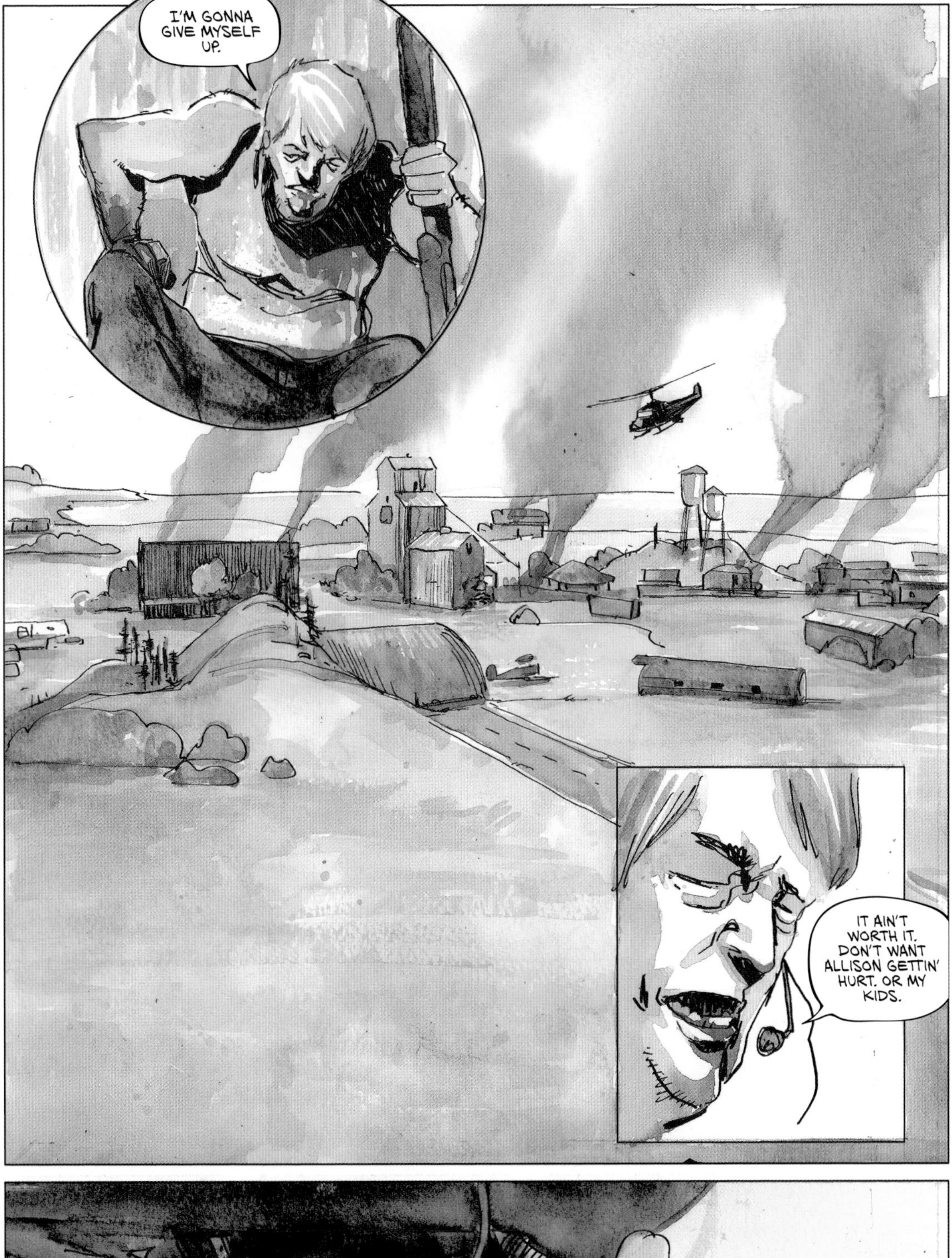
I'M GONNA GIVE MYSELF UP.
IT AIN'T WORTH IT. DON'T WANT ALLISON GETTIN' HURT. OR MY KIDS.

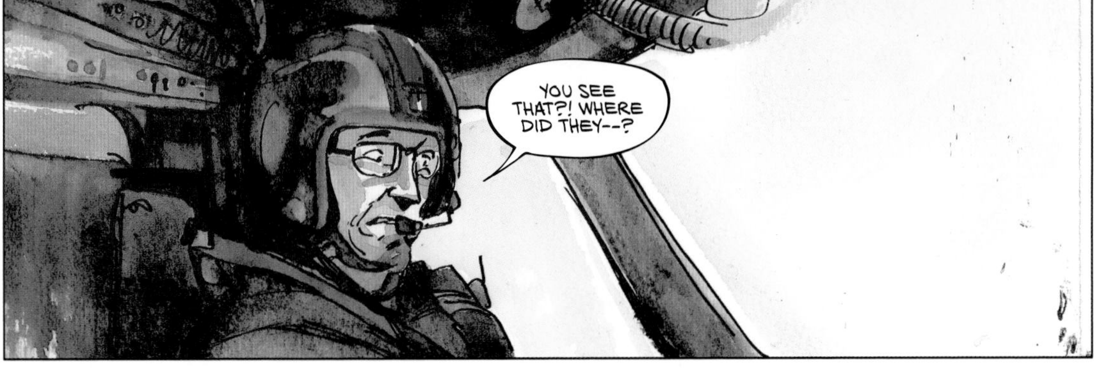
YOU SEE THAT?! WHERE DID THEY--?

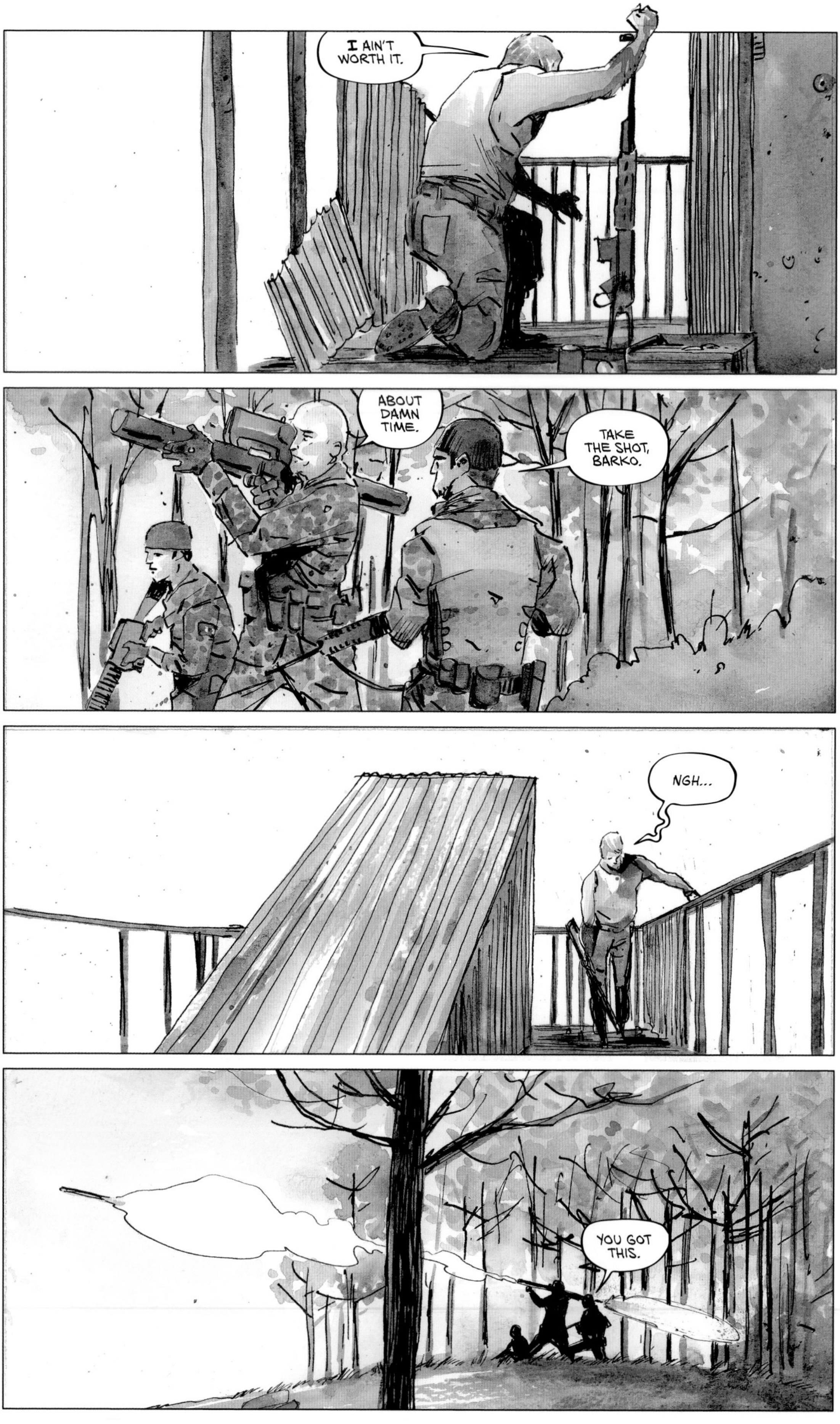
I AIN'T WORTH IT.
ABOUT DAMN TIME.
TAKE THE SHOT, BARKO.
NGH...
YOU GOT THIS.

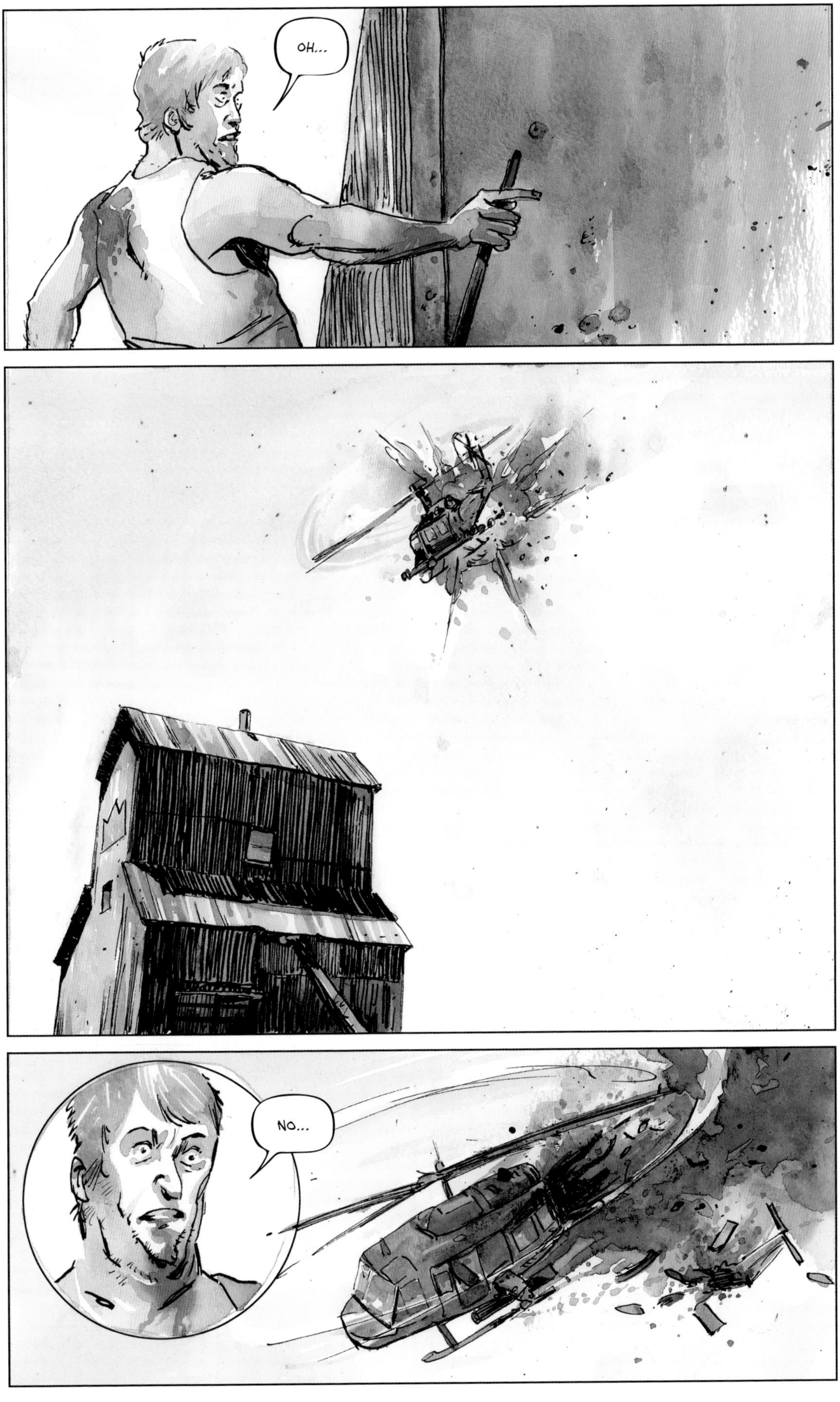
OH...
NO...

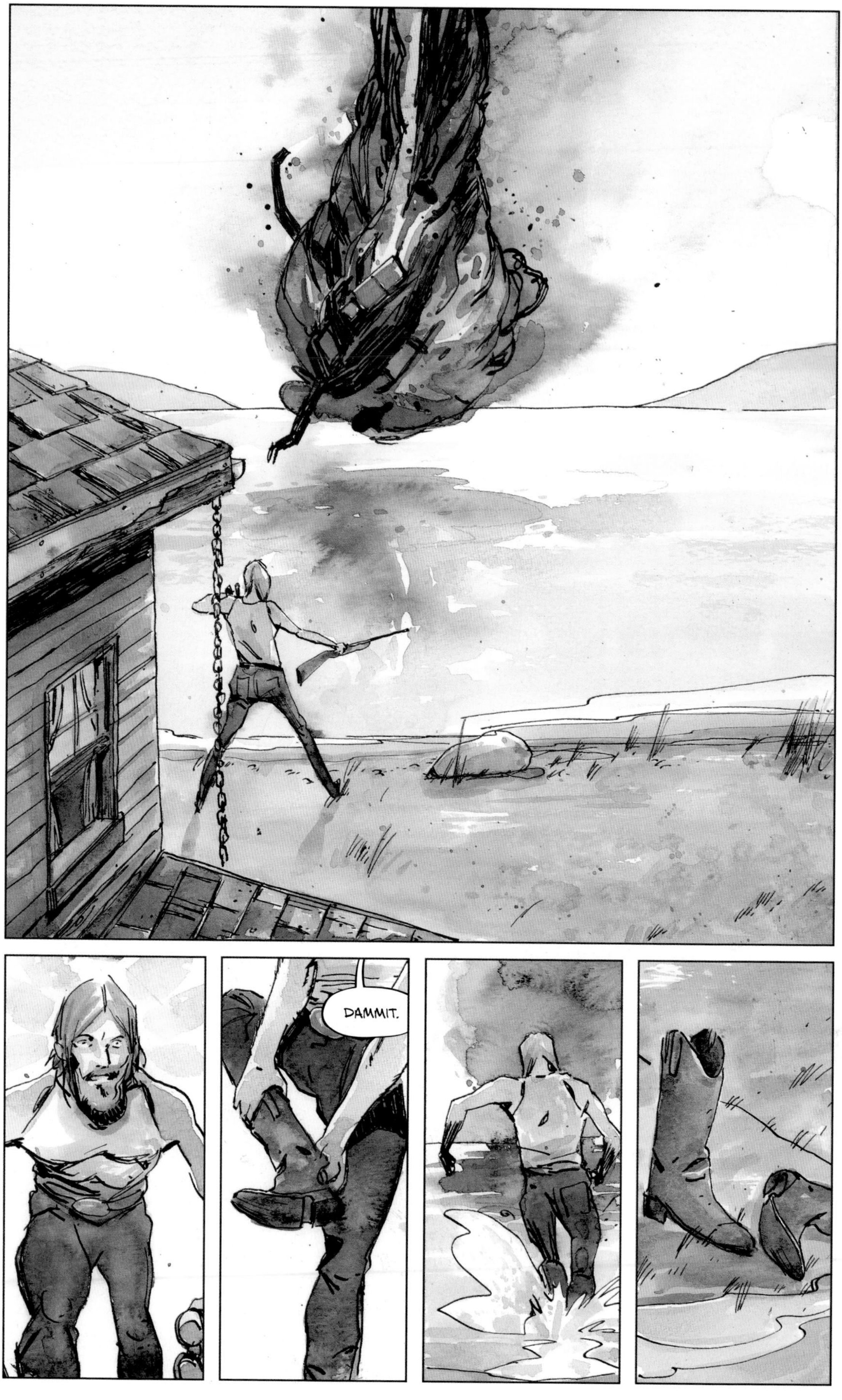
DAMMIT.

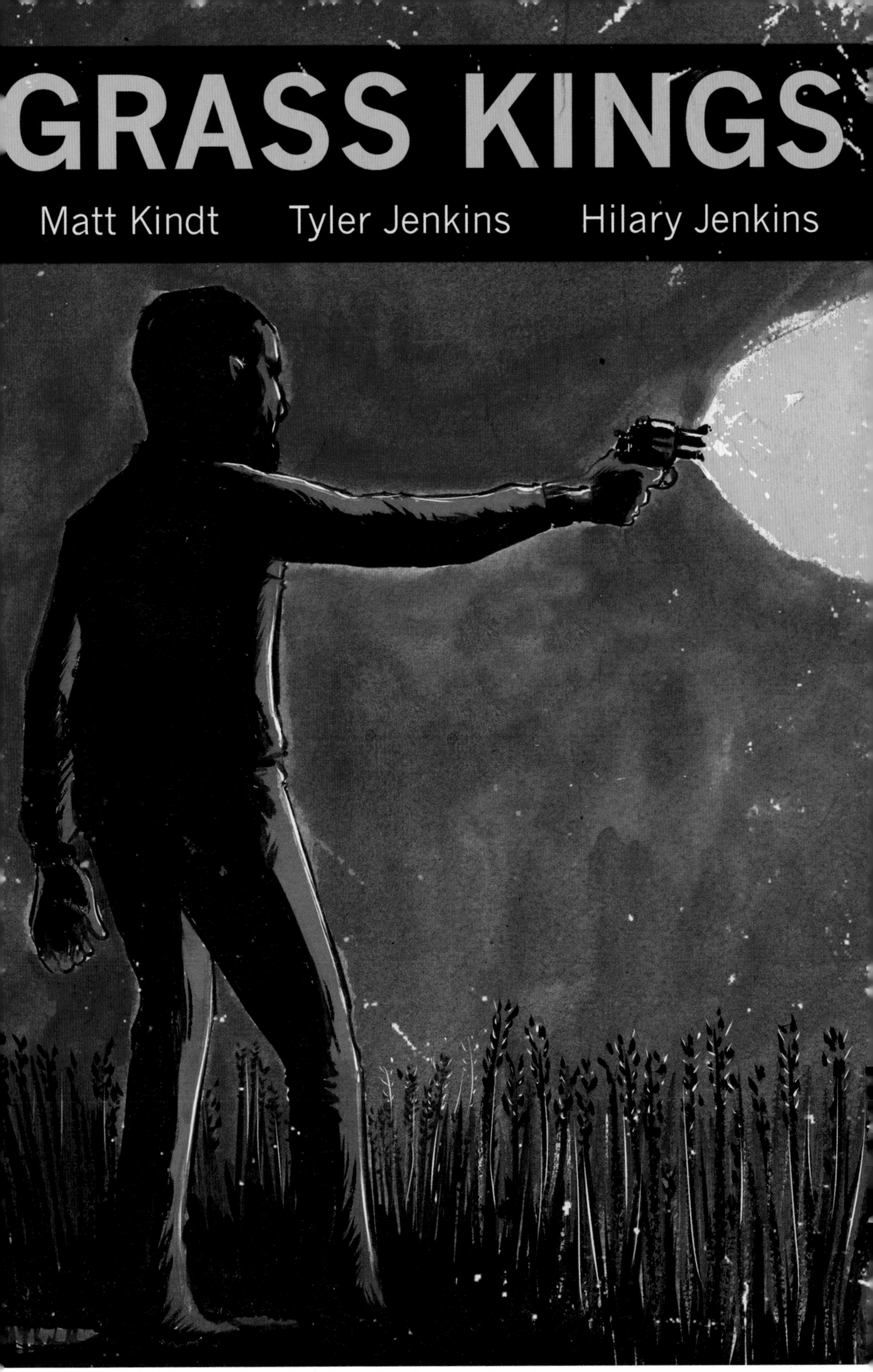
GRASS KINGS
Matt Kindt
Tyler Jenkins
Hilary Jenkins

issue #13 cover by matt kindt

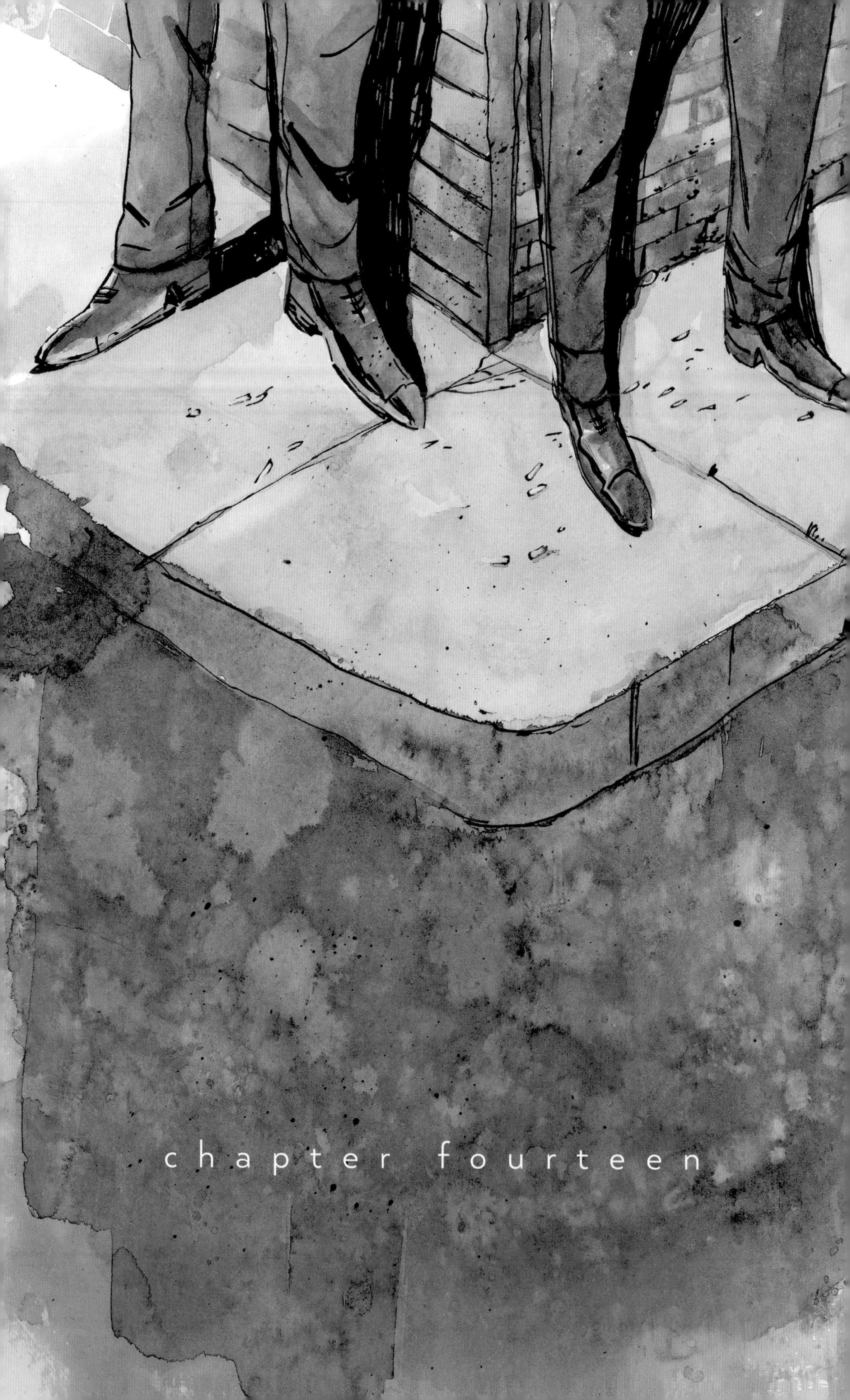
chapter fourteen

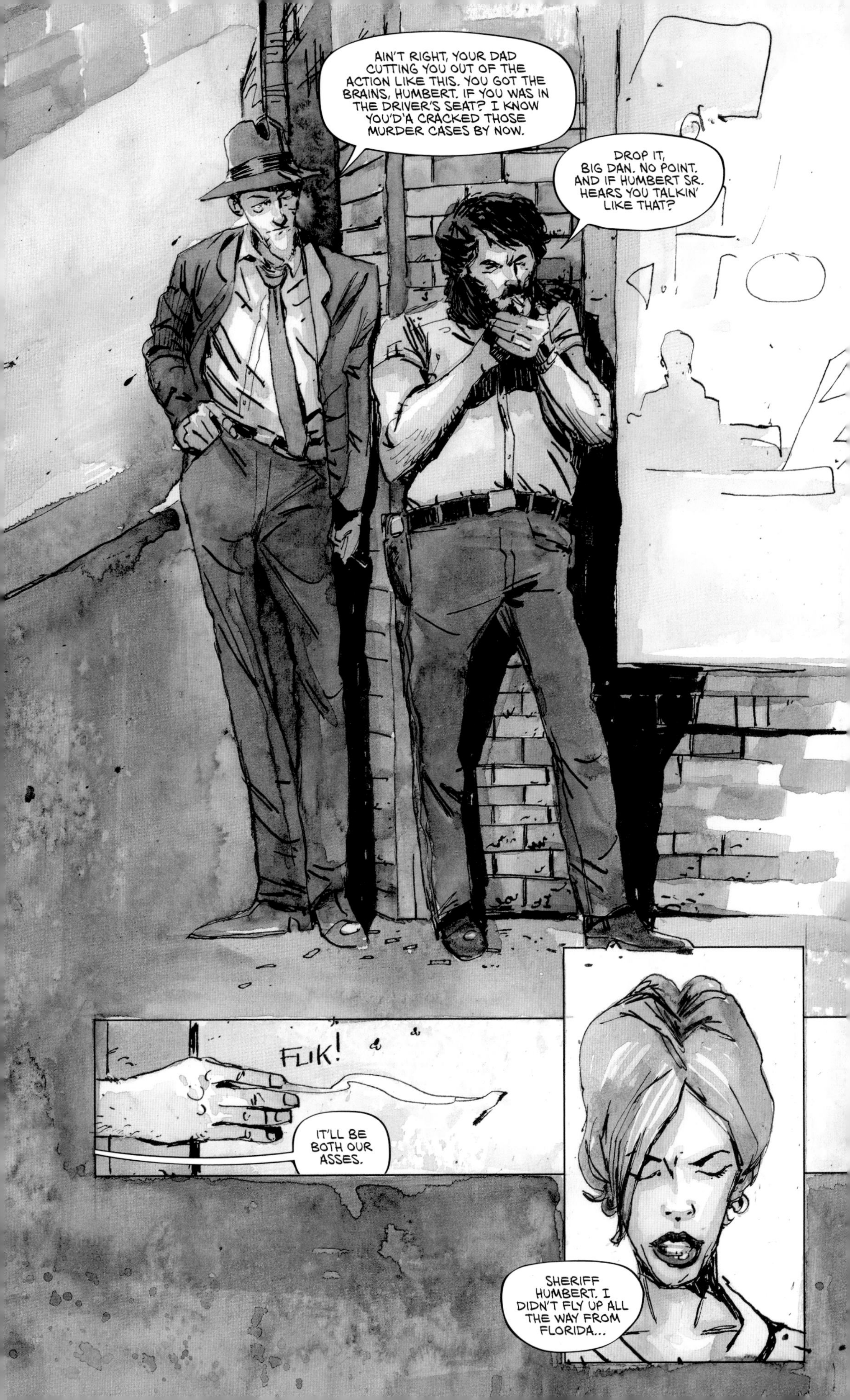
AIN'T RIGHT, YOUR DAD CUTTING YOU OUT OF THE ACTION LIKE THIS. YOU GOT THE BRAINS, HUMBERT. IF YOU WAS IN THE DRIVER'S SEAT? I KNOW YOU'D'A CRACKED THOSE MURDER CASES BY NOW.
DROP IT, BIG DAN. NO POINT. AND IF HUMBERT SR. HEARS YOU TALKIN' LIKE THAT?
FLIK!
IT'LL BE BOTH OUR ASSES.
SHERIFF HUMBERT. I DIDN'T FLY UP ALL THE WAY FROM FLORIDA...

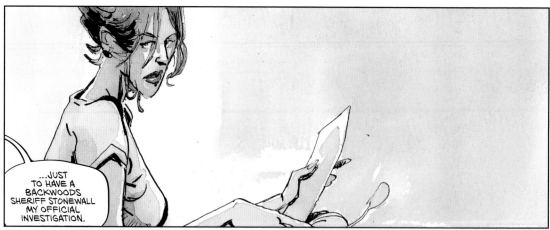

...JUST TO HAVE A BACKWOODS SHERIFF STONEWALL MY OFFICIAL INVESTIGATION.

THERE'S BEEN A KILLING DOWN IN FLORIDA THAT MATCHES THE M.O. OF THE KILLER YOU HAVE AROUND HERE, SHERIFF HUMBERT. THE COMPUTER FLAGGED IT.

WELL, CONGRATULATIONS TO YOUR "COMPUTER," FIELD AGENT HUMPHREY. MAYBE THEY SHOULD'A SENT **IT** UP HERE.

SHERIFF. I CAME UP HERE BY MYSELF. I USUALLY FIND THAT A LIGHTER TOUCH IS BEST WHEN EXTENDING THE REACH OF THE FEDERAL GOVERNMENT.

BUT DON'T MISUNDERSTAND. WE HAVE JURISDICTION AND I WILL COME IN HARD AND HEAVY IF YOU FORCE MY HAND.

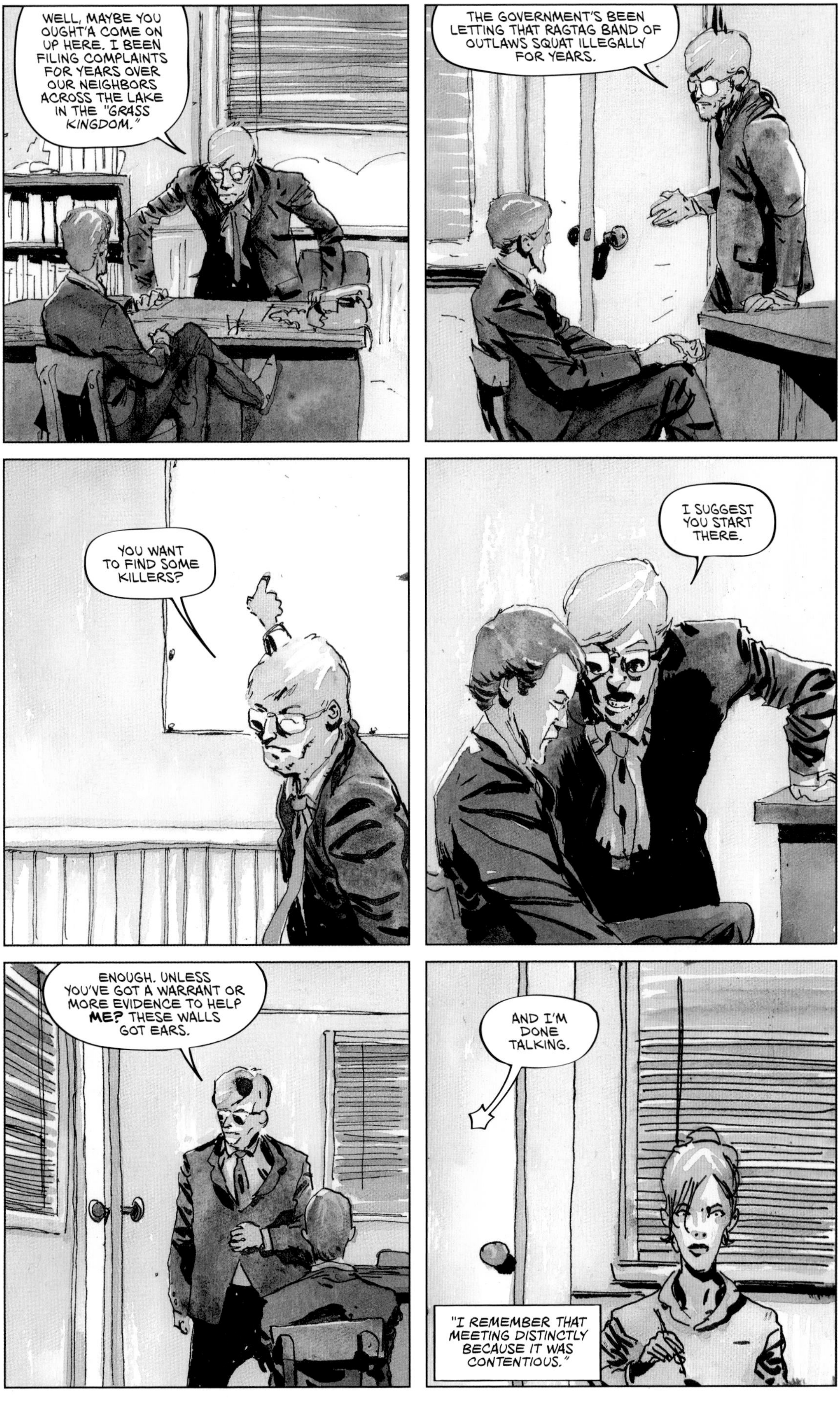
WELL, MAYBE YOU OUGHT'A COME ON UP HERE. I BEEN FILING COMPLAINTS FOR YEARS OVER OUR NEIGHBORS ACROSS THE LAKE IN THE "GRASS KINGDOM."
THE GOVERNMENT'S BEEN LETTING THAT RAGTAG BAND OF OUTLAWS SQUAT ILLEGALLY FOR YEARS.
YOU WANT TO FIND SOME KILLERS?
I SUGGEST YOU START THERE.
ENOUGH. UNLESS YOU'VE GOT A WARRANT OR MORE EVIDENCE TO HELP **ME?** THESE WALLS GOT EARS.
AND I'M DONE TALKING.
"I REMEMBER THAT MEETING DISTINCTLY BECAUSE IT WAS CONTENTIOUS."

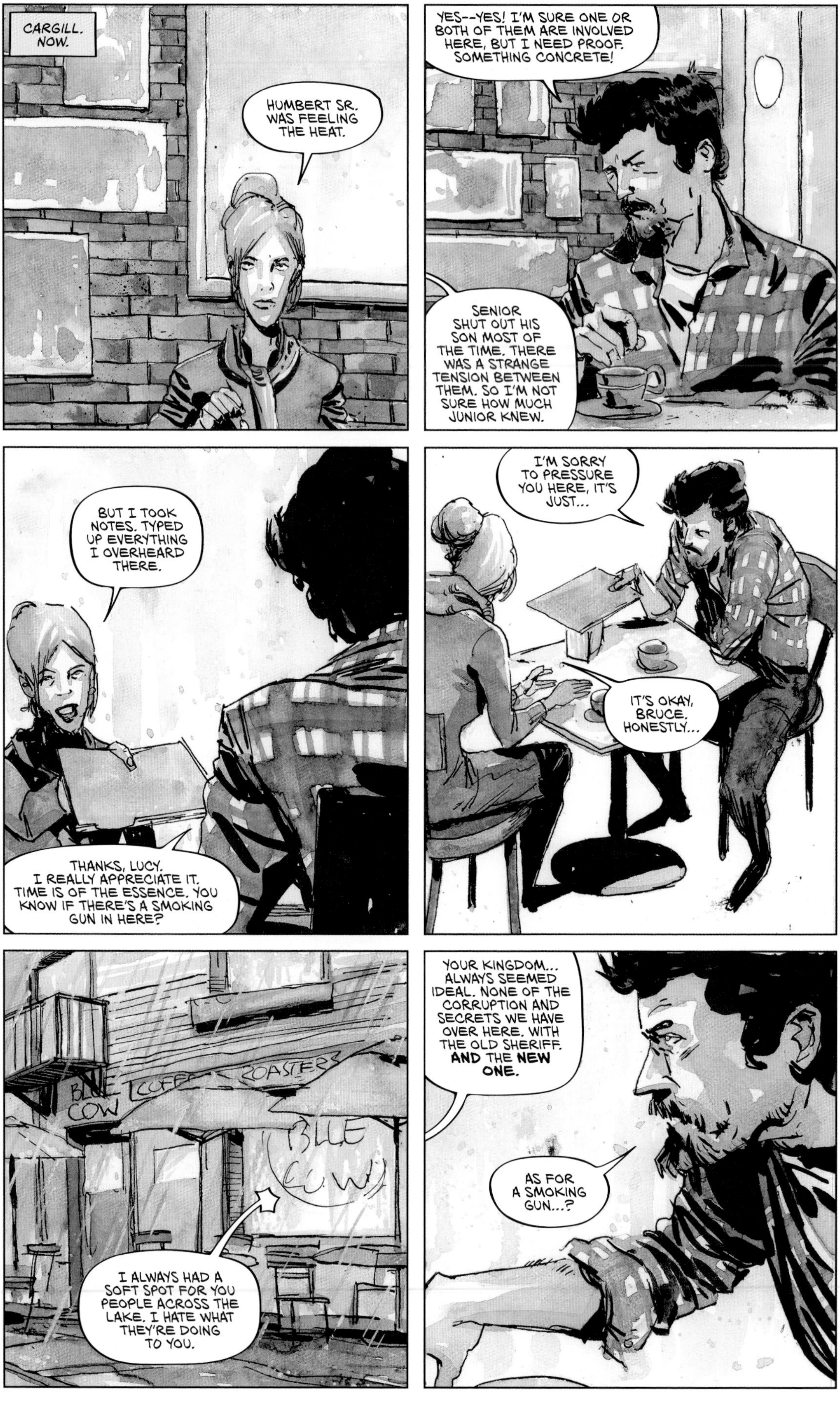
CARGILL. NOW.
HUMBERT SR. WAS FEELING THE HEAT.
YES--YES! I'M SURE ONE OR BOTH OF THEM ARE INVOLVED HERE, BUT I NEED PROOF. SOMETHING CONCRETE!
SENIOR SHUT OUT HIS SON MOST OF THE TIME. THERE WAS A STRANGE TENSION BETWEEN THEM. SO I'M NOT SURE HOW MUCH JUNIOR KNEW.
BUT I TOOK NOTES. TYPED UP EVERYTHING I OVERHEARD THERE.
THANKS, LUCY. I REALLY APPRECIATE IT. TIME IS OF THE ESSENCE. YOU KNOW IF THERE'S A SMOKING GUN IN HERE?
I'M SORRY TO PRESSURE YOU HERE, IT'S JUST...
IT'S OKAY, BRUCE. HONESTLY...
BLUE COW COFFEE ROASTERS
I ALWAYS HAD A SOFT SPOT FOR YOU PEOPLE ACROSS THE LAKE. I HATE WHAT THEY'RE DOING TO YOU.
YOUR KINGDOM... ALWAYS SEEMED IDEAL. NONE OF THE CORRUPTION AND SECRETS WE HAVE OVER HERE. WITH THE OLD SHERIFF. **AND THE NEW ONE.**
AS FOR A SMOKING GUN...?

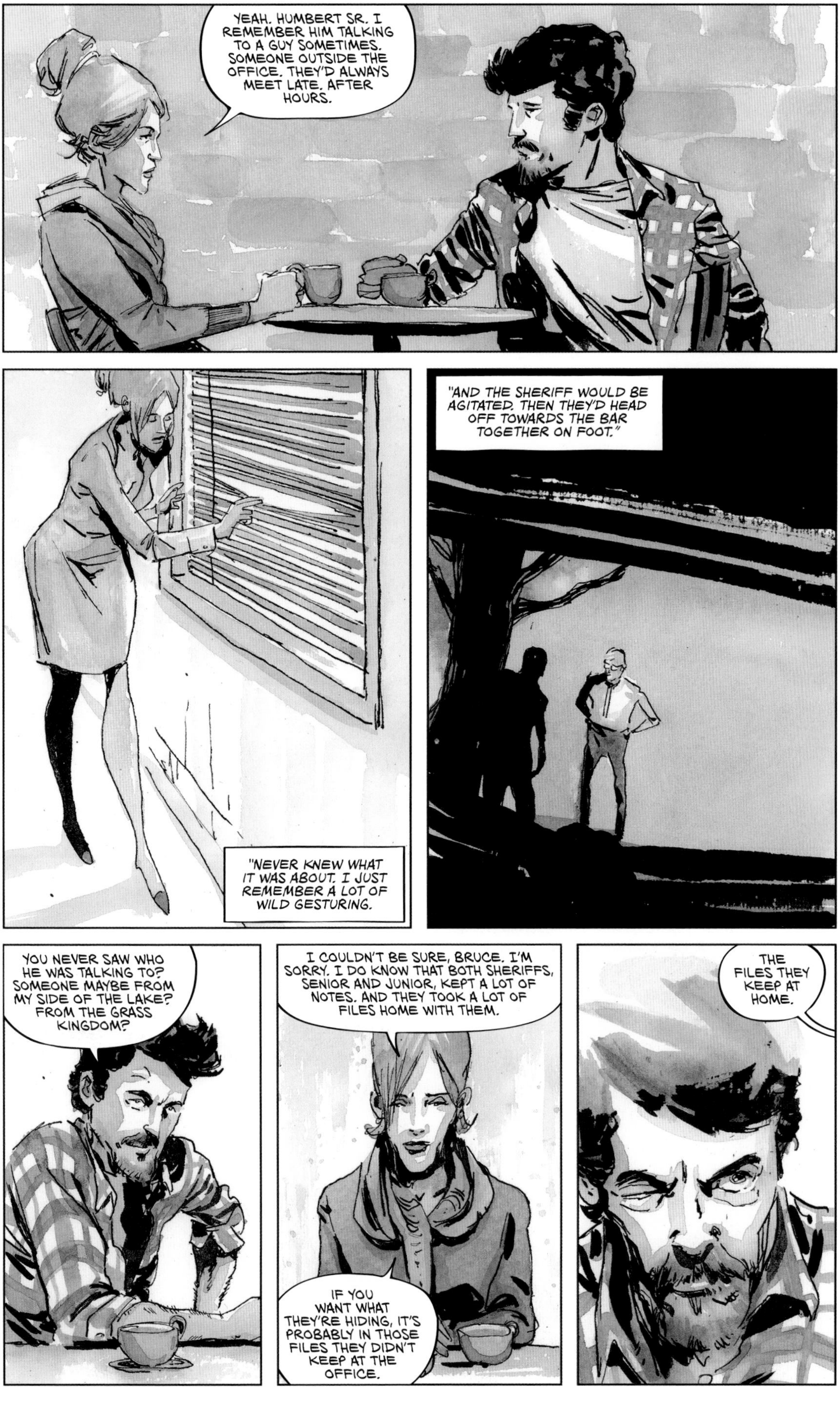
YEAH. HUMBERT SR. I REMEMBER HIM TALKING TO A GUY SOMETIMES. SOMEONE OUTSIDE THE OFFICE. THEY'D ALWAYS MEET LATE. AFTER HOURS.
"NEVER KNEW WHAT IT WAS ABOUT. I JUST REMEMBER A LOT OF WILD GESTURING.
"AND THE SHERIFF WOULD BE AGITATED. THEN THEY'D HEAD OFF TOWARDS THE BAR TOGETHER ON FOOT."
YOU NEVER SAW WHO HE WAS TALKING TO? SOMEONE MAYBE FROM MY SIDE OF THE LAKE? FROM THE GRASS KINGDOM?
I COULDN'T BE SURE, BRUCE. I'M SORRY. I DO KNOW THAT BOTH SHERIFFS, SENIOR AND JUNIOR, KEPT A LOT OF NOTES. AND THEY TOOK A LOT OF FILES HOME WITH THEM.
IF YOU WANT WHAT THEY'RE HIDING, IT'S PROBABLY IN THOSE FILES THEY DIDN'T KEEP AT THE OFFICE.
THE FILES THEY KEEP AT HOME.

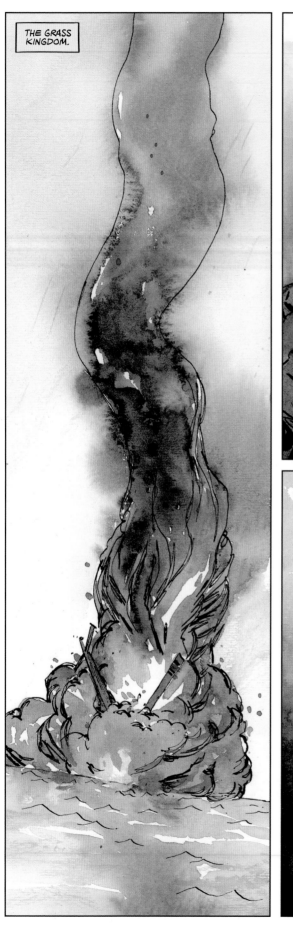

THE GRASS
KINGDOM.

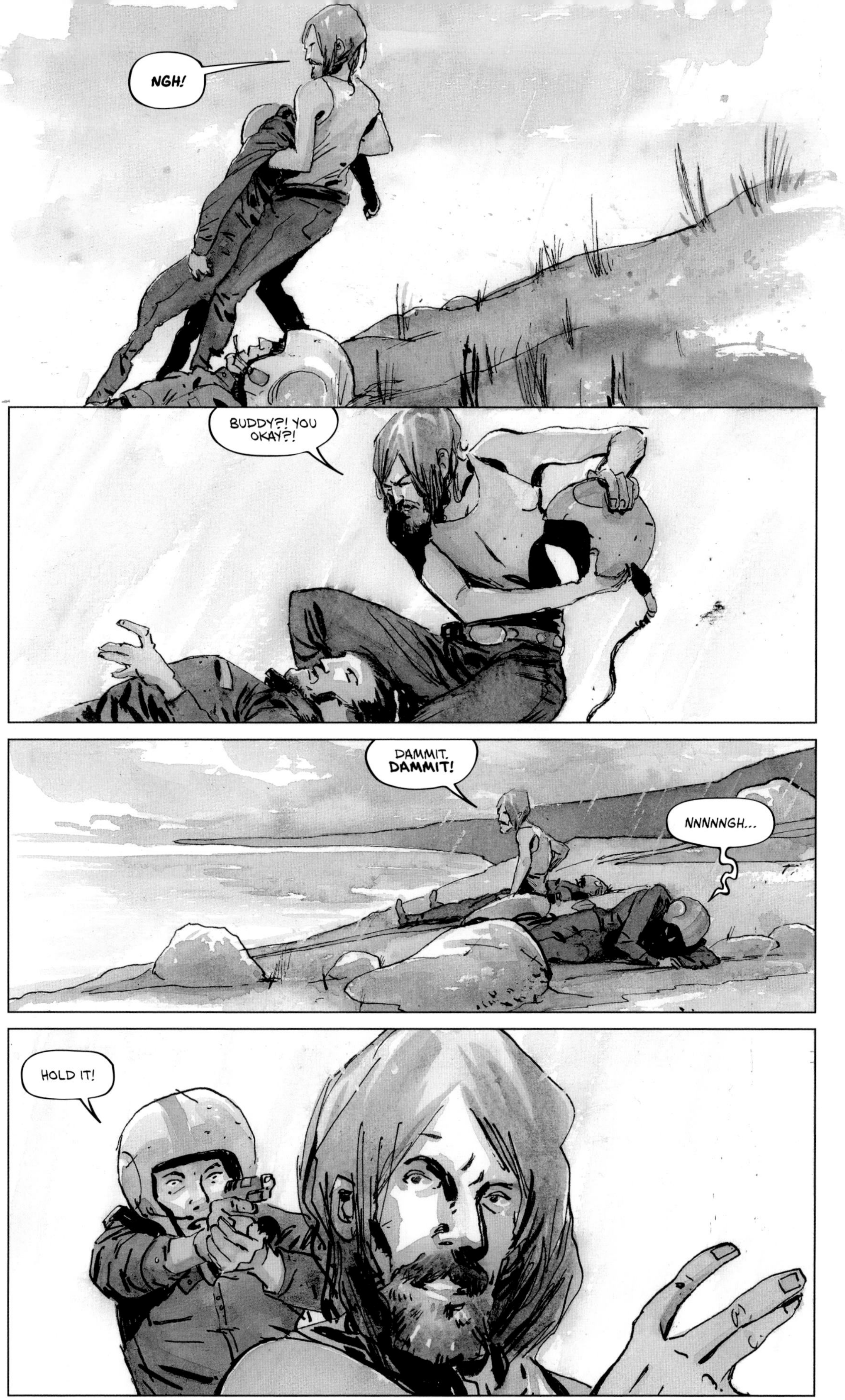
NGH!
BUDDY?! YOU OKAY?!
DAMMIT. DAMMIT!
NNNNNGH...
HOLD IT!

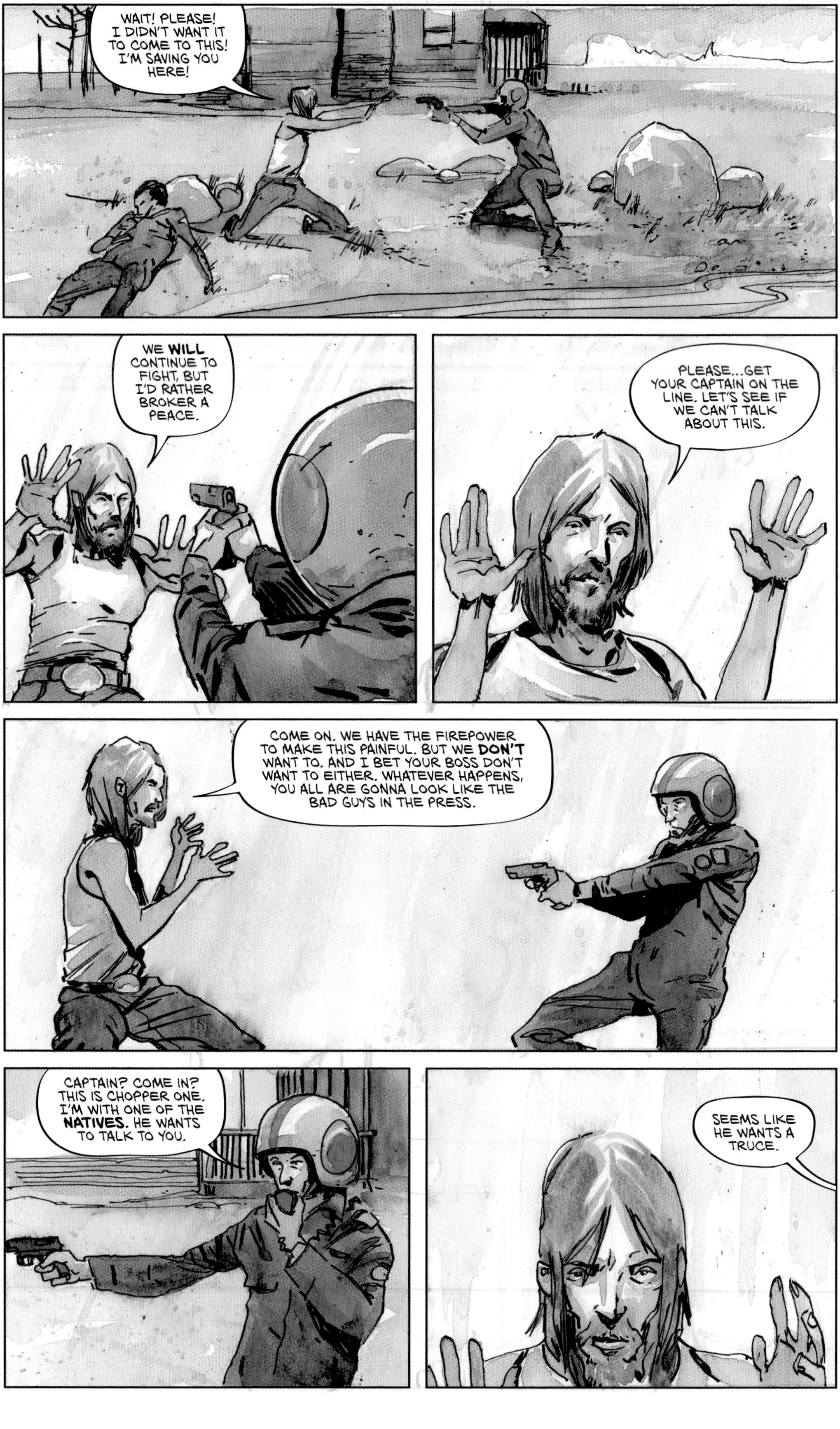
WAIT! PLEASE! I DIDN'T WANT IT TO COME TO THIS! I'M SAVING YOU HERE!
WE **WILL** CONTINUE TO FIGHT, BUT I'D RATHER BROKER A PEACE.
PLEASE...GET YOUR CAPTAIN ON THE LINE. LET'S SEE IF WE CAN'T TALK ABOUT THIS.
COME ON. WE HAVE THE FIREPOWER TO MAKE THIS PAINFUL. BUT WE **DON'T** WANT TO. AND I BET YOUR BOSS DON'T WANT TO EITHER. WHATEVER HAPPENS, YOU ALL ARE GONNA LOOK LIKE THE BAD GUYS IN THE PRESS.
CAPTAIN? COME IN? THIS IS CHOPPER ONE. I'M WITH ONE OF THE **NATIVES.** HE WANTS TO TALK TO YOU.
SEEMS LIKE HE WANTS A TRUCE.

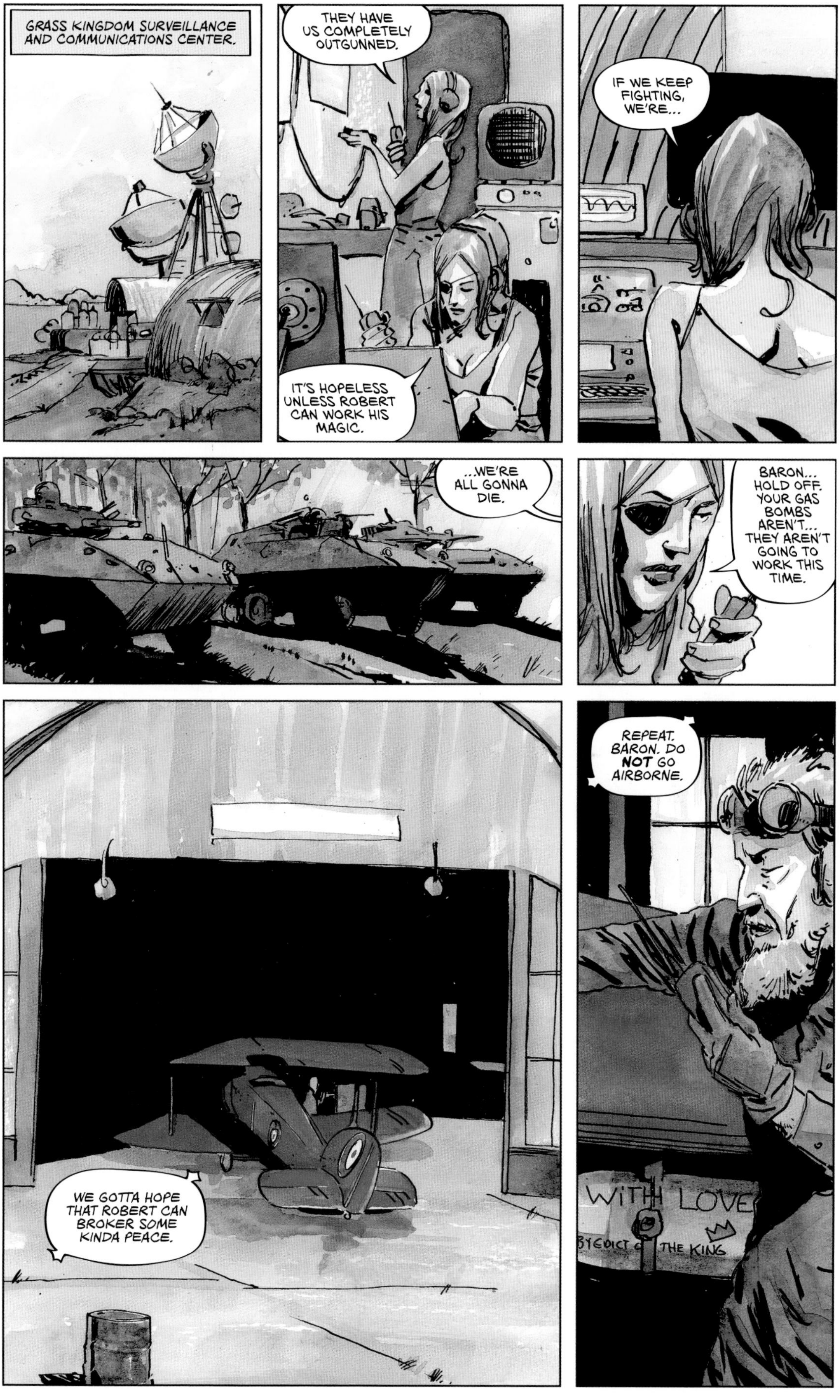
GRASS KINGDOM SURVEILLANCE AND COMMUNICATIONS CENTER.
THEY HAVE US COMPLETELY OUTGUNNED.
IT'S HOPELESS UNLESS ROBERT CAN WORK HIS MAGIC.
IF WE KEEP FIGHTING, WE'RE...
...WE'RE ALL GONNA DIE.
BARON... HOLD OFF. YOUR GAS BOMBS AREN'T... THEY AREN'T GOING TO WORK THIS TIME.
WE GOTTA HOPE THAT ROBERT CAN BROKER SOME KINDA PEACE.
REPEAT. BARON. DO **NOT** GO AIRBORNE.
WITH LOVE
BY EDICT OF THE KING

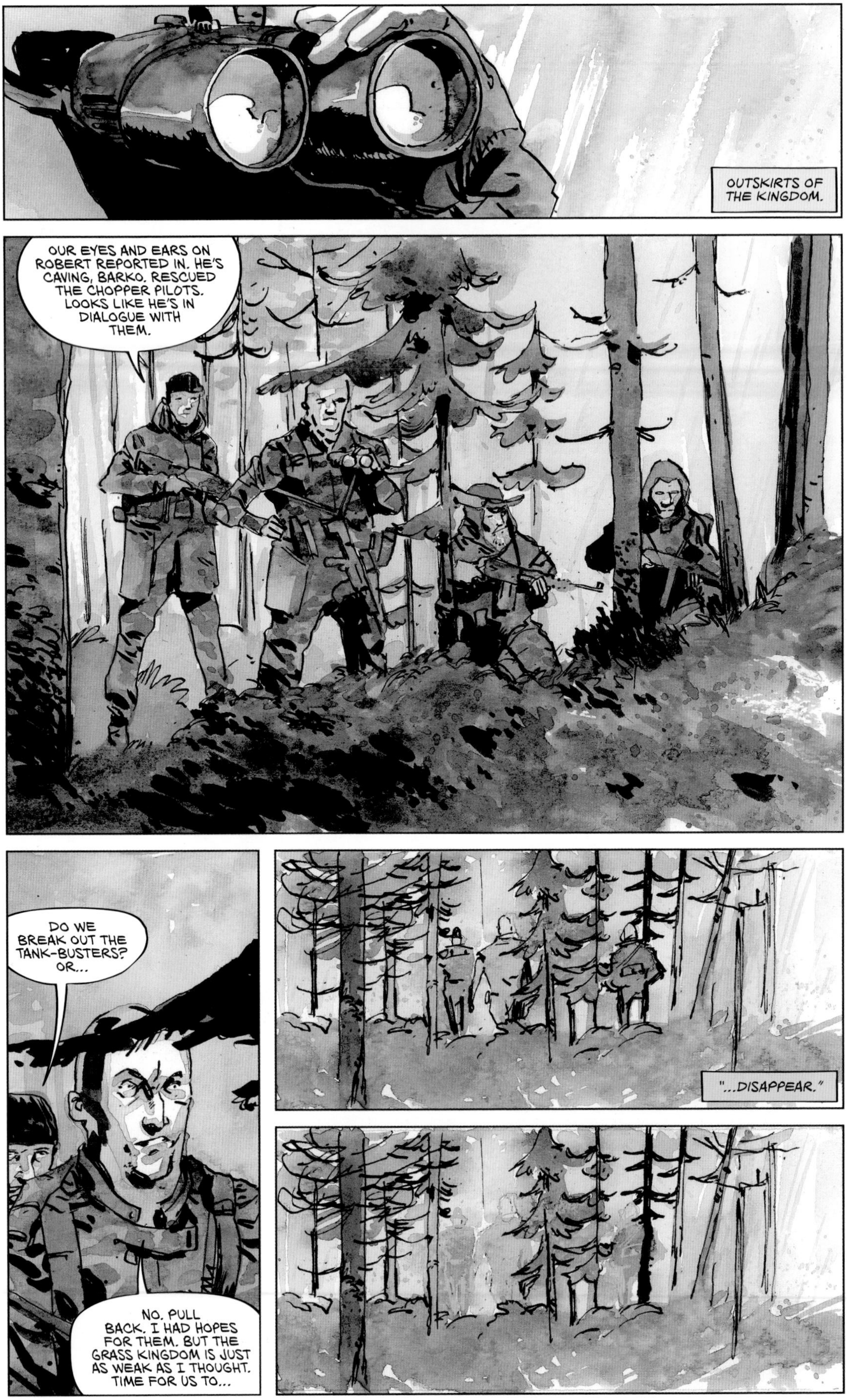
OUTSKIRTS OF THE KINGDOM.
OUR EYES AND EARS ON ROBERT REPORTED IN. HE'S CAVING, BARKO. RESCUED THE CHOPPER PILOTS. LOOKS LIKE HE'S IN DIALOGUE WITH THEM.
DO WE BREAK OUT THE TANK-BUSTERS? OR...
NO. PULL BACK. I HAD HOPES FOR THEM. BUT THE GRASS KINGDOM IS JUST AS WEAK AS I THOUGHT. TIME FOR US TO...
"...DISAPPEAR."

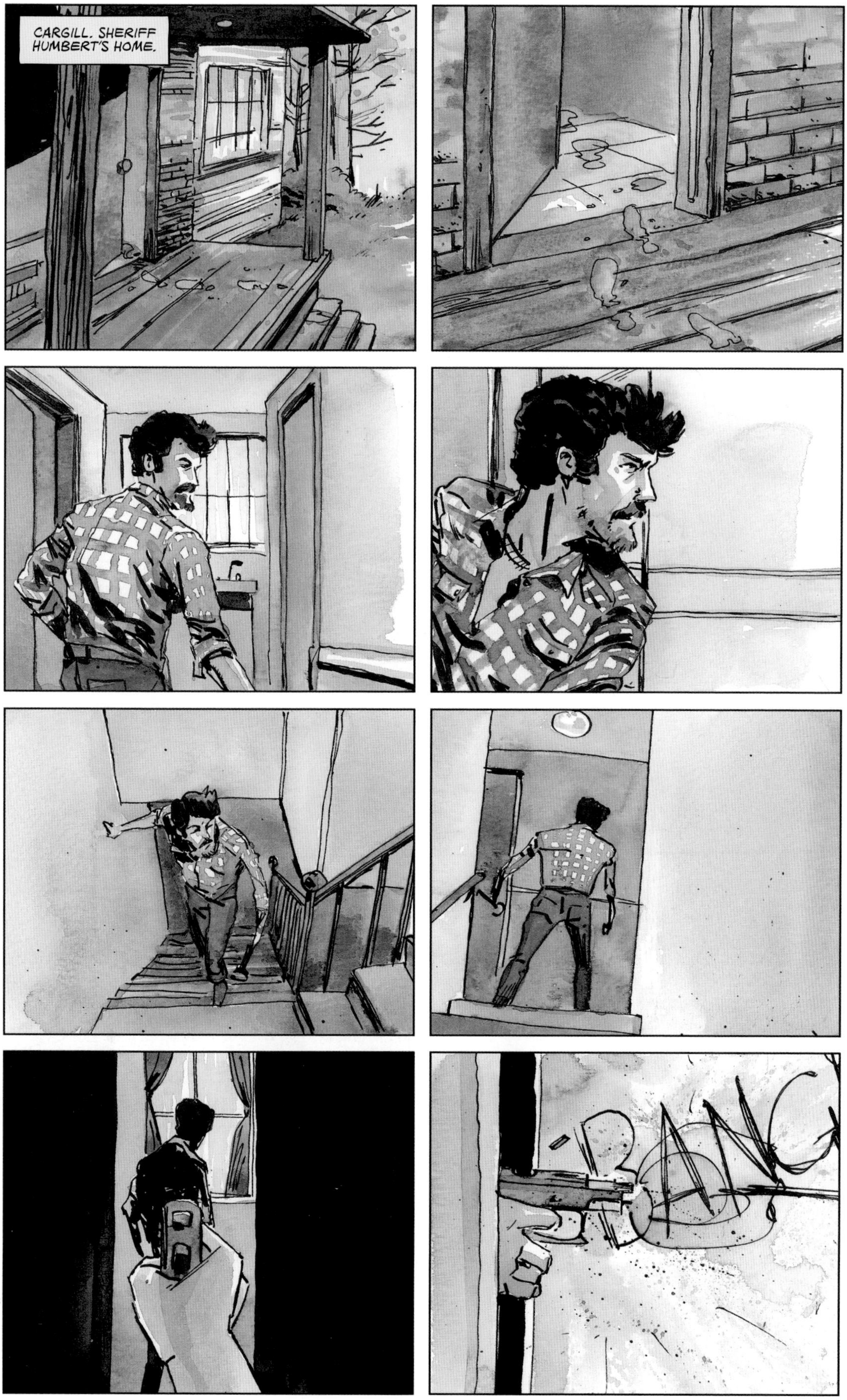
CARGILL. SHERIFF HUMBERT'S HOME.
BANG

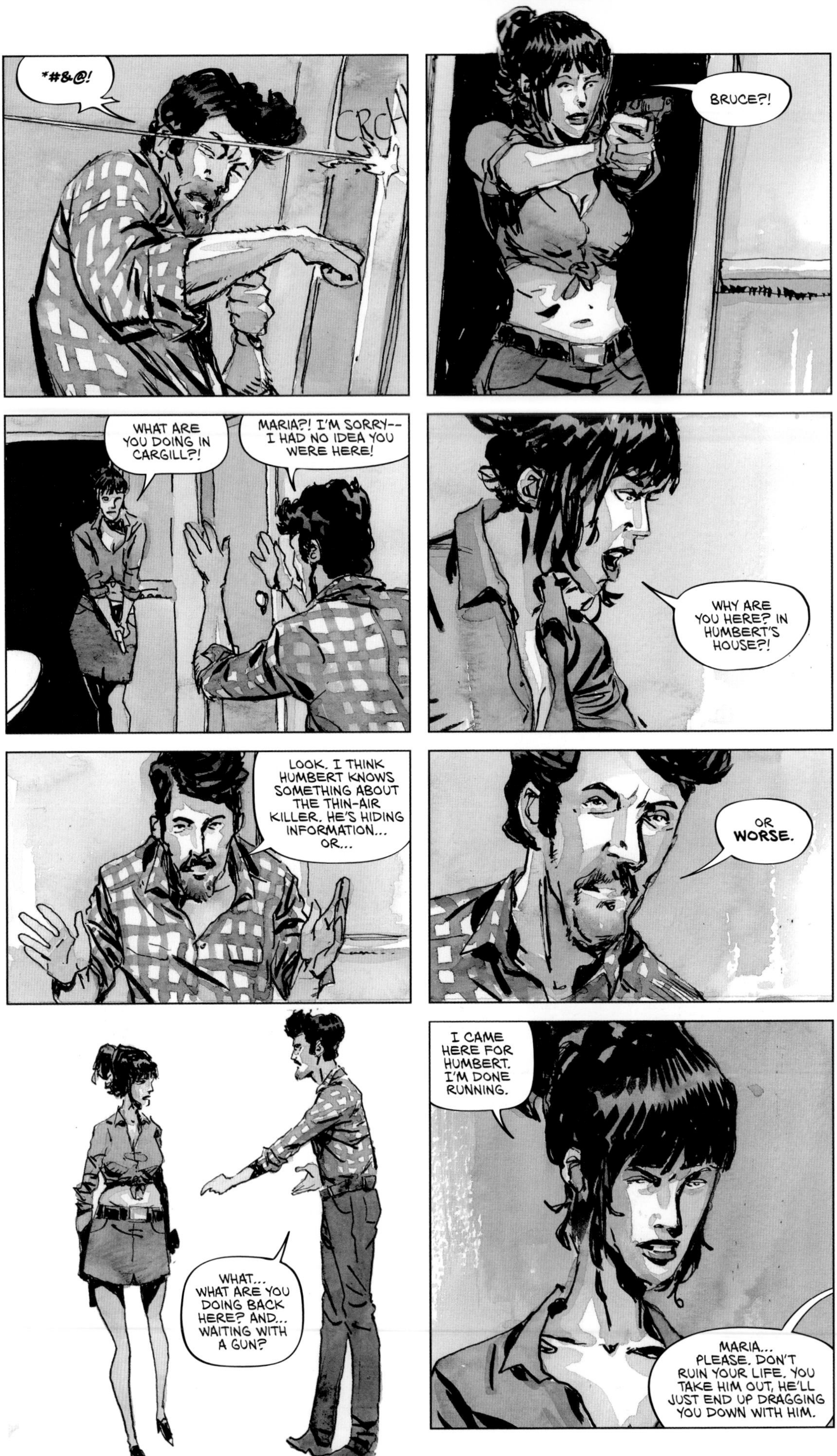
*#&@!
CRCH
BRUCE?!
WHAT ARE YOU DOING IN CARGILL?!
MARIA?! I'M SORRY-- I HAD NO IDEA YOU WERE HERE!
WHY ARE YOU HERE? IN HUMBERT'S HOUSE?!
LOOK. I THINK HUMBERT KNOWS SOMETHING ABOUT THE THIN-AIR KILLER. HE'S HIDING INFORMATION... OR...
OR **WORSE.**
WHAT... WHAT ARE YOU DOING BACK HERE? AND... WAITING WITH A GUN?
I CAME HERE FOR HUMBERT. I'M DONE RUNNING.
MARIA... PLEASE. DON'T RUIN YOUR LIFE. YOU TAKE HIM OUT, HE'LL JUST END UP DRAGGING YOU DOWN WITH HIM.

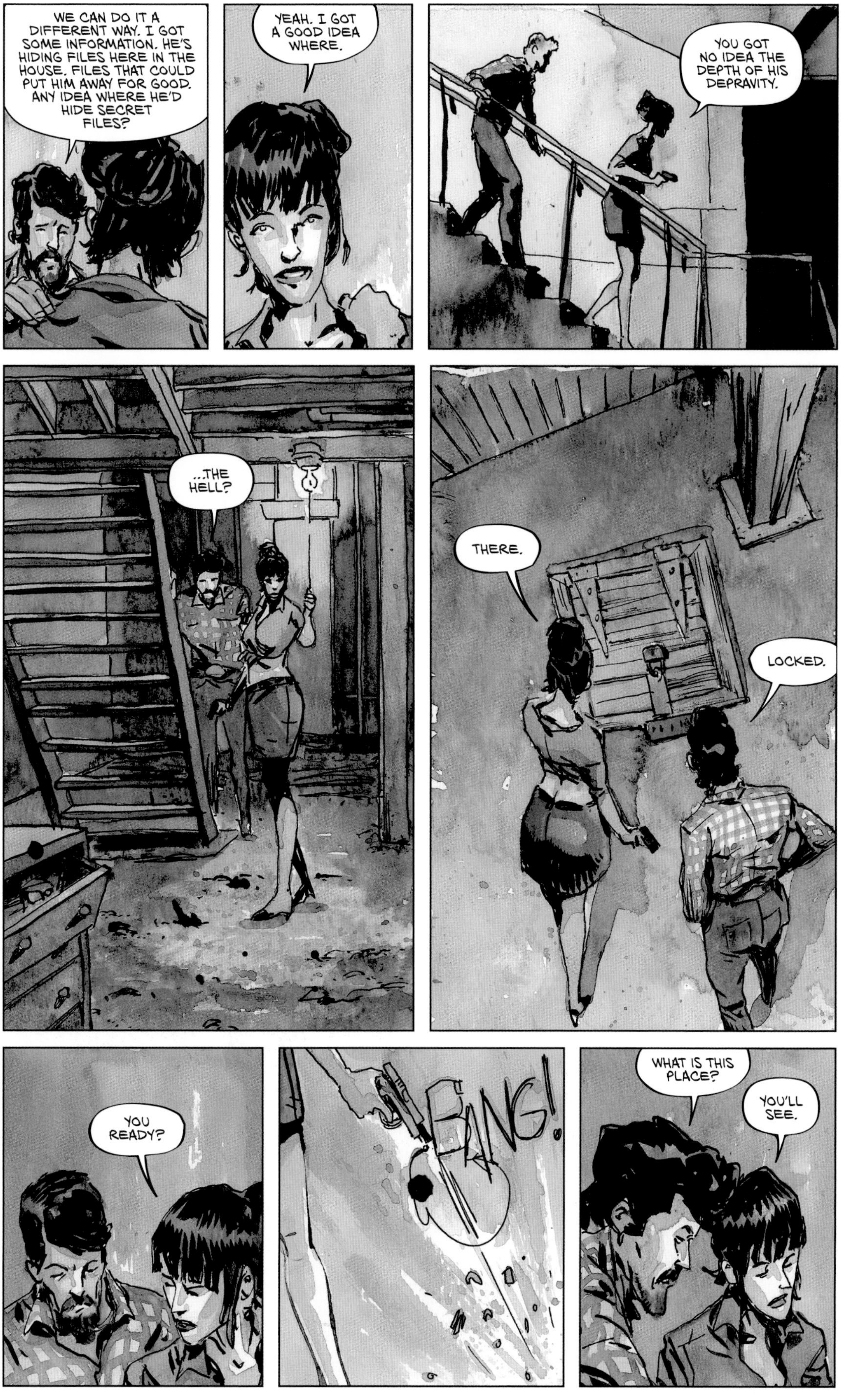
WE CAN DO IT A DIFFERENT WAY. I GOT SOME INFORMATION. HE'S HIDING FILES HERE IN THE HOUSE. FILES THAT COULD PUT HIM AWAY FOR GOOD. ANY IDEA WHERE HE'D HIDE SECRET FILES?
YEAH. I GOT A GOOD IDEA WHERE.
YOU GOT NO IDEA THE DEPTH OF HIS DEPRAVITY.
...THE HELL?
THERE.
LOCKED.
YOU READY?
BANG!
WHAT IS THIS PLACE?
YOU'LL SEE.

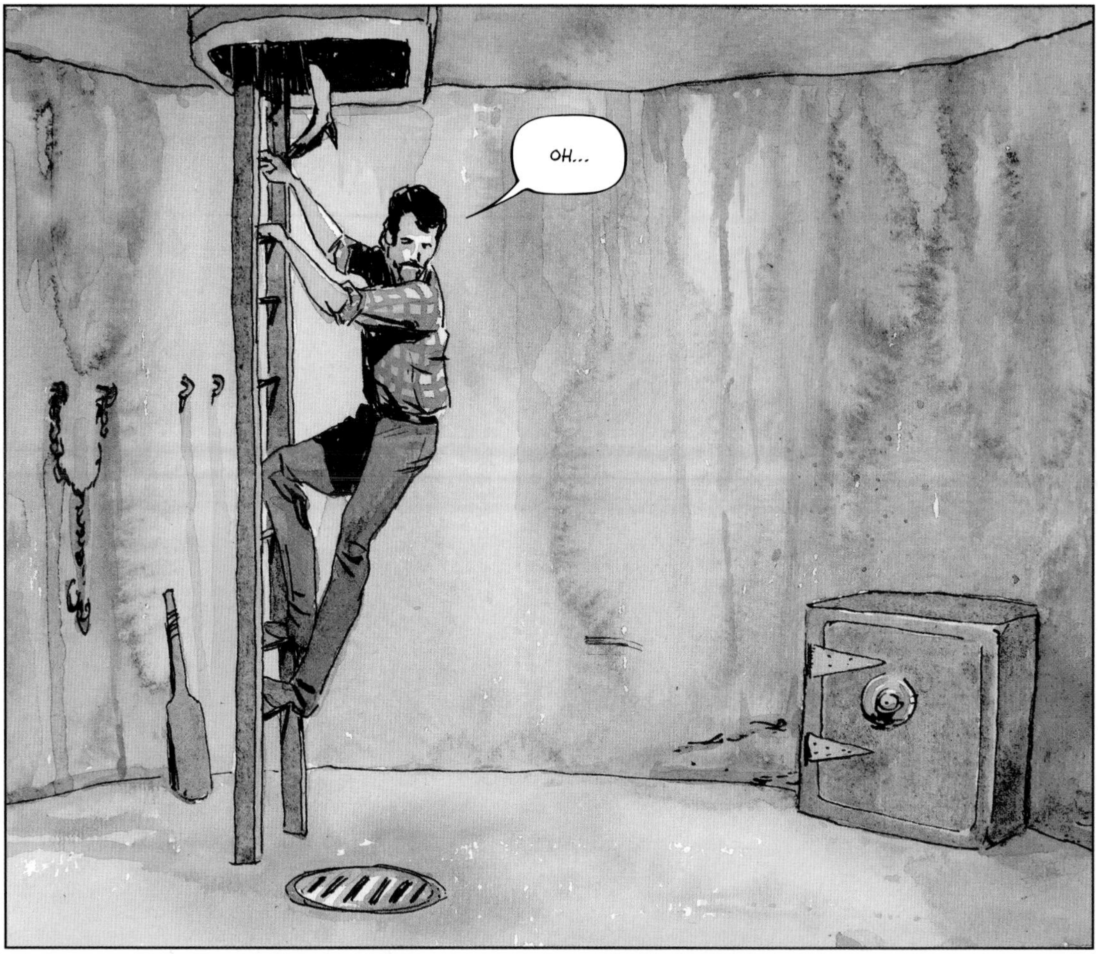
OH...

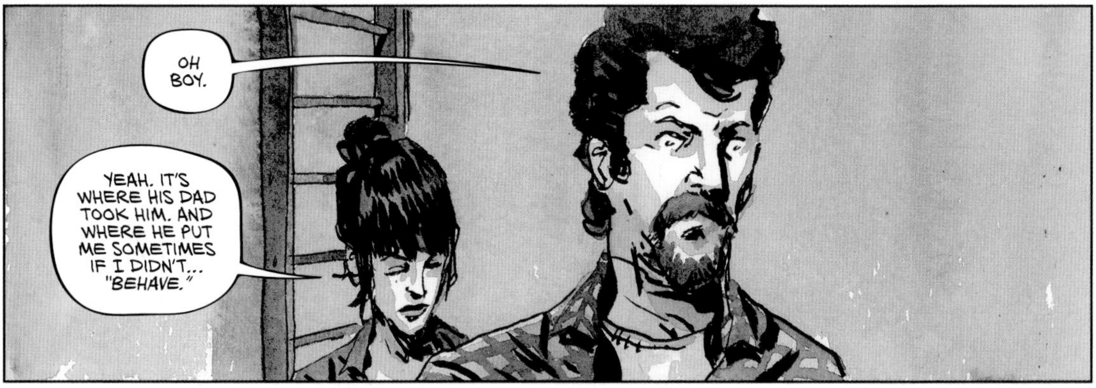
OH BOY.
YEAH. IT'S WHERE HIS DAD TOOK HIM. AND WHERE HE PUT ME SOMETIMES IF I DIDN'T... "BEHAVE."

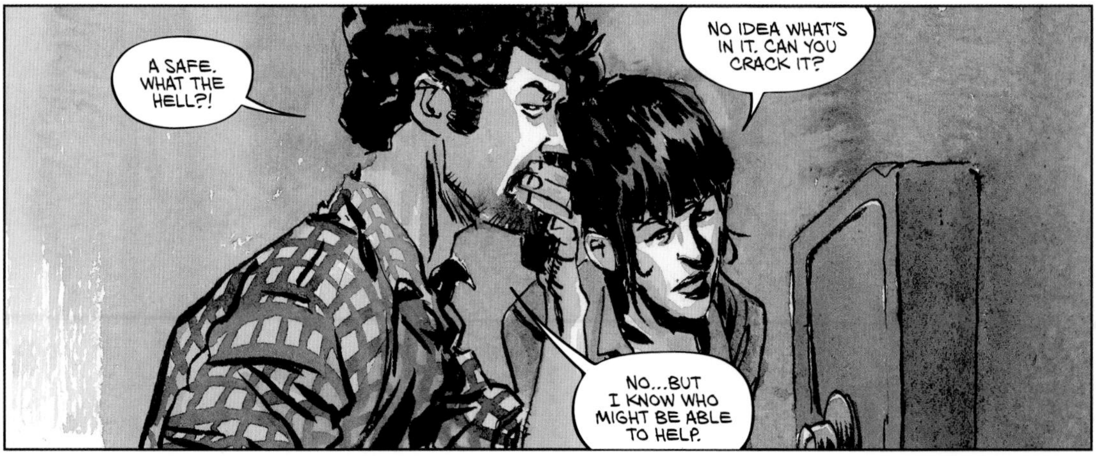
A SAFE. WHAT THE HELL?!
NO IDEA WHAT'S IN IT. CAN YOU CRACK IT?
NO...BUT I KNOW WHO MIGHT BE ABLE TO HELP.

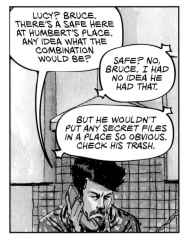

LUCY? BRUCE. THERE'S A SAFE HERE AT HUMBERT'S PLACE. ANY IDEA WHAT THE COMBINATION WOULD BE?

SAFE? NO, BRUCE. I HAD NO IDEA HE HAD THAT.

BUT HE WOULDN'T PUT ANY SECRET FILES IN A PLACE SO OBVIOUS. CHECK HIS TRASH.

BOTH HUMBERTS WERE PARANOID ABOUT DYING AND SOMEONE FINDING THEIR SECRETS.

HUMBERT WOULD PUT THINGS IN THE TRASH, SO IF HE DIED THE FILES WOULD END UP BEING EVENTUALLY JUST THROWN AWAY.

HE HAVE AN OFFICE HERE?

FOLLOW ME.

I'LL CHECK THE CABINET.

HOW WILL WE KNOW WHEN WE FIND IT?

WHAT THE HELL?!

FOUND IT.

OH MY GOD... THIS...?

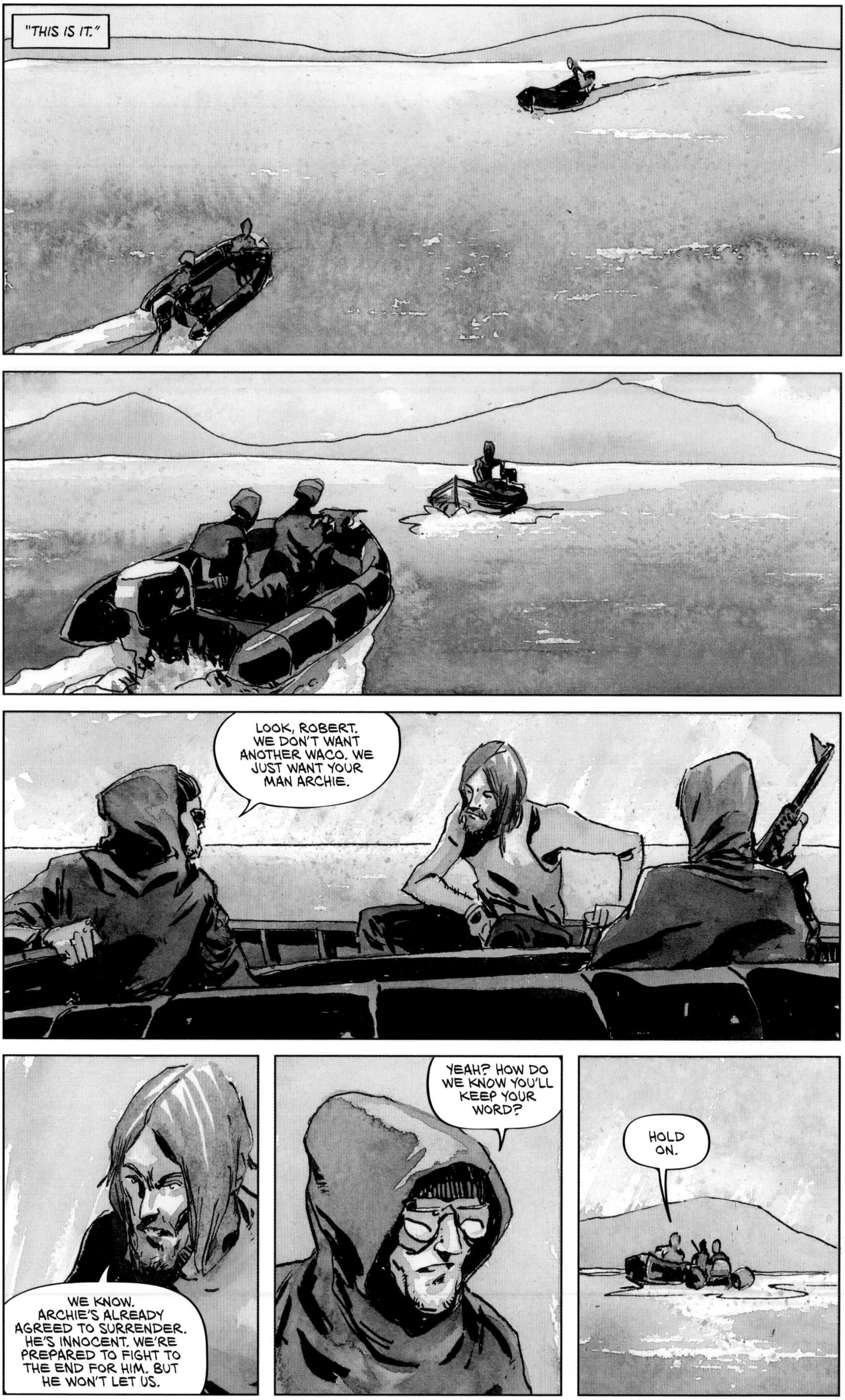
"THIS IS IT."
LOOK, ROBERT. WE DON'T WANT ANOTHER WACO. WE JUST WANT YOUR MAN ARCHIE.
WE KNOW. ARCHIE'S ALREADY AGREED TO SURRENDER. HE'S INNOCENT. WE'RE PREPARED TO FIGHT TO THE END FOR HIM. BUT HE WON'T LET US.
YEAH? HOW DO WE KNOW YOU'LL KEEP YOUR WORD?
HOLD ON.

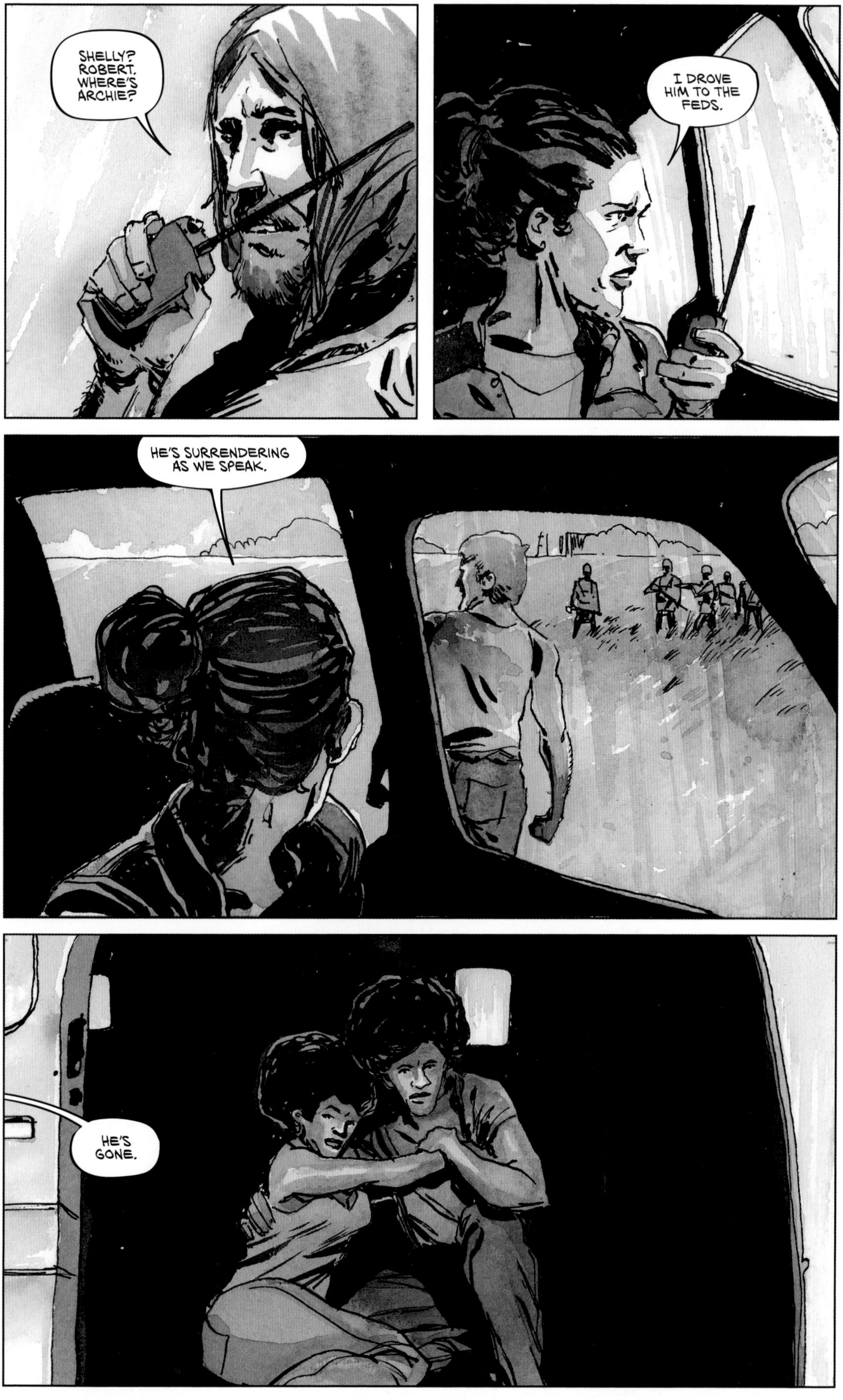
SHELLY? ROBERT. WHERE'S ARCHIE?
I DROVE HIM TO THE FEDS.
HE'S SURRENDERING AS WE SPEAK.
HE'S GONE.

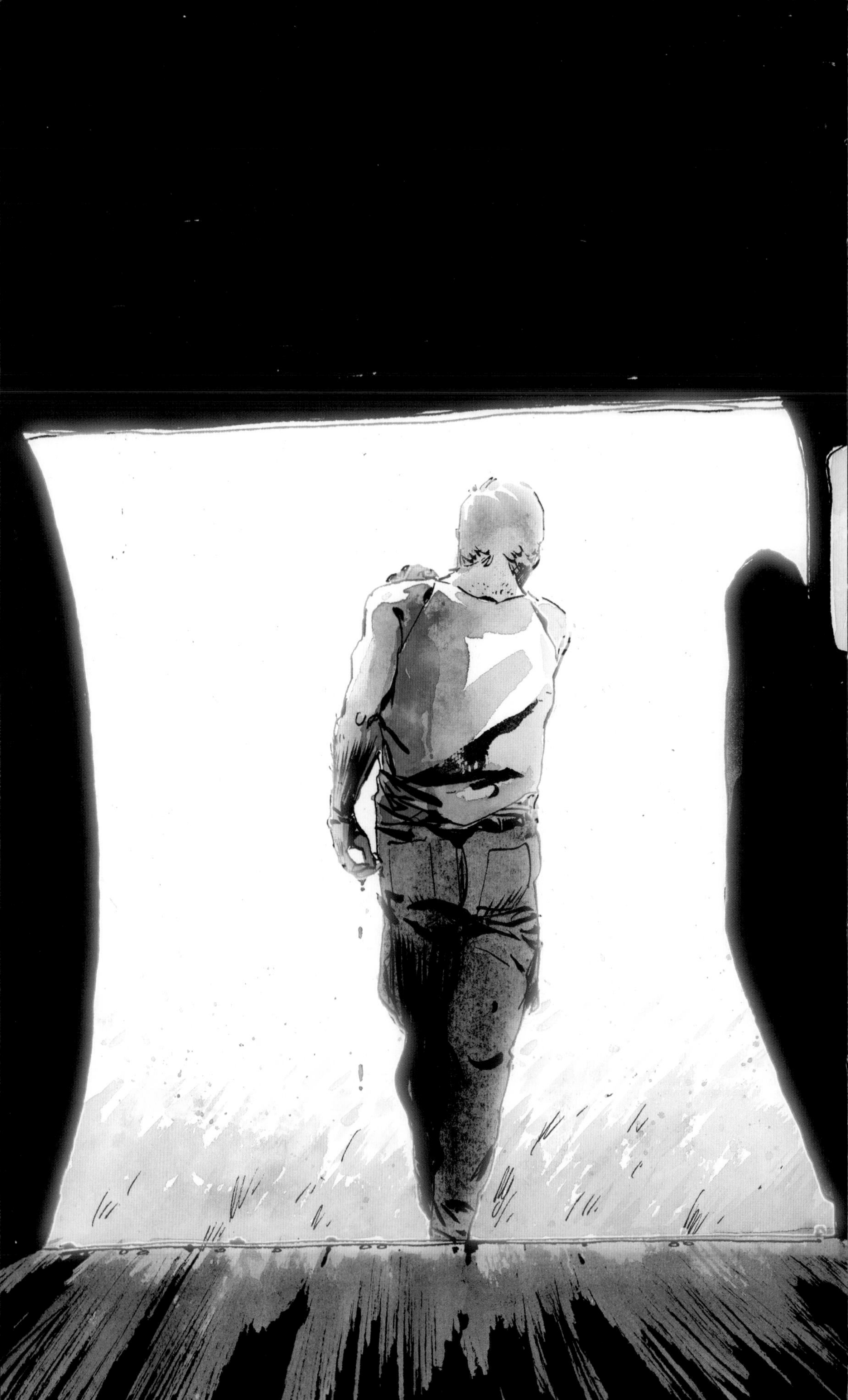

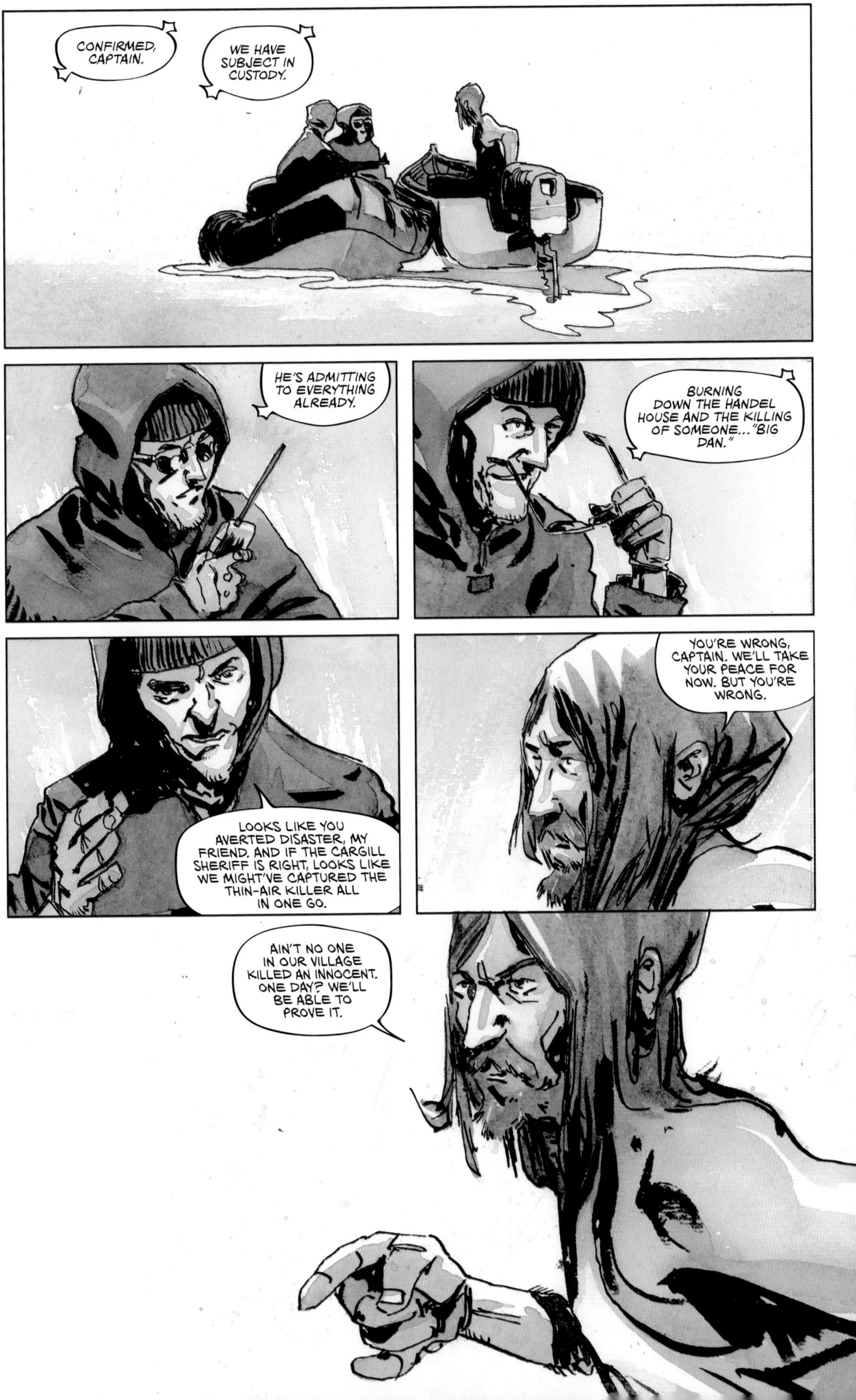
CONFIRMED, CAPTAIN.
WE HAVE SUBJECT IN CUSTODY.
HE'S ADMITTING TO EVERYTHING ALREADY.
BURNING DOWN THE HANDEL HOUSE AND THE KILLING OF SOMEONE... "BIG DAN."
LOOKS LIKE YOU AVERTED DISASTER, MY FRIEND. AND IF THE CARGILL SHERIFF IS RIGHT, LOOKS LIKE WE MIGHT'VE CAPTURED THE THIN-AIR KILLER ALL IN ONE GO.
YOU'RE WRONG, CAPTAIN. WE'LL TAKE YOUR PEACE FOR NOW. BUT YOU'RE WRONG.
AIN'T NO ONE IN OUR VILLAGE KILLED AN INNOCENT. ONE DAY? WE'LL BE ABLE TO PROVE IT.

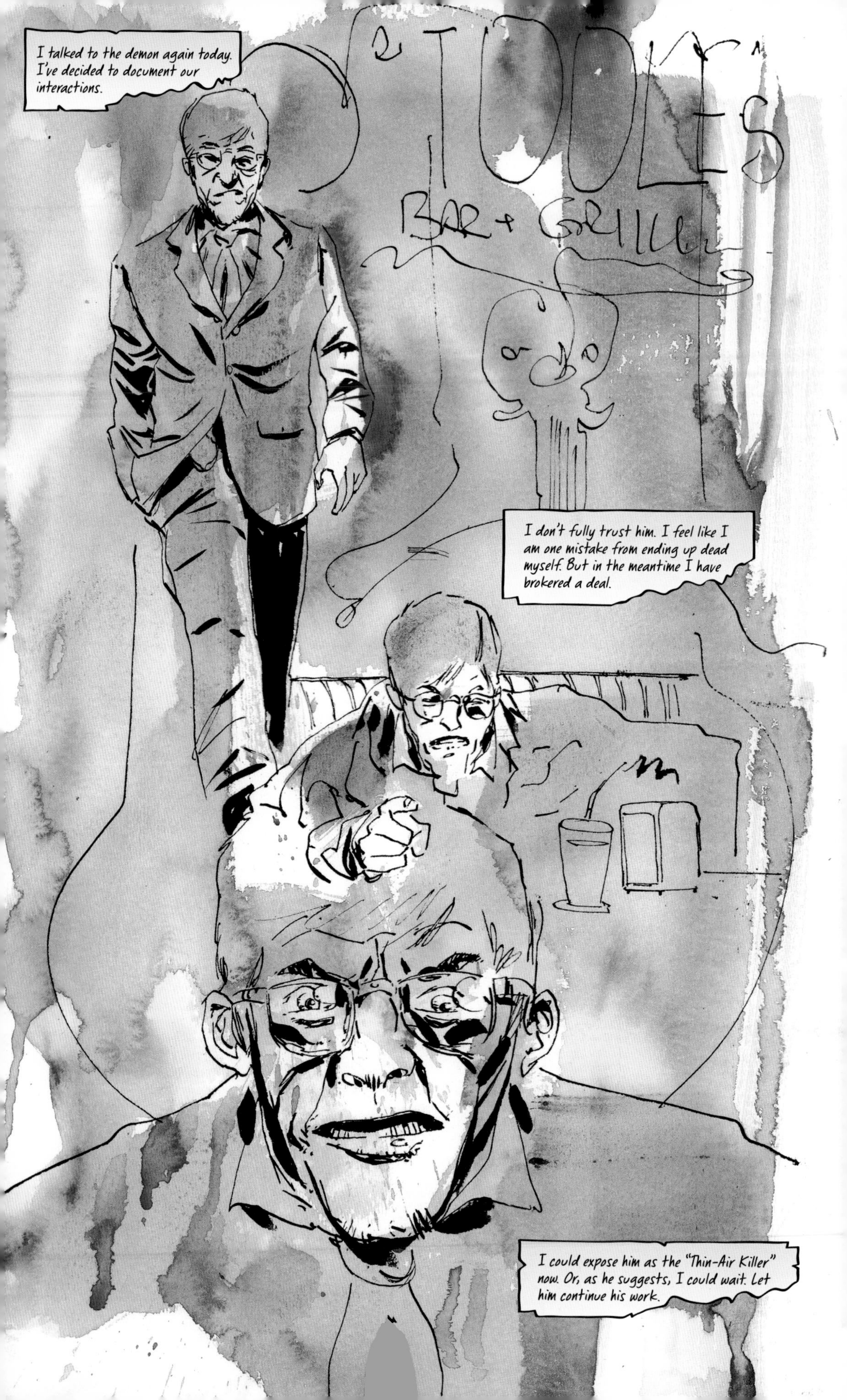
I talked to the demon again today. I've decided to document our interactions.
O'TOOLE'S
BAR + GRILL
I don't fully trust him. I feel like I am one mistake from ending up dead myself. But in the meantime I have brokered a deal.
I could expose him as the "Thin-Air Killer" now. Or, as he suggests, I could wait. Let him continue his work.

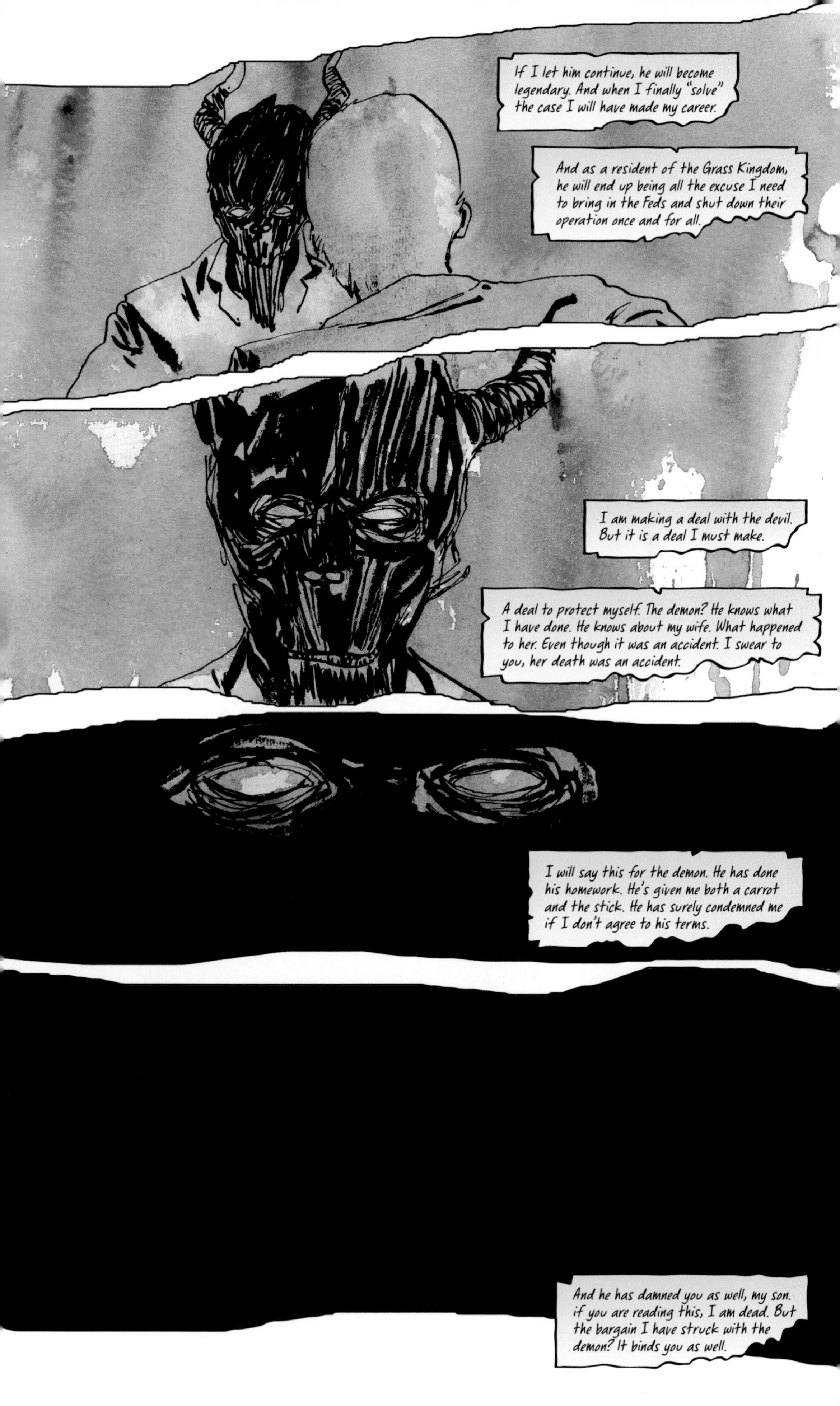
If I let him continue, he will become legendary. And when I finally "solve" the case I will have made my career.
And as a resident of the Grass Kingdom, he will end up being all the excuse I need to bring in the Feds and shut down their operation once and for all.
I am making a deal with the devil. But it is a deal I must make.
A deal to protect myself. The demon? He knows what I have done. He knows about my wife. What happened to her. Even though it was an accident. I swear to you, her death was an accident.
I will say this for the demon. He has done his homework. He's given me both a carrot and the stick. He has surely condemned me if I don't agree to his terms.
And he has damned you as well, my son. if you are reading this, I am dead. But the bargain I have struck with the demon? It binds you as well.

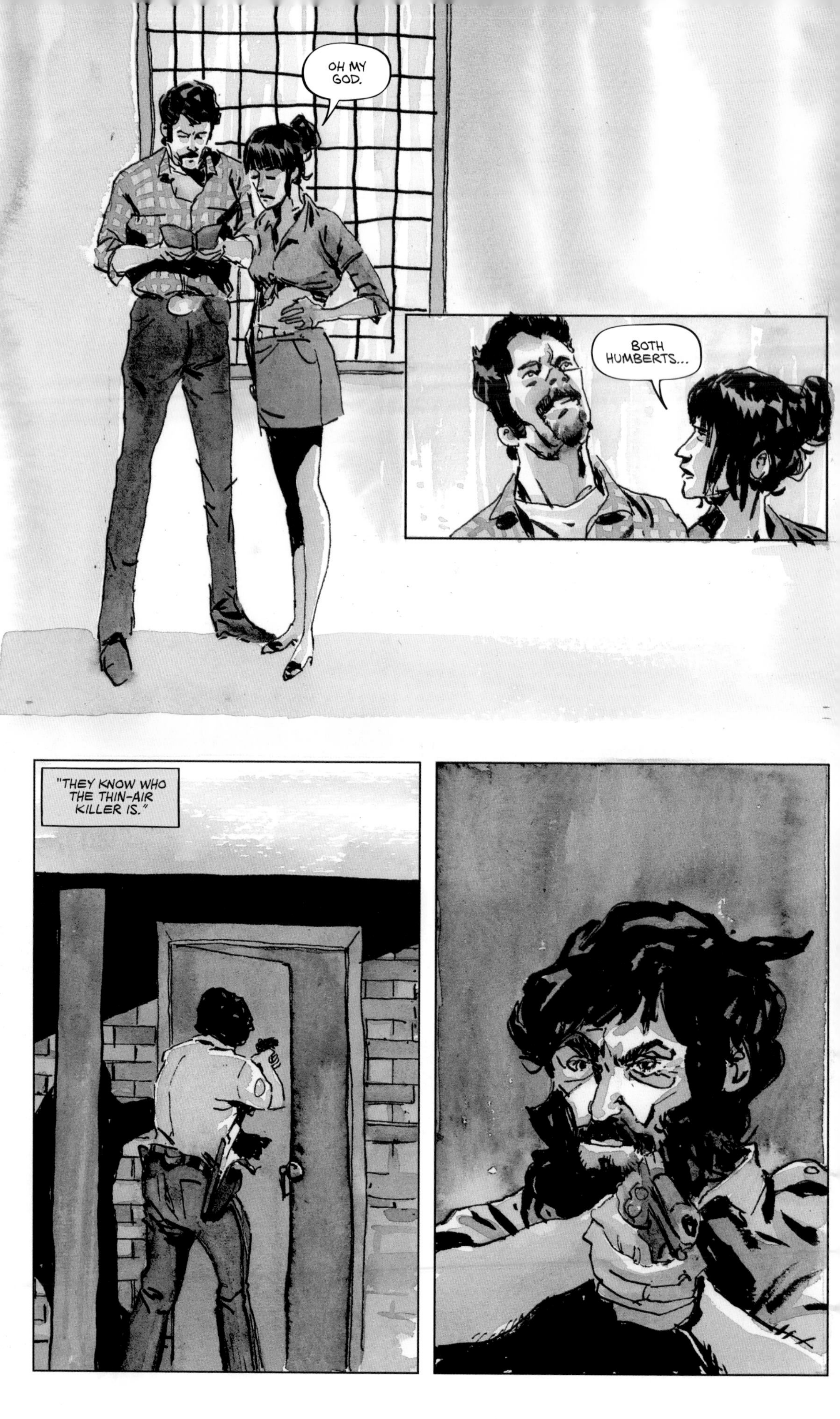
OH MY GOD.
BOTH HUMBERTS...
"THEY KNOW WHO THE THIN-AIR KILLER IS."

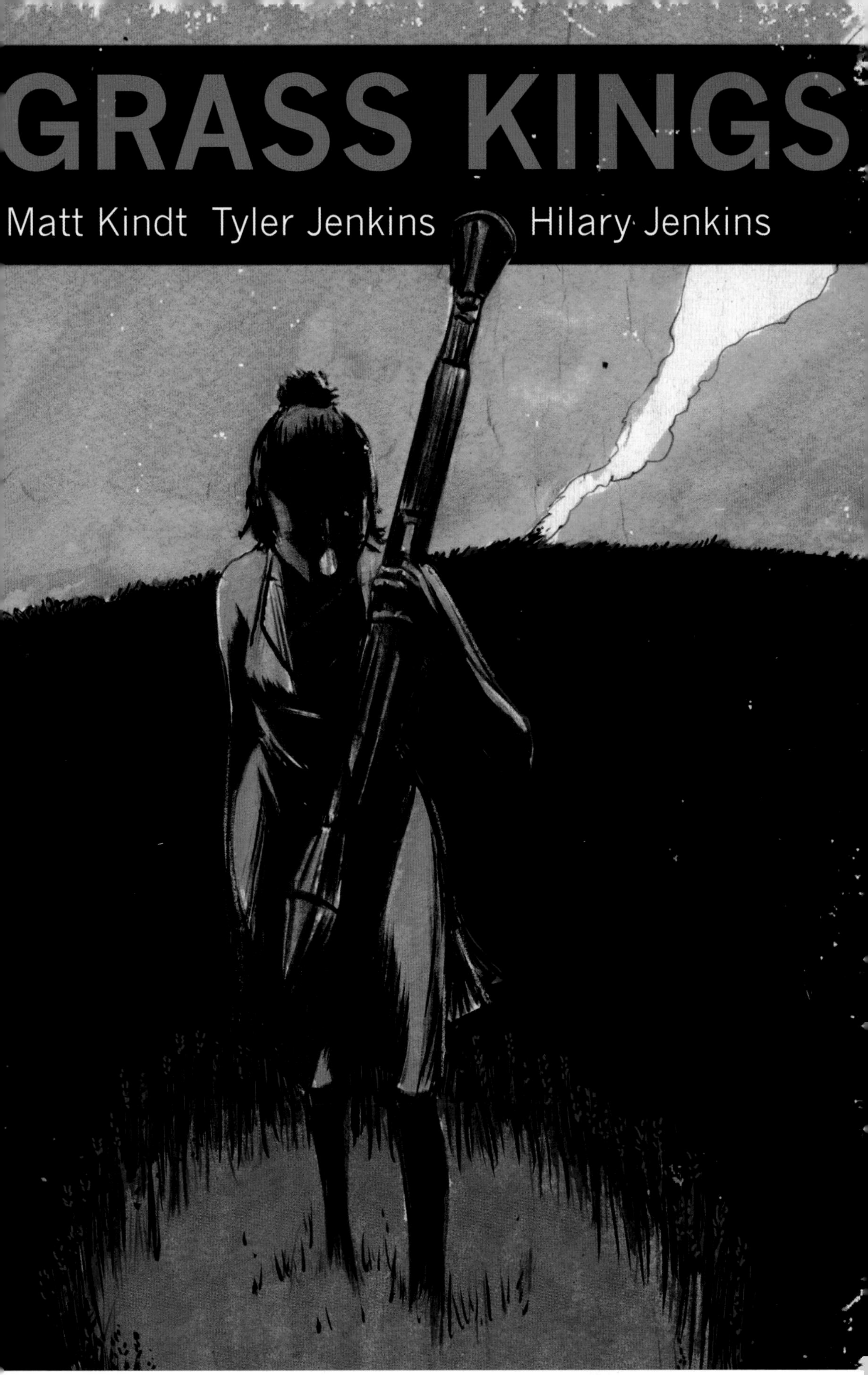
GRASS KINGS
Matt Kindt Tyler Jenkins Hilary Jenkins

issue #14 cover by matt kindt

chapter fifteen

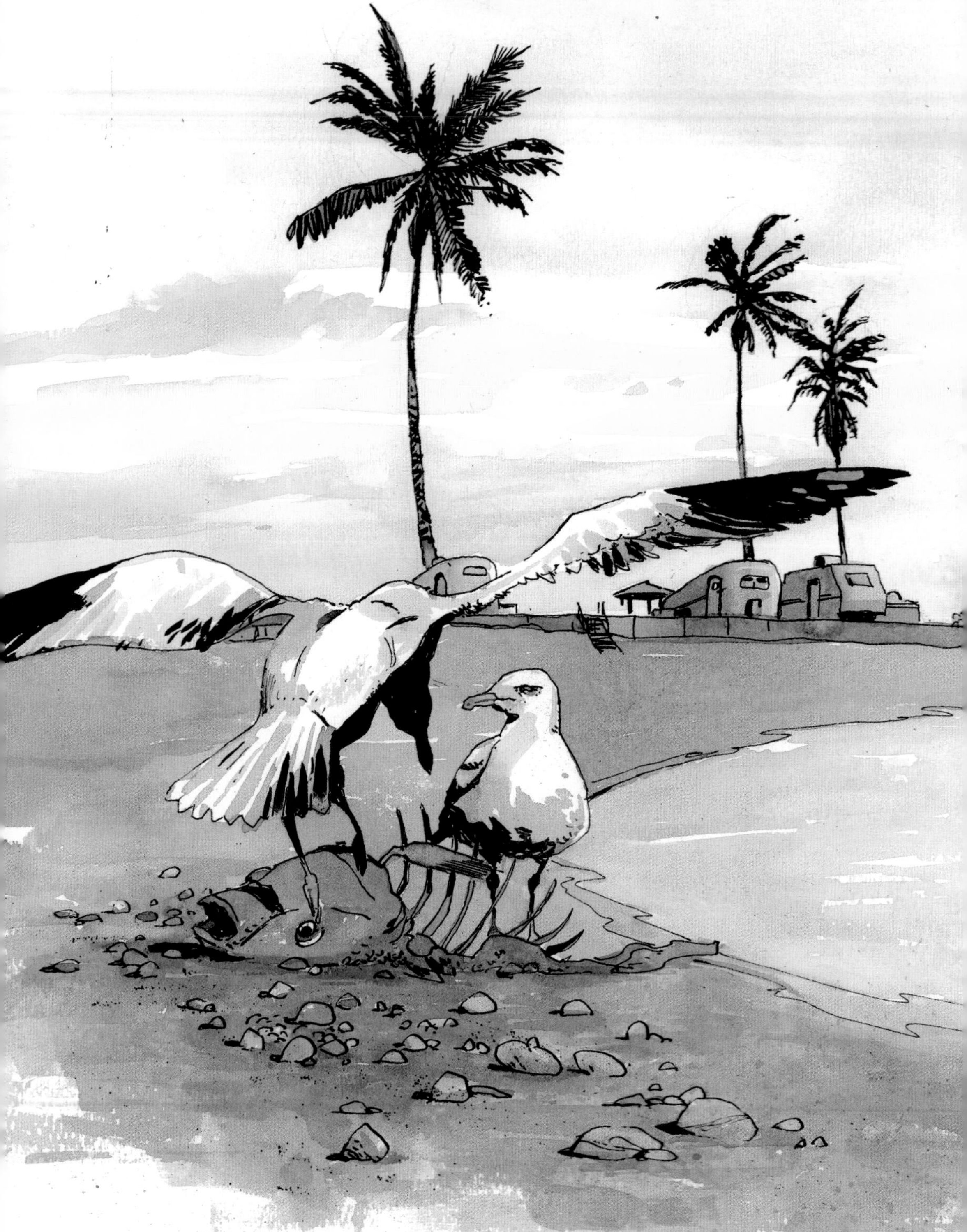

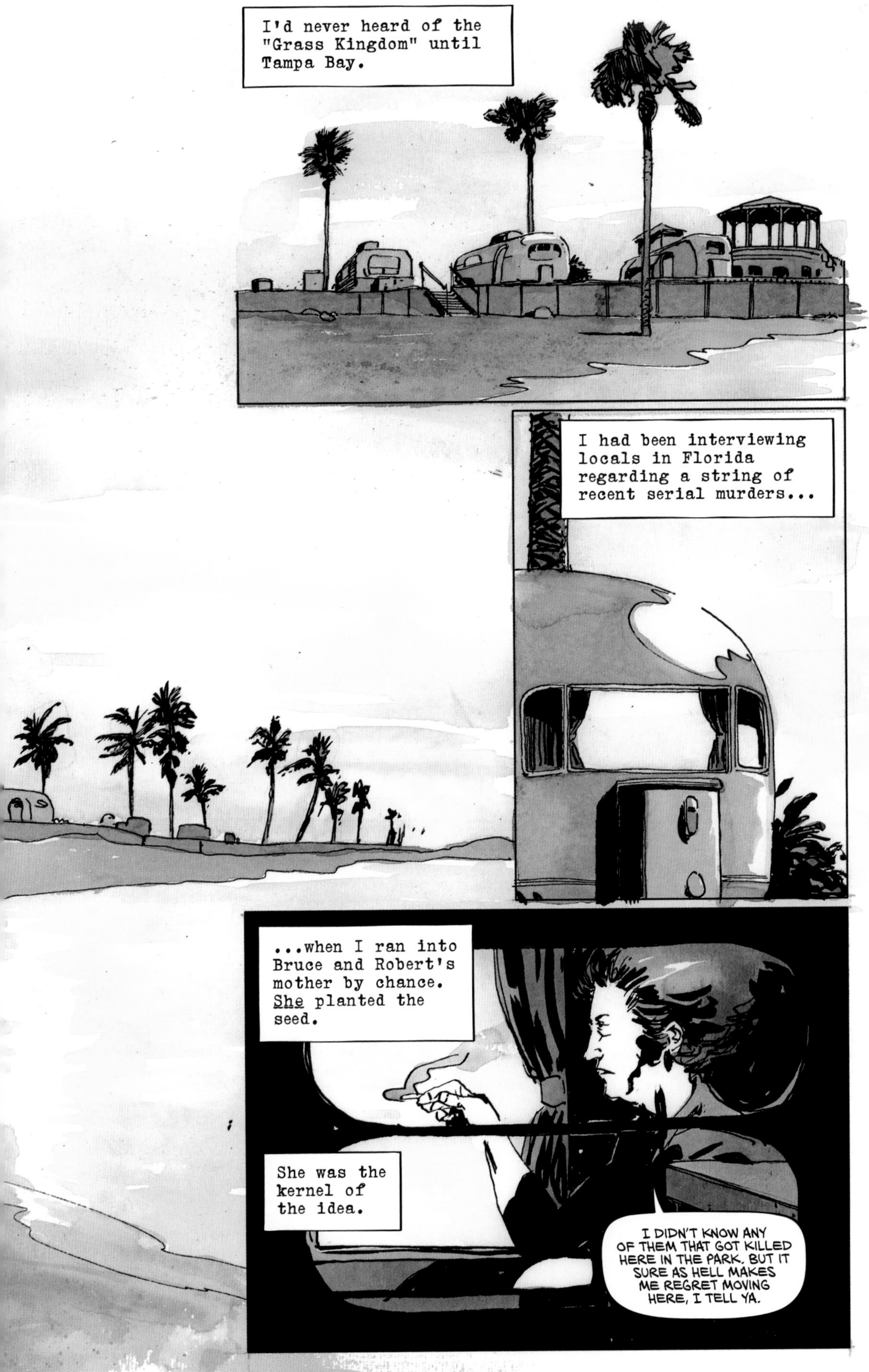
I'd never heard of the "Grass Kingdom" until Tampa Bay.
I had been interviewing locals in Florida regarding a string of recent serial murders...
...when I ran into Bruce and Robert's mother by chance. She planted the seed.
She was the kernel of the idea.
I DIDN'T KNOW ANY OF THEM THAT GOT KILLED HERE IN THE PARK, BUT IT SURE AS HELL MAKES ME REGRET MOVING HERE, I TELL YA.

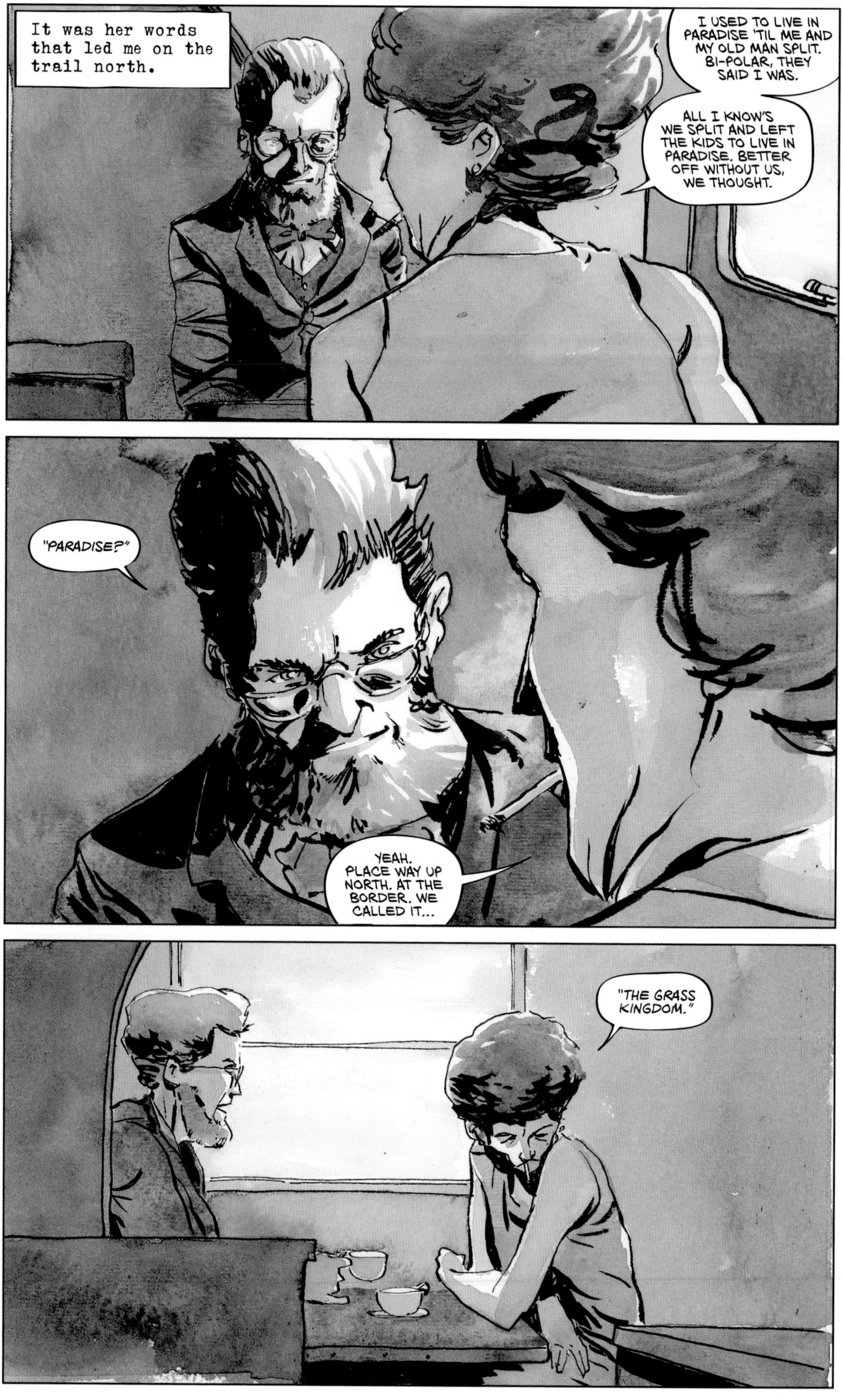
It was her words that led me on the trail north.
I USED TO LIVE IN PARADISE 'TIL ME AND MY OLD MAN SPLIT. BI-POLAR, THEY SAID I WAS.
ALL I KNOW'S WE SPLIT AND LEFT THE KIDS TO LIVE IN PARADISE. BETTER OFF WITHOUT US, WE THOUGHT.
"PARADISE?"
YEAH. PLACE WAY UP NORTH. AT THE BORDER. WE CALLED IT...
"THE GRASS KINGDOM."

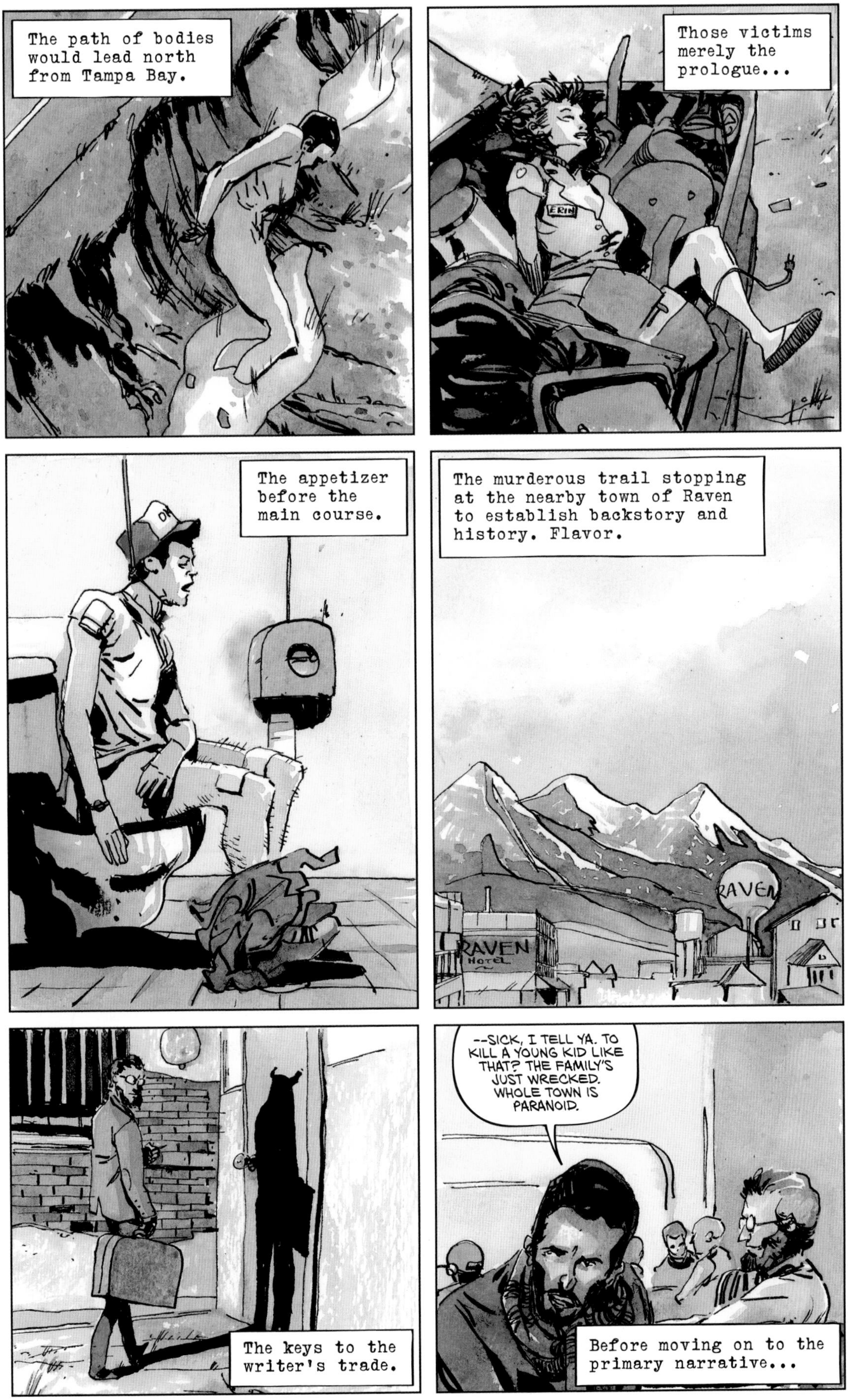
The path of bodies would lead north from Tampa Bay.
Those victims merely the prologue...
ERIN
The appetizer before the main course.
The murderous trail stopping at the nearby town of Raven to establish backstory and history. Flavor.
RAVEN
RAVEN HOTEL
The keys to the writer's trade.
--SICK, I TELL YA. TO KILL A YOUNG KID LIKE THAT? THE FAMILY'S JUST WRECKED. WHOLE TOWN IS PARANOID.
Before moving on to the primary narrative...

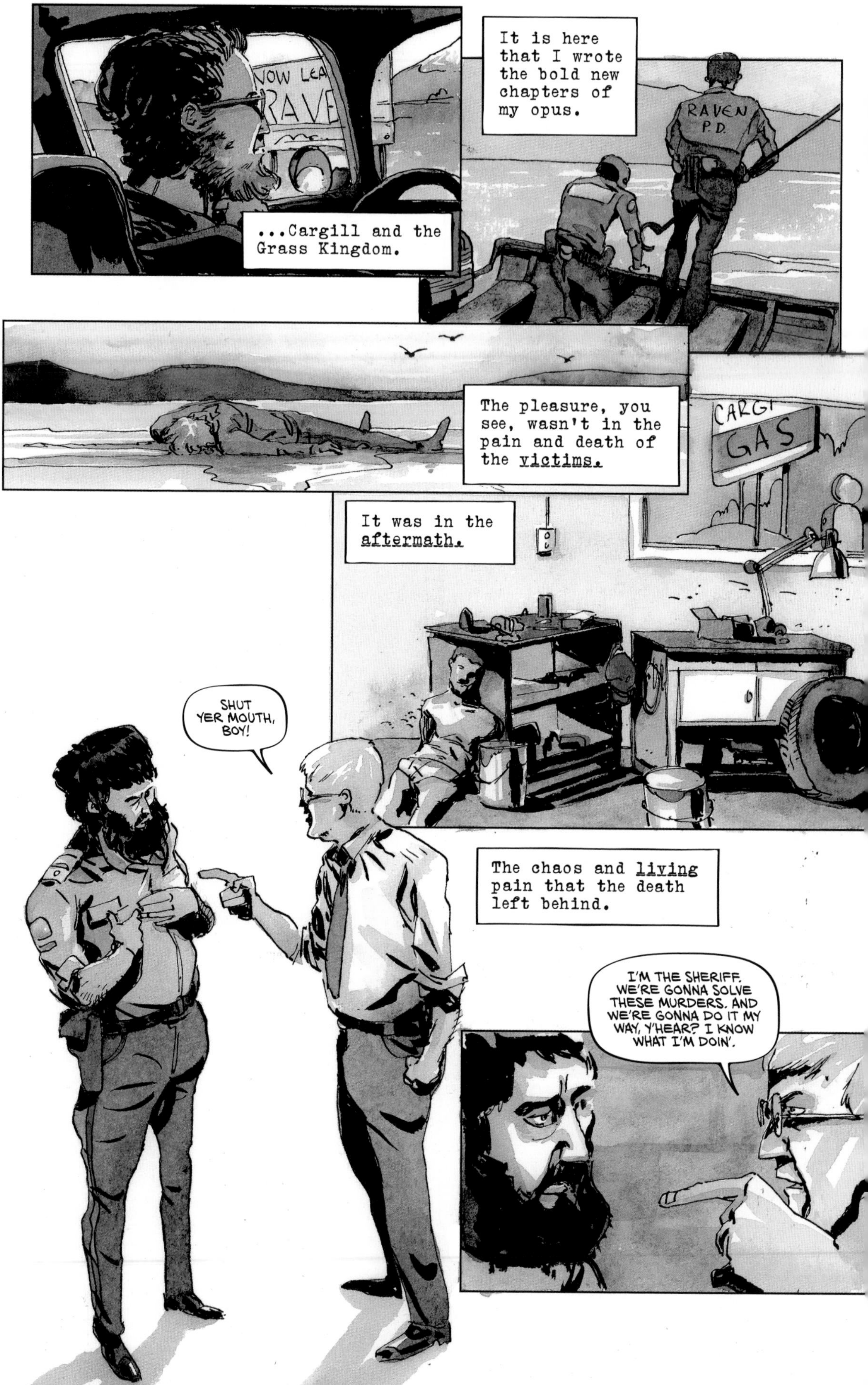
NOW LEA
RAVE
...Cargill and the Grass Kingdom.
It is here that I wrote the bold new chapters of my opus.
RAVEN P.D.
The pleasure, you see, wasn't in the pain and death of the victims.
CARGI
GAS
It was in the aftermath.
SHUT YER MOUTH, BOY!
The chaos and living pain that the death left behind.
I'M THE SHERIFF. WE'RE GONNA SOLVE THESE MURDERS. AND WE'RE GONNA DO IT MY WAY, Y'HEAR? I KNOW WHAT I'M DOIN'.

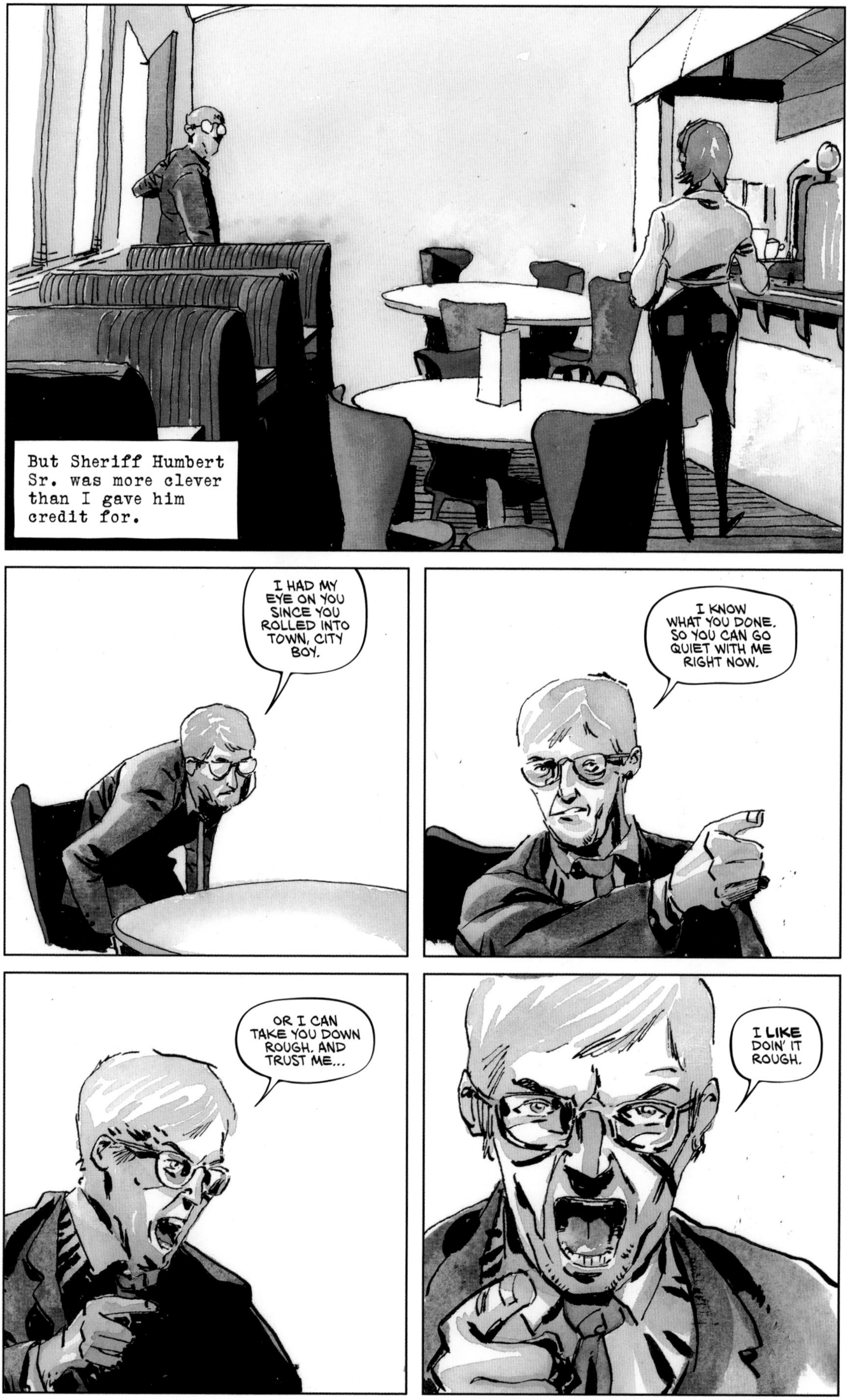
But Sheriff Humbert Sr. was more clever than I gave him credit for.
I HAD MY EYE ON YOU SINCE YOU ROLLED INTO TOWN, CITY BOY.
I KNOW WHAT YOU DONE. SO YOU CAN GO QUIET WITH ME RIGHT NOW.
OR I CAN TAKE YOU DOWN ROUGH. AND TRUST ME...
I LIKE DOIN' IT ROUGH.

I'M WELL AWARE THAT YOU LIKE IT ROUGH, SHERIFF HUMBERT.

I DID SOME DIGGING OF MY OWN. THE NATURE OF **MY** WORK MAKES ME SOMETHING OF A FORENSIC EXPERT.

I KNOW THAT YOUR WIFE DIED A WHILE BACK. "HEART ATTACK," THE AUTOPSY SAYS. BUT I DID A LITTLE... DIGGING.

YOUR WIFE HAD MULTIPLE LACERATIONS ON HER BACK. STRANGULATION MARKS ON HER NECK.

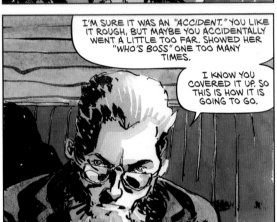

I'M SURE IT WAS AN "ACCIDENT." YOU LIKE IT ROUGH, BUT MAYBE YOU ACCIDENTALLY WENT A LITTLE TOO FAR. SHOWED HER "WHO'S BOSS" ONE TOO MANY TIMES.

I KNOW YOU COVERED IT UP. SO THIS IS HOW IT IS GOING TO GO.

I'LL MOVE TO THE GRASS KINGDOM. CONTINUE MY...WORK. YOU SIT TIGHT. WHEN THE TIME COMES, YOU GET TO PIN THE MURDER ON SOMEONE IN THE GRASS KINGDOM.

YOU CAN TAKE THE ENTIRE KINGDOM DOWN, CATCH THE "THIN-AIR KILLER" AND MAKE YOUR CAREER.

OR YOU CAN DO SOMETHING STUPID, AND I SEND A FILE ON **YOU** TO THE FEDS.

Humbert Sr. and I would eventually come to an understanding that would be mutually beneficial...

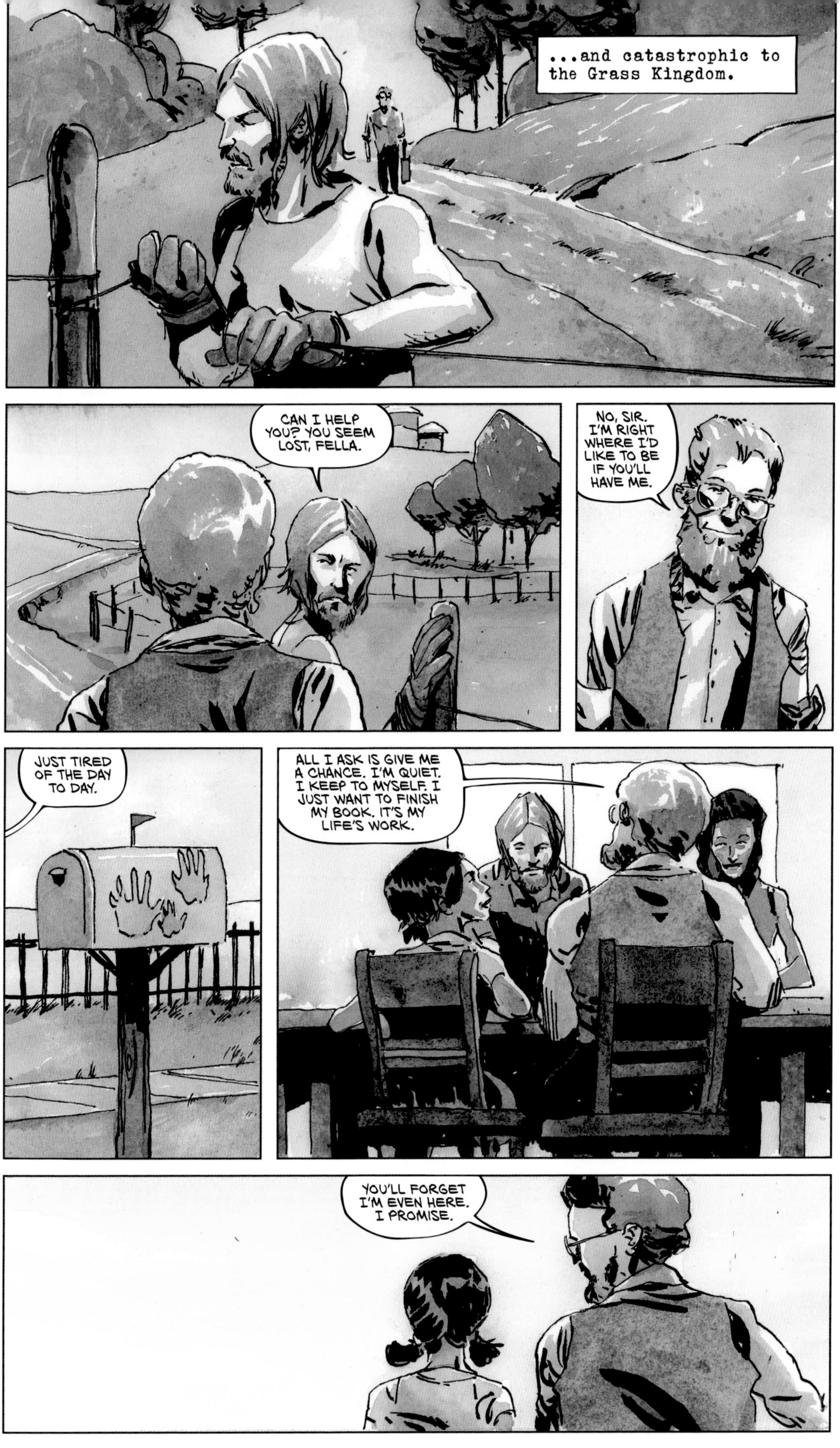
...and catastrophic to the Grass Kingdom.
CAN I HELP YOU? YOU SEEM LOST, FELLA.
NO, SIR. I'M RIGHT WHERE I'D LIKE TO BE IF YOU'LL HAVE ME.
JUST TIRED OF THE DAY TO DAY.
ALL I ASK IS GIVE ME A CHANCE. I'M QUIET. I KEEP TO MYSELF. I JUST WANT TO FINISH MY BOOK. IT'S MY LIFE'S WORK.
YOU'LL FORGET I'M EVEN HERE. I PROMISE.

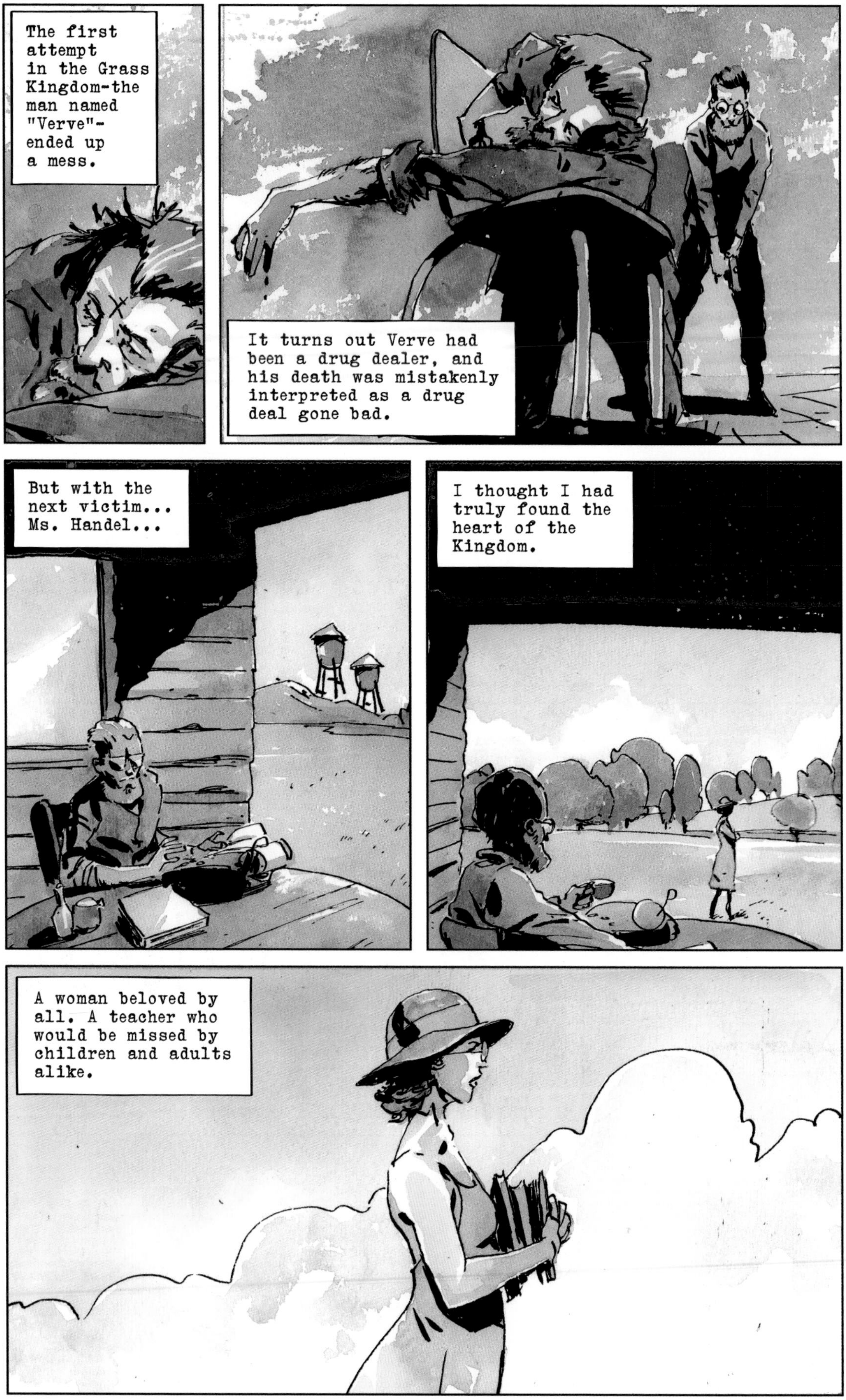

The first attempt in the Grass Kingdom-the man named "Verve"- ended up a mess.
It turns out Verve had been a drug dealer, and his death was mistakenly interpreted as a drug deal gone bad.
But with the next victim... Ms. Handel...
I thought I had truly found the heart of the Kingdom.
A woman beloved by all. A teacher who would be missed by children and adults alike.

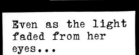
Even as the light faded from her eyes...

I could predict the ensuing grief and pain that would fill those around her.

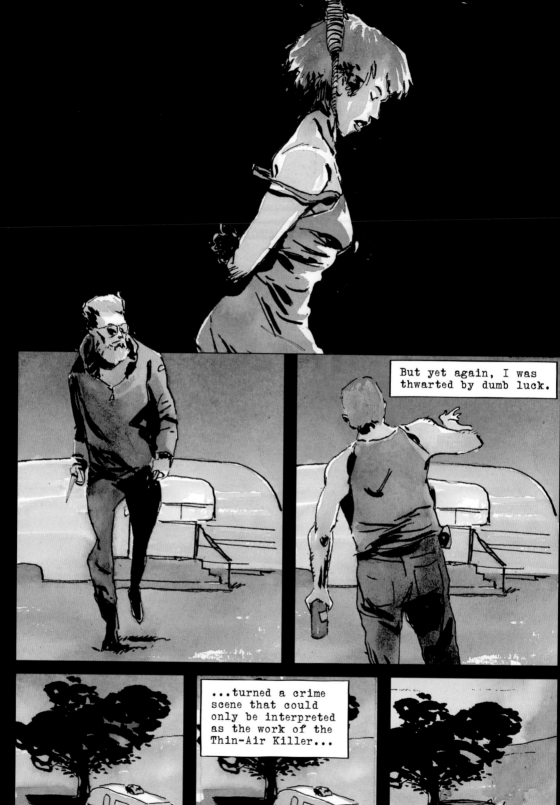

But yet again, I was thwarted by dumb luck.

...turned a crime scene that could only be interpreted as the work of the Thin-Air Killer...

As a drunken infatuated fool...

...into a pile of ashes.

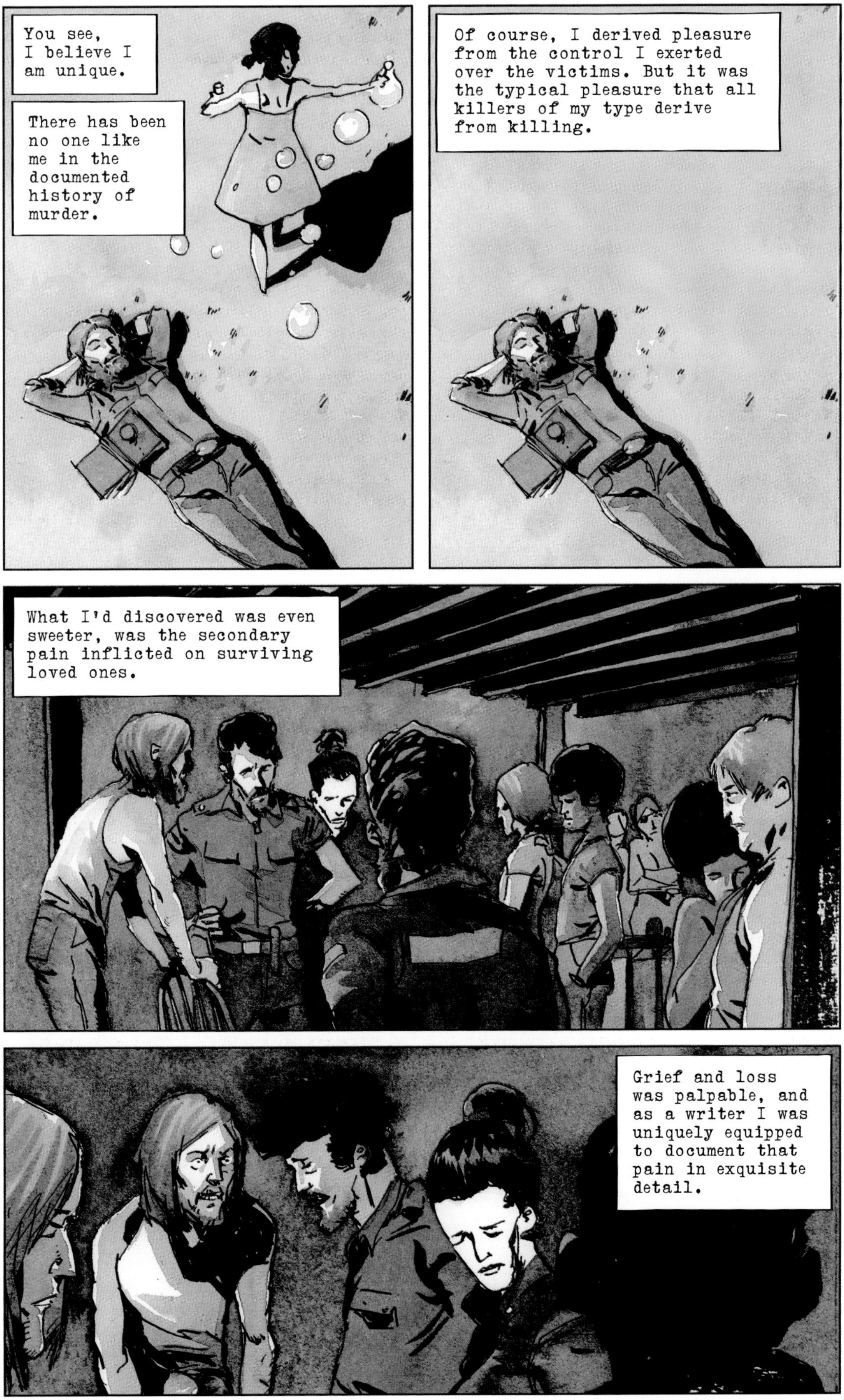
You see, I believe I am unique.
There has been no one like me in the documented history of murder.
Of course, I derived pleasure from the control I exerted over the victims. But it was the typical pleasure that all killers of my type derive from killing.
What I'd discovered was even sweeter, was the secondary pain inflicted on surviving loved ones.
Grief and loss was palpable, and as a writer I was uniquely equipped to document that pain in exquisite detail.

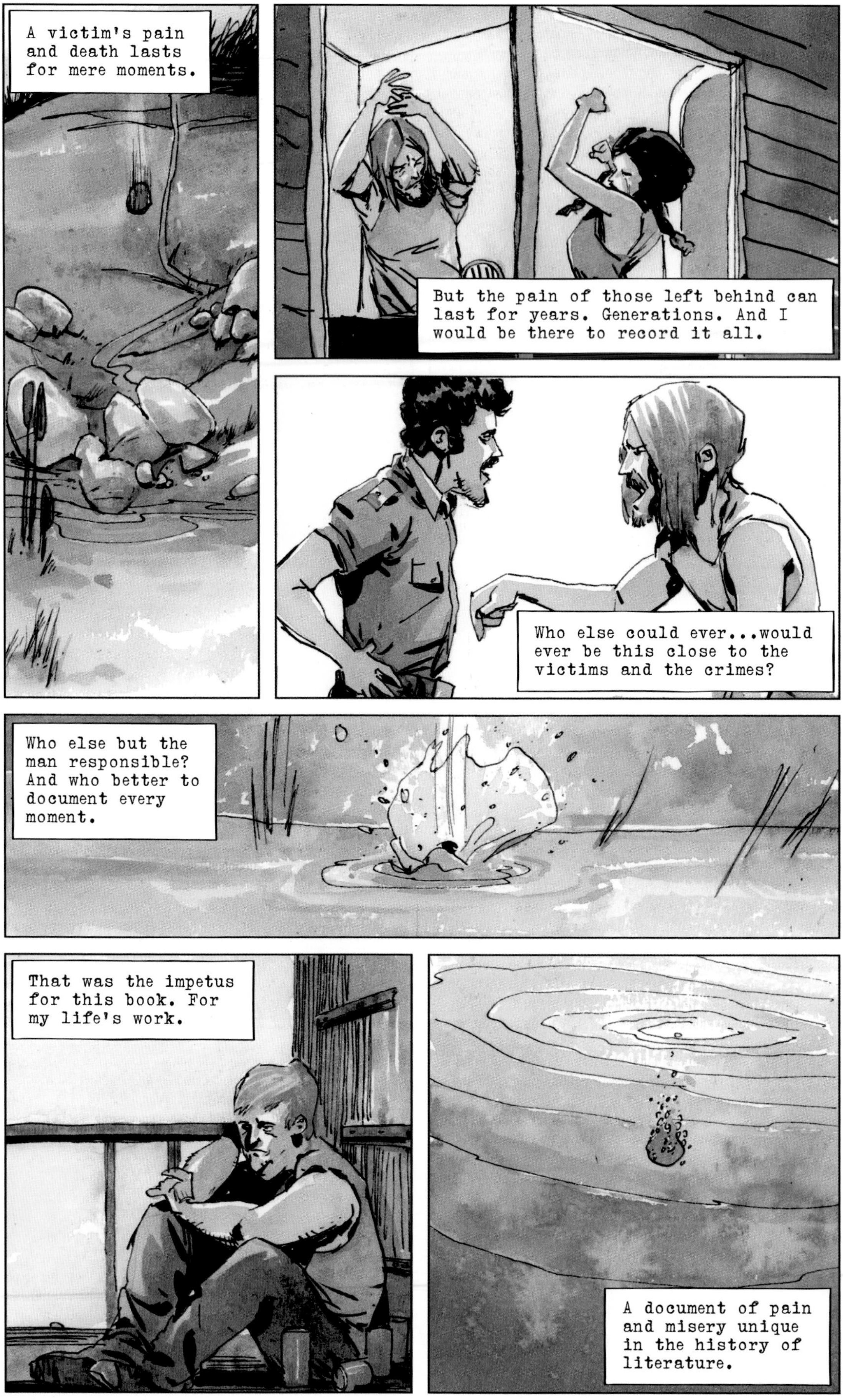
A victim's pain and death lasts for mere moments.
But the pain of those left behind can last for years. Generations. And I would be there to record it all.
Who else could ever...would ever be this close to the victims and the crimes?
Who else but the man responsible? And who better to document every moment.
That was the impetus for this book. For my life's work.
A document of pain and misery unique in the history of literature.

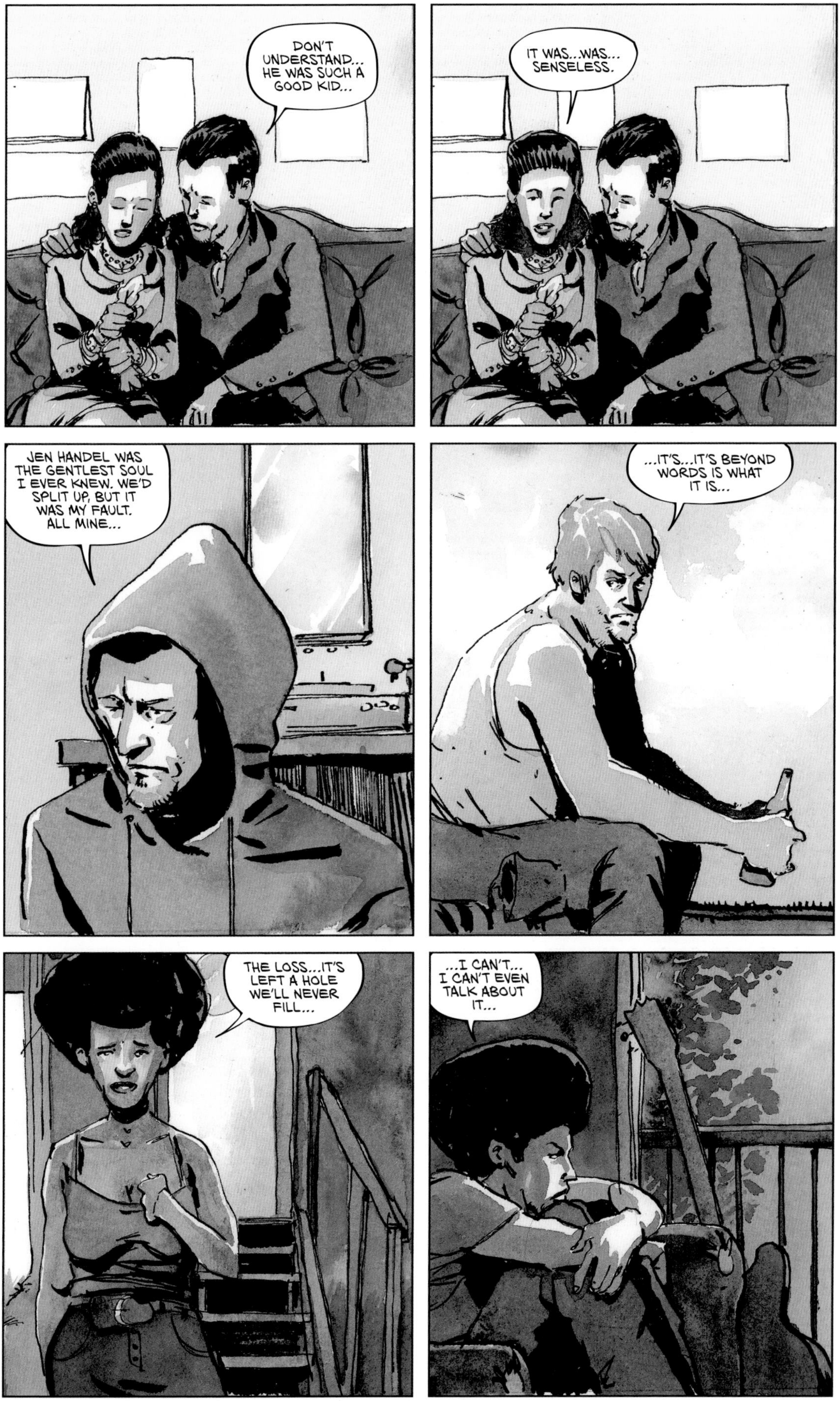
DON'T UNDERSTAND... HE WAS SUCH A GOOD KID...
IT WAS...WAS... SENSELESS.
JEN HANDEL WAS THE GENTLEST SOUL I EVER KNEW. WE'D SPLIT UP, BUT IT WAS MY FAULT. ALL MINE...
...IT'S...IT'S BEYOND WORDS IS WHAT IT IS...
THE LOSS...IT'S LEFT A HOLE WE'LL NEVER FILL...
...I CAN'T... I CAN'T EVEN TALK ABOUT IT...

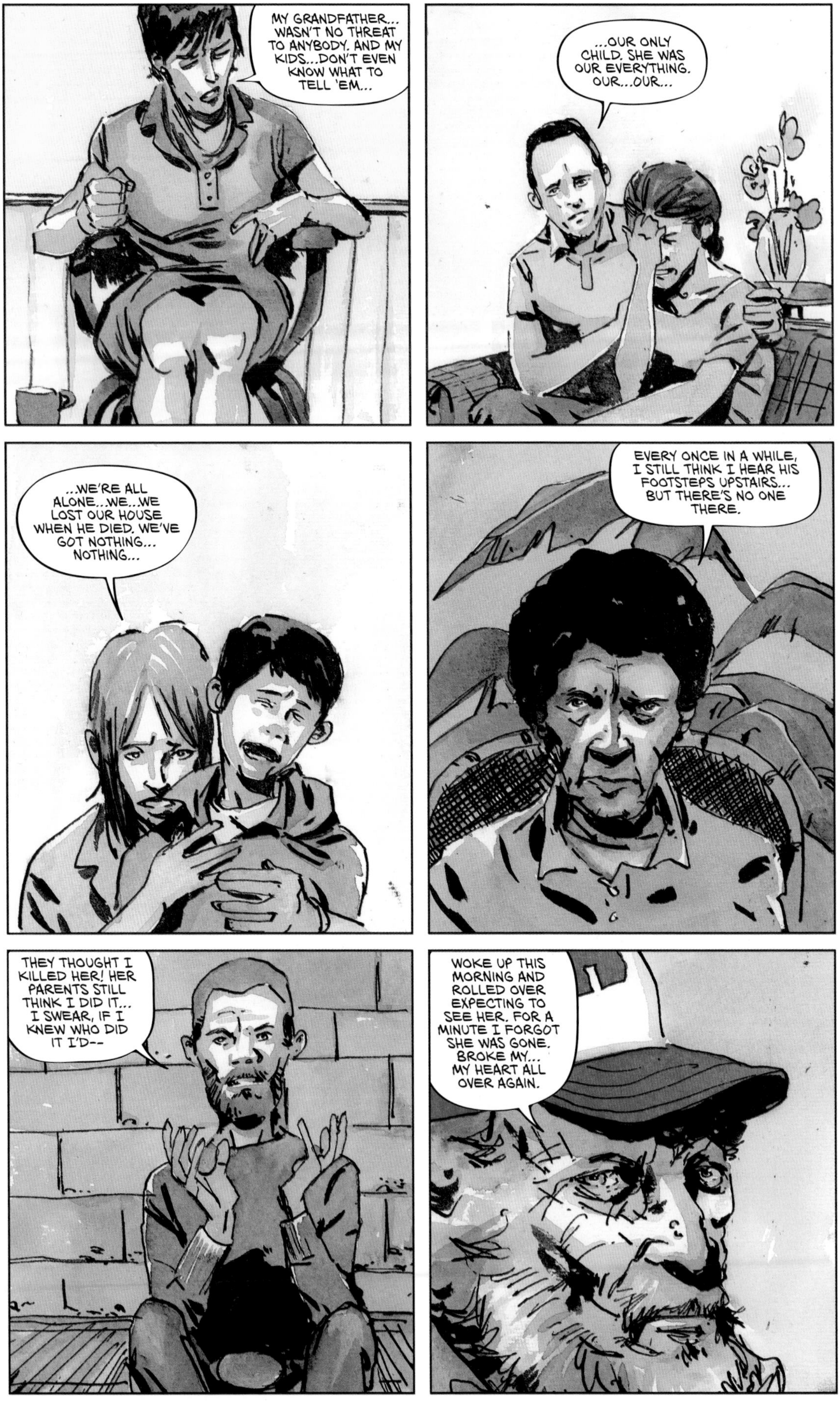
MY GRANDFATHER... WASN'T NO THREAT TO ANYBODY. AND MY KIDS...DON'T EVEN KNOW WHAT TO TELL 'EM...
...OUR ONLY CHILD. SHE WAS OUR EVERYTHING. OUR...OUR...
...WE'RE ALL ALONE...WE...WE LOST OUR HOUSE WHEN HE DIED. WE'VE GOT NOTHING... NOTHING...
EVERY ONCE IN A WHILE, I STILL THINK I HEAR HIS FOOTSTEPS UPSTAIRS... BUT THERE'S NO ONE THERE.
THEY THOUGHT I KILLED HER! HER PARENTS STILL THINK I DID IT... I SWEAR, IF I KNEW WHO DID IT I'D--
WOKE UP THIS MORNING AND ROLLED OVER EXPECTING TO SEE HER. FOR A MINUTE I FORGOT SHE WAS GONE. BROKE MY... MY HEART ALL OVER AGAIN.

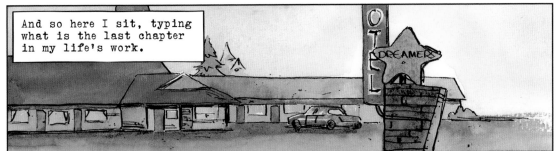

And so here I sit, typing what is the last chapter in my life's work.

The most comprehensive document of pure human suffering.

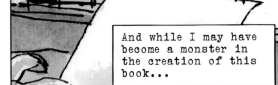

And while I may have become a monster in the creation of this book...

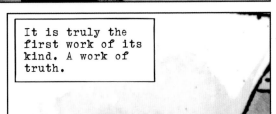

It is truly the first work of its kind. A work of truth.

≈YAWN≈ FINALLY.

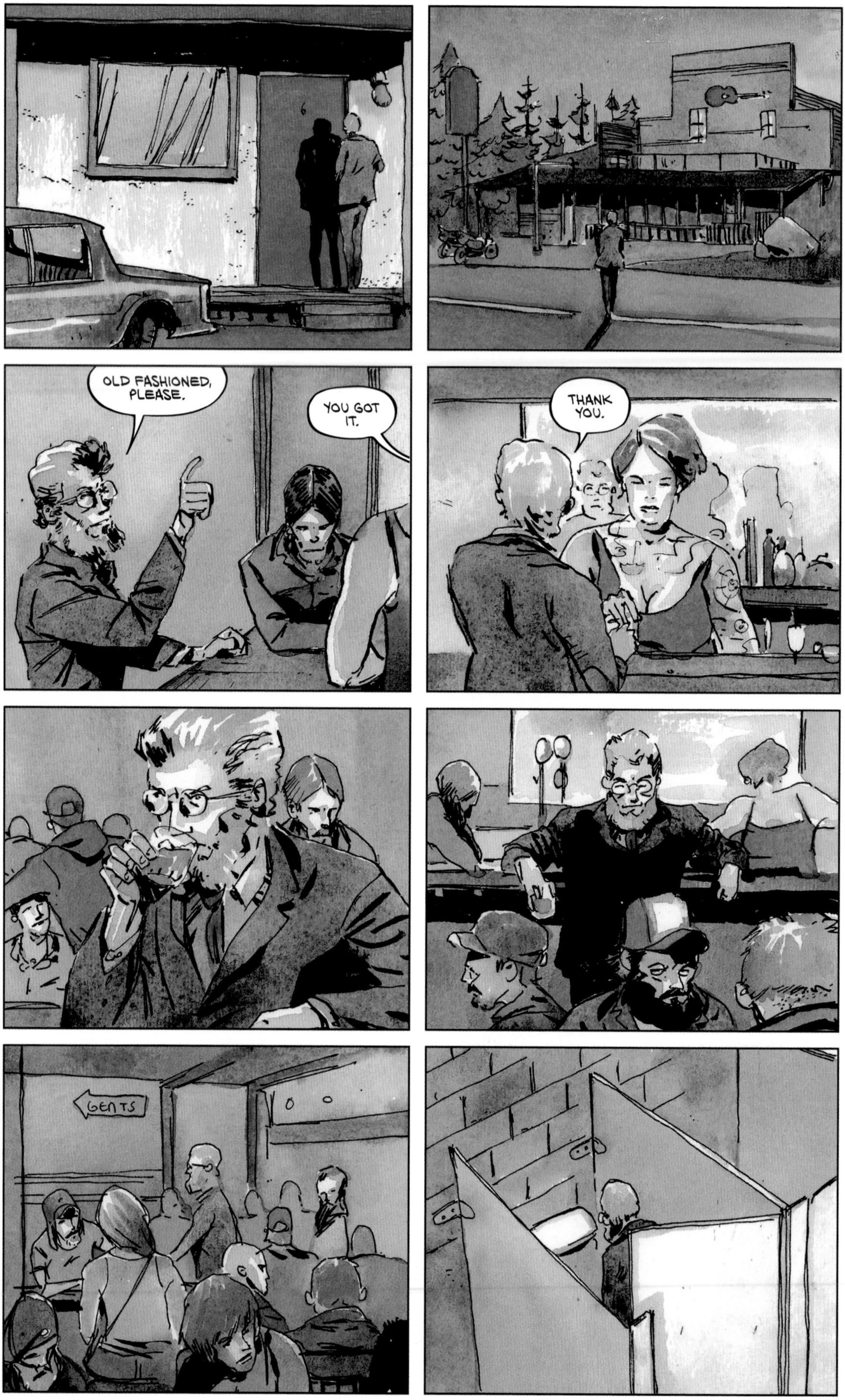
OLD FASHIONED, PLEASE.
YOU GOT IT.
THANK YOU.
GENTS

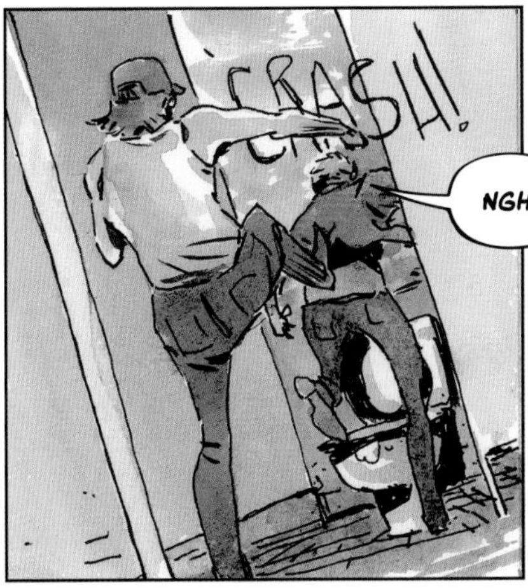
CRASH!
NGH!

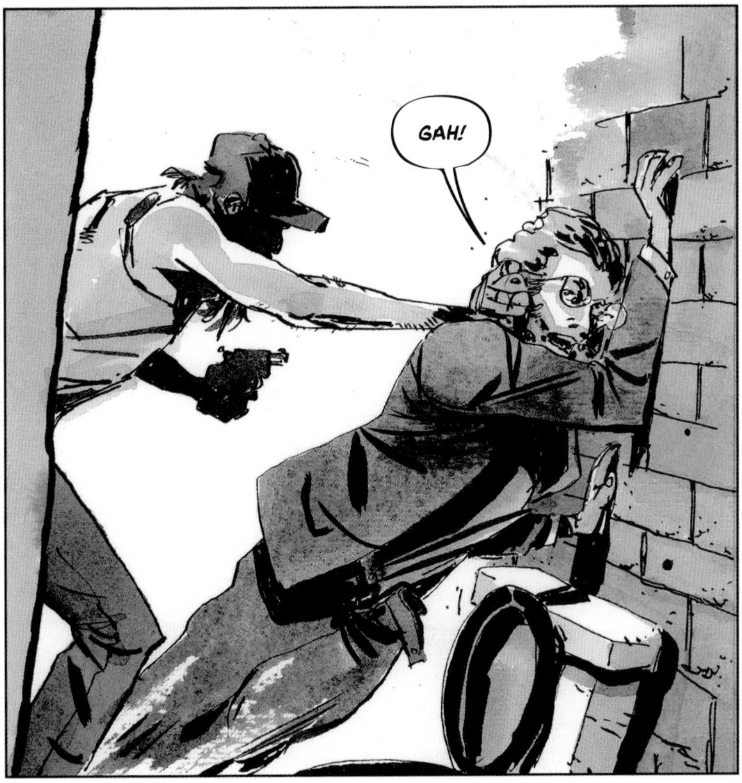
GAH!

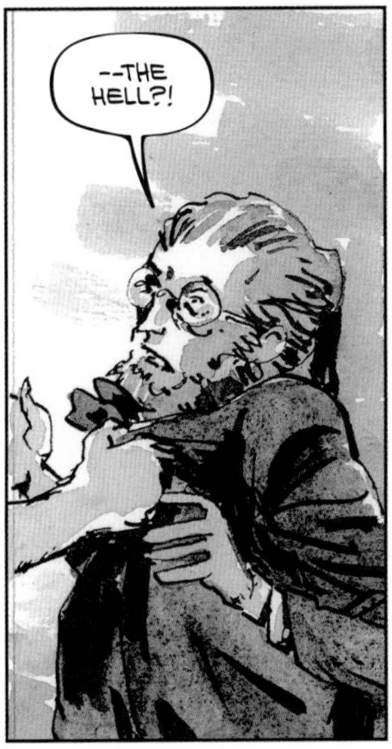
--THE HELL?!

SHUT YOUR MOUTH, "HEMINGWAY."
I DON'T UNDERSTAND, ROBERT. I--
SHUT UP.

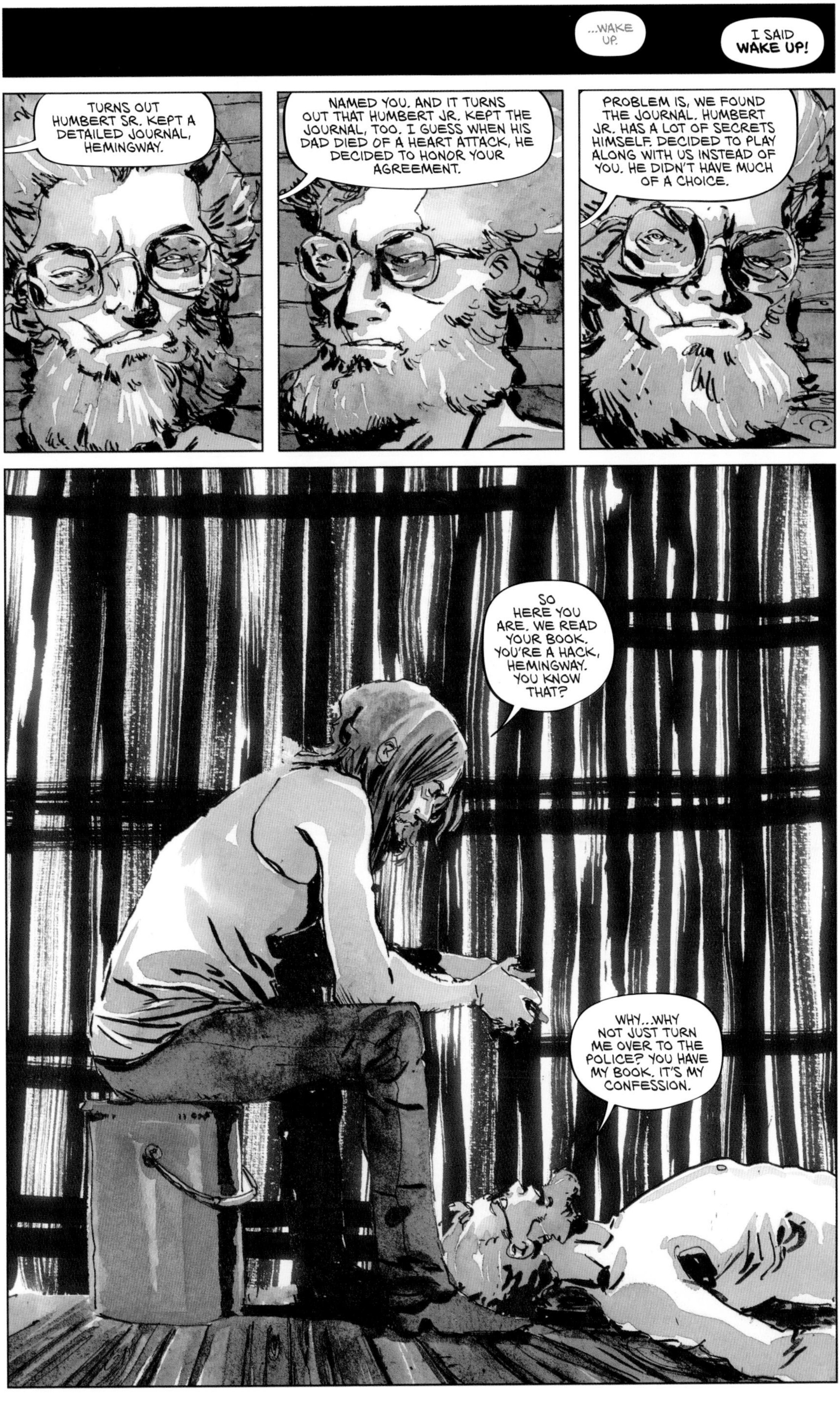
...WAKE UP.
I SAID WAKE UP!
TURNS OUT HUMBERT SR. KEPT A DETAILED JOURNAL, HEMINGWAY.
NAMED YOU. AND IT TURNS OUT THAT HUMBERT JR. KEPT THE JOURNAL, TOO. I GUESS WHEN HIS DAD DIED OF A HEART ATTACK, HE DECIDED TO HONOR YOUR AGREEMENT.
PROBLEM IS, WE FOUND THE JOURNAL. HUMBERT JR. HAS A LOT OF SECRETS HIMSELF. DECIDED TO PLAY ALONG WITH US INSTEAD OF YOU. HE DIDN'T HAVE MUCH OF A CHOICE.
SO HERE YOU ARE. WE READ YOUR BOOK. YOU'RE A HACK, HEMINGWAY. YOU KNOW THAT?
WHY...WHY NOT JUST TURN ME OVER TO THE POLICE? YOU HAVE MY BOOK. IT'S MY CONFESSION.

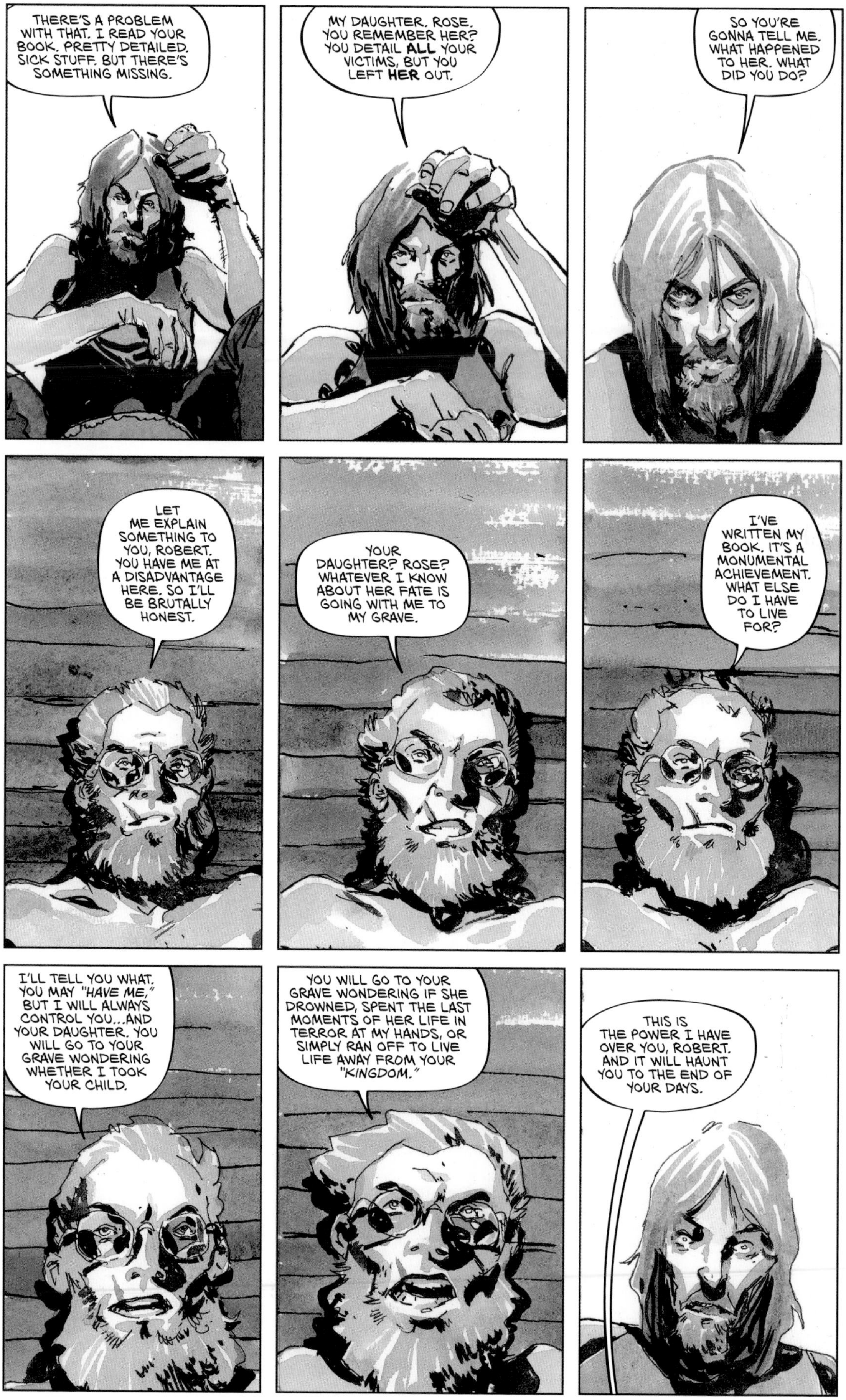

THERE'S A PROBLEM WITH THAT. I READ YOUR BOOK. PRETTY DETAILED. SICK STUFF. BUT THERE'S SOMETHING MISSING.
MY DAUGHTER. ROSE. YOU REMEMBER HER? YOU DETAIL **ALL** YOUR VICTIMS, BUT YOU LEFT **HER** OUT.
SO YOU'RE GONNA TELL ME. WHAT HAPPENED TO HER. WHAT DID YOU DO?
LET ME EXPLAIN SOMETHING TO YOU, ROBERT. YOU HAVE ME AT A DISADVANTAGE HERE. SO I'LL BE BRUTALLY HONEST.
YOUR DAUGHTER? ROSE? WHATEVER I KNOW ABOUT HER FATE IS GOING WITH ME TO MY GRAVE.
I'VE WRITTEN MY BOOK. IT'S A MONUMENTAL ACHIEVEMENT. WHAT ELSE DO I HAVE TO LIVE FOR?
I'LL TELL YOU WHAT. YOU MAY *"HAVE ME,"* BUT I WILL ALWAYS CONTROL YOU...AND YOUR DAUGHTER. YOU WILL GO TO YOUR GRAVE WONDERING WHETHER I TOOK YOUR CHILD.
YOU WILL GO TO YOUR GRAVE WONDERING IF SHE DROWNED, SPENT THE LAST MOMENTS OF HER LIFE IN TERROR AT MY HANDS, OR SIMPLY RAN OFF TO LIVE LIFE AWAY FROM YOUR *"KINGDOM."*
THIS IS THE POWER I HAVE OVER YOU, ROBERT. AND IT WILL HAUNT YOU TO THE END OF YOUR DAYS.

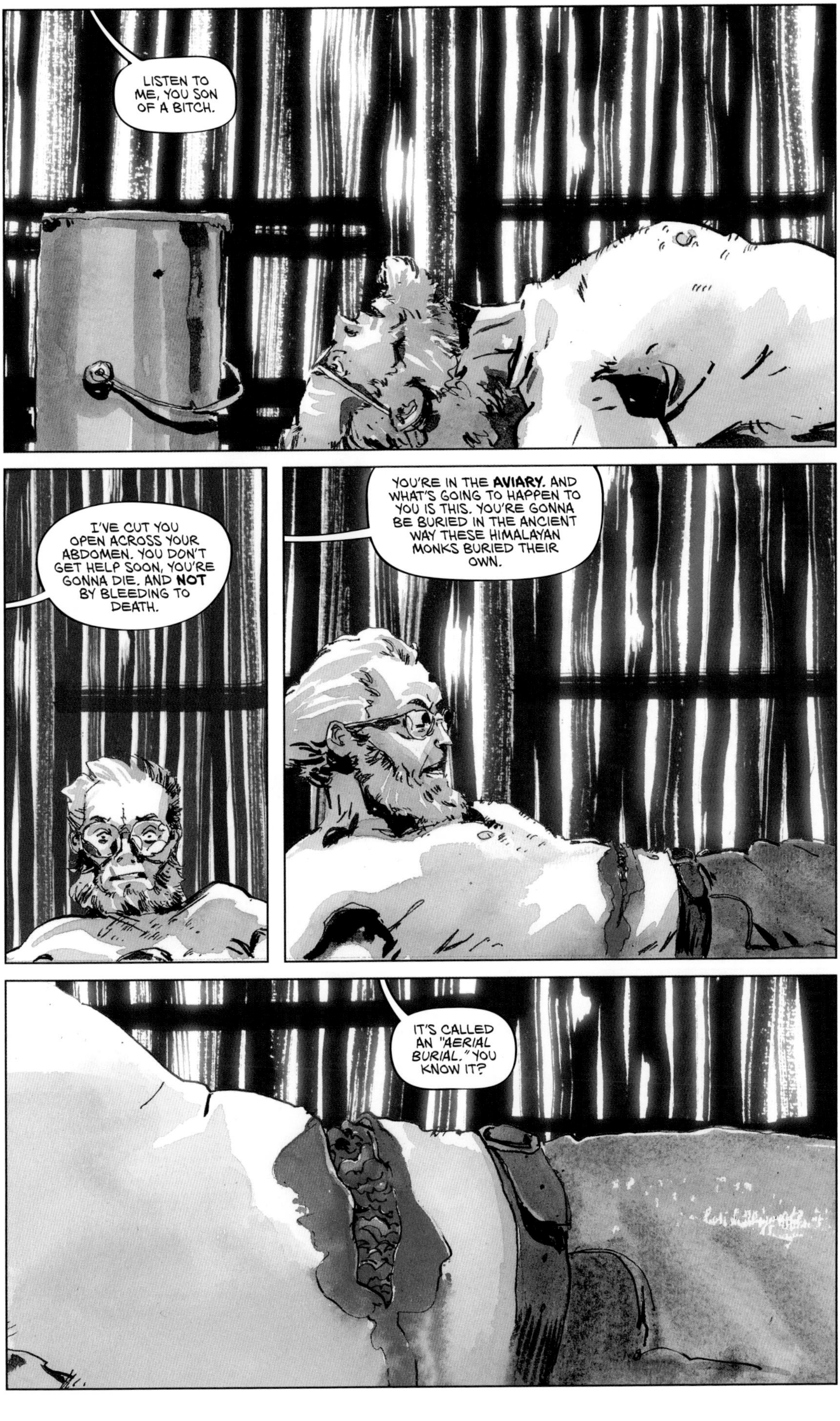
LISTEN TO ME, YOU SON OF A BITCH.
I'VE CUT YOU OPEN ACROSS YOUR ABDOMEN. YOU DON'T GET HELP SOON, YOU'RE GONNA DIE. AND **NOT** BY BLEEDING TO DEATH.
YOU'RE IN THE **AVIARY.** AND WHAT'S GOING TO HAPPEN TO YOU IS THIS. YOU'RE GONNA BE BURIED IN THE ANCIENT WAY THESE HIMALAYAN MONKS BURIED THEIR OWN.
IT'S CALLED AN "AERIAL BURIAL." YOU KNOW IT?

THEY PUT THE DECEASED MONK ON THE TOP OF A MOUNTAIN AND LET THE BIRDS CARRY THE PIECES OF THE BODY AWAY.

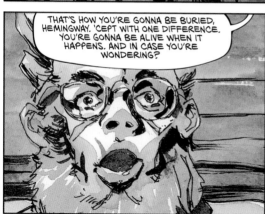

THAT'S HOW YOU'RE GONNA BE BURIED, HEMINGWAY. 'CEPT WITH ONE DIFFERENCE. YOU'RE GONNA BE ALIVE WHEN IT HAPPENS. AND IN CASE YOU'RE WONDERING?

WE **DESTROYED** YOUR BOOK. ARCHIE TOOK THE BLAME FOR EVERYTHING YOU DID.

...NGH...

NO ONE IS EVER GOING TO SEE IT. NO ONE IS GOING TO REMEMBER YOU.

NGAHHHHHHH!

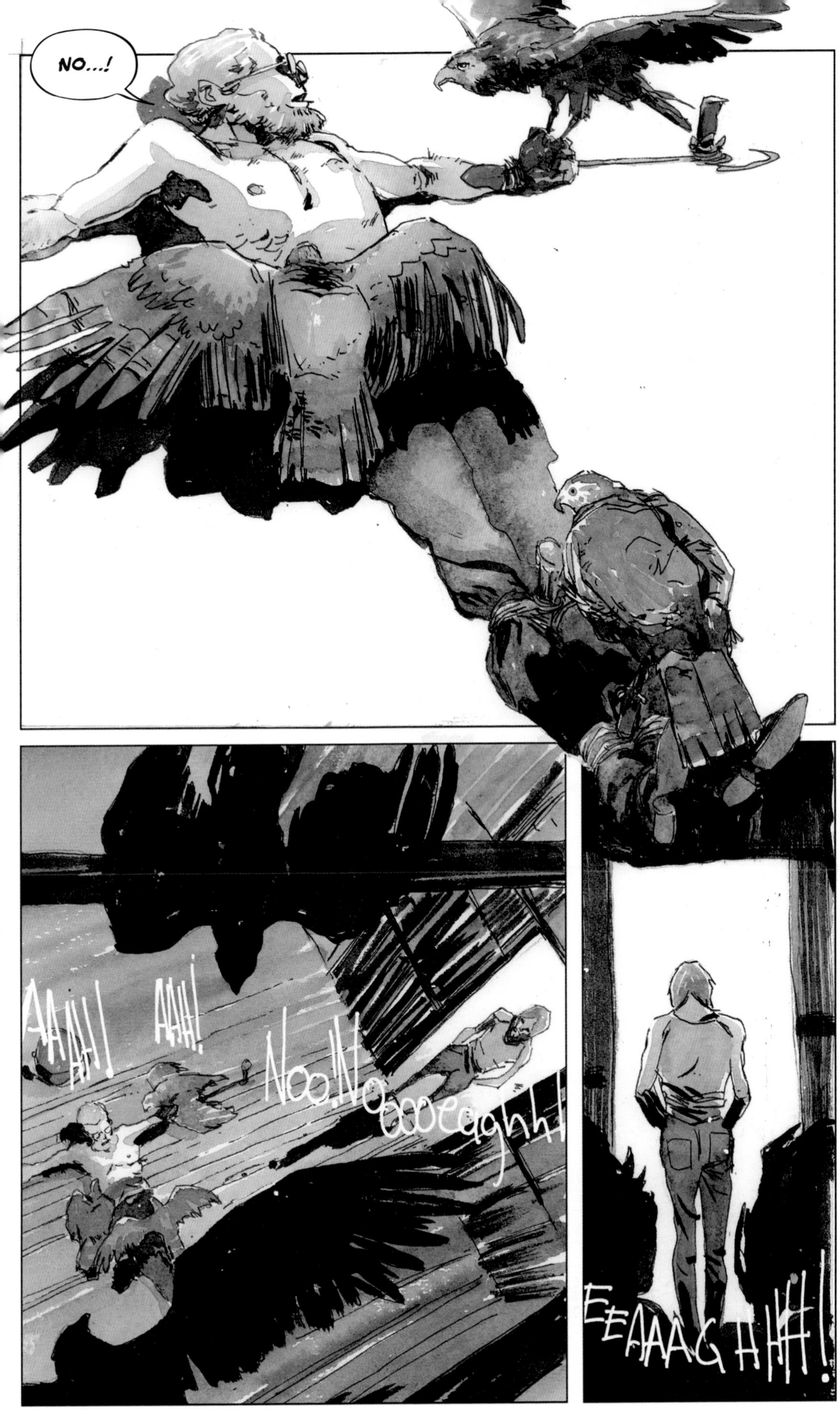
NO...!
AAAH!
AAAH!
Noo! Noooooeaghh!
EEAAAGHHH!

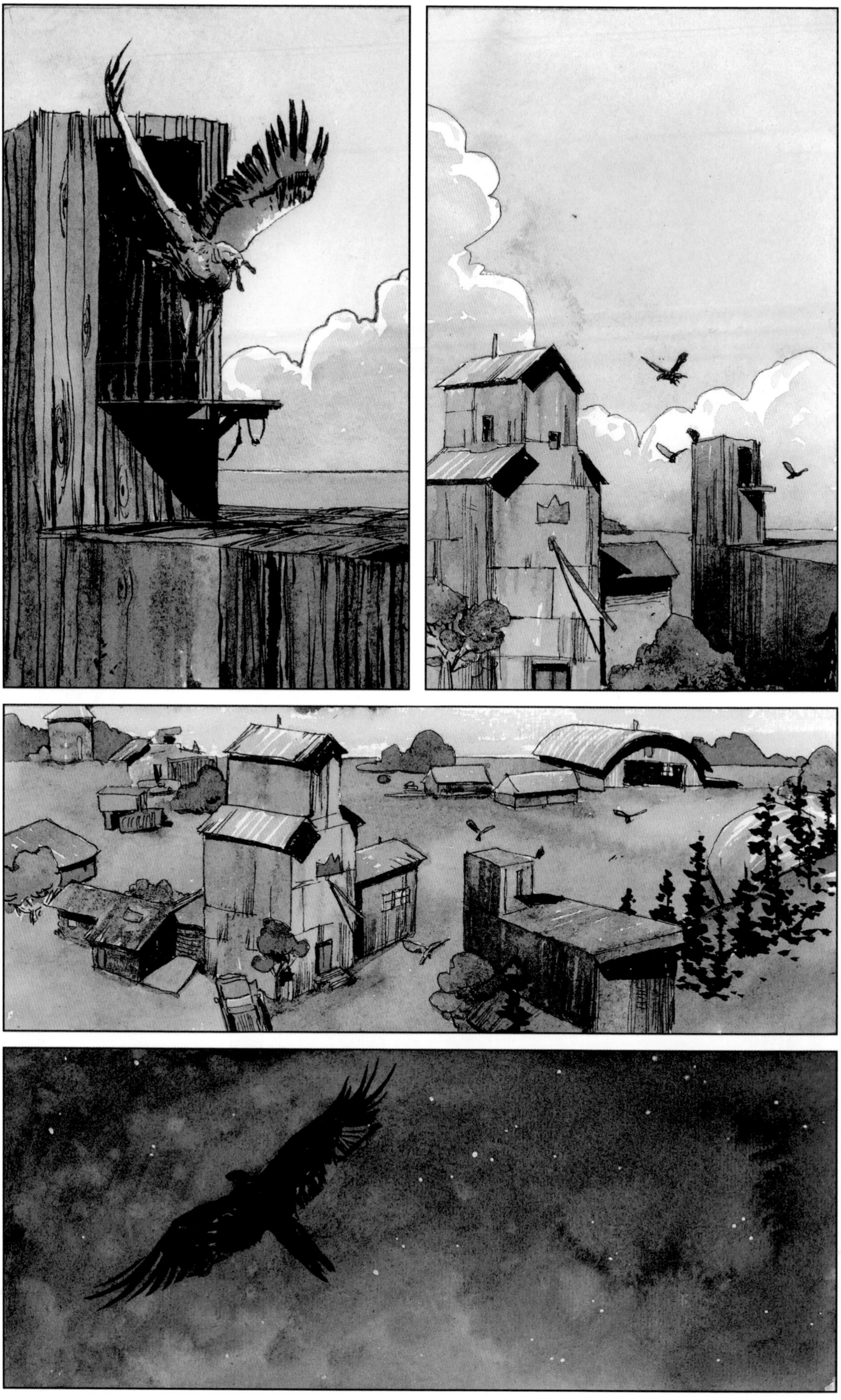

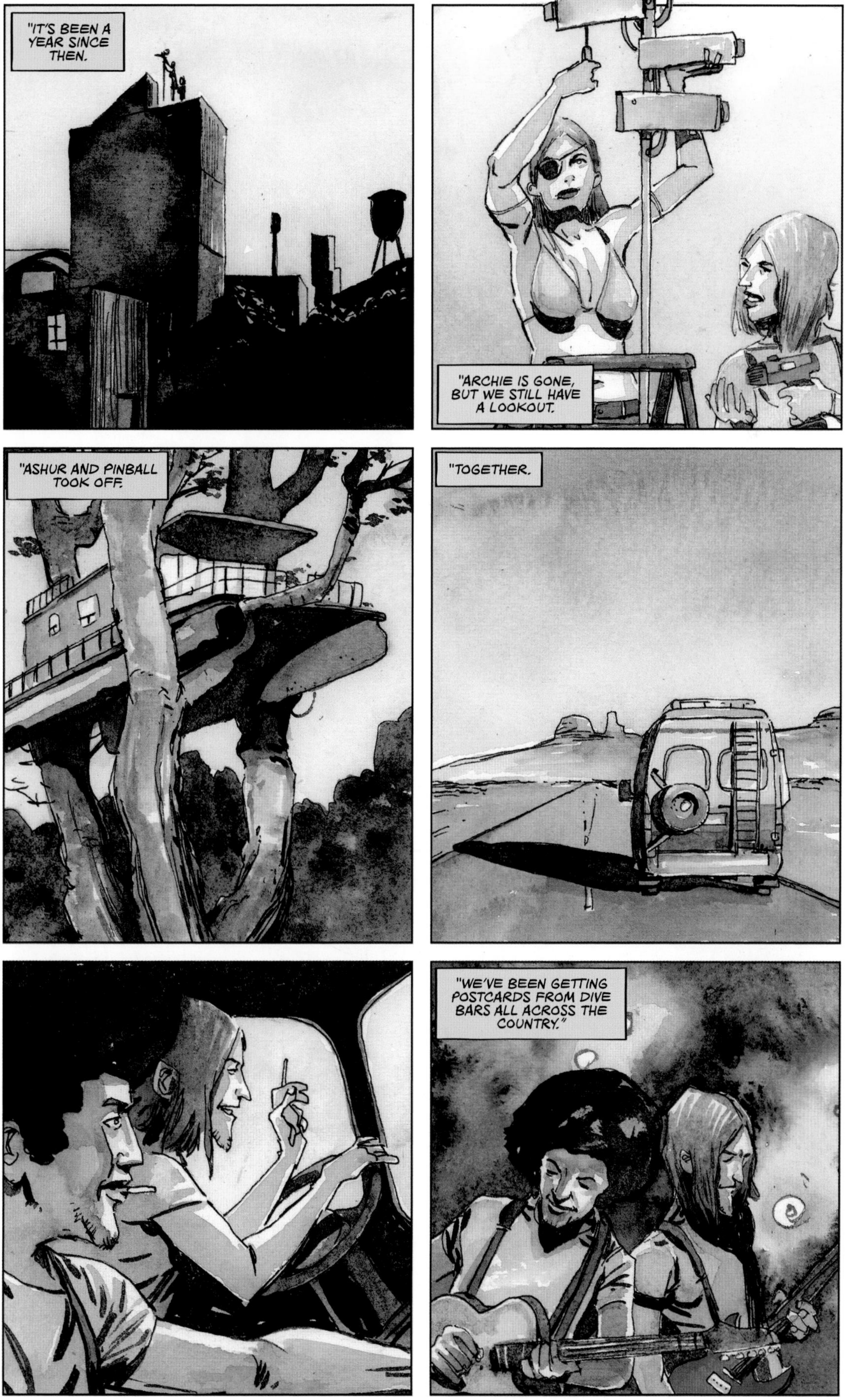
"IT'S BEEN A YEAR SINCE THEN.
"ARCHIE IS GONE, BUT WE STILL HAVE A LOOKOUT.
"ASHUR AND PINBALL TOOK OFF.
"TOGETHER.
"WE'VE BEEN GETTING POSTCARDS FROM DIVE BARS ALL ACROSS THE COUNTRY."

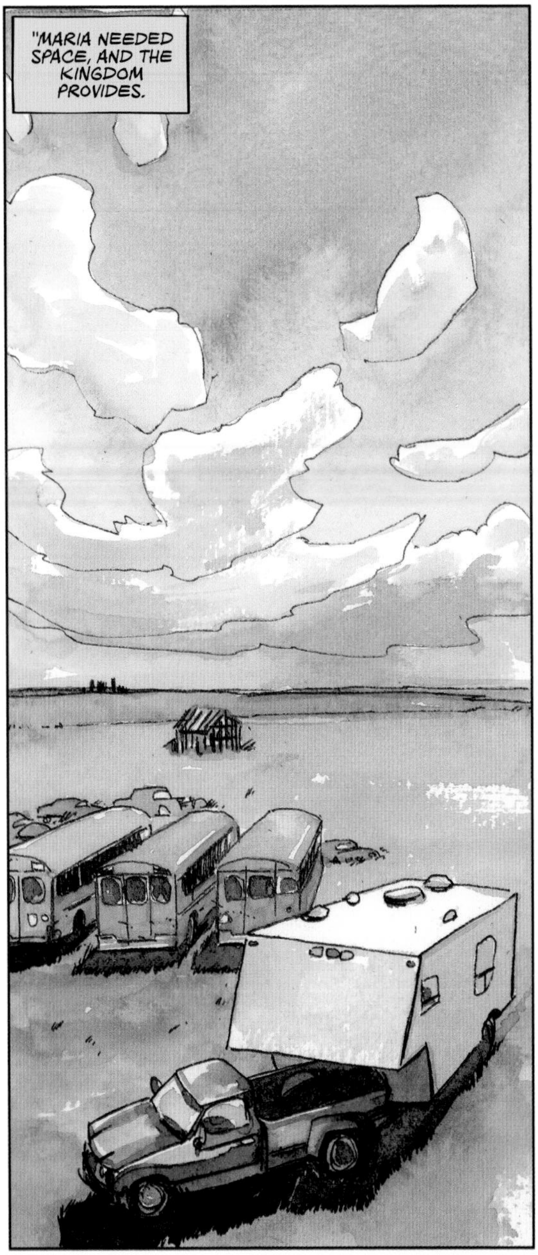
"MARIA NEEDED SPACE, AND THE KINGDOM PROVIDES.

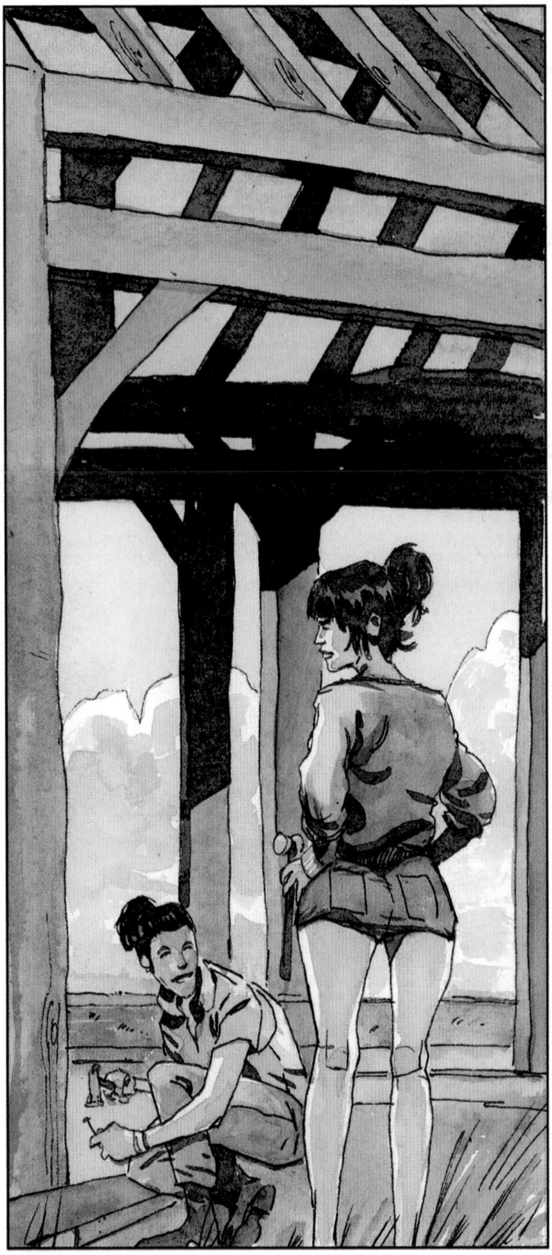

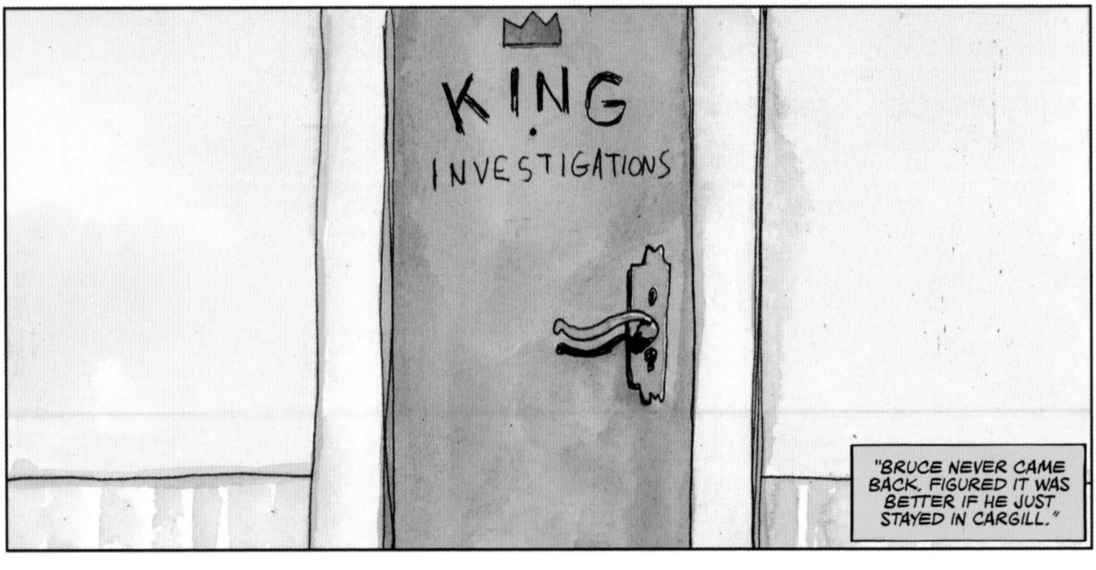
KING
INVESTIGATIONS
"BRUCE NEVER CAME BACK. FIGURED IT WAS BETTER IF HE JUST STAYED IN CARGILL."

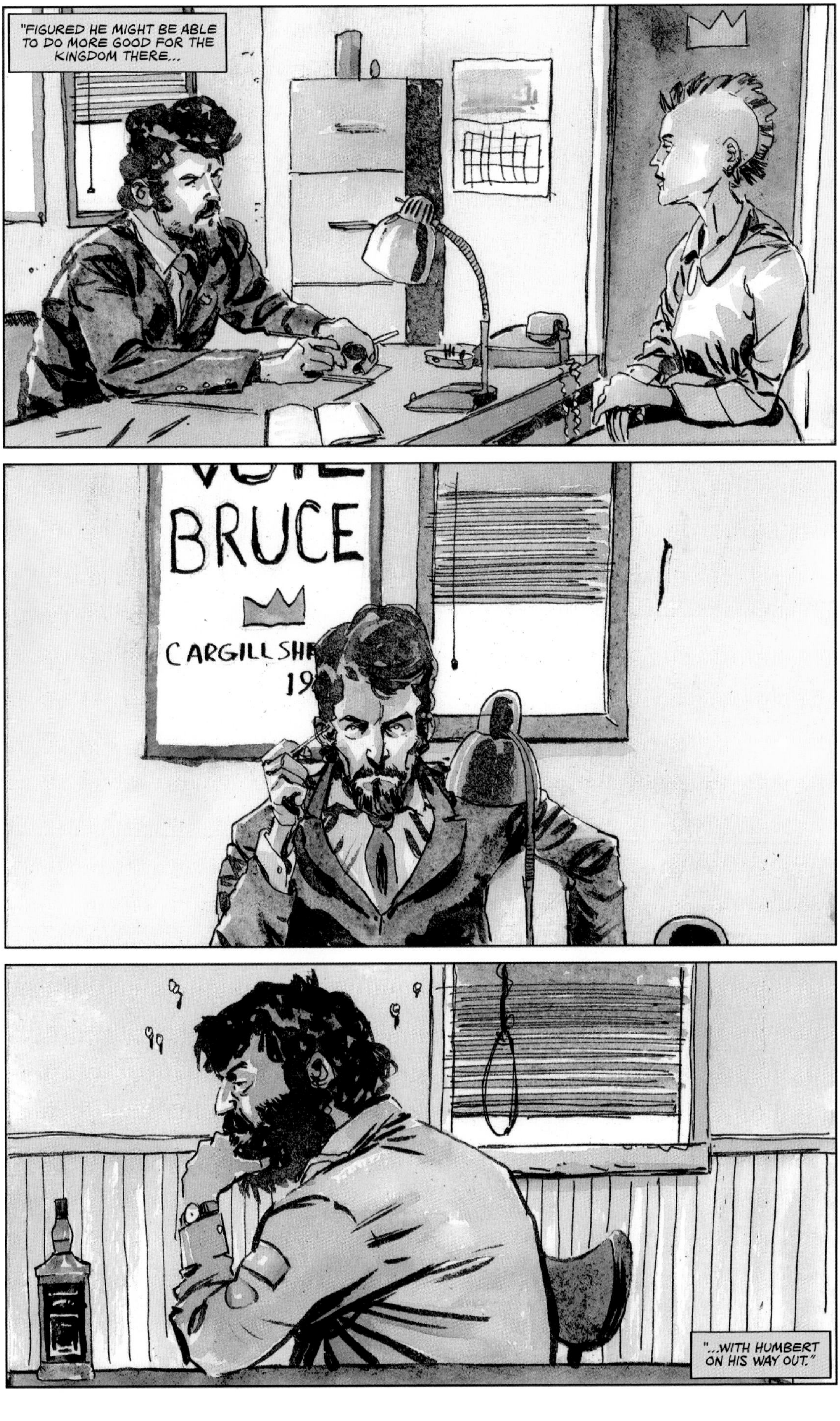
"FIGURED HE MIGHT BE ABLE TO DO MORE GOOD FOR THE KINGDOM THERE...
BRUCE
"...WITH HUMBERT ON HIS WAY OUT."

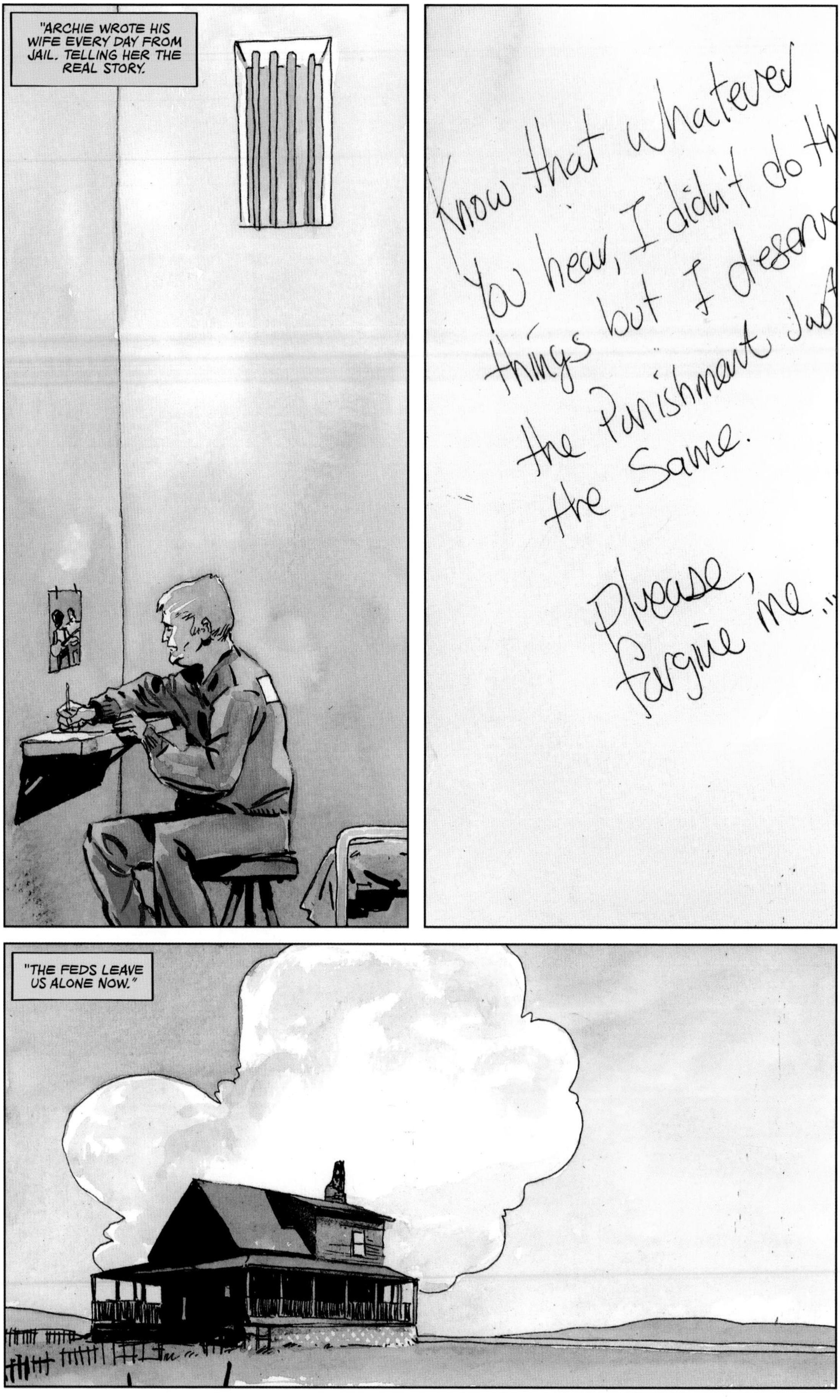
"ARCHIE WROTE HIS WIFE EVERY DAY FROM JAIL. TELLING HER THE REAL STORY.
Know that whatever
You hear, I didn't do th
things but I deserv
the Punishment Jus
the Same.
Please,
forgive me...
"THE FEDS LEAVE US ALONE NOW."

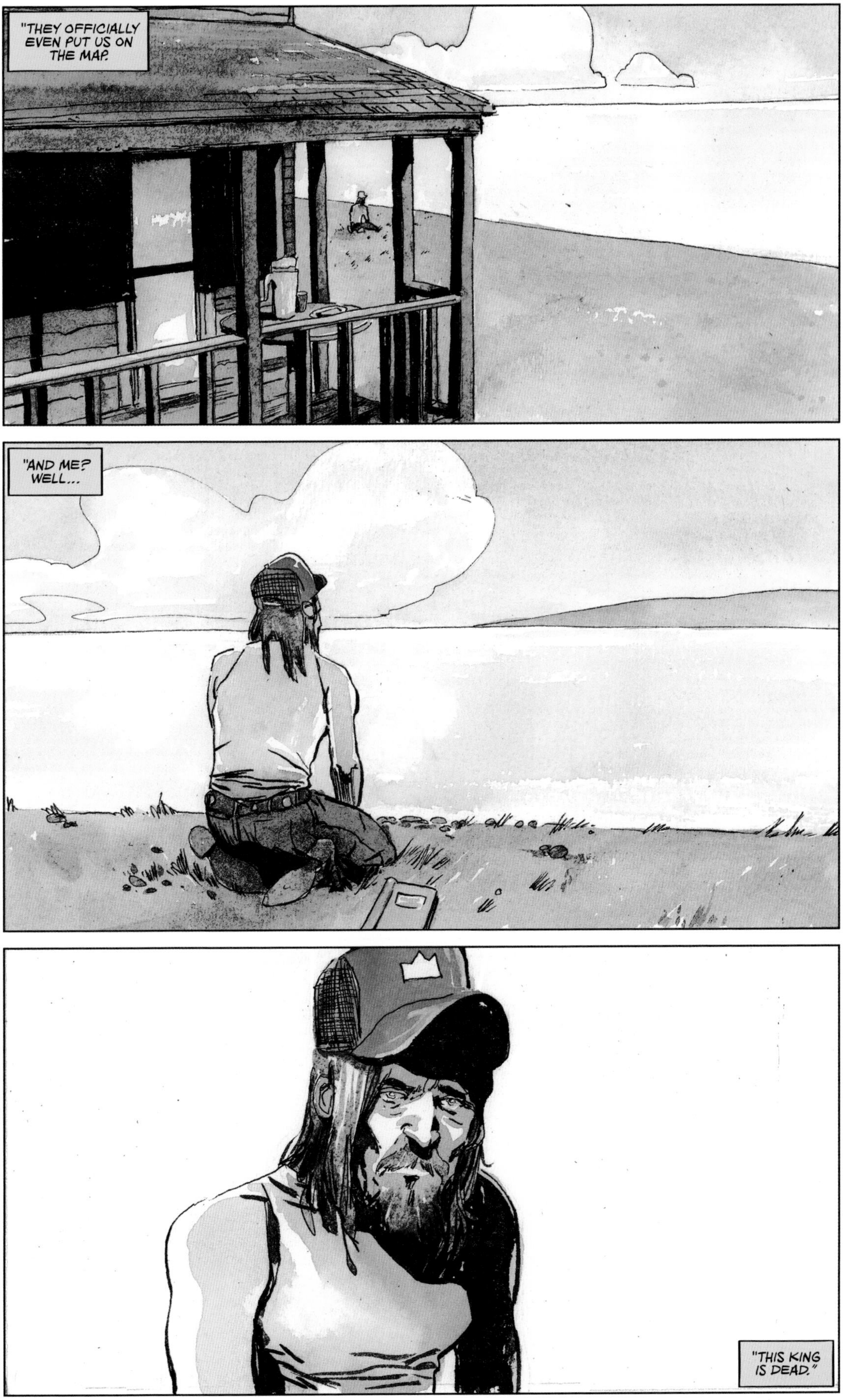
"THEY OFFICIALLY EVEN PUT US ON THE MAP.
"AND ME? WELL...
"THIS KING IS DEAD."

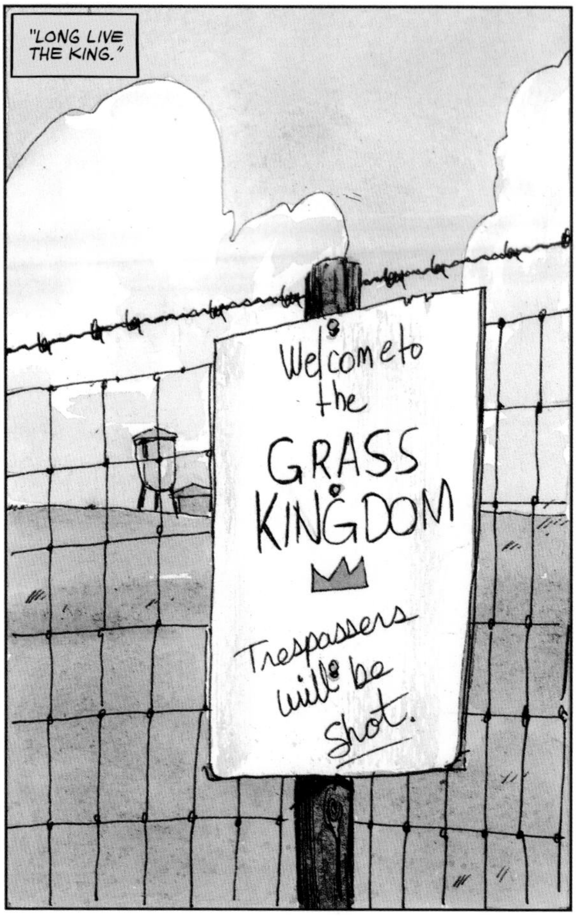
"LONG LIVE THE KING."
Welcome to the GRASS KINGDOM
Trespassers will be Shot.

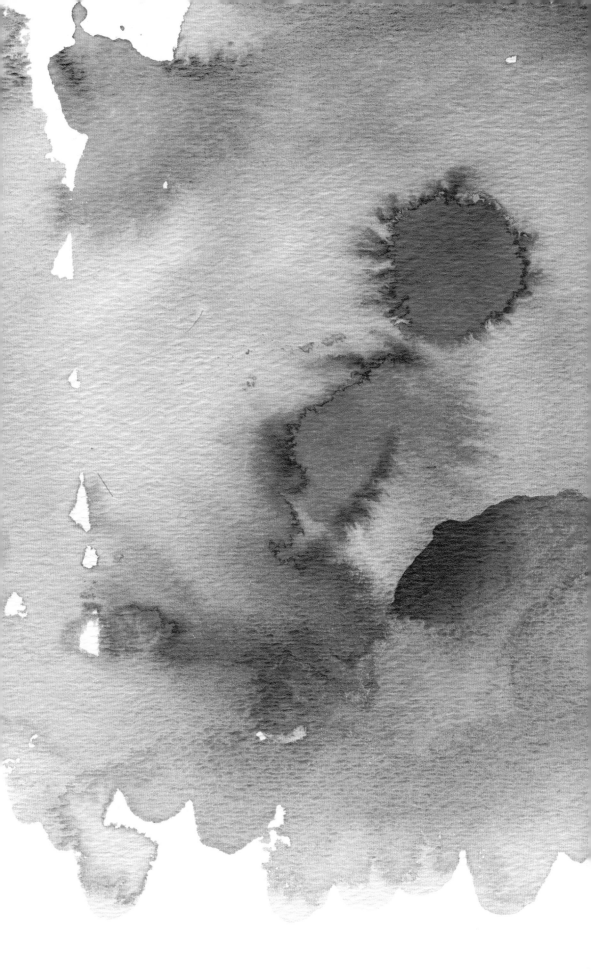

behind the scenes

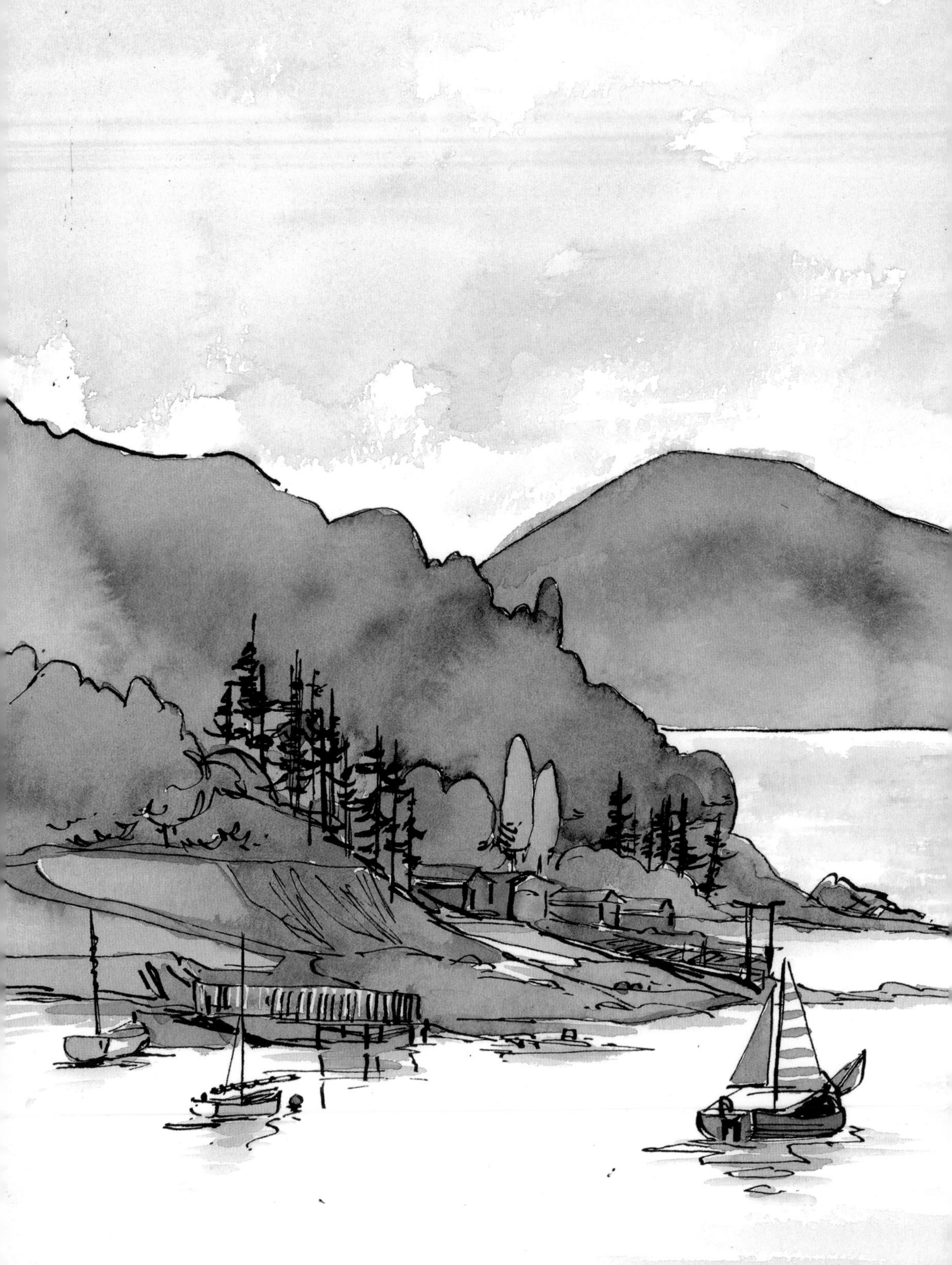

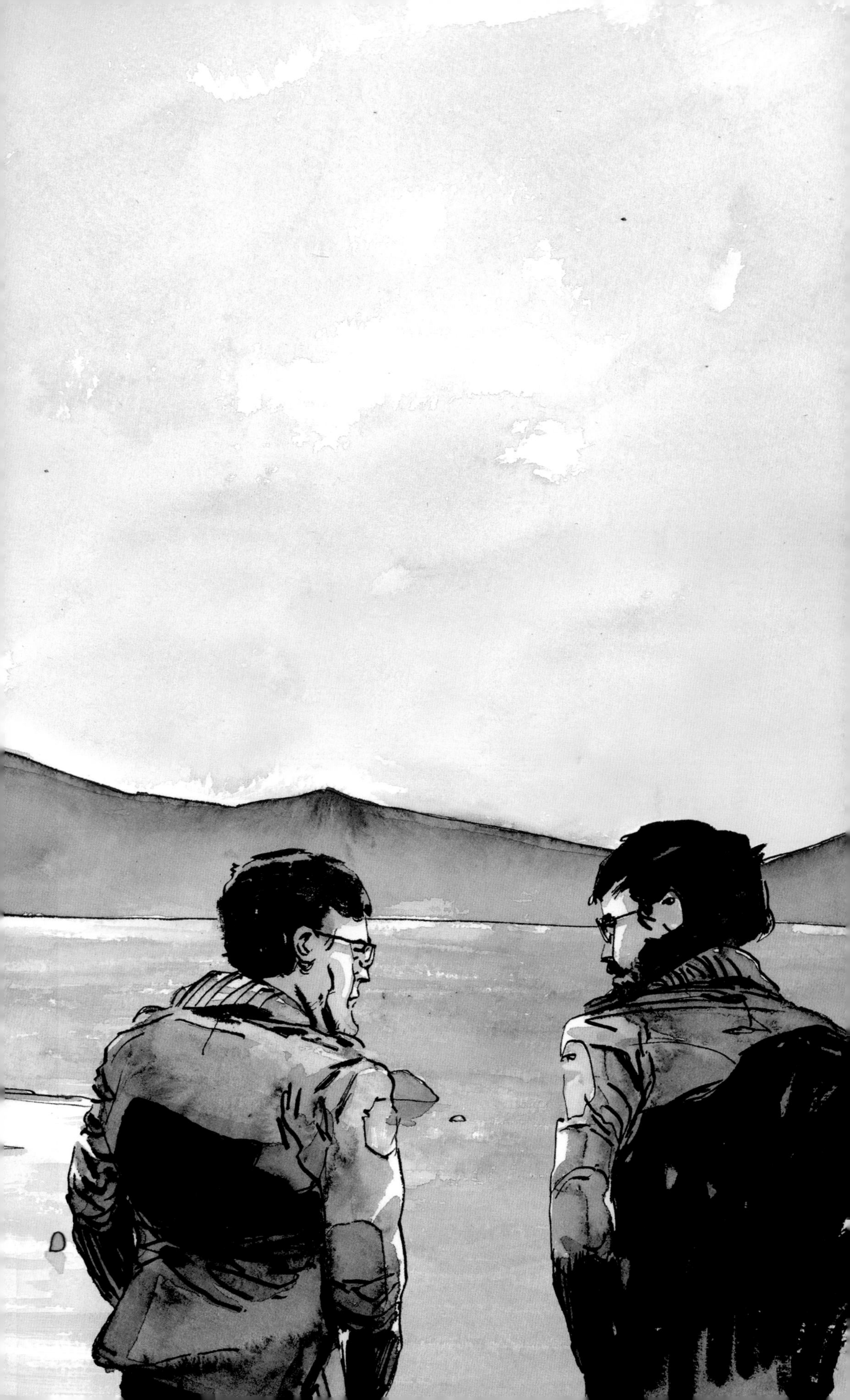

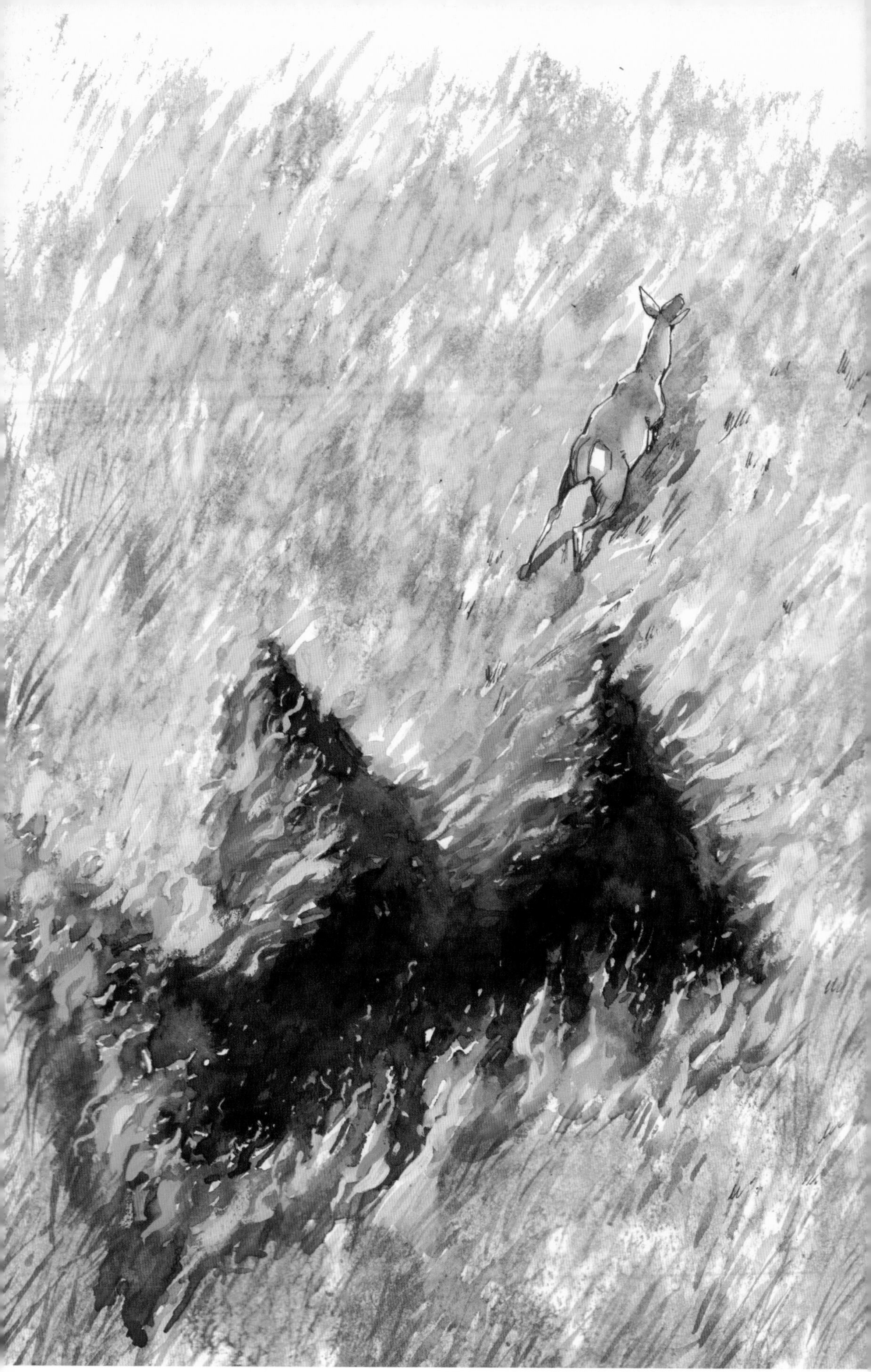

issue #12 cover by tyler jenkins

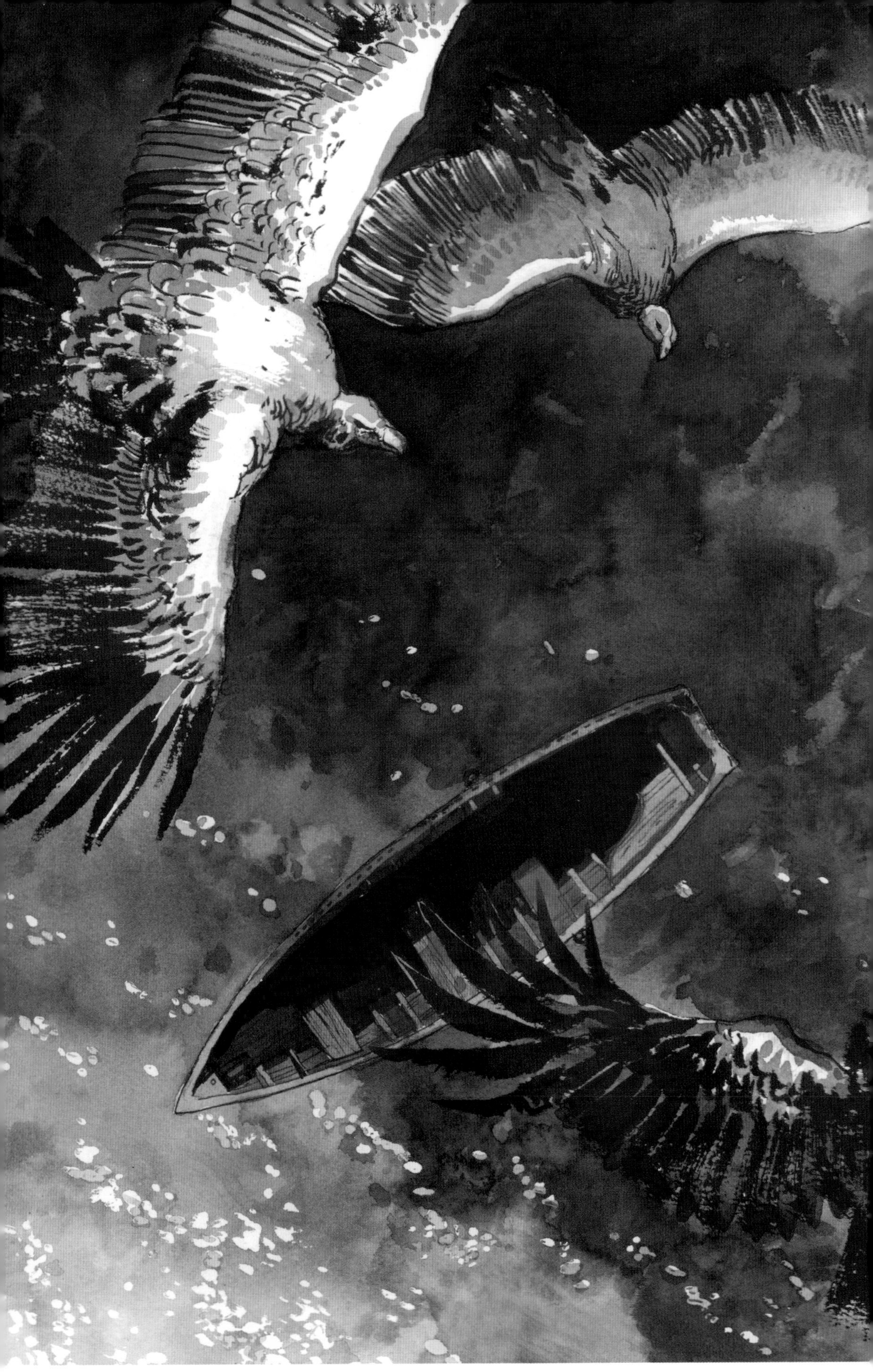

issue #13 cover by tyler jenkins

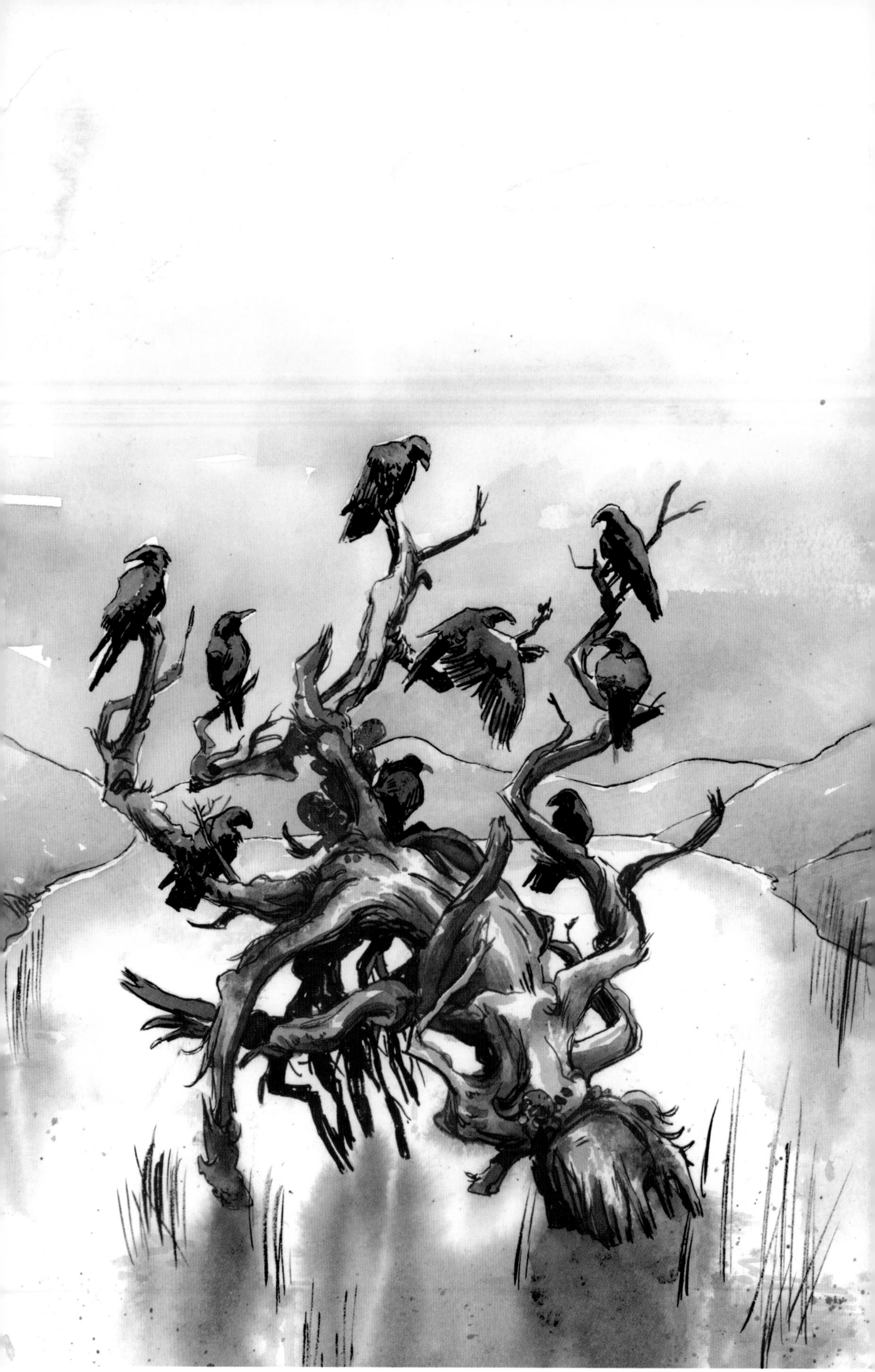

issue #14 cover by tyler jenkins

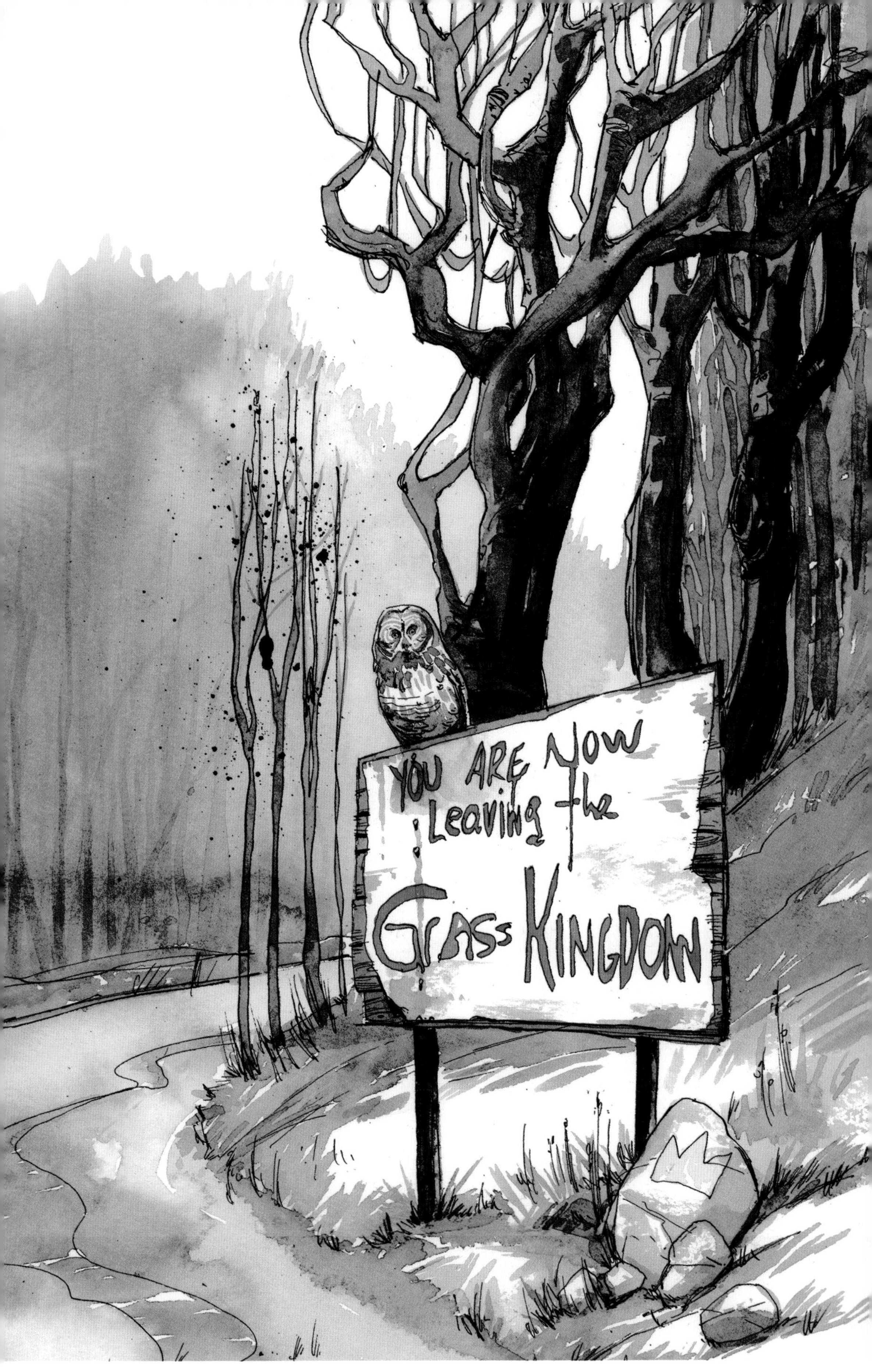
YOU ARE NOW
Leaving the
GRASS KINGDOM

issue #15 cover by tyler jenkins

GRASS KINGS

Matt Kindt Tyler Jenkins Hilary Jenkins

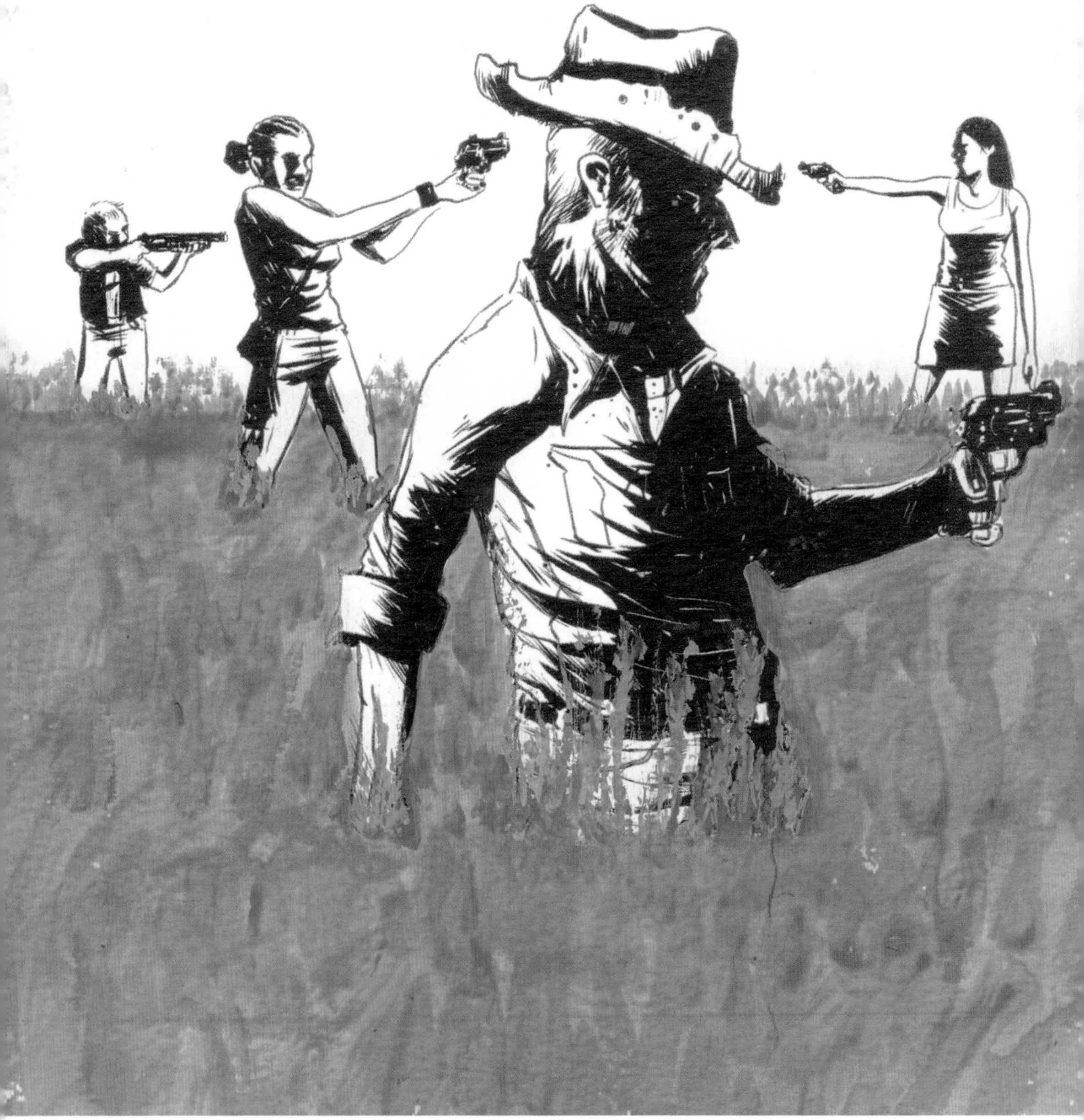

issue #15 cover by matt kindt

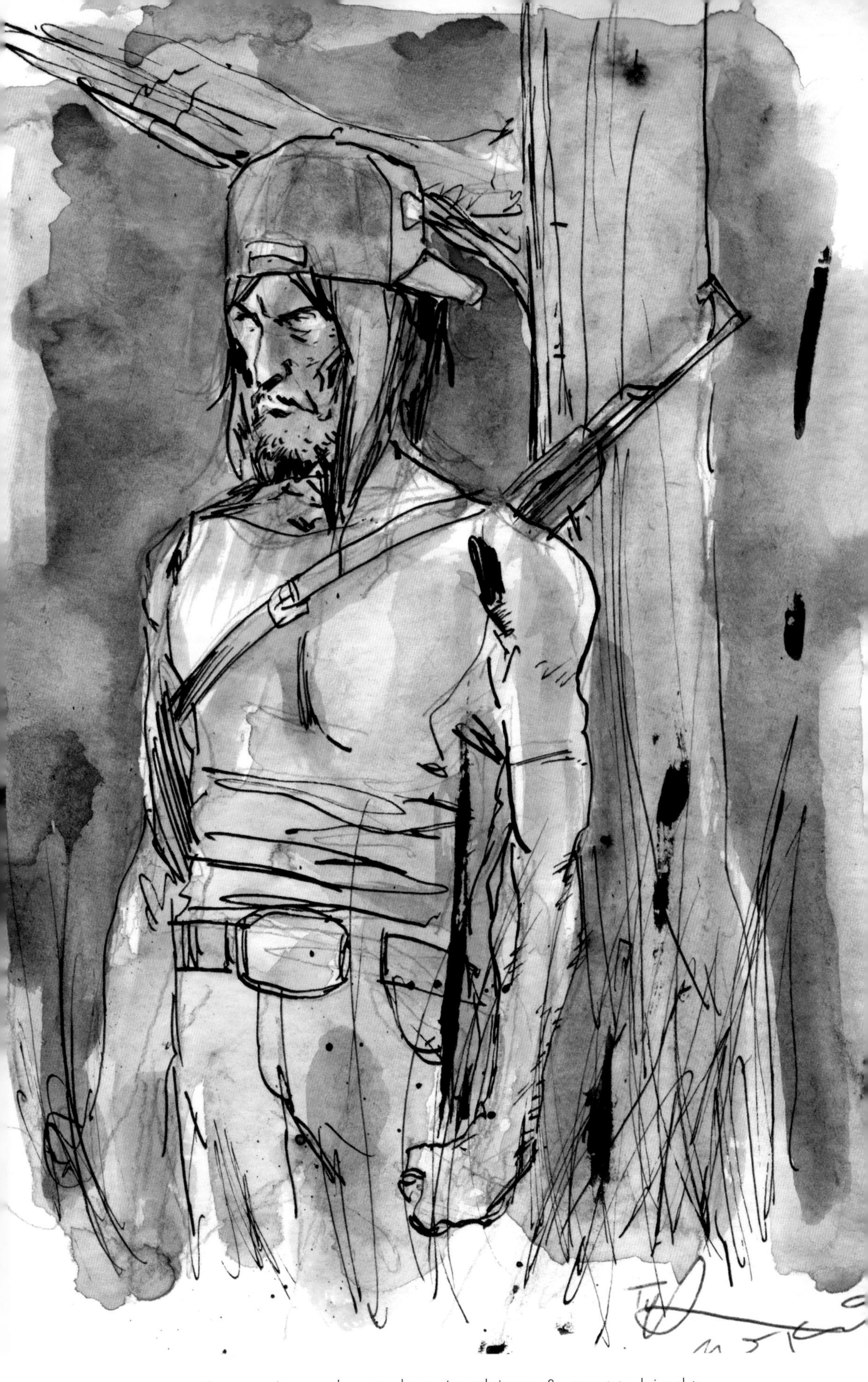

eccc jam piece by tyler jenkins & matt kindt

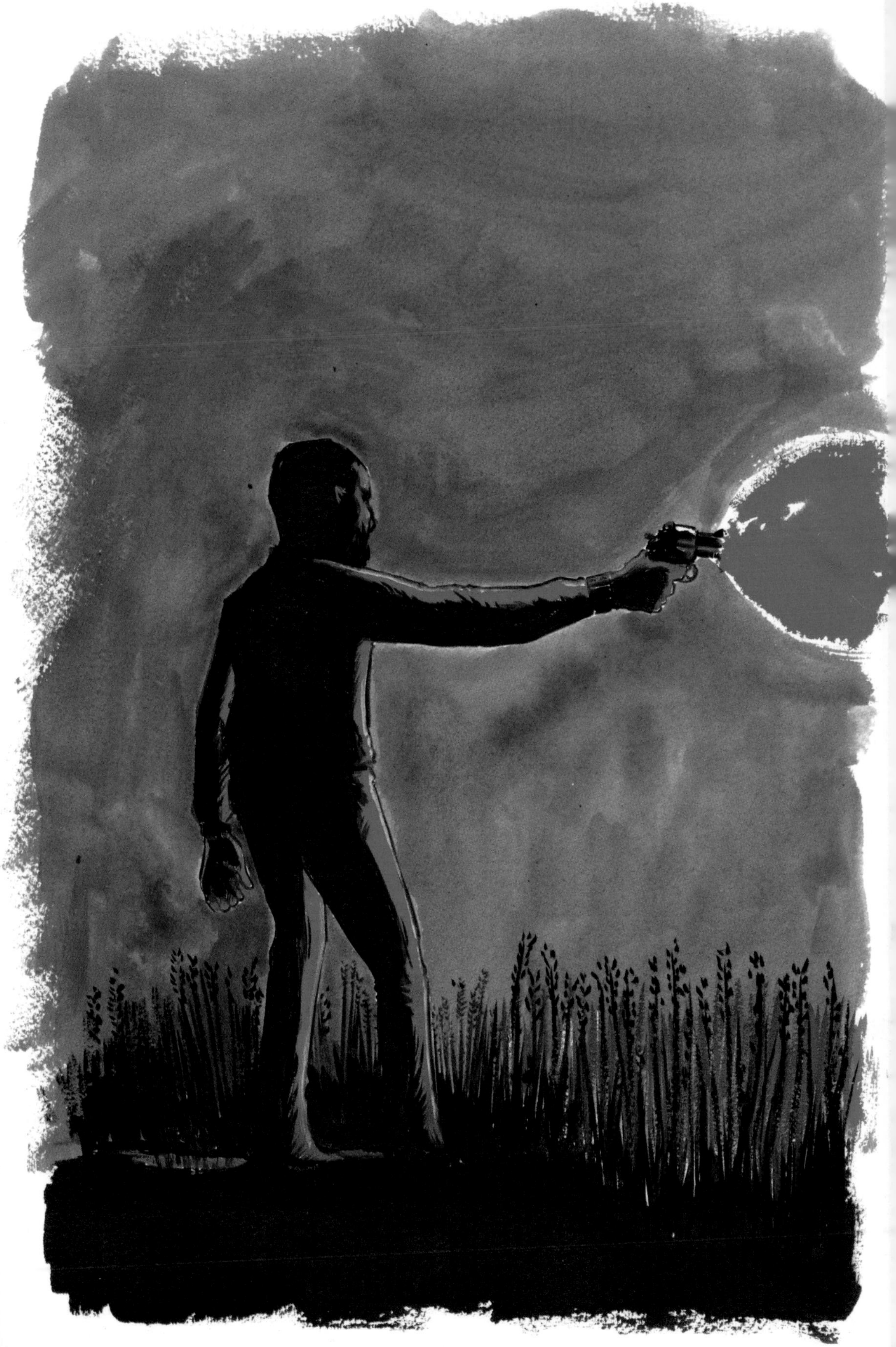

#13 cover process by matt kindt

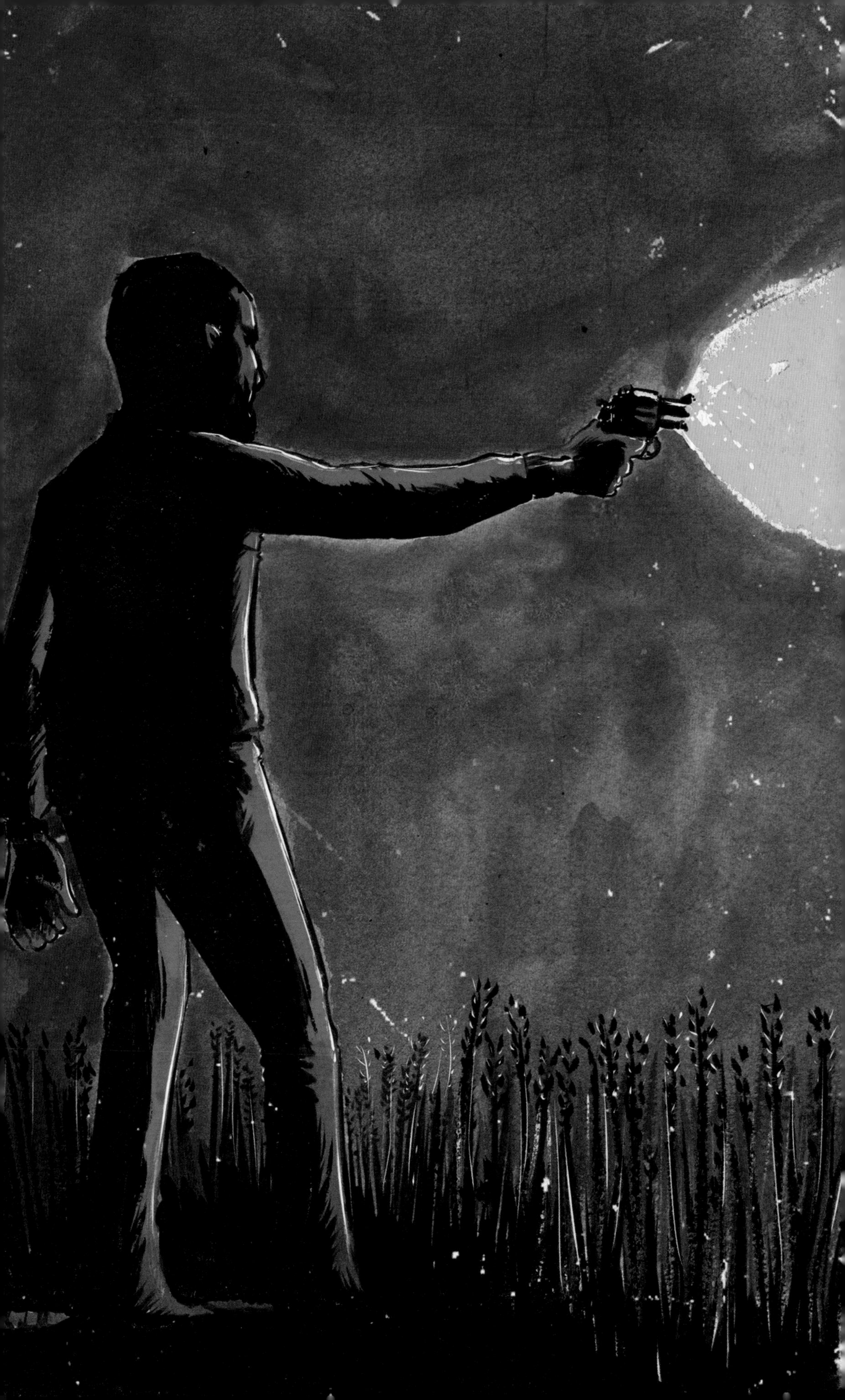

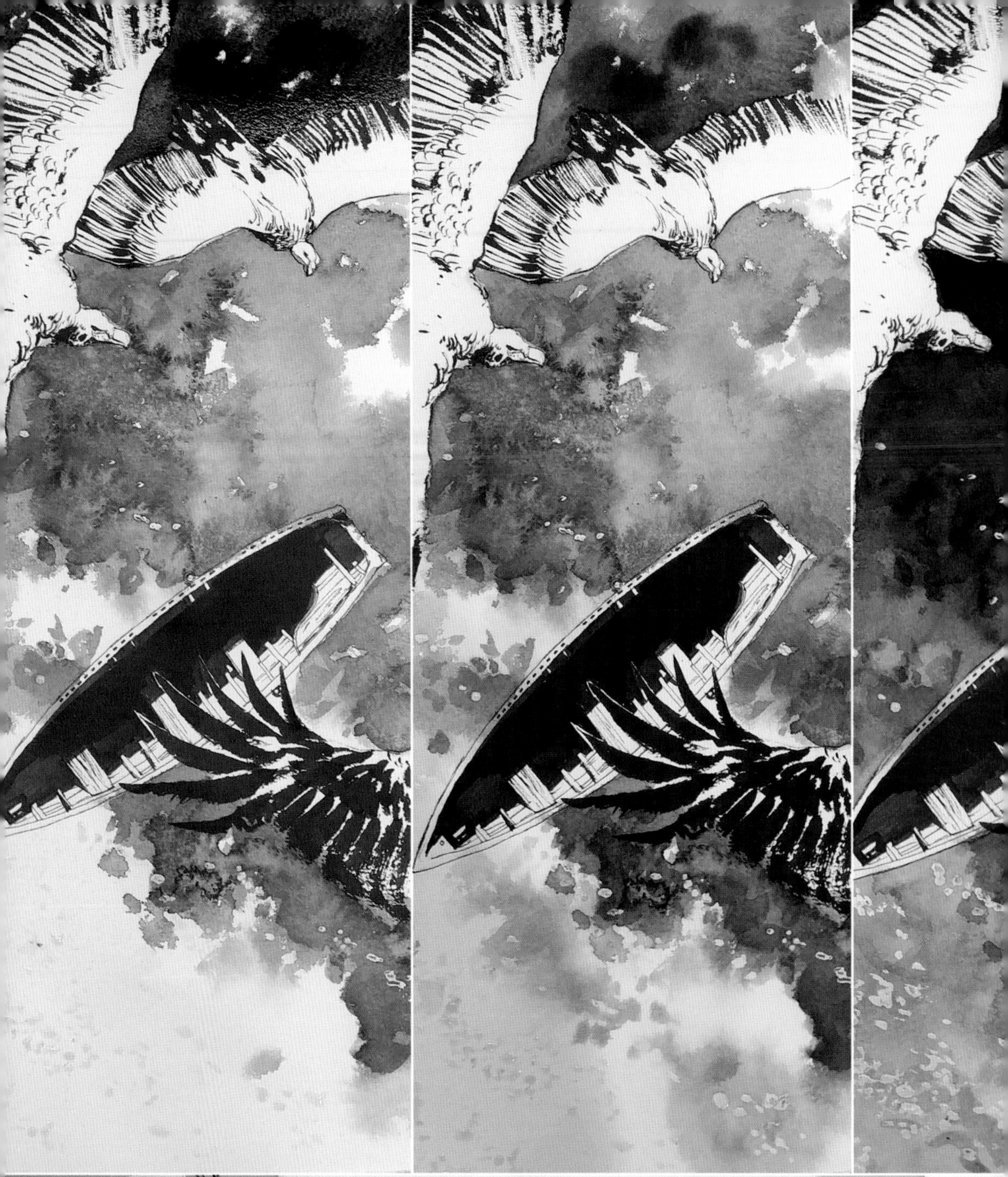

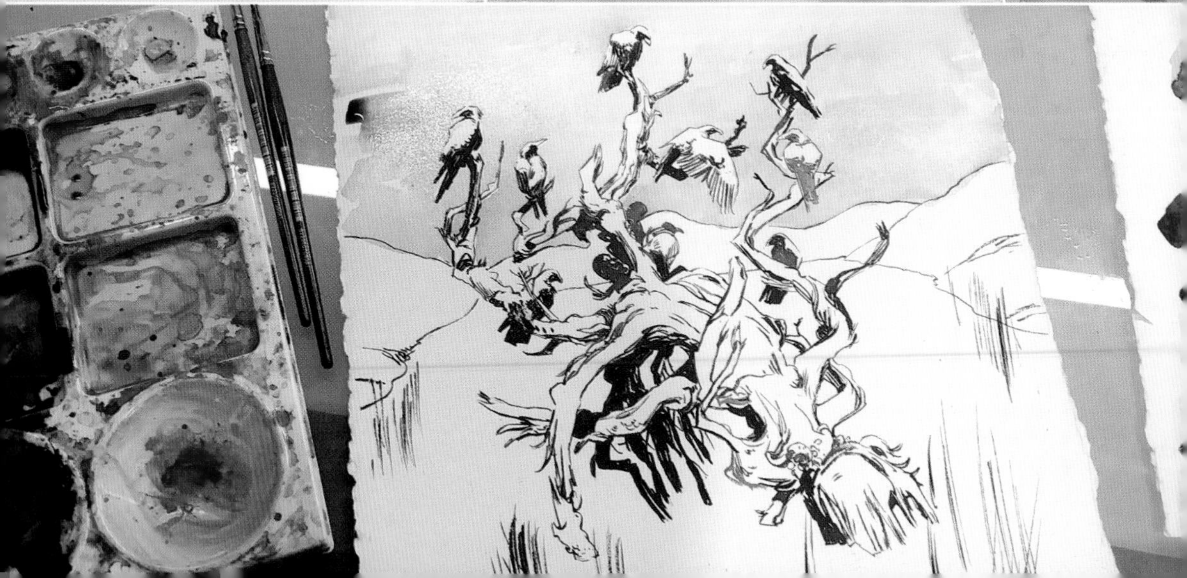

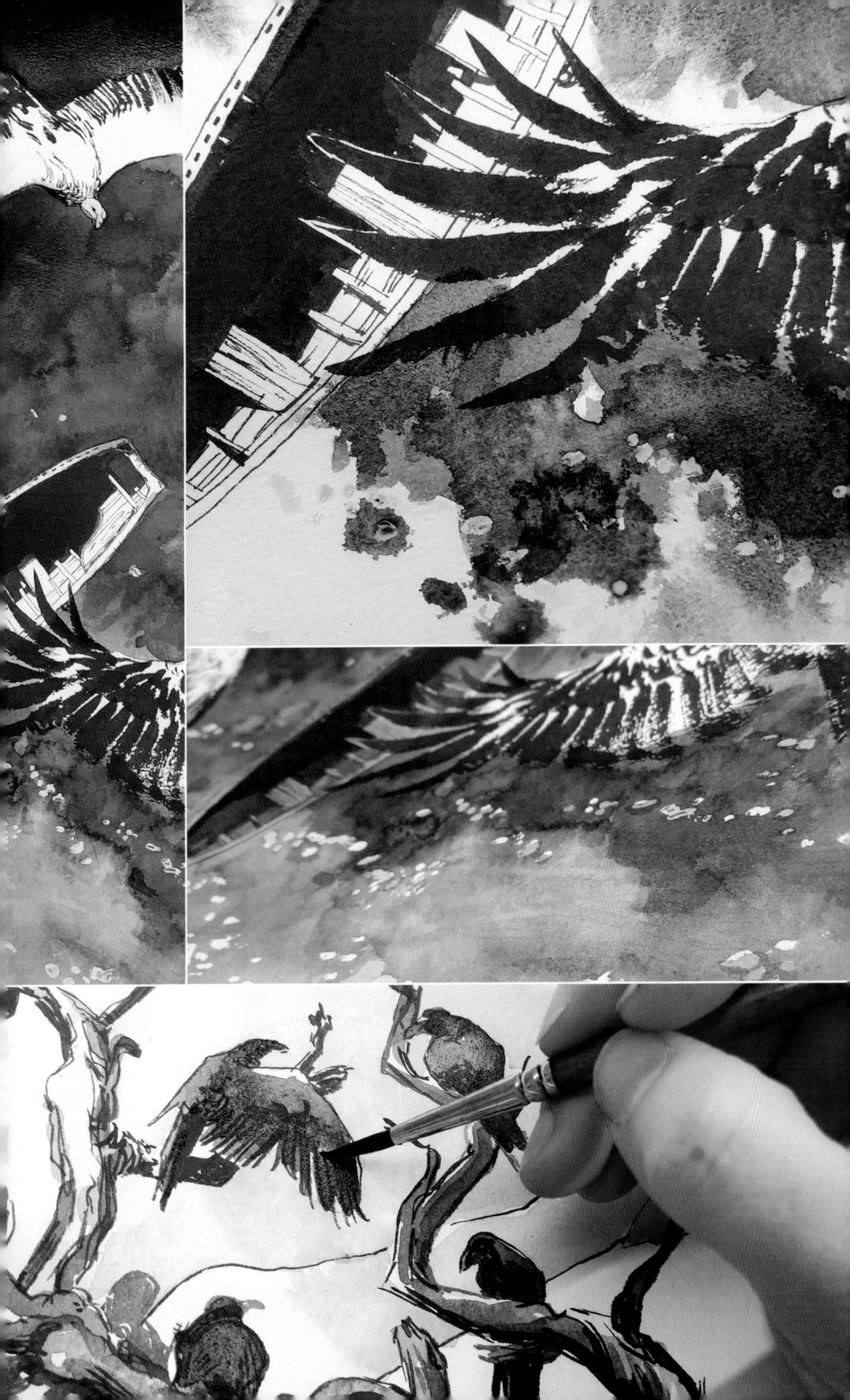

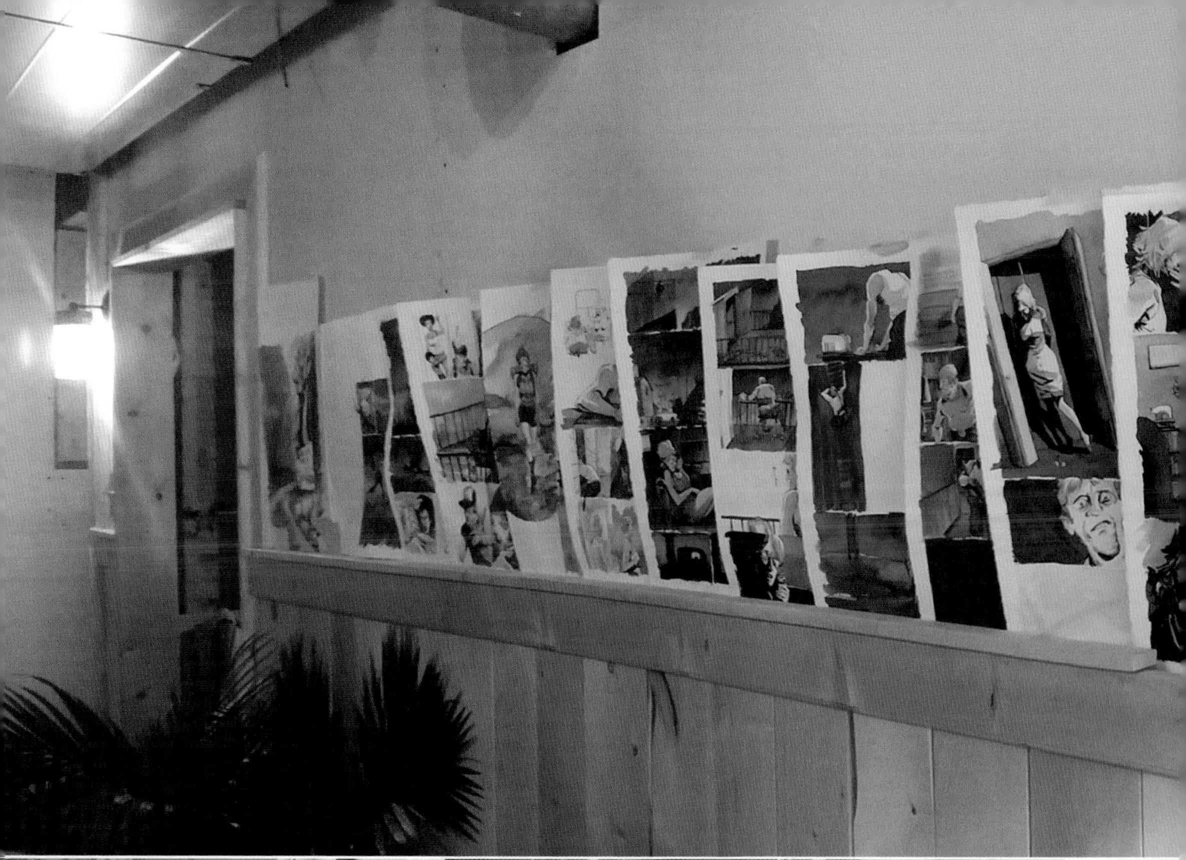

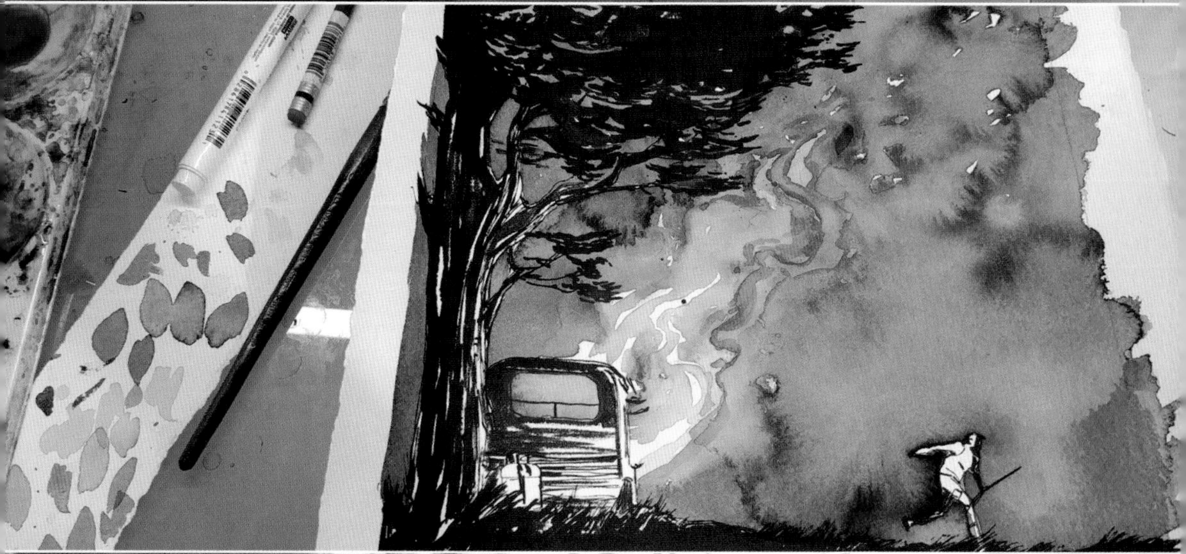

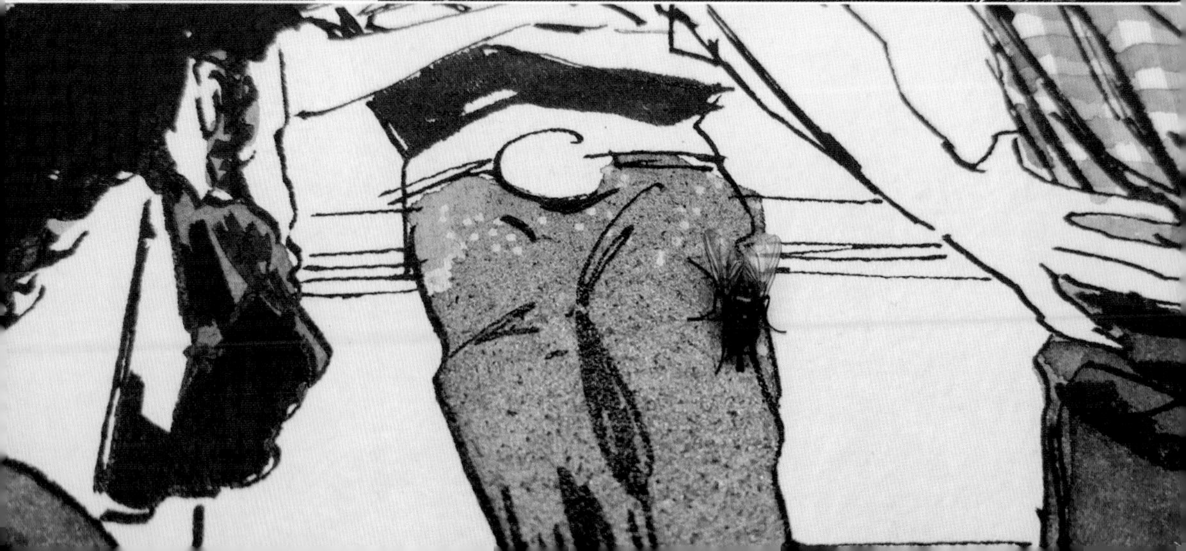

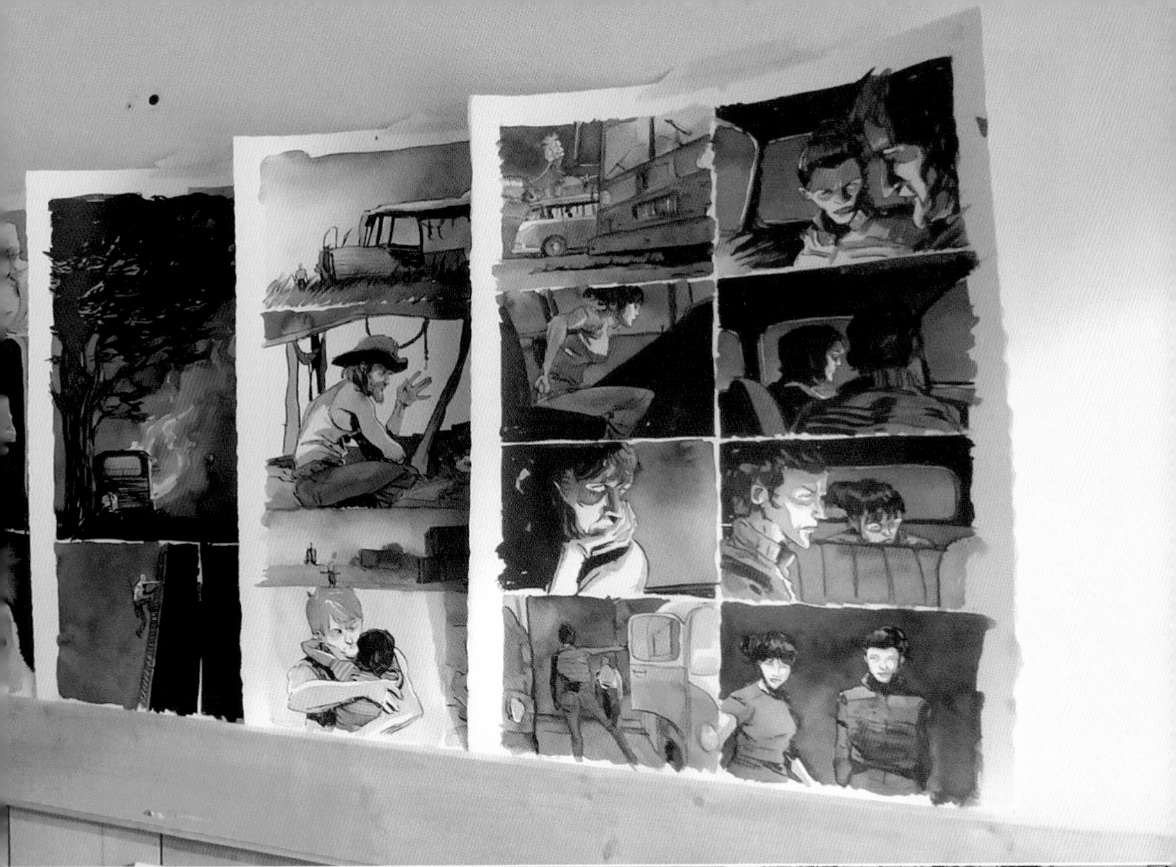

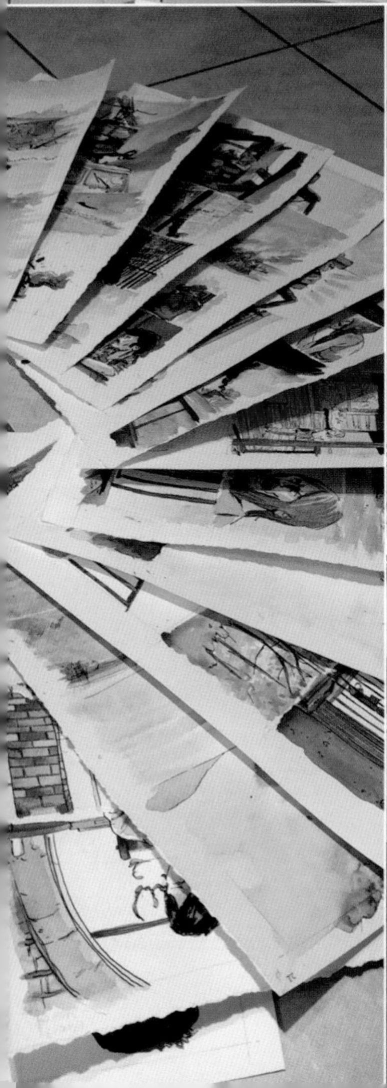

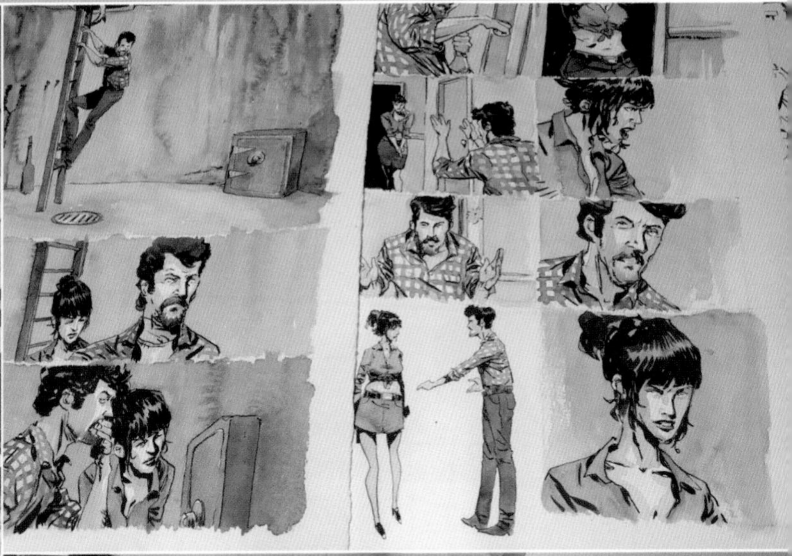

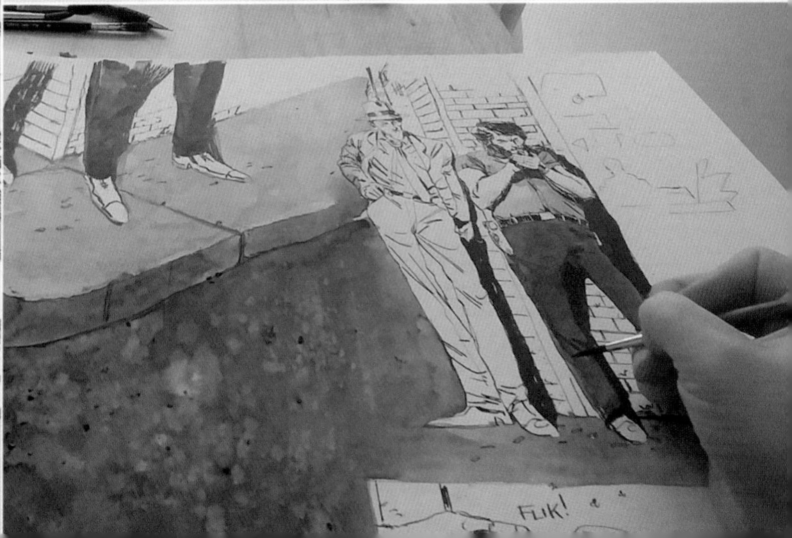
FLIK!

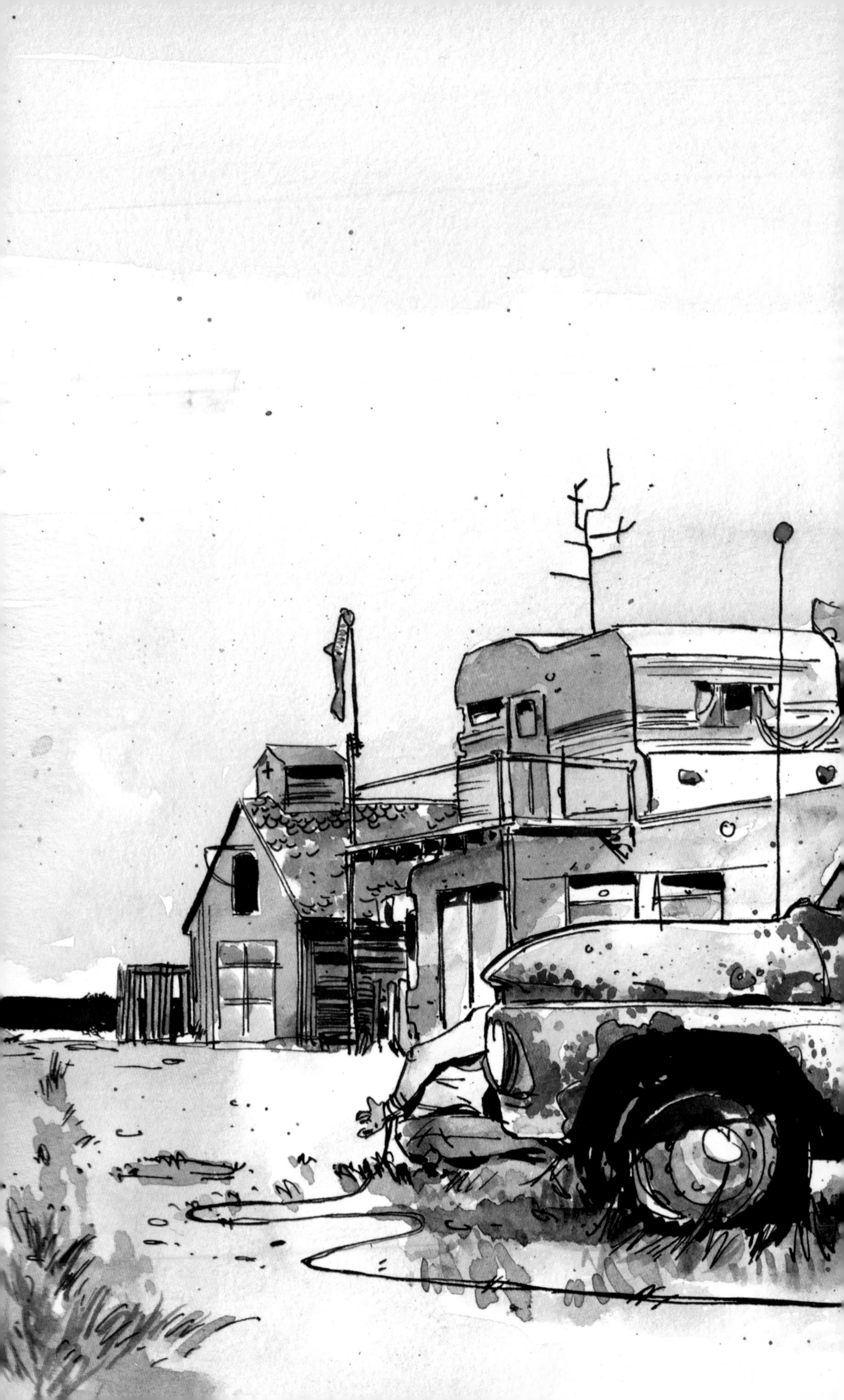

about the authors

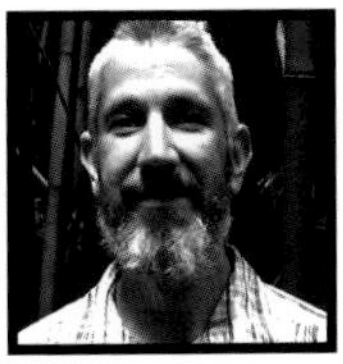

Matt Kindt is the *New York Times* best-selling writer and artist of the comics and graphic novels *Dept. H, Mind MGMT, Revolver, 3 Story, Super Spy, 2 Sisters,* and *Pistolwhip,* as well as the writer of *Grass Kings, Ether, Justice League of America* (DC), *Spider-Man* (Marvel), *Unity, Ninjak, Rai,* and *Divinity* (Valiant). He has been nominated for six Eisner and six Harvey Awards (and won once). His work has been published in French, Spanish, Italian, German and Korean.

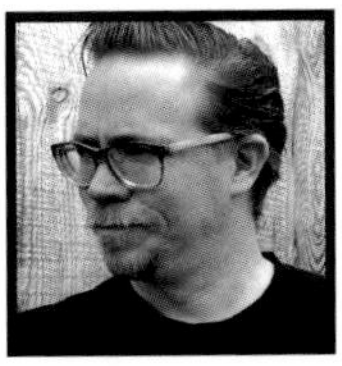

Tyler Jenkins is a dude who draws comics, makes art and music, and on occasion barbecues a mean back of ribs. Tyler is best known for creating *Grass Kings* with Matt Kindt and *Peter Panzerfaust* with Kurtis Wiebe, and handling art duties on *Snow Blind* with Ollie Masters and *Neverboy* with Shaun Simon. Tyler lives in rural Alberta, Canada, with his wife, three small child-like creatures, and more gophers than you can shove in a tin pail. Find him at tylerjenkinsprojects on Instagram.

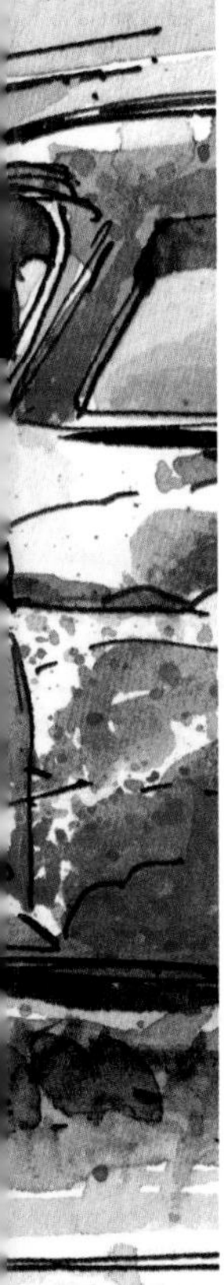

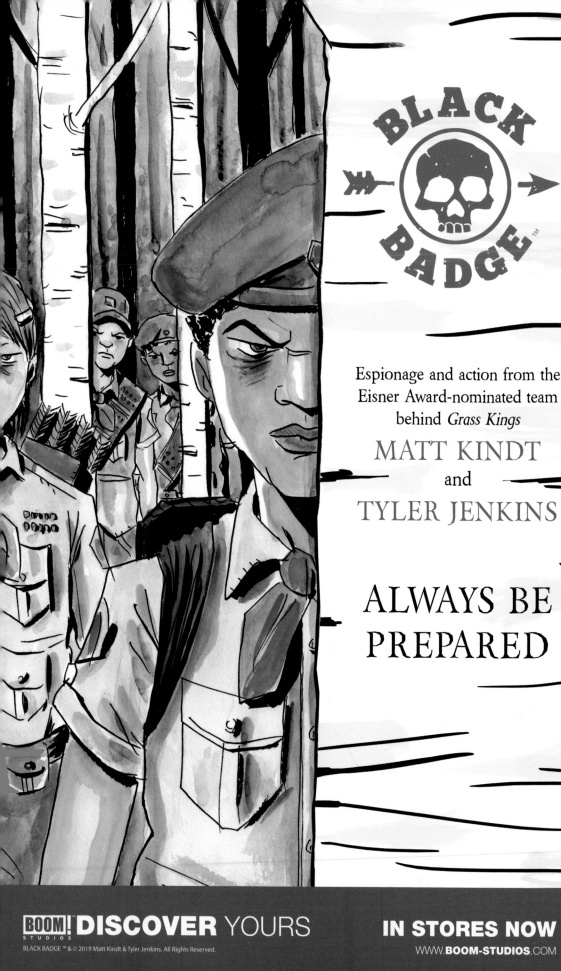